Godplayer

Also by Robin Cook

The Year of the Intern
Coma
Sphinx
Brain
Fever

GODPLAYER

□□□

ROBIN COOK

MACMILLAN LONDON

ISBN 0 333 35327 7

First published 1983 by
G. P. Putnam's Sons,
New York

First published 1983 in Great Britain by
Macmillan London Limited
London and Basingstoke

Associated companies in Auckland, Dallas,
Delhi, Dublin, Hong Kong, Johannesburg,
Lagos, Manzini, Melbourne, Nairobi,
New York, Singapore, Tokyo, Washington
and Zaria

Printed in Hong Kong

To Barbara and Fluffy—
my constant companions
and
my most willing listeners.

Godplayer

PROLOGUE

BRUCE WILKINSON WENT from dead asleep to full awake with such suddenness that he felt overwhelmed with a sense of fear, like a child awakening from a nightmare. He had no idea what had awakened him but guessed it was some noise or movement. He wondered if something had touched him. He stayed still, holding his breath, and stared straight ahead, listening. At first he was disoriented, but as his mind took in his limited field of vision, he remembered he was in the Boston Memorial Hospital: in room 1832 to be exact. At about the same instant that he realized where he was, Bruce perceived that it was the middle of the night. The hospital was clothed in a heavy stillness.

On his current admission for cardiac bypass surgery, Bruce had been in the hospital for over a week. But a month or so before he'd spent three weeks several floors down, recovering from his unexpected heart attack. As a consequence Bruce had become accustomed to the hospital routine. Such things as the squeak of the nurse's medication cart as it was pushed up the hall, or the distant sounds of an arriving ambulance, or even the hospital page calling a doctor's name had become reassuring phenomena. In fact, Bruce could often tell merely by listening to these familiar sounds what time of day it was without looking at his watch. They all signified that help for any medical emergency was close at hand.

Bruce had never worried much about his health even though he was a victim of multiple sclerosis. The problem with his vision that had brought him to the doctor five years ago had cleared, and Bruce had made a conscious effort to forget the diagnosis because hospitals and doctors tended to frighten him. Then, out of the blue, came the heart attack with its attendant hospitalization and the current major surgery. His doctors assured him that the heart problem was not related to the multiple sclerosis, but that disclaimer had done little to buoy his sagging courage.

Now, as Bruce awoke in the middle of the night and heard none of the usual reassuring hospital sounds, the hospital seemed like an ominous and lonely place, evoking fear rather than hope. The silence was intimidating, providing no immediate explanation for his sudden wakefulness. Bruce felt himself inexplicably paralyzed by a sensation of acute terror.

As the seconds passed, Bruce's mouth became dry, exactly as it had been after his preop medication five days earlier. He attributed this to fear, as he continued to lie perfectly still like a wary animal, his senses straining for any disturbance. He'd done the same thing as a boy after awakening in the night from bad dreams. If he didn't move, perhaps the monsters would not see him. Lying on his back, he couldn't see much of the room, especially since the only illumination came from a small floor-level night-light behind his bed. All he could see was the indistinct juncture of ceiling and wall. Silhouetted against it was the magnified shadow of his IV pole, bottle, and tubing. The bottle seemed to be swaying slightly.

Trying to dismiss his fears, Bruce began monitoring his internal messages. The big question loomed in his mind: Am I all right? Having been rudely betrayed by his body by the heart attack, he wondered if some new catastrophe had awakened him. Could his stitches have split? That had been one of his fears immediately after the operation. Could the bypass have come loose?

Bruce could feel his pulse in his temples, and, despite a clamminess to his palms and a somewhat disagreeable sensation in his head that he associated with fever, he felt okay. At least there was no pain, particularly not the crushing, searing pressure that had come with the initial heart attack.

Tentatively Bruce took a breath. There was no stabbing knifelike pain although it seemed to take extra effort to inflate his lungs.

In the semidarkness, a throaty, phlegm-laden cough reverberated within the confines of the room. Bruce felt a new surge of fright, but he quickly realized that it was just his roommate. Perhaps Mr. Hauptman's coughing had been the sound that had awakened him, Bruce thought, feeling a modicum of relief. The old man coughed anew, then noisily turned over in his sleep.

Bruce entertained the idea of calling a nurse to check Mr. Hauptman, more for the opportunity for Bruce to speak to someone than because he thought there was a real problem. The truth of the matter was that Mr. Hauptman coughed like that all the time.

The disagreeable feverish sensation became more intense and began to spread. Bruce could feel it in his chest like a hot liquid. The concern that something had gone wrong on the "inside" reasserted itself.

Bruce tried to turn to locate the nurse's call button that was looped through the side rails of the bed. His eyes moved, but his head felt heavy. Out of the corner of his eye he saw quick, staccato movement. Looking up he could see his IV bottle. The movement he'd seen was coming from the rapid running of his IV. The drops in the micropore chamber were falling in quick succession, and the night-light glinted off the liquid with an explosive sparkle.

That was strange! Bruce knew that his IV was only being maintained for emergencies and was supposed to run as slowly as possible. It should not be running quickly. Bruce could remember having checked it as he always did before turning out his reading light.

He tried to reach out and find the nurse's call button. But he couldn't move. It was as if his right arm had not gotten the command. He tried again with the same result.

Bruce felt his terror become panic. Now he was certain something terrible was happening to him! He was surrounded by the best medical care but unable to reach it. He had to get help. He had to get help instantly. It was like a nightmare from which he could not awaken.

Yanking his head off the pillow, Bruce screamed for a nurse. His voice surprised him with its weakness. He'd intended to yell but instead he whispered. At the same time he became aware that his head felt tremendously heavy, requiring all his strength to keep it off the pillow. The exertion caused a trembling that rattled the bed.

With a barely audible sigh, Bruce collapsed back onto his pillow, compounding his panic. Trying again to call out, he heard an incomprehensible hiss almost devoid of vocalization. Whatever was wrong with him was rapidly worsening. He felt as if an invisible lead blanket was settling over him, pressing him flat against the bed. His attempts to breathe were pitiful, uncoordinated heaves of his chest. With utter terror Bruce comprehended he was being suffocated.

Somehow he organized his thoughts enough to remember again the nurse's call button. With horrendous effort he lifted his arm from the bed, and in an uncoordinated, spastic fashion pulled it across his chest. It was as if he were immersed in some viscous liquid. His fingers brushed the rails, and he grasped vainly for the button. It wasn't there. With the last vestiges of strength, he heaved himself onto his left side, rolling over and thudding up against the rail. His face pressed heavily against the cold steel, occluding the view from his right eye, but he did not have the strength to move. With his left eye he saw the emergency button. It was on the floor, curled on itself like a snake.

Panic and desperation filled Bruce's consciousness, but the oppressive weight on his body increased, precluding all movement. In his terror he guessed that something had happened to his heart; perhaps all the stitches had burst. The sense of being smothered intensified as Bruce's brain screamed for life-giving oxygen. Yet Bruce was totally paralyzed, able only to grunt in agony as he desperately tried to breathe. Yet through all of this, Bruce's senses were sharp, his mind painfully clear. He knew he was dying. There was a ringing in his ears, a sense of revolving, nausea. Then blackness . . .

□

Pamela Breckenridge had been working from eleven to seven for over a year. It wasn't a popular shift, but she liked it. She felt it gave her more freedom. During the summer she'd go to the beach by day and sleep in the evenings. In the winter she slept days. Her body had no problem making the adjustment as long as she slept at least seven hours. And as far as her work was concerned, she preferred night duty. There was less hassle. Days sometimes made a nurse feel like a traffic cop, trying to get patients to and from their numerous X rays, EKGs, lab tests, and surgeries. Besides, Pamela liked the responsibility of being alone.

Tonight as she walked down the empty, darkened corridor all she heard were a few murmurs, the hiss of a respirator, and her own footsteps. It was 3:45. No doctors were immediately on hand, nor even other RNs for that matter. Pamela worked with two LPNs, both skilled veterans of the ward. The three of them had learned to deal with any number of potential catastrophies.

Passing room 1832, Pamela stopped. During report that evening, the charge nurse going off the shift had mentioned that Bruce Wilkinson's IV was probably low enough to think about hanging a new bottle of D5W before morning. Pamela hesitated. It was probably a job she should delegate, but since she was right outside the room and no stickler for protocol, she decided to do it herself.

A wet cough rattled a greeting in the dimly lit room, making Pamela want to clear her own throat. Silently she slipped alongside Wilkinson's bed. The level of the bottle was low, and she was startled to see the IV running at a very rapid rate. A fresh bottle of D5W was on the nightstand. As she changed the IV and adjusted its rate, she felt something hard under her foot. She looked down and saw the call button. It was only as she bent to retrieve it that she looked at the patient, noticing his face pressed up against the side rail. Something was wrong. Gently she eased Bruce onto his back. Instead of the expected resistance, Bruce flopped over like a rag doll, his right hand coming to rest in a totally unnatural position. She bent closer. The patient was not breathing!

With trained efficiency, Pamela pressed the call button, switched on the bedside light, and pulled the bed away from the wall. Under the harsh fluorescent light, she saw that Bruce's skin was a deep grayish blue like a fine Chinese porcelain, suggesting that he had choked on something and had asphyxiated himself. Immediately Pamela bent over, pulled Bruce's chin back with her left hand, covered his nose with her right hand, and forcefully blew into his mouth. Expecting an airway obstruction, Pamela was surprised when Bruce's chest rose effortlessly. Obviously if he had choked on something, it was no longer in his trachea.

She felt Bruce's wrist for a pulse: nothing. She tried for a carotid pulse: nothing. Taking the pillow from beneath Bruce's head, she struck his chest with the palm of her hand. Then she bent over and reinflated the lungs.

The two practical nurses raced into the room at the same time. Pamela said one word, "code," and they went into action like a crack drill team. Rose quickly had the emergency paged over the loudspeaker while Trudy got the sturdy two-by-three-foot board used for support under a patient during cardiac massage. As soon as Bruce was settled on the board, Rose climbed onto the bed and began to compress his chest. After every fourth compression Pamela reinflated Bruce's lungs. Meanwhile, Trudy ran for the emergency crash cart and EKG machine.

Four minutes later when the medical resident, Jerry Donovan, arrived, Pamela, Rose, and Trudy had the EKG machine hooked up and running. Unfortunately it traced a flat, monotonous line. On the positive side, Bruce's color had improved slightly from its former grayish blue.

Jerry saw the flat EKG indicating no electrical activity, and, like Pamela, he hit the patient on the chest. No response. He checked the pupils: widely dilated and fixed. Behind Jerry was an intern named Peter Matheson, who climbed up on the bed and relieved Trudy. A disheveled medical student with long hair stood by the door.

"How long has this been going on?" asked Jerry.

"It's been five minutes since I found him," replied Pamela. "But I have no idea when he arrested. He wasn't on the monitor. His skin was dark blue."

Jerry nodded. For a split second he debated continuing resuscitation. He suspected the patient was already brain dead. But he still hadn't come to terms with denying treatment. It was easier to go ahead.

"I want two amps of bicarbonate and some epinephrine," barked Jerry as he took an endotracheal tube from the crash cart. Stepping behind the bed, he let Pamela inflate the lungs once more. Then he inserted the laryngoscope, an endotracheal tube, and attached an ambu bag, which he connected to the wall oxygen source. Resting his stethoscope on the patient's chest and telling Peter to hold up for a second, he compressed the ambu bag. Bruce's chest rose immediately.

"At least his airway is clear," said Jerry, as much to himself as anyone.

The bicarbonate and epinephrine were given.

"Let's give him calcium chloride," said Jerry, watching Bruce's face slowly turn a normal pink.

"How much?" asked Trudy, standing behind the crash cart.

"Five ccs of a ten-percent solution." Turning back to Pamela he said, "What's the patient in for?"

"Bypass surgery," said Pamela. Rose had brought down the chart and Pamela flipped it open. "He's four days postop. He's been doing well."

"Was doing well," corrected Jerry. Bruce's color looked almost normal but the pupils stayed widely dilated and the EKG ran out a flat line.

"Must have had a massive heart attack," said Jerry. "Maybe a pulmonary embolus. Did you say he was blue when you found him?"

"Dark blue," Pamela affirmed.

Jerry shook his head. Neither diagnosis should have produced deep cyanosis. His thoughts were interrupted by the arrival of a surgical resident, groggy with sleep.

Jerry outlined what he was doing. As he spoke, he held up a syringe of epinephrine to get rid of the air bubbles, then pushed it into Bruce's chest, perpendicular to the skin. There was an audible snap as the needle broke through some fascia. The only other sound was the EKG machine spewing out paper with the straight line. When Jerry pulled back on the plunger, blood entered the syringe. Confident he was in the heart, Jerry injected. He motioned for Peter to recommence compressing the chest and for Rose to reinflate the lungs.

Still there was no cardiac activity. As Jerry opened the outer cover of the sterile packaging holding a transvenous pacemaker electrode, he wished he had never begun the charade. Intuitively he knew the patient was too far gone. But now he had started, he had to finish.

"I'm going to need a fourteen-gauge intercath," said Jerry. With betedine on a cotton sponge, he began to prepare the entry site on the left side of Bruce's neck.

"Would you like me to do that?" asked the surgical resident, speaking for the first time.

"I think we have it under control," said Jerry, trying to project more confidence than he felt.

Pamela began helping him on with a pair of surgical gloves. They were just about to drape the patient when a figure appeared at the doorway and pushed past the medical student. Jerry's attention was drawn by the surgical resident's response: the ass-kisser did everything but salute. Even the nurses had perceptively straightened up as Thomas Kingsley, the hospital's most noted cardiac surgeon, strode into the room.

He was dressed in scrub clothes, obviously having come directly from the OR. He approached the bed and softly laid a hand on Bruce's forearm as if through the mere touch he could divine the problem.

"What are you doing?" he asked Jerry.

"I'm passing a transvenous pacemaker," said Jerry, shocked and impressed by Dr. Kingsley's presence. Staff members usually did not respond to cardiac arrests, especially in the middle of the night.

"Looks like total cardiac standstill," said Dr. Kingsley, running a portion of the voluminous EKG tape through his hands. "No evidence of any type of AV block. The chance of a transvenous pacemaker being successful is infinitesimally small. I think you're wasting your time." Dr. Kingsley then felt for a pulse at Bruce's groin. Glancing up at Peter, who was perspiring by this time, Dr. Kingsley said, "Pulse is strong. You must be doing a good job." Turning to Pamela he said: "Size eights, please."

Pamela produced the gloves without delay. Dr. Kingsley pulled them on and asked for the crash cart scalpel.

"Could you pull off the dressing?" said Dr. Kingsley to Peter. To Pamela he said he needed some sterile heavy dressing scissors.

Peter glanced at Jerry for confirmation, then paused in his massage, and pulled off the tangle of adhesive and gauze over the patient's sternum. Dr. Kingsley stepped up to the bed and fingered the scalpel. Without further delay he buried the tip of the knife in the top of the healing wound and decisively drew it down to the base. There was an audible snap as he cut each of the translucent blue nylon sutures. Peter slid off the bed to get out of the way.

"Scissors," said Dr. Kingsley calmly as his audience watched in shocked silence. This was the kind of scene they'd read about but had never seen.

Dr. Kingsley snipped through the wire sutures holding the split sternum together. Then he pushed both hands into the wound and forcibly pulled the sternum apart. There was a sharp cracking noise. Jerry Donovan tried to glance into Bruce's chest but Dr. Kingsley had obscured the view. The one thing Jerry could tell was that there was no bleeding whatsoever.

Dr. Kingsley eased his hand, fingers first, into Bruce's chest and cupped the apex of the heart. Rhythmically he began to compress it, nodding to Rose when she should inflate the lungs. "Check the pulse now," said Dr. Kingsley.

Peter dutifully stepped forward. "Strong," he said.

"I'd like some epinephrine, please," said Dr. Kingsley. "But it doesn't look good. I think this patient arrested some time ago."

Jerry Donovan thought about saying he had the same impression but decided against it.

"Call the EEG lab," said Dr. Kingsley, continuing to massage the heart. "Let's see if there's any brain activity at all."

Trudy went to the phone.

Dr. Kingsley injected the epinephrine but could see that there was no effect on the EKG. "Whose patient is this?" he asked.

"Dr. Ballantine's," said Pamela.

Bending over, Dr. Kingsley peered into the wound. Jerry guessed he was assessing the surgical repair. It was common hospital knowledge that on a scale of one to ten, as far as operative technique was concerned, Kingsley was a ten, and Ballantine, despite the fact that he was chief of the cardiac surgery department, was about a three.

Dr. Kingsley abruptly looked up and stared at the medical student as if he'd seen him for the first time. "How can you tell at the moment this isn't a case of an AV block, Doctor?"

All color drained from the student's face. "I don't know," he managed finally.

"Safe answer," smiled Dr. Kingsley. "I wish I had had the courage to admit not knowing something when I was a medical student." Turning to Jerry he asked: "What are his pupils doing?"

Jerry moved over and lifted Bruce's eyelids. "Haven't budged."

"Run in another amp of bicarbonate," ordered Dr. Kingsley. "I assume you gave some calcium."

Jerry nodded.

For the next few minutes there was silence as Dr. Kingsley massaged the heart. Then a technician appeared at the doorway with an ancient EEG machine.

"I just want to know if there's any electrical activity in the brain," said Dr. Kingsley. The technician attached the scalp electrodes and turned on the machine. The brain wave tracings were flat, just like the EKG.

"Unfortunately, that's that," said Dr. Kingsley as he withdrew his hand from Bruce's chest and stripped off his gloves. "I think someone better call Dr. Ballantine. Thank you for your help." He strode from the room.

For a moment no one spoke or moved. The EEG technician was first. Self-consciously he said he'd better get back to the lab. He unhooked his paraphernalia and left.

"I've never seen anything like that," said Peter, staring at Bruce's gaping chest.

"Me neither," agreed Jerry. "Kinda takes your breath away."

Both men stepped up to the bed and peered into the wound.

Jerry cleared his throat. "I don't know what you need more, competence or self-confidence, to cut into someone like that."

"Both," said Pamela, pulling the plug on the EKG machine. "How about you fellows giving us some room to get this place in order. By the way, one thing I forgot to mention. When I found Mr. Wilkinson, his IV was running rapidly. It should have been barely open." Pamela shrugged. "I don't know if it was important or not but I thought I'd let you know."

"Thanks," said Jerry absently. He wasn't listening. Daintily he stuck his index finger into the wound and touched Bruce's heart. "People say Dr. Kingsley is an arrogant son of a bitch, but there is one thing I know for sure. If I needed a bypass tomorrow, he is the one I'd have do it."

"Amen," said Pamela, pushing her way between Jerry and the bed to begin preparation of the body.

CHAPTER

1

"THERE WAS ONE new admission last night," said Cassandra Kingsley, glancing down at her preliminary work-up. She felt distinctly ill at ease, having been thrust into the spotlight of the early morning team meeting on the psychiatry ward, Clarkson Two. "His name is Colonel William Bentworth. He's a forty-eight-year-old Caucasian male, thrice divorced, who'd been admitted through the ER after an altercation in a gay bar. He was acutely intoxicated and abusive to the ER personnel."

"My God!" laughed Jacob Levine, the chief psychiatric resident. He took off his round, wire-rimmed glasses and rubbed his eyes. "Your first night on psychiatry call and you get Bentworth!"

"Trial by fire," said Roxane Jefferson, the black, no-nonsense head nurse for Clarkson Two. "No one can say psychiatry at the Boston Memorial is a boring rotation."

"He wasn't my idea of a perfect patient," admitted Cassi with a weak smile. Jacob's and Roxane's comments made her feel a bit more relaxed, sensing that if she made an ass of herself with her presentation, everyone would excuse her. Bentworth was no foreigner to Clarkson Two.

Cassi had been a psychiatry resident for less than a week. November wasn't the usual time for people to begin a residency, but Cassi had not decided to switch from pathology to psychiatry until after the beginning of the medical year in July and had only been able to do so because one of the first-year residents had quit. At the time Cassi thought she'd been extraordinarily lucky. But now she wasn't so sure. Starting a residency without other colleagues equally as inexperienced was more difficult than she'd anticipated. The other first-year residents had almost a five-month jump on her.

"I bet Bentworth had some choice words for you when you showed up," sympathized Joan Widiker, a third-year resident who was currently running the psychiatric consultation service and who had taken an immediate liking to Cassi.

"I wouldn't want to repeat them," admitted Cassi, nodding toward Joan. "In fact he refused to talk with me at all, other than to tell me what he thought of psychiatry and psychiatrists. He did ask for a cigarette, which I gave him, thinking it might relax him, but instead of smoking it he proceeded to press the lighted end against his arms. Before I could get some help, he'd burned himself in six places."

"He's a charmer all right," said Jacob. "Cassi, you should have called me. What time did he come in?"

"Two-thirty A.M.," said Cassi.

"I take that back," said Jacob. "You did the right thing."

Everyone laughed, including Cassi. For once there wasn't that substratum of hostile competition that had colored all her years of training. And none of the half-respectful, half-jealous commentary that had surrounded her relations at Boston Memorial since her marriage to Thomas Kingsley. Cassi hoped she would be able to repay their support.

"Anyway," she said, trying to organize her thoughts. "Mr. Bentworth, or I should say Colonel Bentworth, U.S. Army, presented with acute alcohol intoxication, diffuse anxiety alternating with a depressionlike state, fulminating anger, self-mutilating behavior, and an eight-pound chart of his previous hospitalizations."

The group erupted with renewed laughter.

"One point to Colonel Bentworth's credit," said Jacob, "is that he has helped train a generation of psychiatrists."

"I had that feeling," admitted Cassi. "I tried to read the most important parts of the chart. I think it's about the same length as *War and Peace*. At least it kept me from making a fool of myself and hazarding a diagnosis. He's been classified as a borderline personality disorder with occasional brief psychotic states.

"On physical examination he had multiple contusions on his face and a small laceration of his upper lip. The rest of the physical examination was normal except for his recent self-inflicted burns. There were slight scars across both wrists. He refused to cooperate for a full neurological exam, but he was oriented to time, place, and person. Since the present admission mirrored the last admission in terms of symptoms and since amytal sodium was used on the previous admission with such success, half a gram was given slowly IV."

At almost the exact instant that Cassi finished her presentation, her name floated out of the hospital page system. By reflex she started to get up, but Joan restrained her, saying the ward clerk would answer.

"Did you think Colonel Bentworth was a suicide risk?" asked Jacob.

"Not really," said Cassi, knowing she was hedging. Cassi was well aware that her ability to estimate suicide risk was approximately the same as the man in the street's. "Burning himself with his cigarette was self-mutilating rather than self-destructive."

Jacob twirled a lock of his frizzed hair and glanced at Roxane, who had been on Clarkson Two longer than anyone else. She was recognized as an authority of sorts. That was another reason why Cassi enjoyed the psychiatry service. There wasn't the stiff structure that existed elsewhere in the hospital, with physicians implacably at the top. Doctors, nurses, aides, everyone was part of the Clarkson Two team and respected as such.

"I've tended to ignore the distinction," said Roxane, "but I suppose there is a difference. Still we should be careful. He's an extremely complex man."

"That's an understatement," said Jacob. "The guy had a meteoric rise in the military, especially during his multiple tours of duty in Vietnam. He was even decorated several times, but when I looked into his army record, it always seemed as if a disproportionate number of his own men were killed. His psychiatric problems didn't seem to show up until he'd reached his present rank of colonel. It was as if success destroyed him."

"Getting back to the risk of suicide," said Roxane, turning to Cassi. "I think the degree of depression is the most important point."

"It wasn't typical depression," said Cassi, knowing she was venturing out on thin ice. "He said he felt empty rather than sad. One minute he acted depressed and the next he'd erupt with anger and abusive language. He was inconsistent."

"There you go," said Jacob. It was one of his favorite phrases, and its meaning was related to how he stressed the words. In this instance he was pleased. "If you had to pick one word to characterize a borderline patient, I think 'inconsistency' would be the most appropriate."

Cassi happily absorbed the praise. Her own ego had had very little to feed on during the previous week.

"Well, then," said Jacob. "What are your plans for Colonel Bentworth?"

Cassi's euphoria vanished.

Then one of the residents said, "I think Cassi should get him to stop smoking."

The group laughed and her tension evaporated.

"My plans for Colonel Bentworth," said Cassi, "are . . ." she paused, "that I'm going to have to do a lot of reading over the weekend."

"Fair enough," said Jacob. "In the meantime I'd recommend a short course of a major tranquilizer. Borderlines don't do well on extended medication, but it can help them over transient psychotic states. Now then, what else happened last night?"

Susan Cheaver, one of the psychiatric nurses, took over. With her usual efficiency, Susan summarized all the significant events that had taken place since late afternoon the previous day. The only happening out of the ordinary was an episode of physical abuse suffered by a patient called Maureen Kavenaugh. Her husband had come for one of his infrequent visits. The meeting had seemingly gone well for a while, but then there were angry words followed by a series of vicious open-handed slaps by Mr. Kavenaugh. The episode occurred in the middle of the patient lounge and severely upset the other patients. Mr. Kavenaugh had to be subdued and escorted from the ward. His wife had been sedated.

"I've spoken with the husband on several occasions," said Roxane. "He's a truck driver with little or no understanding of his wife's condition."

"And what do you suggest?" asked Jacob.

"I think," said Roxane, "that Mr. Kavenaugh should be encouraged to visit his wife but only when someone can be with them. I don't think Maureen will be able to retain a remission unless he's brought into the therapy in some capacity, and I think it's going to be hard to get him to cooperate."

Cassi watched and listened as the whole psychiatric team participated. After Susan had finished, each of the residents had an opportunity to discuss their patients. Then the occupational therapist, followed by the psych social worker, had a chance to speak. Finally Dr. Levine asked if there were any other problems. No one moved.

"Okay," said Dr. Levine, "see you all at afternoon rounds."

Cassi did not get up immediately. She closed her eyes and took a deep breath. The anxiousness engendered by the team meeting had hidden her exhaustion, but now that the excitement was over she felt it with a vengeance. She'd had only three hours of sleep. And for Cassi rest was important. Oh, how nice it would have felt to just lay her head down on her arm right there on the conference table.

"I bet you're tired," said Joan Widiker, placing her hand on Cassi's arm. It was a warm, reassuring gesture.

Cassi managed a smile. Joan was genuinely interested in other people. More than anyone, she had taken time to make Cassi's first week as a psychiatry resident as easy as possible.

"I'll make it," said Cassi. Then she added: "I hope."

"You'll make it fine," assured Joan. "In fact you did marvelously this morning."

"Do you really think so?" asked Cassi. Her hazel eyes brightened.

"Absolutely," said Joan. "You even drew a compliment of sorts out of Jacob. He liked your description of Colonel Bentworth as inconsistent."

"Don't remind me," said Cassi forlornly. "The truth is I wouldn't know a borderline personality disorder if I met one at dinner."

"You probably wouldn't," agreed Joan. "Nor would many other people, provided the patient was not having a psychotic episode. Borderlines can be fairly well compensated. Look at Bentworth. He's a colonel in the army."

"That did bother me," said Cassi. "It didn't seem to be consistent, either."

"Bentworth can upset anyone," said Joan, giving Cassi's arm a supportive squeeze. "Come on. I'll buy you some coffee in the coffee shop. You look like you could use it."

"I can use it all right," agreed Cassi. "But I'm not sure I should take the time."

"Doctor's orders," said Joan, getting up. As they walked down the corridor, she added, "I got Bentworth when I was a first-year resident, and I had the same experience as you did. So I know how you feel."

"No kidding," said Cassi, encouraged. "I didn't want to admit it at the meeting, but I found the colonel frightening."

Joan nodded. "Look, Bentworth's trouble. He's vicious, and he's smart. Somehow he knows just how to get at people: find their weaknesses. That power, combined with his pent-up anger and hostility, can be devastating."

"He made me feel completely worthless," said Cassi.

"As a psychiatrist," corrected Joan.

"As a psychiatrist," agreed Cassi. "But that's what I'm supposed to be. Maybe if I could find some similar case histories to read."

"There is plenty of literature," said Joan. "Too much. But it's a little like learning to ride a bike. You could read everything about bicycles, for years, yet when you finally tried to ride it yourself, you wouldn't be able to. Psychiatry is as much a process as it is knowledge. Come on, let's get that coffee."

Cassi hesitated. "Maybe I should get to work."

"You don't have any scheduled patient meetings right now, do you?" asked Joan.

"No, but . . ."

"Then you're coming." Joan took her arm and they started walking again.

Cassi allowed herself to be led. She wanted to spend a little time with Joan. It was encouraging as well as instructive. Maybe Bentworth would be willing to talk after a night's rest.

"Let me tell you something about Bentworth," said Joan, as if reading Cassi's mind. "Everyone that I know who has taken care of him, myself included, was certain they would cure him. But borderlines in general and Colonel Bentworth in particular don't get cured. They can get progressively better compensated but not cured."

As they passed the nurses' station, Cassi left Bentworth's chart and asked about her page. "It was Dr. Robert Seibert," said the aide. "He asked for you to call as soon as possible."

"Who's Dr. Seibert?" asked Joan.

"He's a resident in pathology," answered Cassi.

"As soon as possible sounds like you'd better call," said Joan.

"Do you mind?"

Joan shook her head, and Cassi went around the counter to use the phone next to the chart rack. Roxane came over to Joan. "She's a nice kid," the nurse said. "I think she's going to be a real addition around here." Joan nodded, and they both agreed that Cassi's insecurity and anxiety were a function of her commitment and dedication.

"But she worries me a little," added Roxane. "She seems to have a special vulnerability."

"I think she'll be fine," said Joan. "And she can't be too weak being married to Thomas Kingsley."

Roxane grinned and walked down the hall. She was a tall, elegant black woman who commanded respect for her intellect and sense of style. She'd worn her hair braided in corn rows long before it was fashionable.

As Cassi put down the phone, Joan eyed her carefully. Roxane was right. Cassi did seem delicate. Perhaps it was her pale, almost translucent skin. She was slender but graceful, only slightly over five-feet-two. Her hair was fine and varied in color from a shiny walnut to blond depending upon the angle and the light. At work she wore it loosely piled on her head, held in place with small combs and hairpins. But because of its texture, wisps spilled down around her face in gossamer strands. Her features were small and narrow, and her eyes turned up ever so slightly at the outer corners, giving them a mildly exotic appearance. She wore little makeup, which made her look younger than her twenty-eight years. Her clothes were always neat even if she'd been up most of the night, and today she was dressed in one of her many high-necked white blouses. To Joan, Cassi appeared like a young woman in an old Victorian photograph.

"Instead of going for coffee," said Cassi with enthusiasm, "how about coming with me to pathology for a few minutes?"

"Pathology," said Joan, with some reluctance.

"I'm sure we can get coffee up there," said Cassi, as if

that was the explanation of Joan's hesitation. "Come on. You might find it interesting."

Joan allowed herself to be led down the main corridor to the heavy fire door which led into the hospital proper. There were no locked doors on Clarkson Two. It was an "open" ward. Many of the patients were not allowed to leave the floor, but compliance was up to them. They knew if they ignored the rules they risked being sent to the State Hospital. There the environment was significantly different and much less pleasant.

As the door closed behind her, Cassi felt a sense of relief. In sharp contrast to the psychiatry ward, here in the main hospital building it was easy to distinguish the doctors and nurses from the patients. The doctors wore either suit jackets or their white coats; the nurses, their white uniforms; and the patients, their hospital johnnies. Back in Clarkson Two everyone wore street clothes.

As Cassi and Joan threaded their way toward the central elevators, Joan asked, "What was it like being a resident in pathology? Did you like it?"

"I loved it," said Cassi.

"I hope you don't take this as an insult," laughed Joan. "But you don't look like any pathologist I know."

"It's the story of my life," said Cassi. "First nobody would believe I was a medical student, then they said I looked too young to be a doctor, and last night Colonel Bentworth was kind enough to tell me I didn't look like a psychiatrist. What do you think I look like?"

Joan didn't answer. The truth was Cassi looked more like a dancer or a model than a doctor.

They joined the crowd of people in front of the bank of elevators serving Scherington, the main hospital building. There were only six elevators, which turned out to be an architectural blunder. Sometimes you could wait ten minutes for a car and then have to stop at every floor.

"What made you switch residencies?" asked Joan. As soon as the question left her lips, she regretted it. "You don't have to answer that. I don't mean to pry. I guess it's the psychiatrist in me."

"It's quite all right," said Cassi equably. "And actually it's quite simple. I have juvenile diabetes. In choosing my medical specialty, I've had to keep that reality in mind. I've tried to ignore it, but it is a definite handicap."

Joan's embarrassment was increased by Cassi's candor. Yet as uncomfortable as Joan felt, she thought it would be worse not to respond to Cassi's honesty. "I would have thought under the circumstances pathology would have been a good choice."

"I thought so too, at first," said Cassi. "But unfortunately during the past year I began to have trouble with my eyes. In fact, at the moment I can only distinguish light and dark with my left eye. I'm sure you know all about diabetic retinopathy. I'm not a defeatist but if worse comes to worst, I could practice psychiatry even if I became blind. Not so with pathology. Come on, let's get that first elevator."

Cassi and Joan were swept into the car. The door closed, and they started up.

Joan had not felt so uncomfortable in years, but she

felt she had to respond. "How long have you had diabetes?" she asked.

The simple question hurled Cassi back in time. Back to when she was eight and her life began to change. Up to that point, Cassi had always liked school. She was an eager, enthusiastic child who seemed to look forward to new experiences. But in the middle of the third grade it all changed. In the past she'd always been ready for school early; now she had to be pushed and cajoled by her mother. Her concentration dwindled and notes to that effect began to arrive from her teacher. One of the central issues, something that no one recognized, not even Cassi herself, was that Cassi had to use the girls' room more and more frequently. After a time the teacher, Miss Rossi, began on occasion to refuse Cassi's requests, suspecting that she was using trips to the toilet to avoid her work. When this happened, Cassi experienced the awful fear that she would lose control of her bladder. In her mind's eye she could picture what it would look like if she had "an accident," and her urine dripped down from her seat and puddled under her desk. The fear brought on anger and the anger, ostracism. The kids began to make fun of Cassi.

At home an episode of bedwetting surprised and shocked both Cassandra and her mother. Mrs. Cassidy demanded an explanation, but Cassandra had none and was, in fact, equally appalled. When Mr. Cassidy suggested they consult the family doctor, Mrs. Cassidy was too mortified to do so, convinced as she was that the whole affair was a behavioral disorder.

Various punishments had no effect. If anything they

exacerbated the problem. Cassi began to throw temper tantrums, lost her few remaining friends, and spent most of her time in her room. Mrs. Cassidy reluctantly began to think about the need for a child psychologist.

Things came to a head in the early spring. Cassi could remember the day vividly. Only a half hour after a recess, she began to experience a combination of mounting bladder pressure and thirst. Anticipating Miss Rossi's response so close to recess, Cassi tried vainly to wait for class to end. She squirmed in her seat and clutched her hands into tight fists. Her mouth became so dry she could barely swallow, and despite all her efforts, she felt the release of a small amount of urine.

In terror she walked pigeon-toed up to Miss Rossi and asked to be excused. Miss Rossi, without a glance, told her to take her seat. Cassi turned and walked deliberately to the door. Miss Rossi heard it open and looked up.

Cassi fled to the girls' room with Miss Rossi at her heels. She had her panties down and her dress bunched in her arms before Miss Rossi caught up to her. With relief, the little girl sank onto the toilet. Miss Rossi stood her ground, putting her hands on her hips, and waited with an expression that said: "You'd better produce or else . . ."

Cassi produced. She began to urinate and continued for what seemed like an incredible duration of time. Miss Rossi's angry expression mellowed. "Why didn't you go during recess?" she demanded. "I did," said Cassi plaintively.

"I don't believe you," said Miss Rossi. "I just don't

believe you, and this afternoon after school, we are going to march down to Mr. Jankowski's office."

Back in the classroom, Miss Rossi made Cassi sit by herself. She could still remember the dizziness that came over her. First she couldn't see the blackboard. Then she felt strange all over and thought she was going to vomit. But she didn't. Instead she passed out. The next thing Cassi knew was that she was in the hospital. Her mother was bending over her. She told Cassi she had diabetes.

Cassi turned to Joan, bringing her mind back to the present.

"I was hospitalized when I was nine," said Cassi hurriedly, hoping Joan hadn't noticed the fact that she had been daydreaming. "The diagnosis was made then."

"That must have been a difficult time for you," said Joan.

"It wasn't so bad," said Cassi. "In some respects it was a relief to know that the symptoms I had been having had a physical basis. And once the doctors stabilized my insulin requirements, I felt much better. By the time I reached my teens I even got used to giving myself the injections twice a day. Ah, here we are." Cassi motioned them off the elevator.

"I'm impressed," said Joan with sincerity. "I doubt if I'd have been able to handle my medical training if I had had diabetes."

"I'm certain you would have," said Cassi casually. "We're all more adaptable than we give ourselves credit for."

Joan wasn't sure she agreed, but she let it go. "What

about your husband? Having known a few surgeons in my life, I hope he's understanding and supportive."

"Oh, he is," said Cassi, but she answered too quickly for Joan's analytical mind.

Pathology was its own world, completely separate from the rest of the hospital. As a psychiatric resident, Joan hadn't visited the floor in the two years she'd been at Boston Memorial. She had prepared herself for the dark, nineteenth-century appearance of the department of pathology in her medical school, complete with dingy glass-fronted cabinets filled with round specimen jars containing bits of horror in yellowing Formalin. Instead, she found herself in a white, futuristic world composed of tile, Formica, stainless steel, and glass. There were no specimens and no clutter and no strangely repulsive smells. At the entrance there were a number of secretaries with earphones typing onto word-processing screens. To the left were offices, and down the center was a long white Formica table supporting double-headed microscopes.

Cassi led Joan into the first office where an impeccably dressed young man leaped up from his desk and greeted Cassi with a big, unprofessional hug. Then the man thrust Cassi away so he could look at her.

"God, you look good," he said. "But wait. You haven't colored your hair, have you?"

"I knew you'd notice," laughed Cassi. "No one else has."

"Of course I'd notice. And this is a new blouse. Lord and Taylor?"

"No, Saks."

"It's wonderful." He fingered the material. "It's all cotton. Very nice."

"Oh, I'm sorry!" said Cassi, remembering Joan and introducing her. "Joan Widiker, Robert Seibert, second-year pathology resident."

Joan took Robert's outstretched hand. She liked his engaging, forthright smile. His eyes twinkled, and Joan had the feeling she'd been instantly inspected.

"Robert and I went to the same medical school," explained Cassi as Robert put his arm around her again. "And then by chance we both ended up here at the Boston Memorial for first-year pathology."

"You two look like you could be brother and sister," said Joan.

"People have said that," said Robert, obviously pleased. "We had an immediate affinity for each other for a lot of reasons including the fact that we both had serious childhood diseases. Cassi had diabetes, and I had rheumatic fever."

"And we're both terrified of surgery," said Cassi, causing herself and Robert to burst out laughing.

Joan assumed it was some kind of private joke.

"Actually, it's not so funny," said Cassi. "Instead of mutually supporting each other, we've ended up making each other more scared. Robert is supposed to have his wisdom teeth removed, and I'm supposed to have the hemorrhage in my left eye cleared."

"I'm going to have mine taken care of soon," said Robert defiantly. "Now that I've got you out of my hair."

"I'll believe that when it happens," laughed Cassi.

"You'll see," said Robert. "But meanwhile let's get

down to business. I've saved the autopsy until you got here. But first I promised to call the medical resident who tried to resuscitate the patient."

Robert stepped back to his desk and picked up his phone.

"Autopsy!" Joan whispered, alarmed. "I didn't bargain on an autopsy. I'm not sure I'm up for that."

"It might be worthwhile," said Cassi innocently, as if watching an autopsy was something people did for amusement. "During my time as a pathology resident, Robert and I became interested in a series of cases that we've labeled SSD, for sudden surgical death. What we found was a group of cardiac surgery patients who had died less than a week after their operations even though most had been doing well and who, on autopsy, had no anatomical cause of death. A few might be understandable, but counting what turned up in the records for the last ten years, we found seventeen. The case Robert is going to autopsy now could make eighteen."

Robert returned from the phone saying Jerry Donovan would be right down and offered his guests coffee. Before they had a chance to drink it, Jerry arrived on the run. The first thing he did was give Cassi a hug. Joan was impressed. Cassi seemed to be on friendly terms with everyone. Then he slapped Robert on the shoulder and said, "Hey, man, thanks for the call."

Robert winced at the impact of the blow and forced a smile.

To Joan, Jerry was dressed like the usual house officer. His white jacket, rumpled and soiled, hung askew due to the weight of an overstuffed black notebook in the right pocket. His pants were spotted with a line of bloodstains across the thighs. Next to Robert, Jerry looked like a floor sweeper in a meat-packing house.

"Jerry went to the same medical school as Robert and I," explained Cassi. "Only he was an upper classman."

"A distinction that is still painfully obvious," kidded Jerry.

"Let's go," said Robert. "I've had one of the autopsy rooms on hold long enough."

Robert left first, followed by Joan. Jerry stepped aside for Cassi, then caught up to her.

"You'll never guess who I had the pleasure of watching do his thing last night," said Jerry as they skirted the microscope table.

"I wouldn't even try," said Cassi, expecting some off-color humor.

"Your husband! Dr. Thomas Kingsley."

"Really?" said Cassi. "What was a medicine man like you doing in the OR?"

"I wasn't," said Jerry. "I was on the surgical floor trying to resuscitate the patient we're going to autopsy. Your husband responded to the code. I was impressed. I don't think I've ever seen such decisiveness. He ripped this guy's chest open and gave open heart massage right on the bed. It blew my mind. Tell me, is your husband that impressive at home?"

Cassi shot Jerry a harsh glance. If that comment had come from anybody but Jerry, she probably would have snapped back. But she expected off-color humor and there it was. So why make an issue? She decided to let it drop.

Ignoring Cassi's less-than-positive reaction, Jerry

continued: "The thing that impressed me was not the actual cutting open of the guy's chest but rather the decision to do it in the first place. It's so goddamn irreversible. It's a decision I don't know how anybody could make. I agonize over whether or not to start a patient on antibiotics."

"Surgeons get used to that sort of thing," said Cassi. "That kind of decision making becomes a tonic. In a sense they enjoy it."

"Enjoy it?" echoed Jerry with disbelief. "That's pretty hard to believe, but I suppose they must; otherwise we wouldn't have any surgeons. Maybe the biggest difference between an internist and a surgeon is the ability to make irreversible decisions."

Entering the autopsy room, Robert donned a black rubber apron and rubber gloves. The others grouped around the pale corpse whose chest still gaped open. The edges of the wound had darkened and dried. Except for an endotracheal tube that stuck rudely out of the mouth, the patient's face looked serene. The eyes were thankfully closed.

"Ten to one it was a pulmonary embolism," said Jerry confidently.

"I'll put a dollar on that," said Robert, positioning a microphone which hung from the ceiling at a convenient height. It was operated by a foot pedal. "You told me yourself the patient initially had been very cyanotic. I don't think we're going to find an embolism. In fact, if my hunch is correct, we're not going to find anything."

As Robert began his examination, he started dictating into the mike. "This is a well-developed, well-nourished Caucasian male weighing approximately one hundred sixty-five pounds and measuring seventy inches in length who appears to be of the stated age of forty-two . . ."

As Robert went on to describe the other visible evidence of Bruce Wilkinson's surgery, Joan stared at Cassi, who was placidly sipping her coffee. Joan looked down at her own cup. The idea of drinking it made her stomach turn.

"Have all these SSD cases been the same?" asked Joan, trying not to look at the table where Robert was arranging scalpels, scissors, and bone clippers in preparation of opening and eviscerating the corpse.

Cassi shook her head. "No. Some have been cyanotic like this case, some seemed to have died from cardiac arrest, some from respiratory failure, and some from convulsions."

Robert began the usual Y-shaped autopsy incision, starting high on the shoulder and connecting with the open-chest incision. Joan could hear the blade scrape across the underlying bony structures.

"What about the kind of surgery?" asked Joan. She heard ribs crack and closed her eyes.

"They've all had open-heart surgery but not necessarily for the same condition. We've checked anesthesia, duration of pump time, whether or not hypothermia was used. There were no correlations. That's been the frustrating part."

"Well, why are you trying to relate them?"

"That's a good question," said Cassi. "It has to do with the mentality of a pathologist. After you've done an autopsy, it's very unsatisfying not to have a definitive cause of death. And when you have a series of such cases, it's demoralizing. Solving the puzzle is what makes pathology rewarding."

Involuntarily Joan's eyes stole a quick glance at the table. Bruce Wilkinson appeared as if he'd been un-zipped. The skin and subcutaneous structures of the chest and thorax had been folded back like the leaves of a gigantic book. Joan felt herself swaying.

"The knowledge is important," Cassi went on, un-aware of Joan's difficulties. "It can have a direct benefit to future patients if some preventable cause is dis-covered. And in this situation, we've noticed an alarm-ing trend. The initial patients seemed to have been older and much sicker. In fact, most were in irreversible coma. Lately though, the patients have been under fifty and generally healthier, like Mr. Wilkinson here. Joan, what's the matter?" Cassi had turned and finally noticed that her friend seemed about to faint.

"I'm going to wait outside," said Joan. She turned and started for the door, but Cassi caught her arm.

"Are you all right?" asked Cassi.

"I'll be fine," said Joan. "I just need to sit down." She fled through the stainless steel door.

Cassi was about to follow when Robert called for her to look at something. He pointed at a quarter-sized con-tusion on the surface of the heart.

"What do you think of that?" asked Robert.

"Probably from the resuscitation attempt," said Cassi.

"At least we agree on that," said Robert as he di-rected his attention back to the respiratory system and the larynx. Deftly he opened the breathing passages.

"No obstruction of any sort. If there had been, that would have explained the deep cyanosis."

Jerry grunted and said, "Goin' to be pulmonary embolism. I'm sure of it."

"It's a bad bet," said Robert, shaking his head.

Switching his attention lower, Robert examined the main pulmonary vessels and the heart itself. "These are the bypass vessels sewn in place." He leaned back so Cassi and Jerry could take a look.

Hefting a scalpel, Robert said: "Okay, Dr. Donovan. Better put your money on the table." Robert bent over and opened the pulmonary arteries. There were no clots. Next he opened the right atrium of the heart. Again the blood was liquid. Finally he turned to the vena cava. There was a bit of tension as the knife slipped into the vessels, but they too were clear. There were no emboli.

"Crap!" said Jerry in disgust.

"That's ten dollars you owe me," said Robert smugly.

"What the hell could have bumped this guy off?" asked Jerry.

"I don't think we're going to find out," said Robert. "I think we've got number eighteen here."

"If we are going to find anything," said Cassi, "it will be inside the head."

"How do you figure?" asked Jerry.

"If the patient was really cyanotic," said Cassi, "and we haven't found a right-to-left circulatory shunt, then the problem has to be in the brain. The patient stopped breathing, but the heart kept pumping unoxygenated blood. Thus cyanosis."

"What's that old saying?" said Jerry. "Pathologists know everything and do everything but too late."

"You forgot the first part," said Cassi. "Surgeons know nothing but do everything. Internists know everything but do nothing. Then comes the part about pathologists."

"And what about psychiatrists?" asked Robert.

"That's easy," laughed Jerry. "Psychiatrists know nothing and do nothing!"

Quickly Robert finished the autopsy. The brain appeared normal on close examination. No sign of clot or other trauma.

"Well?" asked Jerry, staring at the glistening convolution of Bruce's brain. "Do you two hotshots have any other bright ideas?"

"Not really," said Cassi. "Maybe Robert will find evidence of a heart attack."

"Even if I do," said Robert, "it wouldn't explain the cyanosis."

"That's true," said Jerry, as he scratched the side of his head. "Maybe the nurse was wrong. Maybe the guy was just ashen."

"Those nurses on cardiac surgery are awfully competent," said Cassi. "If they said the patient was dark blue, he was dark blue."

"Then I give up," said Jerry, taking out a ten-dollar bill and slipping it into the pocket of Robert's white jacket.

"You don't have to pay me," said Robert. "I was just kidding."

"Bullshit," said Jerry. "If it had been a pulmonary

embolism I'd have taken your money." Jerry walked over to where he'd hung his white jacket.

"Congratulations, Robert," said Cassi. "Looks like you got case number eighteen. Compared to the number of open-heart surgery cases they've done over the last ten years, that's getting close to being statistically significant. You'll get a paper out of this yet."

"What do you mean 'me'?" asked Robert. "You mean 'us,' don't you?"

Cassi shook her head. "No, Robert. This whole thing has been your idea from the start. Besides, now that I've switched to psychiatry, I can't hold up my end of the work."

Robert looked glum.

"Cheer up," said Cassi. "When the paper comes out, you'll be glad you didn't have to share authorship with a psychiatrist."

"I was hoping this study would get you to come up here frequently."

"Don't be silly," said Cassi. "I'll still come up, especially when you find new SSD cases."

"Cassi, let's go," called Jerry impatiently. He had the door held open with his foot.

Cassi gave Robert a peck on the cheek and ran out. Jerry took a playful swipe at her as she passed through the door. Not only did she evade the blow, but she managed to give Jerry's necktie a sharp tug as she passed.

"Where's your woman friend?" asked Jerry as they reached the main part of the pathology department. He was still struggling to straighten his tie.

"Probably in Robert's office," said Cassi. "She said

she needed to sit down. I think the autopsy was a little much for her."

Joan had been resting with her eyes closed. When she heard Cassi she got unsteadily to her feet. "Well, what did you learn?" She tried to sound casual.

"Not much," said Cassi. "Joan, are you all right?"

"Just a mortal wound to my pride," said Joan. "I should have known better than watch an autopsy."

"I'm terribly sorry . . ." began Cassi.

"Don't be silly," said Joan. "I came voluntarily. But I'd just as soon leave if you're ready."

They walked down to the elevators where Jerry decided to use the stairs since it was only four flights to the medical floor. He waved before disappearing into the stairwell.

"Joan," said Cassi, turning back to her. "I really am sorry I forced you up here. I'd gotten so accustomed to autopsies as a path resident that I'd forgotten how awful they can be. I hope it didn't upset you too much."

"You didn't force me up here," said Joan. "Besides, my squeamishness is my problem, not yours. It's just plain embarrassing. You'd think after four years of medical school I'd have gotten over it. Anyway, I should have admitted it and waited for you in Robert's office. Instead I acted like a fool. I don't know what I was trying to prove."

"Autopsies were hard for me at first," said Cassi, "but gradually it became easier. It is astounding what you can get used to if you do it enough, especially when you can intellectualize it."

"For sure," said Joan, eager to change the subject. "By the way, your men friends do run the gamut.

What's the story with Jerry Donovan? Is he available?"

"I think so," said Cassi, punching the elevator button again. "He was married back in med school but then divorced."

"I know the story," said Joan.

"I'm not sure if he's dating anyone in particular," said Cassi. "But I could find out. Are you interested?"

"I wouldn't mind asking him to dinner," said Joan pensively. "But only if I could be sure he'd put out on the first date."

It took a moment for Joan's comment to penetrate before Cassi burst out laughing. "I think you sized him up pretty well," she said.

"The macho medicine man," said Joan. "What about Robert?" Joan lowered her voice as they got on the elevator. "Is he gay?"

"I suppose so," said Cassi. "But we've never discussed it. He's been such a good friend, it has never mattered. He used to rate my boy friends back in medical school, and I used to listen until I met my husband because Robert was always right. But he must have been jealous of Thomas because he never liked him."

"Does he still feel that way?" asked Joan.

"I can't say," said Cassi. "That's the only other subject that we never talk about."

CHAPTER

2

"THE PATIENT IS READY for you in No. 3 cardiac cath room," said one of the X-ray technicians. She didn't come into the office but rather just stuck her head around the door. By the time Dr. Joseph Riggin turned to acknowledge the information, the girl was gone.

With a sigh, Joseph lifted his feet off his desk, tossed the journal he'd been reading onto the bookshelf, and took one last slug of coffee. From a hook behind the door he lifted his lead apron and put it on.

The radiology corridor at 10:30 A.M. reminded Joseph of a sale day at Bloomingdale's. There were people everywhere waiting in chairs, waiting in lines, and waiting on gurneys. Their faces had a blank, expectant look. Joseph felt an unwelcome sense of boredom. He'd been doing radiology now for fourteen years and he was beginning to admit to himself that the excitement had gone out of it. Every day was like every other day. Nothing unique ever happened anymore. If it hadn't been for the arrival of the CAT scanner a number of years ago, Joseph wondered if he'd have quit. As he pushed into No. 3, he tried to imagine what he could do if he left clinical radiology. Unfortunately he didn't have any bright ideas.

The No. 3 cath room was the largest of the five rooms so equipped. It had the newest equipment as well as its own built-in viewer screens. As Joseph entered, he saw that someone else's X rays had been left up. If he'd told his technicians once, he'd told them a thousand times that he wanted his room cleared of previous films before he did a study. Then, as if that wasn't enough, Joseph noticed there was no technician.

Joseph felt his blood pressure soar. It was a cardinal rule that no patients were ever to be left unattended. "Dammit," snarled Joseph under his breath. The patient was lying on the X-ray table, covered by a thin white blanket. He looked about fifteen years old, with a broad face and close-cropped hair. His dark eyes were watching Joseph intently. Next to the table was an IV bottle, and the plastic tube snaked under the blanket.

"Hello," said Joseph, forcing a smile despite his frustration.

The patient did not stir. As Joseph took the chart, he noticed that the boy's neck was thick and muscular. Another glance at the boy's face suggested that this was no ordinary patient. His eyes were abnormally tilted and his tongue, which partially protruded from his lips, was enormous.

"Well, what do we have here?" said Joseph with a

wave of uneasiness. He wished the boy would say something or at least look away. Joseph flipped open the chart and read the admitting note.

"Sam Stevens is a twenty-two-year-old muscular Caucasian male institutionalized since age four with undiagnosed mental retardation, who is admitted for definitive work-up and repair of his congenital cardiac abnormality thought to be a septal defect . . ."

The door to the cath room banged open, and Sally Marcheson breezed in carrying a stack of cassettes. "Hi, Dr. Riggin," she called.

"Why has this patient been left alone?"

Sally stopped short of the X-ray machine. "Alone?"

"Alone," repeated Joseph with obvious anger.

"Where's Gloria? She was supposed . . ."

"For Christ's sake, Sally," shouted Joseph. "Patients are never to be left alone. Can't you understand that?"

Sally shrugged. "I've only been gone fifteen or twenty minutes."

"And what about all these X rays? Why are they out?"

Sally glanced at the viewers. "I don't know anything about them. They weren't here when I left."

Quickly Sally began pulling the X rays down and stuffing them in the envelope on the countertop. It was someone's coronary angiogram, and she had no idea whatsoever why the X rays were there.

Still grumbling to himself, Joseph opened a sterile gown and pulled it on. Glancing back at the patient, he saw that the boy had not moved. His eyes still followed him wherever he moved.

With a frightful banging noise, Sally succeeded in loading the cassettes into the machine, then came back to pull off the sterile cover over the cath tray.

While Joseph pulled on rubber gloves, he moved over closer to the patient's face. "How are you doing, Sam?" For some reason, knowing the boy was retarded made Joseph think he should speak louder than usual. But Sam didn't respond.

"Do you feel okay, Sam?" called Joseph. "I'm going to have to stick you with a little needle, okay?"

Sam acted as if he were carved from granite.

"I want you to stay very still, okay?" persisted Joseph.

True to form, Sam didn't budge. Joseph was about to return his attention to the cath tray when Sam's tongue once again caught his attention. The protruding portion was cracked and dried. Looking closer, Joseph could see that Sam's lips weren't much better off. The boy looked like he'd been wandering around in a desert.

"You a little thirsty, Sam?" queried Joseph.

Joseph glanced up at the IV, noticing that it wasn't running. With a flick of his wrist he turned it on. No sense in the kid becoming dehydrated.

Joseph stepped over to the cath tray and took the gauze out of the prep dishes.

A high-pitched, inhuman scream shattered the stillness of the cath room. Joseph whirled around, his heart in his mouth.

Sam had thrown off his blanket and was clawing at the arm that had the IV. His feet began to hammer up and down on the X-ray table. A shrill cry still issued from his lips.

Joseph collected himself enough to pull the fluoroscopy unit back away from Sam's thrashing legs. He reached up and put his hands on Sam's shoulders to push him back onto the table. Instead Sam grasped Joseph's arm with such power that Joseph yelped out in pain. Powerless to prevent it, Joseph watched with horror as Sam pulled Joseph's hand up to his mouth, then sank his teeth into the base of Joseph's thumb.

It was now Joseph's turn to scream. He struggled to pull his arm from Sam's grasp, but the boy was far too strong. In desperation Joseph lifted a foot to the side of the X-ray table and pushed. He stumbled back and fell, pulling Sam on top of him.

Joseph felt Sam release his arm only to feel the boy's hands close around his throat. Pressure built up inside of his head as the boy squeezed. Desperately he tried to pull Sam's hands away, but they were like steel. The room began to spin. With a last reserve of strength, Joseph brought his knee up into the boy's groin.

Almost simultaneously, Sam's body heaved with a sudden contraction. It was rapidly followed by another and then another. Sam was having a grand mal seizure, and Joseph lay pinned to the floor beneath the heaving, convulsing body.

Sally finally recovered from shock and helped Joseph squirm free. Sam's eyes had disappeared inside his head and blood sprayed in a gradually widening circle from his mangled tongue

"Get help," gasped Joseph as he grasped his own wrist to stem the bleeding. Within the jagged edges of the wound he could see the glistening surface of exposed bone.

Before help arrived, Sam's wrenching spasms weakened and all but stopped. By the time Joseph realized the boy was not breathing, the medical emergency team arrived. They worked feverishly but to no avail. After fifteen minutes, a reluctant Dr. Joseph Riggin was led away to have his hand sutured while Sally Marcheson removed the misplaced X rays.

□

As Thomas Kingsley scrubbed, he felt the surge of excitement that always possessed him before an operation. He had known he was born to be a surgeon the first time he'd assisted in the OR as an intern, and it hadn't been long before his skill had been acknowledged throughout the hospital. Now as Boston Memorial's foremost cardiovascular surgeon, he had an international reputation.

Rinsing off the suds, Thomas lifted his hands to prevent water from running down his arms. He opened the OR door with his hip. As he did so, he could hear the conversation in the room trail off into awed silence. He accepted a towel from the scrub nurse, Teresa Goldberg. For a second their eyes met above their face masks. Thomas liked Teresa. She had a wonderful body that even the bulky surgical gown she was wearing could not hide. Besides, he could yell at her if need be, knowing she wouldn't burst into tears. She was also smart enough not only to recognize that Thomas was the best surgeon at the Memorial but to tell him so.

Thomas methodically dried his hands while he checked out the patient's vital signs. Then, like a general reviewing his troops, he moved around the room, nodding to Phil Baxter, the perfusionist, who stood behind his heart-lung machine. It was primed and humming, ready to take over the job of oxygenating the patient's blood and pumping it around the body while Thomas did his work.

Next Thomas eyed Terence Halainen, the anesthesiologist.

"Everything is stable," said Terence, alternately squeezing the breathing bag.

"Good," said Thomas.

Disposing of the towel, Thomas slipped on the sterile gown held by Teresa. Then he thrust his hands into special brown rubber gloves. As if on cue, Dr. Larry Owen, the senior cardiac surgery fellow, looked up from the operative field.

"Mr. Campbell is all ready for you," said Larry, making room for Thomas to approach the OR table. The patient lay with his chest fully opened in preparation for the famous Dr. Kingsley to do a bypass procedure. At Boston Memorial it was customary for the senior resident or fellow to open as well as close such operations.

Thomas stepped up to his position on the patient's right. As he always did at this point, he slowly reached into the wound and touched the beating heart. The wet surface of his rubber gloves offered no resistance, and he could feel all the mysterious movement in the pulsating organ.

The touch of the beating heart took Thomas's mind back to his first major case as a resident in thoracic surgery. He had been involved in many operations prior to that, but always as the first assistant, or second assistant, or somewhere down the line of authority. Then a patient named Walter Nazzaro had been admitted to the hospital. Nazzaro had had a massive heart attack and was not expected to live. But he did. Not only did he survive his heart attack, but he survived the rigorous evaluation that the house staff doctors put him through. The results of the work-up were impressive. Everyone wondered how Walter Nazzaro had lived as long as he had. He had occlusive disease in his main left coronary artery, which had been responsible for his heart attack. He also had occlusive disease in his right coronary artery with evidence of an old heart attack. In addition he had mitral and aortic valve disease. Then, as if that weren't enough, Walter had developed an aneurysm, or a ballooning of the wall, of his left ventricle of his heart as a result of the most recent heart attack. He also had an irregular heart rhythm, high blood pressure, and kidney disease.

Since Walter was such a fund of anatomic and physiologic pathology, he was presented at all the conferences with everyone offering various opinions. The only aspect of his case that everyone agreed upon was the fact that Walter was a walking time bomb. No one wanted to operate except a resident named Thomas Kingsley, who argued that surgery was Walter's only chance to escape the death sentence. Thomas continued to argue until everyone was sick of hearing him. Finally the chief resident agreed to allow Thomas to do the case.

On the day of surgery, Thomas, who had been working with an experimental method of aiding cardiac function, inserted a helium-driven counterpulsation balloon into Walter's aorta. Anticipating trouble with Walter's left ventricle, Thomas wanted to be prepared. Only after the operation had begun did the reality of the situation dawn on him. Excitement had changed to anxiety as Thomas began to follow the plan he had outlined in his mind. He would never forget the sensation he experienced when he stopped Walter's heart and held the quivering mass of sick muscle in his hand. At that moment he knew it was in his power to restore life. Refusing to consider the possibility of failure, Thomas first performed a bypass, an experimental procedure in those days. Then he excised the ballooned area of Walter's heart, oversewing the defect with rows of heavy silk. Finally, he replaced both the mitral and aortic valves.

The instant the repair was complete, Thomas tried to take Walter from the heart-lung machine. By this time, unknown to Thomas, a significant audience had gathered. There was a murmur of sadness when it was obvious that Walter's heart did not have the strength to pump the blood. Undaunted, Thomas started the counterpulsation device he had positioned before the operation.

He would always remember his elation when Walter's heart responded. Not only was Walter taken off the heart-lung machine, but three hours later in the recovery room even the counterpulsation assist was no longer needed. Thomas felt as if he had created life. The excitement was like a fix. For months afterward he was carried away by open-heart surgery. Reaching in, touching the heart, defying death with his own two hands—it was like playing God. Soon he found he became deeply depressed without the excitement of several such operations a week. When he went into practice he scheduled one, two, three such procedures a day. His reputation was so great that there was an endless stream of patients. As long as the hospital allowed him sufficient time in the OR, Thomas was supremely happy. But if another department or the boys in full-time academic medicine attempted to cut back his operating hours, Thomas became as tense and angry as an addict deprived of his daily drug. He needed to operate in order to survive. He needed to feel Godlike in order not to consider himself a failure. He needed the awed approval of other people, the unquestioning approval that was in Larry Owen's eyes this moment as he asked, "Have you decided if you're going to do a double or triple bypass?"

The question brought Thomas back to the present.

"It's a good exposure," said Thomas, appreciating Larry's work. "We might as well do three provided you got enough saphenous vein."

"More than enough," said Larry with enthusiasm. Prior to opening the chest, Larry had carefully removed a length of vein from Mr. Campbell's leg.

"All right," said Thomas with authority. "Let's get this show on the road. Is the pump ready?"

"All ready," said Phil Baxter, checking his dials and gauges.

"Forceps and scalpel," said Thomas.

Swiftly but without haste, Thomas began to work. Within minutes the patient was on the heart-lung machine. Thomas's operative technique was deliberate and without wasted motion. His knowledge of the anatomy was encyclopedic, as was his sense of feel for the tissue. He handled sutures with an economy of precise motion that was a joy for the aspiring surgeons to watch. Every stitch was perfectly placed. He'd done so many bypass procedures, he could almost function by rote, but the excitement of working on the heart never failed to stir him.

When he was through and convinced the bypasses were all sound and there was no excessive bleeding, Thomas stepped back from the table and snapped off his gloves.

"I trust you'll be able to put back the chest wall the way you found it, Larry," said Kingsley, turning to leave. "I'll be available if there is any trouble." As he left, he heard an audible sigh of appreciation from the residents.

Outside the operating room, the corridor was jammed with people. At that time of day, midafternoon, most of the thirty-six operating rooms were still occupied. Patients, either going to or coming from their surgery, were wheeled through on gurneys, sometimes with teams of people in attendance. Thomas moved among the crowd, occasionally hearing his name whispered.

As he passed the clock outside of central supply, he realized that he'd done Mr. Campbell in less than one hour. In fact, he'd done three bypass cases that day in the time it took most surgeons to do one or two at best.

Thomas told himself that he could have scheduled another operation although he recognized this was not true. The reason he had scheduled only three cases was the bothersome new rule that all surgeons attend Friday

afternoon cardiac surgical conference, a relatively recent creation of the chief of the department, Dr. Norman Ballantine. Thomas went, not because he was ordered to do so, but because it had become the ad hoc
admitting committee for the department of cardiac surgery. Thomas tried not to think about the situation,
because whenever he did so, it made him furious.

"Dr. Kingsley," called a harsh voice, interrupting
Thomas's thoughts.

Priscilla Grenier, the overbearing director of the
OR, was waving a pen at him. Thomas gave her credit
for being a hard worker and putting in long hours. It
was no picnic keeping the thirty-six operating rooms at
the Boston Memorial working smoothly. Yet he could
not tolerate it when she insinuated herself in his affairs,
something that she seemed eager to do. She always had
some order or instruction.

"Dr. Kingsley," called Priscilla. "Mr. Campbell's
daughter is in the waiting room, and you should go
down and see her before you change." Without waiting
for a reply, Priscilla turned back to her desk.

With difficulty, Thomas contained his annoyance
and continued down the hall without acknowledging
the comment. Some of the euphoria he had felt in the
OR left him. Lately he found the pleasure in each surgical success increasingly fleeting.

At first Thomas thought he'd ignore Priscilla,
change into his suit, then stop in to see Mr. Campbell's
daughter. However, the fact remained that he felt obligated to remain in his scrub clothes until Mr. Campbell
had reached the recovery room, just in case there were
unforeseen complications.

Banging open the door to the surgical lounge with his hand, Thomas stopped at the coat rack and rummaged for a long white coat to put over his scrub clothes. As he pulled it on, he thought about the unnecessary frustrations he was forced to endure. The quality of the nurses had definitely gone down. And Priscilla Grenier! It seemed like only yesterday that people like her knew their place. And compulsory Friday afternoon conferences . . . God!

In a distracted state, Thomas walked down to the waiting room. This was a relatively new addition to the hospital, which had been created out of an old storeroom. As the number of bypass procedures done by the department had soared, it was decided that there should be a special room close by where family members could stay until their loved ones were out of the OR. It had been the brainchild of one of the assistant administrators and turned out to be a gold mine for public relations.

When Thomas entered the room, which was tastefully decorated with pale blue walls and white trim, his attention was caught by an emotional outburst in the corner.

"Why, why?" shouted a small, distraught woman.

"There, there," said Dr. George Sherman, trying to calm the sobbing woman. "I'm sure they did all they could to save Sam. We knew his heart was not normal. It could have happened at any time."

"But he'd been happy at the home. We should have let him be. Why did I let you talk me into bringing him here. You told me there was some risk if you operated.

You never told me there was a risk during the catheterization. Oh God."

The woman's tears overwhelmed her. She began to
sag, and Dr. Sherman reached out to catch her arm.

Thomas rushed over to George's side and helped
support the woman. He exchanged glances with George,
who rolled his eyes at the outburst. As a member of the
full-time cardiac staff, Thomas did not have a high regard for Dr. George Sherman, but under the circumstances he felt obligated to lend a hand. Together they sat
the bereaved mother down. She buried her face in her
hands, her hunched-over shoulders jerking as she continued to sob.

"Her son arrested down in X ray during a catheterization," whispered George. "He was badly retarded
and had physical problems as well."

Before Thomas could respond, a priest and another
man, who was apparently the woman's husband, arrived. They all embraced, which seemed to give the
woman renewed strength. Together they hurriedly left
the room.

George straightened up. It was obvious that the situation had unnerved him. Thomas felt like repeating the
woman's question about why the child had been taken
from the institution where he'd apparently been happy,
but he didn't have the heart.

"What a way to make a living," said George self-
consciously as he left the room.

Thomas scanned the faces of the people remaining.
They were looking at him with a mixture of empathy
and fear. All of them had family members currently

undergoing surgery, and such a scene was extremely disquieting. Thomas looked for Campbell's daughter. She was sitting by the window, pale and expectant, arms on her knees, hands clasped. Thomas walked over to her and looked down. He'd seen her once before in his office and knew her name was Laura. She was a handsome woman, probably about thirty, with fine light brown hair pulled back from her forehead in a long ponytail.

"The case went fine," he said gently.

In response, Laura leaped to her feet and threw herself at Thomas, pressing herself against him and flinging her arms around his neck. "Thank you," she said, bursting into tears. "Thank you."

Thomas stood stiffly, absorbing the display of emotion. Her outburst had taken him by complete surprise. He realized that other people were watching and tried to disengage himself, but Laura refused to let go. Thomas remembered that after his first open-heart success, Mr. Nazzaro's family had been equally hysterical in their thanks. At that time Thomas had shared their happiness. The whole family had hugged him and Thomas had hugged them back. He could sense the respect and gratitude they felt toward him. It had been an unbelievably heady experience, and Thomas recalled the event with strong nostalgia. Now he knew his reactions were more complicated. He often did three to five cases a day. More often than not he knew little or nothing about his patients save for their preoperative physiological data. Mr. Campbell was a good example.

"I wish there was something I could do for you,"

whispered Laura, her arms still tightly wrapped around Thomas's neck. "Anything."

Thomas looked down at the curve of her buttocks, accentuated by the silk dress that hugged her form. Disturbingly he could feel her thighs pressed against his own, and he knew he had to get away.

Reaching up, he detached Laura's encircling arms.

"You'll be able to talk with your father in the morning," said Thomas.

She nodded, suddenly embarrassed by her behavior.

Thomas left her and walked from the waiting room with a feeling of anxiety that he did not understand. He wondered if it was fatigue, although he had not felt tired earlier even though he'd been up a good portion of the previous night on an emergency operation. Returning the white coat to the rack, he tried to shrug off his mood.

Before going into the lounge, Thomas paid a visit to the recovery room. His two previous cases, Victor Marlborough and Gwendolen Hasbruck, were stable and doing predictably well, but as he looked down at their faces he felt his anxiety increase. He wouldn't have recognized them in a crowd although he'd held their hearts in his hand just hours before.

Feeling distracted and irritated by the forced camaraderie of the recovery room, Thomas retreated to the surgical lounge. He didn't particularly care for the taste of coffee, but he poured himself a cup and took it over to one of the overstuffed leather armchairs in the far corner. The living section of the *Boston Globe* was on the floor, and he picked it up, more as a defense than for what it contained. Thomas didn't feel like being trapped into small talk with any of the OR personnel. But the ploy didn't work.

"Thanks for the help in the waiting room."

Thomas lowered the paper and looked up into the broad face of George Sherman. He had a heavy beard, and by that time in the afternoon it appeared as if he'd forgotten to shave that morning. He was a stocky, athletic-looking man an inch or two shorter than Thomas's six feet, but his thick, curly hair made him look the same height. He had already changed back to his street clothes, which included a wrinkled blue button-down shirt that appeared as if it had never felt the flat surface of an iron, a striped tie, and a corduroy jacket somewhat threadbare on the elbows.

George Sherman was one of the few unmarried surgeons. What put him in a unique class was that at age forty he'd never been married. The other bachelors were either separated or divorced. And George was a particular favorite among the younger nurses. They loved to tease him about his errant bachelor's life, offering help in various ways. George's intelligence and humor took all this in stride, and he milked it for all it was worth. Thomas found it all exceedingly irritating.

"The poor woman was pretty upset," said Thomas. Once again he had to refrain from making some comment concerning the advisability of bringing such a case into the hospital. Instead he raised his paper.

"It was an unexpected complication," said George, undeterred. "I understand that good-looking chick in the waiting room was your patient's daughter."

Thomas slowly lowered his paper again.

"I didn't notice she was particularly attractive," Thomas said shortly.

"Then how about sharing her name and phone number?" said George with a chuckle. When Thomas failed to respond, George tactfully changed the subject. "Did you hear that one of Ballantine's patients arrested and died during the night?"

"I was aware of it," said Thomas.

"The guy was an admitted homosexual," said George.

"That I didn't know," said Thomas with disinterest. "I also didn't know that the presence or absence of homosexuality was part of a routine cardiac surgical work-up."

"It should be," said George.

"And why do you think so?" asked Thomas.

"You'll find out," said George, raising an eyebrow. "Tomorrow in Grand Rounds."

"I can't wait," said Thomas.

"See you in conference this afternoon, sport," said George, giving Thomas a playful thump on the shoulder.

Thomas watched the man saunter away from him. It annoyed him to be touched and pummeled like that. It seemed so juvenile. While he watched, George joined a group of residents and scrub nurses slumped over several chairs near the window. Laughter and raised voices drifted across the room. The truth was that Thomas could not stand George Sherman. He was convinced George was a man bent on accumulating the trappings of success to cover a basic mediocrity in surgical skill. It was all too familiar to Thomas. One of the seemingly inadvertent evils of the academic medical center was that appointments were more political than anything else. And George was political. He was quick-witted, a good conversationalist, and socialized easily. Most important, he thrived within the bureaucratic committee system of hospital politics. He'd learned early that for success it was more important to study Machiavelli than Halstead.

Thomas knew that the root of the problem was an antagonism between the doctors on the teaching staff like himself, who had private practices and earned their incomes by billing their patients, and the doctors like George Sherman, who were full-time employees of the medical school and received salaries instead of fees for service. The private doctors had substantially higher incomes and more freedom. They did not have to submit to a higher authority. The full-time doctors had more impressive titles and easier schedules, but there was always someone over them to tell them what to do.

The hospital was caught in the middle. It liked the high census and money brought in by the private doctors, and, at the same time, it enjoyed the credibility and status of being part of the university medical school.

"Campbell's chest is closed," said Larry, interrupting Thomas's thoughts. "The residents are closing the skin. All signs are stable and normal."

Tossing the newspaper aside, Thomas got up from the chair and followed Larry toward the dressing room. As he passed behind George, Thomas could hear him talking about forming some kind of new teaching committee. It never stopped! Nor did the pressure that George, as head of the teaching service, and Ballantine, as head of the department, applied to Thomas, trying to convince him to give up his practice and join the full-time staff. They tried to entice him by offering him a full professorship, and although there'd been a time when that might have interested Thomas, now it held no appeal whatsoever. He'd keep his practice, his autonomy, his income, and his sanity. Thomas knew if he went full time it would only be a matter of time before he was told who he could and who he could not operate on. Before long he'd be assigned ridiculous cases like the poor mentally retarded kid in the cath room.

Tense and angry, Thomas went into the dressing area and opened his locker. As he pulled off his scrub clothes and tossed them into the hamper, he recalled Laura Campbell's pliant body pressed against his own. It was a welcome and pleasant image and had the effect of mollifying his frazzled nerves. Ever since he'd left the OR, his pleasure in operating had dissipated, leaving him increasingly tense.

"As usual, you did a superb job today," said Larry, noting Thomas's grim face and hoping to please him.

Thomas didn't respond. In the past he would have loved such a compliment, but now it didn't seem to make any difference.

"It's too bad that people can't appreciate the details," said Larry, buttoning his shirt. "They'd have a totally different idea of surgery if they did. They'd also be more careful who they let operate on them."

Thomas still did not say anything, although he nodded at the truth of the comment. As he pulled on his own shirt, he thought of Norman Ballantine, that white-haired, friendly old doc whom everyone loved and applauded. The fact of the matter was that Ballantine probably shouldn't still be operating, although no one had the nerve to tell him. It was common knowledge in the department that one of the chief thoracic resident's jobs was to assign himself to all of Ballantine's cases so that he could help the chief when he blundered. So much for academic medicine, thought Thomas. Ballantine, thanks to the residents, got reasonable results, and his patients and their families worshipped him despite what went on when the patient was anesthetized.

Thomas had to agree with Larry's comment. He also thought that it would be infinitely more appropriate if he, Dr. Thomas Kingsley, was chief. After all, he did most of the surgery, for God's sake. It was he, more than any other single person, who had made Boston Memorial the place to have any cardiac surgery. Even *Time* magazine had said as much.

Yet Thomas did not know if he wanted to be chief any longer. At one time it was all he could think about. It had been one of his driving forces, pushing him on to greater efforts and more personal sacrifice. It had seemed part of a natural progression, and colleagues had started talking about it while he was still a fellow. But that was quite a few years ago, before all the administrative bullshit had reared its ugly head and showed just how much it could interfere in his practice.

Thomas stopped dressing and stared ahead into the distance. He felt an emptiness inside of him. Comprehending that one of his long sought-after goals was potentially no longer attractive was depressing, especially when the goal was finally within his grasp. Maybe there was no place to go . . . maybe he'd reached his apogee. God, what an awful thought!

"I'm awfully sorry to hear about your wife," said Larry as he sat down to put on his shoes. "It really is a shame."

"What do you mean?" asked Thomas, pronouncing each word with deliberate precision. He took immediate offense that a subordinate like Larry would presume to be so familiar.

Larry, oblivious to Thomas's response, bent to tie his shoes. "I mean about her diabetes and her eye problem. I heard she's got to have a vitrectomy. That's terrible."

"The surgery is not definite," snapped Thomas.

Hearing the anger in Thomas's voice, Larry looked up. "I didn't mean it was necessarily definite," he managed. "I'm sorry I brought it up. It must be difficult for you. I just hoped that she was okay."

"My wife is perfectly fine," said Thomas angrily. "Furthermore, I don't think that her health is any of your business."

"I'm sorry."

There was an uncomfortable silence as Larry quickly finished with his shoes. Thomas tied his tie and splashed on Yves St. Laurent cologne with rapid, irritated motions.

"Where did you hear this rumor?" asked Thomas.

"From a pathology resident," said Larry. "Robert Seibert."

Larry closed his locker and told Thomas he'd be in the recovery room if he was needed.

Thomas ran a comb through his hair, trying to calm

down. It just wasn't his day. Everyone seemed intent on upsetting him. The idea that his wife's ill health was a topic of idle conversation among the resident staff seemed inexplicably galling. It was also humiliating.

Placing the comb back in his locker, Thomas noticed a small plastic container. Feeling a rising inner tension and the stirrings of a headache, he flipped open the lid of the bottle. Snapping one of the scored yellow tablets in two, he popped the half into his mouth. Hesitant, he then popped in the other half as well. After all, he deserved it.

The tablets tasted bitter, and he needed a drink from the fountain to wash them down. But almost immediately he felt relief from his growing anxiety.

☐

The Friday afternoon cardiac surgery conference was held in the Turner surgical teaching room diagonally across the hall from the surgical intensive care unit. It had been donated by the wife of a Mr. J. P. Turner, who'd died in the late nineteen-thirties, and the decor had an Art Deco flavor. The room provided seating for sixty, half the medical school class size in 1939. In the front there was a raised podium, a dusty blackboard, an overhead rack of ancient anatomy charts, and a standing skeleton.

It had been at Dr. Norman Ballantine's insistence that the Friday meeting be held in the Turner teaching room because it was close to the ward, and, as Dr. Ballantine put it, "It is the patients that it's all about." But the small group of a dozen or so looked lost among the sea of empty seats and distinctly uncomfortable behind the spartanly designed desks.

"I think we should get the meeting under way," called Dr. Ballantine over the hum of conversation. The people took their seats. Present at the meeting were six of the eight cardiac surgeons on staff, including Ballantine, Sherman, and Kingsley, as well as various other doctors and administrators, and a relatively new addition, Rodney Stoddard, philosopher.

Thomas watched Rodney Stoddard sit down. He looked like he was in his late twenties despite the fact that he was mostly bald and his remaining hair was such a light color that it was difficult to see it. He wore thin wire-rimmed glasses and an expression of constant self-satisfaction. To Thomas it seemed as if the man were saying, "Ask me about your problem because I know the answer."

Stoddard had been hired at the university's insistence. Until recently doctors were committed to trying to save all their patients. But now, with the advent of such expensive and complicated procedures as open-heart surgery, transplants, and artificial organs, hospitals had to pick and choose to whom to give these life-saving operations. For the time being, these techniques were limited by extraordinary costs and by the space available in the sophisticated units needed for aftercare. In general the teaching staff tended to favor patients with multisystemic disease, who did not always do well, while private physicians such as Thomas leaned toward otherwise healthy, productive members of society.

Looking at Rodney, Thomas allowed an ironic smile

to steal across his face. He wondered just how self-confident Rodney would feel if he held a man's heart in his hand. That was a time for decision, not discussion. As far as Thomas was concerned, Rodney's presence at the meeting was one more indication of the bureaucratic soup in which medicine was drowning.

"Before we start," said Dr. Ballantine, extending his arms with hands spread out as if to quiet a crowd, "I want to be sure that everyone has seen the article in this week's *Time* magazine rating the Boston Memorial as *the* center for cardiac bypass surgery. I think we deserve it, and I want to thank each and every one of you for helping us reach this position." Ballantine clapped, followed by George and a smattering of others.

Thomas, who'd sat near the door in case he was called to the recovery room, glowered. Ballantine and the other doctors were taking credit for something that was due largely to Thomas and to a lesser extent to two other private surgeons who happened to be absent. When he had gone into surgery, Thomas thought he would avoid the bullshit that surrounded most other professions. It was going to be him and the patient against disease! But as Thomas looked around the room, he realized that almost everyone at the meeting could interfere with his work because of one aggravating problem—the limited number of cardiac surgical beds and associated OR time. The Memorial had become so famous that it seemed as if everyone wanted to have their bypass there. People literally had to wait in line. Especially in Thomas's practice. He had been limited to nineteen OR slots a week and he had a backlog of more than a month.

"While George passes out the schedule for next week," said Dr. Ballantine, extending a stack of stapled papers to George, "I'd like to recap this week."

He droned on as Thomas turned his attention to the schedule. His own patients were scheduled by his nurse, who collated the necessary information and got it over to Ballantine's secretary, who typed it up. It contained a capsule medical history of each patient, a listing of significant diagnostic data, and an explanation of the need for surgery. The idea was that everyone at the conference would go over each patient and make sure that the operation was needed or advisable. But in reality it rarely happened, except if you missed the meeting. Once when Thomas had been absent, the anesthesiology department had canceled several of his cases, resulting in a row no one was likely to forget. Thomas continued reviewing the sheets until Ballantine mentioned something about deaths. Thomas looked up.

"Unfortunately there were two surgical deaths this week," said Dr. Ballantine. "The first was a case on the teaching service, Albert Bigelow, an eighty-two-year-old gentleman who could not be weaned from the pump after a double-valve replacement. He'd been scheduled as an emergency. Is there word on the autopsy yet, George?"

"Not yet," said George. "I must point out that Mr. Bigelow was a very sick cookie. His alcoholism had seriously affected his liver. We knew we were taking a risk going to surgery. You win some and you lose some."

There was a silence. Thomas commented sarcastically to himself that Mr. Bigelow's untimely demise had prompted a stimulating discussion. The galling part was that it was this kind of patient that was keeping Thomas's patients waiting.

Ballantine glanced around, and when no one spoke he continued: "The second death was a patient of mine, Mr. Wilkinson. He died last night. He was autopsied this morning."

Thomas saw Ballantine look over at George, who shook his head almost imperceptibly.

Ballantine cleared his throat and said that both cases would be discussed at the next death conference.

Thomas wondered at the silent communication. It brought to mind the weird comment George had made up in the lounge. Thomas shook his head.

Something was going on between Ballantine and George, and Thomas felt a twinge of uneasiness. Ballantine had a unique position in the medical center. As chief of cardiac surgery, he held an endowed chair with the university and was paid a salary. But Ballantine also had a private practice. Ballantine was a holdover from the past, bridging as he did the full-time salaried men like George and the private staff, like Thomas. Of late Thomas had begun to think that Ballantine, whose skills were obviously on the decline, was beginning to favor the prestige of being a professor over the rewards of private practice. If that were true, it could cause trouble by upsetting the balance between the full-time staff and the private physicians, which in the past had always tilted toward the latter.

"Now, if everyone will turn to the last page of the handout," said Dr. Ballantine, "I'd like to point out that there has been a major scheduling change."

There was a simultaneous rustle as everyone flipped

the pages. Thomas did the same, placing the papers on the arm of his chair. He did not like the sound of a major scheduling change.

The last page was divided vertically into four columns, representing the four rooms used for open-heart surgery. Horizontally the page was divided into the five days of the work week. Within each box were the names of the surgeons scheduled for that day. OR No. 18 was Thomas's room. As the fastest and busiest surgeon, he was assigned four cases on each day except Friday when he had three because of the conference. The first thing Thomas checked when he looked at the page was OR No. 18. His eyes widened in disbelief. The schedule suggested that he'd been cut to three cases a day, Monday through Thursday. He'd lost four slots!

"The university has authorized us to hire another full-time attending for the teaching service," Dr. Ballantine was saying proudly, "and we have started a search for a pediatric cardiac surgeon. This, of course, is a major advance for the department. In preparation for this new situation, we are expanding the teaching service by an additional four cases per week."

"Dr. Ballantine," began Thomas, carefully controlling himself. "It appears from the schedule that all four additional teaching slots are being taken from my allotted time. Am I to assume that is just for next week?"

"No," said Dr. Ballantine. "The schedule you see will hold until further notice."

Thomas breathed out slowly before speaking. "I must object. I hardly think it's fair that I should be the sole person to give up OR time."

"The fact of the matter is that you have been controlling about forty percent of the OR time," said George. "And this is a teaching hospital."

"I participate in teaching," snapped Thomas.

"We understand that," said Ballantine. "You're not to take this personally. It is plainly a matter of more equitable distribution of OR time."

"I'm already over a month behind on my patient schedule," said Thomas. "There isn't that kind of demand for teaching cases. There aren't enough patients to fill the current teaching slots."

"Don't worry," said George. "We'll find the cases."

Thomas knew what the real issue was. George, and most of the others, were jealous of the number of cases Thomas did and how much money Thomas earned. He felt like getting up and punching George right in the face. Glancing around the room, Thomas noticed that the rest of the doctors were suddenly busy with their notes, papers, or other belongings. He could not count on any of the people present to back him up.

"What we all have to understand," said Dr. Ballantine, "is that we are all part of the university system. And teaching is a major goal. If you feel pressure from some of your private patients, you could take them to other institutions."

Thomas's anger and frustration made it hard for him to think clearly. He knew, in fact everybody knew, that he could not just pick up and go to another hospital. Cardiac surgery required a trained and experienced team. Thomas had helped build the system at the Memorial, and he depended on the structure.

Priscilla Grenier spoke up, saying they might be able to add an additional OR room if they got an appropriation for another heart-lung machine and perfusionist to run it."

"That's a thought," responded Dr. Ballantine. "Thomas, perhaps you'd be willing to chair an ad hoc committee to look into the advisability of such expansion."

Thomas thanked Dr. Ballantine, struggling to keep his sarcasm to a minimum. He said that with his current workload it was not possible to accept Ballantine's offer immediately, but that he'd think about it. At the moment he had to worry about putting off patients who might die before they had OR time. Patients with a ninety-nine-percent chance of living long, productive lives if they did not find their OR time sacrificed to some sclerotic wino whom the teaching service wished to experiment on!

On that note the meeting was adjourned.

Struggling to keep his temper under control, Thomas went up to Ballantine. George had, of course, beat Thomas to the podium, but Thomas interrupted.

"Could I speak to you for a moment?" asked Thomas.

"Of course," said Dr. Ballantine.

"Alone," said Thomas succinctly.

"I was heading over to the ICU anyway," said George amiably. "I'll be in my office if you need me." George gave Thomas a pat on the shoulder before leaving.

To Thomas, Ballantine was the Hollywood image of the physician, with his soft white hair combed back from a deeply lined but tanned and handsome face. The only feature that somewhat marred the overall effect were the ears. By anyone's standards they were large. Right now Thomas felt like grabbing and shaking them.

"Now, Thomas," said Dr. Ballantine quickly. "I don't want you getting paranoid about all this. You have to understand that the university has been putting pressure on me to delegate more OR time to teaching, especially with the *Time* article. That kind of publicity is doing wonders for the endowment program. And as George pointed out, you have been controlling a disproportionate amount of hours. I'm sorry you had to learn about it like this, but . . ."

"But what?" asked Thomas.

"You are in private practice," said Dr. Ballantine. "Now if you'd agree to come full-time, I can guarantee a full professorship and . . ."

"My title as Assistant Clinical Professor is fine with me," said Thomas. Suddenly he understood. The new schedule was another attempt at pressuring him into giving up his private practice.

"Thomas, you do know that the chief of cardiac surgery who follows me will have to be full-time."

"So I'm to look at this cut in my OR time as a *fait accompli*," said Thomas, ignoring Ballantine's implications.

"I'm afraid so, Thomas. Unless we get another OR, but, as you know, that takes time."

Abruptly Thomas turned to go.

"You'll think about coming aboard full-time, won't you?" called Dr. Ballantine.

"I'll consider it," said Thomas, knowing he was lying.

Thomas left the teaching room and started down the stairs. At the first landing he stopped. Gripping the handrail and closing his eyes as tightly as possible, he let his body shake with sheer anger. It was only for a moment. Then he straightened up. He was back in control. After all, he was a rational individual, and he'd been up against bureaucratic nonsense long enough to deal with it. He'd suspected that Ballantine and George were up to something. Now he knew. But Thomas wondered if that were all. Maybe it was something more than the OR schedule change because he still had the anxious feeling something else was going on that he should know about.

CHAPTER

3

CASSI ALWAYS EXPERIENCED a degree of apprehension when she dipped the test tape into her urine. There was always the chance that the color of the tape would change and indicate she was losing sugar. Not that a little sugar in her urine was all that big a deal, especially if it occurred only once in a while. It was more an emotional thing; if she was spilling sugar, then she was not in control. It was the psychological aspect that was disturbing.

The light in the toilet was poor, forcing Cassi to unlatch the stall door in order to get a good look at the tape. It had not changed its color. Having gotten so little sleep the night before and having cheated that afternoon with a fruit yogurt snack, she wouldn't have been too surprised to see a little sugar. Cassi was pleased that the amount of insulin she was giving herself and her

diet were in balance. Her internist, Dr. Malcolm Mc-
Inery, talked occasionally of switching her to a constant
insulin-infusion device, but Cassi had demurred. She
was reluctant to alter a system that seemed to be working. She did not mind giving herself two injections a
day, one before breakfast and one before dinner. It had
become so routine as to be effortless.

Closing her right eye, Cassi looked at the test tape.
There was just a vague sensation of light as if she were
looking through a wall of ground glass. She wished that
she didn't have the problem with her eye because the
idea of blindness terrified her more, in some ways, than
the idea of death. The possibility of death she could
deny, just like everyone else. But denying the possibility
of blindness was difficult with the condition of her left
eye there to remind her each and every day. The problem had happened suddenly. She'd been told that a
blood vessel had broken, causing blood to enter into the
vitreous cavity.

As she washed her hands, Cassi examined herself in
the mirror. The single overhead light was kind, she decided, giving her skin more color than she knew it possessed. She looked at her nose. It was too small for her
face. And her eyes: they curved unnaturally upwards at
the outer corners as if she had her hair pulled back too
tightly. Cassi tried to look at herself without concentrating on any single feature. Was she really as attractive as
people said? She'd never felt pretty. She had always
thought that diabetes was indelibly stamped in bold letters across her forehead. She was convinced that her
disease was a major flaw that everyone could see.

It hadn't always been that way. In high school Cassi

had tried to reduce it to a small aspect of her life. Something she could compartmentalize. And although she was conscientious about her medicine and diet, she did not want to dwell on it.

Yet this approach made her parents, mostly her mother, understandably concerned. They felt that the only way she would be able to maintain the discipline the disease required was to make it her major focus. At least that was the way Mrs. Cassidy had dealt with the problem.

The conflict came to a head at the time of the senior prom.

Cassi came home from school beside herself with excitement and anticipation. The prom was to be held in a fashionable local country club, followed by a breakfast back at the school. Then the entire class was to head down to the New Jersey shore for the rest of the weekend.

Unexpectedly Cassi had been asked to the prom by Tim Bartholomew, one of the more popular boys in the school. He'd talked with Cassi on a number of occasions following a physics class they shared. But he'd never asked Cassi out, so the invitation came as a total surprise. The thrill of going out with a desirable boy to the biggest social event of the year was almost too much for Cassi to bear.

Cassi's father was the first to hear the good news. As a rather dry professor of geology at Columbia University, he didn't share the same enthusiasm as Cassi but was pleased she was happy.

Cassi's mother was less enthusiastic. Coming in from

the kitchen, she told Cassi that she could go to the prom but had to come home instead of going to the breakfast.

"They don't cook for diabetics at such affairs," said Mrs. Cassidy, "and as far as going to the shore for the weekend, that is completely out of the question."

Not expecting this negative response, Cassi was ill-prepared to deal with it. She protested through tears that she'd demonstrated adequate responsibility toward her medicine and diet and that she should be allowed to go.

Mrs. Cassidy was adamant, telling Cassi that she was only thinking of her welfare. Then she said that Cassi had to accept the fact that she was not normal.

Cassi screamed that she was normal, having emotionally struggled with that very issue for her entire adolescence.

Mrs. Cassidy grasped Cassi's shoulders and told her daughter that she had a chronic, life-long disease and that the sooner she accepted the fact the better off she'd be.

Cassandra flew to her room, locking her door. She refused to talk with anyone until the next day. When she did, she informed her mother that she'd called Tim and told him that she couldn't go to the prom because she was ill. She told her mother that Tim had been surprised because he'd not known she had diabetes.

Staring at her reflection in the hospital mirror, Cassi brought herself back to the present. She wondered to what degree she had overcome her disease intellectually. Oh, she knew a lot about it now and could quote all sorts of facts and figures. But had that knowledge been worth the sacrifices? She didn't know the answer to that question and probably never would. Her eyes strayed up to her hair, which was a mess.

After taking out her combs and hairpins, Cassi gave her head a shake. Her fine hair tumbled down around her face in a disorganized mop. With practiced hands she carefully put it back up, and when she emerged from the bathroom she felt refreshed.

The few things she'd brought with her for the overnight in the hospital fitted easily into her canvas shoulder bag despite the fact that it already contained a large folder of reprinted medical articles. She'd had the bag since college, and although it was soiled and threadbare in places, it was an old friend. It had a large red heart on one side. Cassi had been given a briefcase on graduation from medical school, but she preferred the canvas bag. The briefcase seemed too pretentious. Besides, she could get more into the bag.

Cassi checked her watch. It was five-thirty, which was just about perfect timing. She knew that Thomas would be heading down the stretch, seeing his last office patients. As Cassi hefted her things, she remarked to herself that the regular schedule was another benefit of psychiatry. As a medical intern or pathology resident, she was never finished much before six-thirty or seven, and at times worked to eight or eight-thirty. On psychiatry she could count on being free after the four to five afternoon team meeting, provided she wasn't on call.

Stepping into the corridor, Cassi was initially surprised to find it empty. Then she remembered that it was dinnertime for the patients, and as she passed the common room, she could see most of the patients eating from their trays in front of their TV sets. Cassi ducked into her cubbyhole office and collected the charts she'd been extracting. She only had four patients, including Colonel Bentworth, and she'd spent a portion of the afternoon carefully going over their charts and making three-by-five index cards on each case.

With the canvas bag over her shoulder and the charts in her arms, Cassi went down to the nurses' station. Joel Hartman, who was on call that night, was sitting in the station, talking to the two nurses. Cassi deposited the charts in their respective slots and said good night. Joel told her to have a good weekend and to relax because he'd have her patients cured by Monday. He said he knew just how to handle Bentworth because he had been in ROTC in college.

As she walked down to the first floor, Cassi could feel herself beginning to relax. Her first week on psychiatry had been a trying and difficult period, one that she would not like to relive.

Cassi took the interior pedestrian crosswalk to the Professional Building. Thomas's office was on the third floor. She paused outside the polished oak door, gazing at the shining brass letters: THOMAS KINGSLEY, M.D., CARDIAC AND THORACIC SURGERY, and felt a thrill of pride.

The waiting room was tastefully decorated with Chippendale reproductions and a large Tabriz rug. The walls were powder blue and hung with original art. The door leading to the inner office was guarded by a mahogany desk occupied by Doris Stratford, Thomas's nurse-receptionist. As Cassi entered, Doris looked up briefly, then went back to her typing when she recognized who it was.

Cassi approached the desk.

"How's Thomas doing?"

"Just fine," said Doris, her eyes on her paper.

Doris never looked Cassandra in the eye. But over the years Cassi had become accustomed to the fact that her illness made some people uncomfortable. Doris was obviously one of them.

"Would you let him know I'm here?" said Cassi.

Cassi got a fleeting glimpse of Doris's brown eyes. There was an aura of petulance about her expression. Not enough for Cassi to complain about but enough to let her know that Doris did not appreciate the interruption. She didn't answer Cassi but rather depressed the button on an intercom unit and announced that Dr. Cassidy had arrived. She went directly back to her typing.

Refusing to allow Doris to irritate her, Cassi settled herself on the rose-colored couch and pulled out the articles she wanted on borderline personality. She started to read but found herself looking over the top of the paper at Doris.

Cassi wondered why Thomas kept Doris. Granted she was efficient, but she seemed moody and irritable, hardly the qualities one would like in a physician's office. She was presentable although not overly attractive. She had a broad face with large features and mousy brown hair pulled back in a bun. She did have a good figure; Cassi had to admit that.

Letting her eyes drop back to her paper, Cassi forced herself to concentrate.

☐

Thomas looked across the polished surface of his desk at his last patient of the day, a fifty-two-year-old lawyer named Herbert Lowell. Thomas's office was decorated like his waiting room, except the walls were a forest green. The other difference was that the furniture was authentic Chippendale. The desk alone was worth a small fortune.

Thomas had examined Mr. Lowell on several occasions and had reviewed the coronary arteriograms done by Mr. Lowell's cardiologist, Dr. Whiting. To Thomas the situation was clear. Mr. Lowell had anginal chest pain, a history of a mild heart attack, and radiographic evidence of compromised arterial circulation. The man needed an operation, and Thomas had told Mr. Lowell as much. Now Thomas wanted to terminate the visit.

"It's such an irreversible decision," Mr. Lowell was saying nervously.

"But still a decision that must be made," said Thomas, standing up and closing Mr. Lowell's folder. "Unfortunately I'm on a tight schedule. If you have any further questions you can call." Thomas started for the door like a clever salesman indicating the issue was beyond further negotiation.

"What about the advisability of a second opinion?" asked Mr. Lowell hesitantly.

"Mr. Lowell," said Thomas, "you can get as many

opinions as you'd like. I will be sending a full consult letter back to Dr. Whiting, and you can discuss the case with him." Thomas opened the door leading to the waiting room. "In fact, Mr. Lowell, I would encourage you to see another surgeon because, frankly, I do not feel good about working with people with negative attitudes. Now if you'll excuse me."

Thomas closed the door behind Mr. Lowell, confident the man would schedule the required operation. Sitting down, he gathered the material he needed for his Grand Rounds presentation the following morning, and then started signing the consultation letters Doris had left for him.

When Thomas emerged with the signed correspondence, he was not surprised to find Mr. Lowell in the waiting room. Thomas glanced at Cassi, acknowledging her with a brief nod, then turned to his patient.

"Dr. Kingsley, I've decided to go ahead with the operation."

"Very well," said Thomas. "Give Miss Stratford a call next week, and she'll set it up."

Mr. Lowell thanked Thomas and left, closing the door quietly behind him.

Holding her reports in front of her as if she were reading, Cassi watched her husband going over some notes with Doris. She'd noticed how well he'd handled Mr. Lowell. He never seemed to hesitate. He knew what should be done and he did it. She'd always admired his composure, a quality she felt she lacked. Cassi smiled as her eyes traced the sharp lines of his profile, his sandy hair, and his athletic body. She found him extraordinarily attractive.

After the insecurities of the day, in fact the entire
week, Cassi wanted to rush up and throw her arms
around him. But she knew instinctively that he would
not care for that kind of show of emotion, especially
with Doris there. And Cassi knew he was right. The
office was not the place for such behavior. Instead, she
put the reprint back into the folder and the folder back
into the canvas bag.

Thomas finished with Doris, but it wasn't until the
office door closed behind them that he spoke to Cassi.

"I've got to go to the ICU," he said, his voice flat.
"You can come or wait in the lobby. Your choice. I won't
be long."

"I'll come," said Cassi, already guessing that Thomas's day had not been smooth. She had to quicken her
step to keep up with him.

"Was there trouble with your surgery today?" she
asked tentatively.

"Surgery went fine."

Cassi decided against further questioning. It was difficult to talk as they threaded their way back into the
Scherington Building. Besides, she'd learned from experience that it was usually better to let Thomas volunteer information when he was upset.

In the elevator she watched while he kept his eyes
glued to the floor indicator. He seemed tense and
preoccupied.

"I'll be glad to get home tonight," said Cassi. "I need
a good night's sleep."

"The weirdos keep you busy last night?"

"Let's not have any of your surgeon's opinions about
psychiatry," said Cassi.

Thomas didn't respond, but an ironic smile appeared on his face, and he seemed to relax a little.

The elevator doors opened on seventeen, and they got out. Thomas walked swiftly ahead. No matter how many years Cassi had spent in hospitals, she always had the same reaction when she found herself on the surgical floor. If it wasn't fear, it was close to it. The crisis aspect undermined the elaborate denial she used about the implications of her own illness. What mystified Cassi about the response was that she didn't feel the same way on the medical floor where there invariably were patients with diabetically induced complications.

As Cassi and Thomas neared the ICU, several waiting relatives recognized Thomas. Like a movie or rock star, he was instantly surrounded. One old woman was intent on touching him as if he were some kind of god. Thomas remained composed, assuring everyone that all the surgery had gone routinely and that they would have to wait for further updates by the nursing personnel. With some difficulty he finally detached himself and entered the ICU where no one dared follow him except Cassi.

With its enormous number of machines, oscilloscope screens, and bandages, it intensified all of Cassi's unspoken fears. And in fact, the patients themselves seemed all but forgotten, lost as they were in the tangle of equipment. The nurses and doctors seemed to tend the machines first.

Thomas went from bed to bed. Each patient in the ICU had his own specially trained nurse to whom Thomas spoke, hardly looking at the patient unless the nurse called his attention to some abnormality. He visually checked all the vital signs which could be seen on the read-out equipment. He glanced at the fluid balance logs, held portable chest X rays up to the overhead light, and looked at electrolyte and blood gas values. Cassi knew enough to know how much she didn't know.

As Thomas had promised, he didn't take long. His patients were all doing well. With Larry Owen in command, the resident staff would deal with all the minor problems that arose during the night. When Thomas and Cassi reemerged, the patients' families again set upon him. Thomas said that he regretted he didn't have more time to talk but that everyone was doing well.

"It must be extraordinarily rewarding to get that kind of feedback from families," said Cassi as they were walking toward the elevator.

Thomas didn't respond immediately. Cassi's statement reminded him of the pleasure he had felt years earlier when the Nazzaros had greeted him. Their gratitude had meant something. Then he thought about Mr. Campbell's daughter. He glanced back down the corridor, realizing that he hadn't seen her.

"Oh, it's nice that the relatives are appreciative," said Thomas without much feeling. "But it's not that important. It's certainly not why I do surgery."

"Of course not," said Cassi. "I didn't mean to imply that."

"For me recognition by my teachers and superiors was always more important," said Thomas.

The elevator arrived and they got on.

"The trouble is," continued Thomas, "now I'm the teacher."

Cassi glanced up. To her surprise his voice had an unexpected and uncharacteristic wistfulness. As she watched him, she could see that he was staring ahead, daydreaming.

Thomas's mind flashed back to his thoracic residency, a time of unbelievable excitement and adventure. He remembered that he all but lived in the hospital for three years, going home to his drab two-room apartment only to recharge by sleeping for a few hours. In order to excel he had worked harder than he'd ever thought possible. And in the end he was appointed chief resident. In many respects Thomas felt that event had been the crowning achievement of his life. He'd come out on top of a group of gifted people as committed and competitive as himself. Thomas would never forget the moment that each of his attendings congratulated him. There was no doubt, he thought, that surgery and life in general were more rewarding and more fun then. Thankful relatives were nice, but they were no substitute.

☐

When Cassi and Thomas emerged from the hospital, they were rudely slapped by a wet Boston evening. Gusts of wind lashed the rain in chaotic circles. At six-fifteen it was already dark. The only illumination came from the city lights reflecting off the low, swirling cloud cover. Cassi grasped Thomas about the waist and together they ran for the nearby parking garage.

Once under shelter, they stomped the moisture from their feet and walked more slowly up the concrete ramp. The wet cement had a surprisingly acrid smell. Thomas still wasn't acting normally, and Cassi tried to guess what was bothering him. She had the uncomfortable feeling that it was something she'd done. But she couldn't imagine what. They hadn't seen each other since the ride in to the hospital Thursday morning, and everything had seemed fine at that time.

"Are you tired from working last night?" asked Cassi.

"Yes, I probably am. I haven't thought too much about it, though."

"And your cases? They went okay?"

"I told you, they went fine," said Thomas. "In fact I could have done another bypass if they had allowed me to schedule it. I did three cases in the time it took George Sherman to do two and Ballantine, our fearless chief, to do one."

"Sounds like you should be pleased," said Cassi.

They stopped in front of an anthracite metallic 928 Porsche. Thomas hesitated, looking at Cassi over the top of the car. "But I'm not pleased. As usual there was a host of little things to annoy me, making my work more difficult. It seems to be getting worse, not better, around the Memorial. I'm really fed up. Then, to top it all off, at the cardiac surgery meeting, I was informed that four of my weekly OR slots were being expropriated so George Sherman could schedule more of his goddamn teaching cases. They don't even have enough teaching patients to fill the slots they already have without dredging up patients who have no right to precious space in the hospital."

Thomas unlocked his door, climbed in and reached across to open Cassi's.

"Besides," said Thomas, gripping the steering wheel, "I have a feeling something else is going on in the hospital. Something between George Sherman and Norman Ballantine. God! I've just had it with all the bullshit!"

Thomas gunned the engine, then rammed the car back, then forward, the tires screeching in protest. Cassi braced herself against the dashboard to keep herself upright. When he stopped to stick his card into the slot for the automatic gate, she reached over her shoulder for her seat belt. As she locked it in place, she said, "Thomas, I think you should fasten yours, too."

"For Chrissake," yelled Thomas. "Stop nagging me."

"I'm sorry," said Cassi quickly, now certain that she was in some way partially responsible for her husband's foul mood.

Thomas weaved in and out of traffic, cutting in front of irate commuters. Cassi was afraid to say anything lest she anger him further. It was like a Grand Prix free-for-all.

Once they were north of the city, the traffic thinned out. Despite the fact Thomas was going over seventy, Cassi began to relax.

"I'm sorry I seemed like a pest, especially after an aggravating day," she said finally.

Thomas didn't respond, but his face was less tense and his grip on the steering wheel not as tight. Several times Cassi started to ask if she'd been responsible for upsetting him, but she could not find the right words.

For a while she just watched the rain-slicked road rushing toward them. "Have I done something that's bothered you?" she said at last.

"You have," snapped Thomas.

They rode for a while in silence. Cassi knew it would come sooner or later.

"It seems Larry Owen knows all about our private medical matters," said Thomas.

"It's no secret that I have diabetes," said Cassi.

"It's no secret because you talk about it so often," said Thomas. "I think the less said the better. I don't like us to be the brunt of gossip."

Cassi could not remember mentioning anything to Larry about her medical problems, but of course that wasn't the issue. She was well aware she'd talked to a number of people about her diabetes, including Joan Widiker that very day. Thomas, like her mother, felt Cassi's disease was not a subject to be shared, even with close friends.

Cassi looked over at Thomas. The bands of light and shadow from the oncoming cars moved down his face and obscured his expression.

"I guess I never thought discussing my diabetes affected us," said Cassi. "I'm sorry. I'll be more careful."

"You know how gossip is in a medical center," said Thomas. "It's better not to give them anything to talk about. Larry knew more than just about your diabetes. He knew that you might have to have eye surgery. That's pretty specific. He said he heard it from your friend Robert Seibert."

Now it made sense to Cassi. She knew she hadn't said anything to Larry Owen. "I did talk to Robert," she conceded. "It seemed only natural. We've known each other so long, and he told me about his surgery. He's having impacted wisdom teeth out. With his history of severe rheumatic fever he has to be admitted and treated with IV antibiotics."

They turned north off Route 128, heading toward the ocean. There were unexpected patches of heavy fog, and Thomas slowed down.

"I still don't think talking about such problems is a good idea," said Thomas, squinting through the wind-shield. "Especially to someone like Robert Seibert. It's still beyond me how you can tolerate such an overt homosexual."

"We never talk about Robert's sexual preferences," said Cassi sharply.

"I don't understand how you could avoid the sub-ject," said Thomas.

"Robert is a sensitive, intelligent human being and a damn good pathologist."

"I'm glad he has some redeeming qualities," said Thomas, conscious that he was baiting his wife.

Cassi bit down her reply. She knew that Thomas was angry and was trying to provoke her; she also knew that losing her own temper would accomplish nothing. After a brief silence, she reached across and massaged Thom-as's neck. At first he remained rigid, but after a few minutes she felt him respond.

"I'm sorry I talked about my diabetes," she said, "and I'm sorry I talked about my eye condition."

Maintaining her massage, Cassi stared out the win-dow with unseeing eyes. A cold fear made her wonder if Thomas was getting tired of her illness. Maybe she'd been complaining too much, especially with all the upset about changing residencies. Thinking about it, Cassi had to admit that Thomas had been distancing himself from her in the last few months, acting more impulsive and with less tolerance. Cassi made a vow to talk less about her illness. She knew, more than anyone, how much pressure Thomas put himself under, and she promised herself not to make it worse.

Moving her hand up his neck, Cassi thought it would be wise to change the subject.

"Did anyone say anything about your doing three bypasses while the others did one or two?"

"No. No one says anything because it's always the same. There really isn't anyone for me to compete with."

"What about competing with the best: yourself!" said Cassi with a smile.

"Oh, no!" said Thomas. "Don't give me any of that pseudopsychology."

"Is competition important at this point?" asked Cassi, becoming serious. "Isn't the satisfaction of helping people return to active lives enough?"

"It's a nice feeling," admitted Thomas. "But it doesn't help me get beds or OR time even though the patients I propose are the most deserving both from a physical and sociological standpoint. And their gratitude probably won't make me chief, although I'm not sure I want the position any longer. To tell you the truth, the kick of surgery doesn't last like it used to. Lately I get this empty feeling."

The word "empty" reminded Cassi of something. Had it been a dream? She glanced around the interior of the car, noting the characteristic smell of the leather, listening to the repetitive click of the windshield wipers, letting her mind wander. What was the association? Then she remembered—"empty" was the word Colonel Bentworth used to describe his life in recent years. Angry and empty, that's what he'd said.

Emerging from the leafless woods, they sped across the salt marshes. Through the rain-swept window, Cassi caught glimpses of the bleak November landscape. Fall was gone, its last agonal bits of color driven from the naked tree limbs by the rain. Winter was coming, its arrival heralded by the damp chill of the night. They rounded the last bend, thundered over a wooden bridge, and turned into their driveway. Within the bouncing headlights, Cassi could see the outline of their house. It had originally been built around the turn of the century as a rich man's summer home in the shingle style peculiar to New England. In the nineteen-forties it had been winterized. Its sprawling character and irregular roof line gave it a unique silhouette. Cassi liked the house, perhaps more in summer than in winter. The best part was the location. It was situated directly on a small inlet with a northern view of the sea. Although it was a forty-minute drive north of Boston, Cassi felt the commute was worth it.

As they pulled up the long driveway, Cassi thought back to when she had first started dating Thomas. They had met when she was sent to the Memorial on her internal medicine rotation her third year of medical school. She'd seen Dr. Thomas Kingsley one day on the ward. He and a group of residents who followed after him like puppies were evaluating a heart attack victim in cardiogenic shock. Cassi had watched Dr. Kingsley with fascination. She'd heard about him and was astonished that he looked so young. She found him extremely attractive, but she never thought someone as dashing as Thomas would ever give her a second glance, except perhaps to ask her an embarrassing medical question. If Thomas had seen her on that first day, he'd given no indication whatsoever.

Once within the hospital community, Cassi found that it wasn't as intimidating as she'd feared. She worked very hard and to her amazement suddenly found herself very popular. Previously she had not had time to date, but at the Boston Memorial, work and social life merged. Cassi found herself actively pursued by most of the house staff, who taught her all sorts of things, frivolous and otherwise. Soon even some of the younger attendings began to compete, including a handsome ophthalmologist who could not take no for an answer. Cassi had never met anyone quite so single-minded and persistent, especially in front of his Beacon Hill fireplace. But it had all been fun and not serious until George Sherman asked her out. Without much encouragement from Cassandra, he sent her flowers, small presents, and then, out of the blue, proposed marriage.

Cassi did not turn George down immediately. She liked him even though she didn't think she loved him. While she was still thinking over how best to handle things, something even more unexpected occurred. Thomas Kingsley asked her out.

Cassi remembered the intense excitement she had felt being with Thomas. He had an aura of self-

assurance that some people might have labeled arrogance. But not Cassi. She felt he simply knew what he
wanted and made decisions with bewildering rapidity.
When Cassi tried to talk about her diabetes early in their
relationship, Thomas dismissed the subject as a problem
of the past. He gave her all the confidence she'd lacked
since third grade.

It had been difficult for Cassi to face George and tell
him that not only did she not want to marry him, but she
had fallen in love with his colleague. George took the
news with seeming composure and said he'd still like to
be her friend. When she saw him on occasion in the
hospital afterward, he seemed more concerned about
her happiness than the fact that she had jilted him.

Thomas was charming, considerate, and gallant, a
far cry from what Cassi expected. She'd heard that he
was famous for intense but short relationships. Although he rarely told her that he loved her, he showed
it in many ways. He took Cassi on teaching rounds with
the fellows and had her come to the OR to see special
cases. For their first Christmas together he bought her
an antique diamond bracelet. Then on New Year's Eve
he asked Cassandra to marry him.

Cassi had never intended to get married while in
medical school. But Thomas Kingsley was the kind of
man that she had not even allowed herself to dream
about. She might never meet anyone like him, and since
Thomas was in medicine himself, she was confident it
would not hinder her work. Cassi said yes and Thomas
was ecstatic.

They were married on the lawn in front of Thomas's
house in view of the sea. Most of the hospital staff had

attended and afterward referred to it as the social event of the year. Cassi could remember every moment of that glorious spring day. The sky had been a faraway blue, not unlike Thomas's eyes. The sea had been relatively calm, with small white caps licked by the westerly breeze.

The reception was sumptuously catered, the lawn dotted with medieval-looking tents from the top of which heraldic flags snapped in the wind. Cassi had never been so happy, and Thomas appeared proud, ever mindful of the smallest details.

When everyone had left, Thomas and Cassi walked the beach, mindless of the icy surf grabbing at their ankles.

Cassi had never felt quite so happy nor quite so secure. They spent the night at the Ritz-Carlton in Boston before leaving for Europe.

After they had returned from their honeymoon, Cassi went back to her studies but ever mindful of her powerful mentor. In every conceivable way, Thomas helped Cassi. She'd always been a good student, but with Thomas's help and encouragement, she excelled beyond her wildest expectations. He continued to encourage her to come frequently to the OR to see particularly interesting cases and, while she rotated on surgery, to have her assist, experiences which other medical students could only dream about. Two years later, when it came to graduate study, it was the pathology department that recruited Cassi, not vice versa.

Perhaps the memory that warmed Cassi's heart more than any other was the weekend she graduated from medical school. Thomas had acted subdued from the moment they'd awakened that morning, which Cassi had attributed to a complicated surgical case Thomas was expecting. During dinner the night before, he'd told Cassi about a patient who was scheduled to be flown in from out of state. He'd apologized for not being able to take her to the celebration dinner the evening after the commencement, and although she was disappointed, Cassi had assured Thomas that she understood.

During the ceremony, Thomas had made a fool of himself and embarrassed Cassi by following her to the podium and taking hundreds of flash pictures with his Pentax. Afterward, when Cassi expected him to disappear abruptly to surgery, he led her across the lawn to an awaiting limousine. Confused, Cassi climbed into the long black Cadillac. Inside were two long-stemmed glasses and a chilled bottle of Dom Perignon.

As if in a fantasy, Cassi was whisked out to Logan Airport and hurried aboard a commuter flight to Nantucket. She tried to protest that she had no clothes and could not possibly go without first returning home, but Thomas had assured her that every detail had been attended to and indeed it had. He showed her a bag, packed with all her makeup and medicine, as well as some new clothes, including the sexiest pink silk Ted Lapidus dress Cassi had ever seen.

They only stayed for a single night, but what a night. Their room was the master suite of an old sea captain's mansion that had been converted to a charming country inn. The decor was early Victorian with a huge canopy bed and period wallpaper. There was no television and more importantly, no telephone. Cassi had the delicious sensation of total isolation and privacy.

Never had she felt so in love nor had Thomas ever been so attentive. They spent the afternoon bicycling along country lanes and running in the icy surf on the beach. Dinner was at a nearby French restaurant. Their candlelit table was set within the shelter of a dormer whose window looked out over Nantucket Harbor. The lights from the anchored sailboats flickered across the water like the sparkle of gemstones. Capping the dinner was Cassi's graduation present. To her utter astonishment, she gingerly lifted from a small, velvet-lined box the most beautiful three-strand pearl choker she'd ever seen. It was secured in front by a large emerald surrounded by diamonds. As Thomas helped her put the necklace on, he explained that the clasp was a family heirloom, brought from Europe by his great-grandmother.

Later that night, they discovered that the imposing canopied bed in their room had one unexpected flaw. It squeaked mercilessly whenever they moved. This discovery brought on fits of uncontrolled laughter but did nothing to diminish their enjoyment. If anything, it gave Cassi another wonderful memory of the weekend.

Cassi's reverie was broken by the jerk with which Thomas brought his Porsche to a stop in front of their garage. He reached across and pressed the automatic door button inside the glove compartment.

The garage, also weathered shingle, was completely separate from the house. There was an apartment on the second floor, originally designed for servants, where

Thomas's widowed mother, Patricia Kingsley, resided. She'd moved from the main house when Cassi and Thomas married.

The Porsche thundered into the garage, then with a final roar, died. Cassi got out, careful that the door did not hit her own Chevy Nova that was parked alongside. Thomas loved his car as much as his own right arm. She also closed the door without too much force. She was accustomed to slamming car doors, something which had been a necessity with the old family Ford sedan. On several occasions Thomas had become livid when she'd reverted back to her old habit despite his lectures on the careful engineering of the Porsche.

"It's about time," said Harriet Summer, their house-keeper, when Thomas and Cassi entered the hall. To emphasize her displeasure, she made sure they saw her check her wristwatch. Harriet Summer had worked for the Kingsleys since before Thomas was born. She was very much the old family retainer and had to be treated as such. Cassi had learned that very quickly.

"Dinner will be on the table in a half hour. If you're not there, it will get cold. Tonight's my favorite TV show, Thomas, so I'm leaving here at eight-thirty come what may."

"We'll be down," said Thomas, removing his coat.

"And hang up that coat," said Harriet. "I'm not going to be picking them up all the time."

Thomas did as he was told.

"What about Mother?" asked Thomas.

"She's as she always is," said Harriet. "She lunched well and she's expecting a call for dinner, so get cracking."

As Thomas and Cassi started upstairs, Cassi marveled at the change in her husband. At the hospital he was so aggressive and commanding, but the minute Harriet or his mother asked him to do something, he obeyed.

At the top of the stairs, Thomas turned into his second-floor study, saying that he'd see Cassi in a few moments. He didn't wait for her to reply. Cassi wasn't surprised, and she continued down the hall toward their bedroom. She knew he liked his study, which was something of a mirror image of his office at the hospital except that it had a wonderful view of the picturesque garage and the salt marshes beyond. The problem was that over the last few months Thomas had begun to spend more and more time there, occasionally even sleeping on the couch. Cassi had not commented, knowing that he was troubled with insomnia, but as the number of nights he spent away from her increased, it had begun to distress her more and more.

The master bedroom was at the very end of the hall, on the northeast side of the house. It had French doors giving out onto a balcony that had a commanding view of the lawn down to the sea. Next to the bedroom was a morning room facing east. On nice days the sun would stream through the windows. Between the two rooms was the master bath.

The only part of the house Cassi had redecorated was the bedroom suite. She'd salvaged and repaired the white wicker porch furniture that she had found ignominiously abandoned in the garage. She had chosen bright chintz fabrics for matching comforter, drapes, and seat cushions. The bedroom had been papered with a Victorian-style vertical print; the morning room painted a pale yellow. The combination was bright and cheerful, in sharp contrast with the dark and heavy tones of the rest of the house.

Cassi had essentially taken over the morning room as her study since Thomas had shown no inclination to share it. She'd found an old country-style desk in the basement, which she'd painted white, and had bought several simple pine bookcases, which she'd painted to match. One of the bookcases had a second role; it served to conceal a small refrigerator that contained Cassi's medicines.

After testing her urine again, Cassi went to the refrigerator and removed a package of regular insulin and one of Lente insulin. Using the same syringe, she drew up a half cc of the U100 regular and then one-tenth cc of the U100 Lente. Knowing she had injected herself in her left thigh that morning, she chose a site on her right thigh. The whole procedure took less than five minutes.

After a quick shower, Cassi knocked on the door to Thomas's study. When she entered she sensed that Thomas was more relaxed. He'd just finished buttoning a fresh shirt and ended up with more buttons than buttonholes when he got to the top.

"Some surgeon you must be," teased Cassi, rapidly fixing the problem. "I met a medical resident whom you impressed last night. I'm glad he didn't see you buttoning your shirt." Cassi was eager for light conversation.

"Who was that?" asked Thomas.

"You helped him on a resuscitation attempt."

"It wasn't a very impressive effort. The man died."

"I know," said Cassi. "I watched the autopsy this morning."

Thomas sat down on the sectional sofa, pulling on his loafers.

"Why on earth were you watching an autopsy?" he asked.

"Because it was a post cardiac-surgical case where the cause of death was unclear."

Thomas stood up and began to brush his wet hair. "Did the entire department of psychiatry go up to watch this event?" asked Thomas.

"Of course not," said Cassi. "Robert called me and . . ."

Cassi paused. It wasn't until she'd mentioned Robert's name that she remembered the talk they had had in the car. Fortunately Thomas kept brushing his hair.

"He said that he thought there was another case for the SSD series. You remember. I've spoken to you about that before."

"Sudden surgical death," said Thomas as if he were reciting a lesson in school.

"And he was right," said Cassi. "There was no obvious cause of death. The man had had a bypass operation by Dr. Ballantine . . ."

"I'd say that was a sufficient cause," interrupted Thomas. "The old man probably put a suture right through the Bundle of His. It knocks out the heart's conduction system, and it's happened before."

"Was that your impression when you tried to resuscitate him?" asked Cassi.

"It occurred to me," said Thomas. "I assumed it was some sort of acute arrhythmia."

"The nurses reported the patient was very cyanotic when they found him," she said.

Thomas finished his hair and indicated he was ready for dinner. He gestured toward the hall while he spoke: "That doesn't surprise me. The patient probably aspirated."

Cassi preceded Thomas out into the hall. From the autopsy she already knew the patient's lungs and bronchial tubes had been clear, meaning he had not aspirated anything. But she didn't tell that to Thomas. His tone suggested he'd had enough of the subject.

"I would have thought that beginning a new residency would keep you busy," said Thomas, starting down the stairs. "Even a residency in psychiatry. Aren't they giving you enough work to do?"

"More than enough," said Cassi. "I've never felt quite so incompetent. But Robert and I have been following this SSD series for a year. We were eventually going to publish our findings. Then, of course, I left pathology, but I truly think Robert is onto something. Anyway, when he called me this morning I took the time to go up and watch."

"Surgery is serious business," said Thomas. "Particularly cardiac surgery."

"I know," said Cassi, "but Robert has seventeen of these cases now, maybe eighteen if this new one checks out. Ten years ago SSD only seemed to occur in patients who were in coma. But lately there's been a change. Patients who have come through surgery with flying colors are seemingly dying postop without cause."

"When you consider the number of cardiac cases done at the Memorial," said Thomas, "you must realize how insignificant a percentage you're talking about. The Memorial's death rate is not only well below the average, it's equal to the best."

"I also know that," said Cassi. "But still it's fascinating when you consider the trend."

Thomas suddenly took Cassi's arm. "Listen, it's bad enough that you chose psychiatry as a specialty, but don't try embarrassing the surgical department about our failures. We are aware of our mistakes. That's why we have a death conference."

"I never intended to cause you embarrassment," said Cassi. "Besides, the SSD study is Robert's. I told him today that he was going to have to carry on without me. I just think it's fascinating."

"The competitive climate of medicine always makes other people's mistakes fascinating," said Thomas, gently propelling Cassi through the archway into the dining room, "whether they are legitimate mistakes or acts of God."

Cassi felt a pang of guilt as she thought about the truth of Thomas's last statement. She never considered it that way, but it was true.

As they entered the dining room, Harriet gave them a petulant glance and said that they were late.

Thomas's mother was already seated at the table. "It's about time you two showed up," she said in her strong, raspy voice. "I'm an old woman. I can't go this long before dinner."

"Why didn't you eat earlier?" said Thomas, taking his chair.

"I've been by myself for two days," complained Patricia. "I need some human contact."

"So I'm not human, am I?" said Harriet with annoyance. "The truth has finally come out."

"You know what I mean, Harriet," said Patricia with a wave of her hand.

Harriet rolled her eyes and began serving the casserole.

"Thomas, when are you going to get that hair of yours cut?" said Patricia.

"As soon as I have a little extra time," said Thomas.

"And how many times do I have to tell you to put your napkin on your lap," said Patricia.

Thomas pulled the napkin from the silver holder and threw it onto his lap.

Mrs. Kingsley placed a minute amount of food in her mouth and began chewing. Her bright blue eyes, similar to Thomas's, ranged around the table, following Harriet's progress, waiting for the slightest slip-up. Patricia was a pleasant-looking, white-haired lady with a will of iron. She had smoked Lucky Strikes for years and had deep creases running from her mouth like spokes on a wheel. She was obviously lonely, and Cassi continually wondered why the woman didn't move to some place where she'd have friends her own age. Cassi knew the thought was motivated by her own interests. After more than three years of eating almost every evening meal with Patricia, Cassi longed for a more romantic end to the day. Despite Cassi's strong feelings in this regard, she never said anything. The truth of the matter was that Cassi had always been intimidated by this woman, and she'd been reluctant to offend her and thereby incur Thomas's wrath.

Still and all, Cassi got along passingly well with Mrs.

Kingsley, at least from Cassi's perspective, and she did feel sorry for the woman, living in the middle of nowhere over her son's garage.

After Harriet served, the dinner proceeded in silence, punctuated by silver clanking against china and whispered negatives to Harriet who tried to force seconds on everyone. It wasn't until they were almost finished that Thomas broke the silence: "My surgeries went well today."

"I don't want to hear about death and disease," said Mrs. Kingsley. Then she turned to Cassandra and said, "Thomas is just like his father, always wanting to discuss his business. Never could talk about anything important or cultural. Sometimes I think I would have been better off if I'd never married."

"You can't mean that," said Cassi. "Otherwise you wouldn't have such an extraordinary son."

"Ha!" said Patricia with explosive suddenness. Her laugh echoed in the room, making the Waterford candelabra vibrate. "The only thing truly extraordinary about Thomas is how closely he resembles his father, even to having been born with a clubfoot."

Cassi dropped her fork. Thomas had never mentioned this. The image of him as a tiny baby with a twisted foot triggered a wave of sympathy in Cassi, but it was clear from his expression that Thomas was furious with his mother's revelation.

"He was a wonderful baby," continued Patricia, oblivious to her son's barely suppressed rage. "And a handsome, wonderful child. At least until puberty."

"Mother," said Thomas in a slow, even voice. "I think you've said enough."

"Fiddlesticks, as they used to say," returned Patricia. "It's your turn to be quiet. I've been alone here, except for Harriet, for two days, and I should be able to talk."

With a final glance of exasperation, Thomas bent over his food.

"Thomas," called Patricia after a short silence. "Please remove your elbows from the table."

Thomas pushed back his chair and stood up, his face flushed. Without a word, he threw down his napkin and left the room. Cassi heard him stomping upstairs. Then the door to his study slammed. The Waterford candelabra again tinkled gently.

Caught in the middle, as usual, Cassi hesitated, not knowing what was the best thing for her to do. After a moment of indecision she too stood up, planning on following Thomas.

"Cassandra," said Patricia sharply. Then in a more plaintive voice she said, "Please sit down. Let the child be. Eat. I know people with diabetes have to eat."

Flustered, Cassi sat down.

□

Thomas paced his study, mumbling out loud that it was unfair that he should have to weather such abuse at home after his frustrating day at the hospital. Angrily he wondered why Cassi had stayed with his mother instead of joining him. For a moment he considered returning to the hospital, fantasizing about Mr. Campbell's daughter and the respect that she would be willing to show him. He remembered her comment about wishing there was something she could do for him.

But the cold rain beating on the window made the idea of returning to town seem like too much effort. Instead he picked up the journal from the top of his towering pile of reading and sprawled in the burgundy leather armchair next to the fireplace.

Trying to read, Thomas found his mind wandering. He wondered why his mother could still, after all these years, irritate him so easily. Then Thomas thought about Cassi and the SSD series that she'd been helping Robert Seibert with. There was no doubt in his mind that the kind of publicity that such a study would generate would be extraordinarily detrimental to the hospital. He also knew that Robert just wanted to get his name in print. He didn't care who he hurt.

Thomas threw the unread journal to the side and went into the bathroom off the study. Staring into the mirror, he looked at his eyes. He'd always thought he looked young for his age, but now he was not quite so sure. There were dark circles under his eyes, and the lids seemed red and swollen.

Returning to his study, he sat at his desk and opened the second drawer on the right, removing a plastic bottle. He popped a yellow pill into his mouth and, after a brief hesitation, another. Over at the bar he poured himself a single-malt whiskey and sat down in the leather armchair that had been his father's. He already felt a lessening of his tension. Reaching over to the side table, he picked up the journal again and tried to read.

But he couldn't concentrate. He still felt too much anger. His mind went back to his first week as the chief cardiac surgery resident when he'd been faced with a full intensive care unit and two senior attendings who were demanding space. Without empty available beds, the whole surgical schedule came to a halt.

Thomas remembered how he had gone into the intensive care unit and carefully checked over each patient to see if any could be moved out. In the end he chose two "gorks," patients in irreversible coma. It was true they needed round-the-clock special nursing that could only be given in the ICU, but it was also true they were beyond any hope of recovery. Yet when Thomas ordered them moved, their physicians were livid and the nursing staff refused the order. Thomas could still remember the humiliation he experienced when the nursing staff prevailed and the brain-dead patients stayed in the ICU. Not only hadn't the problem been solved, but Thomas had made additional enemies. It was as if no one understood that surgery, that life-giving process, as well as the costly intensive care unit, were intended for patients who would recover, not the living dead.

Back at the bar, Thomas refreshed his drink. The ice had diluted the Scotch and blunted its taste. Looking back at the burgundy leather chair, Thomas remembered his father, the businessman, and Thomas wondered what the old man would have thought of him had he lived. Thomas had no idea because, like Patricia, Mr. Kingsley had never been particularly appreciative or supportive of Thomas, always more willing to criticize than commend. Would he have approved of Cassi? Thomas guessed that his father probably would not have thought much of a girl with diabetes.

□

Cassi felt anxious after Thomas had left the table. Since he'd already been in a bad mood prior to coming down for dinner, she was afraid he was upstairs seething. Desperately she hunted for conversation but could only elicit "yes" or "no" from Patricia, who acted as if she were pleased she'd driven Thomas away.

"Did Thomas have a bad clubfoot?" Cassi finally asked, hoping to break the silence.

"Terrible. Just like his father, who was crippled for life."

"I had no idea. I never would have guessed."

"Of course not. In contrast to his father, he got treated."

"Thank goodness," said Cassi sincerely. She tried to imagine Thomas with a limp. It was hard for Cassi even to think of Thomas being crippled as a young baby.

"We had to lock the boy in foot braces at night," said Patricia, "which was a strain because he screamed and carried on as if I were torturing him." Patricia dabbed at her lips with her napkin.

Cassi pictured Thomas as an infant, strapped into his confining foot braces. Undoubtedly it had been a type of torture.

"Well," began Patricia, abruptly standing up. "Why don't you go up to him? Obviously he needs someone. He's not such a strong boy despite his aggressive manner. I'd go, but he's obviously chosen you. Men are all the same. You give them everything and they abandon you. Good night, Cassandra."

Dumbfounded by Patricia's rude exit, Cassi sat by herself for a moment. She heard Patricia talking with Harriet, then the front door slammed. The house was quiet except for the squeak of the porch swing as gusts of wind blew it back and forth.

She got up and began to mount the stairs, smiling suddenly at the thought that she and Thomas had shared a point in common while growing up; they both had had childhood afflictions. Knocking on the study door, Cassi wondered what kind of mood Thomas would be in. After the way he'd behaved in the car, combined with Patricia's pestering, she expected the worst. But when she entered the room, she was immediately relieved. Thomas was sitting sideways with his legs draped over one arm of his chair, drink in one hand, medical journal in the other. He looked relaxed and handsome. And more important, he was smiling.

"I trust you and Mother remained cordial," he said, raising his eyebrows as if there were a chance that the opposite had occurred. "I'm sorry for my abrupt departure, but the old woman was about to drive me mad. I didn't quite feel up to a scene." Thomas winked.

"You're so predictably unpredictable," said Cassi, smiling. "Your mother and I had a most interesting conversation. Thomas, I never knew about your clubfoot. Why didn't you tell me?"

She sat down on the arm of his chair, forcing him to swing around into a normal position. He didn't answer, concentrating on his drink.

"It's not important," said Cassi, "but I'm an expert on childhood afflictions. I find it reassuring that we shared such an experience. I think it gives us a special degree of understanding."

"I can't remember anything about a clubfoot," said

Thomas. "As far as I know I never had one. The whole thing is some elaborate delusion of my mother's. She wants you to be impressed by how she suffered bringing me up. Look at my feet: Do they look deformed?"

Thomas took off his shoes and raised his feet.

Looking down, Cassi had to admit both feet looked entirely normal. She knew Thomas had no problem walking and had been something of a college athlete. But she still wasn't sure who had been telling the truth.

"It seems incredible that your mother would make something like that up?" Her tone was more a question than a statement, but Thomas took it as a statement.

Throwing down the medical journal, he leaped to his feet, nearly knocking Cassi to the floor. "Listen, I don't care who you believe," said Thomas. "My feet are fine, have always been fine, and I don't want to hear anything more about a clubfoot."

"All right, all right," said Cassi soothingly. With a professional eye she watched her husband, noting that his equilibrium was slightly off in that he'd overshoot with simple motions that required him to make subtle readjustments. And that wasn't all. His speech was slightly slurred as well. Cassandra had noticed similar episodes over the previous months but she'd ignored them. He had every right to indulge himself with alcohol now and then, and she knew he liked Scotch. What surprised her was how short a time had passed since he'd fled from the dinner table. He must have tossed off quite a few drinks, one after another.

More than anything, Cassi wanted Thomas to relax. If a discussion about a hypothetical clubfoot was going to upset him, she was perfectly willing to drop the subject forever if necessary. Sliding off the chair, she reached up to place her arm around his shoulder.

He fended her off, defiantly taking another sip of Scotch. He looked contentious and eager to quarrel. At close range Cassi noted his pupils were constricted to mere dots of black in his bright blue irises. Suppressing her own irritation at being rejected, Cassi said: "Thomas, you must be exhausted. You need a good night's sleep." She reached up again and this time he permitted her to put her arm around his neck. "Come to bed with me," she said softly.

Thomas sighed but didn't speak. He put down his half-finished drink and let Cassi lead him back down the hall to their bedroom. He started to unbutton his shirt, but Cassi pushed his hands away and did it for him. Slowly she undressed him, discarding his clothes in a careless heap on the floor. Once he was under the covers, she rapidly undressed herself, sliding in next to him. It was a delicious sensation to feel the coolness of the freshly laundered sheets, the comforting weight of the blankets, and the warmth of Thomas's body. Outside the November wind howled and shook the Japanese wind chimes on the balcony.

Cassi began by rubbing his neck and shoulders. Then she slowly worked her way down his body. Beneath her fingers she could feel him relax and respond to her. He stirred and enveloped her in an embrace. She kissed him and gently reached down between his legs. He was flaccid.

The moment Thomas felt Cassi's hand touch him, he sat up and pushed her away. "I don't think it's quite fair to expect that I'd be able to satisfy you tonight."

"I was interested in your pleasure," said Cassi softly, "not my own."

"I'll bet," said Thomas viciously. "Don't try any of your psychiatric bullshit on me."

"Thomas, it doesn't matter if we make love or not."

Throwing his legs over the side of the bed, Thomas grabbed for his discarded clothes with jerky, uncoordinated motions. "I find that hard to believe."

Thomas went into the hall, slamming the door behind him with such force that the storm windows rattled in their frames.

Cassi found herself engulfed in lonely darkness. The howling wind, which moments before had enhanced her sense of security, now did the opposite. The old fear of being abandoned haunted her. Despite the warmth of the blankets, Cassi shivered. What if Thomas left her? Desperately she tried to put the thought out of her mind because she could not bear the possibility. Maybe he had just been drunk. She recalled his lack of equilibrium and slurred speech. In the short time she'd spoken with Patricia, it didn't seem possible that Thomas could have absorbed enough alcohol to cause such an effect, but when she thought about it, she had to admit that there had been several such episodes in the last three or four months.

Rolling onto her back, Cassi stared at the ceiling where an outdoor lamp shining through the leafless tree outside created a pattern like a gigantic spider web. Frightened by the image, she turned on her side only to confront the same scary shadow on the wall across from the window. Was Thomas taking some kind of drug?

Having admitted the possibility, she recognized that she'd been denying the signs for months. It was further evidence that Thomas was unhappy with her, that their life had drastically changed, and that he had changed.

☐

In the bathroom off his study, Thomas stared at his naked body in the mirror. Although he hated to admit it, he did look older. And more worrisome than that was his shriveled penis. To his own touch it felt almost numb, and the lack of sensation filled him with agonizing fear. What was wrong with his sexuality? When Cassi had been massaging him he'd felt the need for sexual release. But obviously his penis had had other ideas.

It must have been Cassi's fault, he reasoned half-heartedly, as he returned to the study and got into his clothes. Rescuing his drink, he sat at his desk and opened the second drawer on the right. In the very back, hidden by his stationery, were a number of plastic bottles. If he was going to sleep, he needed one more pill. Just one! Deftly he flipped one of the small yellow tablets into his mouth, then chased it down with his Scotch. It was amazing how quickly he felt the calming effect.

CHAPTER

4

THE NEXT MORNING Cassi took her insulin and ate breakfast without any sign of Thomas. By eight she was concerned. Their usual schedule on Saturday was to leave by eight-fifteen so that Thomas could see his patients before Grand Rounds and Cassi could catch up on her own work.

Putting down the article she'd been reading at her desk and tightening the belt on her robe, Cassi walked from the morning room down the hall and listened outside Thomas's door. There were no sounds whatsoever. She knocked softly and waited. Still nothing. She tried the door. It was unlocked. Thomas was sound asleep with his alarm clock gripped in his hand. Evidently he'd turned it off and fallen directly back to sleep.

Cassi walked over to him and shook him gently. There was no response. She shook him more forcibly and his heavy-lidded eyes opened, but he looked as if he didn't recognize her.

"I'm sorry to wake you, but it's already after eight. You do want to go to Grand Rounds, don't you?"

"Grand Rounds?" answered Thomas with confusion. Then he seemed to understand. "Of course I want to go. I'll be down for a bite in a few minutes. We'll leave here in twenty at the most."

"I'm not going to the hospital today," said Cassi as brightly as she could. "I'm not expected in psychiatry, and I have an enormous amount to read. I brought home an entire bag full of reprints."

"Suit yourself," said Thomas, pushing himself up to a sitting position. "I'm on call tonight, so I'm not sure when I'll be home. I'll let you know later."

Cassi went down to the kitchen to make something for Thomas to eat in the car.

Thomas sat on the edge of the bed while the room whirled around him. He waited until his vision cleared, feeling each pulse like a hammer in his head. He stumbled first to the desk where he got out one of his plastic containers. Then he made his way into the bathroom.

Avoiding his image in the mirror, Thomas tried to get one of the small, orange triangular pills out of the container. It was no easy task, and it wasn't until he'd dropped several that he got one into his mouth and washed it down. Only then did he venture a glance at his face. It didn't look as bad as he feared nor as bad as he felt. With a bit more agility he took another pill, stepped into the shower, and turned on the water full blast.

□

Cassi stood by the window in the living room watching as Thomas disappeared into the garage. Even through the glass she could hear the roar of the Porsche as it started. She wondered what it sounded like in Patricia's apartment. The thought made her realize that she'd never visited Patricia; not once in the three years Cassi had been living there.

She watched until Thomas's Porsche had accelerated down the driveway and disappeared into the damp morning fog that hung over the salt marsh. Even after the car was out of sight, its low-frequency roar could be heard as Thomas shifted gears. Finally the noise vanished and the stillness of the empty house enveloped Cassi.

Looking at her palms, Cassi noticed they were damp. Her first thought was that she was experiencing a mild insulin reaction. Then she realized it was nervousness. She was going to violate Thomas's study. She'd always felt that trust and privacy were necessary parts of a close relationship, but she simply had to know if Thomas was taking tranquilizers or any other drugs. For months she'd been closing her eyes, hoping her marriage would improve. Now she knew she could not continue to wait passively any longer.

As she opened the door to Thomas's study, she felt like a burglar: a very bad burglar. Each little sound in the house made her jump.

"My God," said Cassi out loud. "You're being an idiot!"

Her own voice had a calming effect. As Thomas's wife she had the right to enter every room in the house. Yet in many ways she still felt like a visitor.

The study was in partial disarray. The sofa bed was still open, the covers piled in a heap on the floor. Cassi eyed the desk but then saw the open bathroom door. She pulled open the medicine cabinet. Inside were shaving gear, the usual litter of patented medicines, several old toothbrushes, and some out-dated Tetracycline antibiotics. She looked through all the packages and containers. There was nothing remotely suspicious.

As she was about to leave, her eye caught a flash of color on the white-tiled floor. Bending down, she found herself holding a small triangular orange pill stamped with SKF-E-19. It looked familiar, but she couldn't place it. Back in Thomas's study she scanned the bookshelves for a *Physician's Desk Reference*. Not finding one, she walked back to the morning room and took out her own. Quickly she turned to the product identification section. It was Dexedrine!

Holding the pill in her hand, Cassi stared out at the sea. There was a lone sailboat about a quarter mile out moving slowly through the swells. Watching it for a moment helped her organize her thoughts. She felt a weird mixture of relief and increased anxiety. The anxiety came from confirming her fear that Thomas might be taking drugs. The relief stemmed from the nature of the pill that she'd found—Dexedrine. Cassi could easily imagine an achiever like Thomas taking an occasional "upper" in order to sustain his almost superhuman performance. Cassi was aware of how much surgery Thomas did. She could understand how he could fall into the trap of taking a pill to sharpen his attention when he was otherwise exhausted. For Cassi it seemed to be in keeping with his personality. But as much as she tried to calm herself, she was still afraid. She knew the dangers of abusing Dexedrine and wondered how much she was to blame for Thomas's need for the drug, and how long he'd been taking it.

She put the innocent pill down on the desk and returned the PDR to the shelf. For a moment she was sorry she'd gone into Thomas's study and found the pill. It would have been easier to ignore the situation. After all, it was most likely a temporary problem, and if she said something to Thomas, he would only get angry.

"You've got to do something," said Cassi, trying to build her resolve. As ridiculous as it seemed, the only person who exerted any kind of authority over Thomas's life was Patricia. Although Cassi was reluctant to discuss the issue with anyone, at least she could expect Patricia to keep Thomas's best interests at heart. Briefly weighing the advantages and disadvantages, she decided to discuss the situation with her mother-in-law. If Thomas had been abusing Dexedrine for a long time, someone should intervene.

The first thing she had to do, Cassi decided, was to make herself presentable. Pulling off her terry robe and her nightgown, she went to the shower.

☐

Thomas enjoyed presenting cases at Grand Rounds. The entire departments of internal medicine and surgery attended, including residents and medical students. Today the MacPherson amphitheater was so full people had even been forced to sit on the steps leading up from the central pit. Thomas always drew a crowd even when, as today, he split the schedule with George.

As Thomas finished his talk, which had been titled "Long-Term Follow-Up of Patients Undergoing Coronary Bypass," the entire amphitheater broke into enthusiastic applause. The sheer volume of Thomas's work was enough to impress anyone, and given his good results, the statistics seemed superhuman.

When he opened up the floor for questions, someone from the upper tier yelled out that he'd like to know what kind of diet Thomas ate that gave him so much energy. The audience laughed heartily, eager for a morsel of humor.

When the laughter died down, Thomas concluded by saying: "I believe from the statistics I've presented there can no longer be any residual doubt as to the efficacy of the coronary bypass procedure."

He gathered his papers and took a chair at the table behind the podium next to Dr. George Sherman.

The topic of George's presentation was "An Interesting Teaching Case."

Thomas inwardly groaned and glanced longingly at the exit. He had a splitting headache that had gotten progressively more intense after his arrival at the hospital. What a ridiculous topic, Thomas thought. He watched with mounting irritation as George made his way over to the podium and blew into the microphone to make sure it was on. As if that weren't enough, he tapped it with his ring. Satisfied, he began to speak.

The case was a twenty-eight-year-old man by the name of Jeoffry Washington who'd contracted acute rheumatic fever at age ten. He'd been a sick child at the time and hospitalized for an extended period. When the acute disease had run its course, the child had been left with a loud holosystolic heart murmur, indicating his mitral valve had been severely damaged. Over the years the problem gradually worsened to the point that an operation was needed to replace the damaged valve.

At that point Jeoffry Washington was wheeled in and presented to the audience. He was a slight, callow-appearing Negro with angular, precise features, bright eyes, and skin the color of blond oak. He held his head back and stared up into the multitude of faces that were looking down at him.

As Jeoffry was wheeled back out, Thomas's and Jeoffry's eyes happened to meet. Jeoffry nodded and smiled. Thomas returned the gesture. Thomas couldn't help feeling sorry for the young man. Yet as tragic as his story was it was also quite common. Thomas had personally operated on hundreds of patients with similar histories.

With Jeoffry gone, George returned to the podium. "Mr. Washington has been scheduled to have a mitral valve replacement, but during the work-up an interesting fact was uncovered. Mr. Washington had an episode of pneumocystic carini pneumonia one year ago."

An excited murmur rippled through the audience.

"I suppose," called George over the babble of voices, "that it is not necessary to remind you that such an illness suggested AIDS, or Acquired Immune Deficiency Syndrome, which was indeed found in this patient. As it turns out, Jeoffry Washington's sexual preferences have placed him in that group of homosexual men whose life-style has apparently led to immuno-suppression."

Thomas now knew what George had meant by his comment in the surgical lounge the previous afternoon. He closed his eyes and tried to control his rising anger. Obviously Jeoffry Washington was an example of the kind of case that was taking OR slots and cardiac surgical beds away from Thomas's patients. Thomas was not alone in his reservations concerning operating on Jeoffry. One of the internists raised his hand and George recognized him. "I would seriously question the rationale for elective heart surgery in light of the patient's having AIDS," said the internist.

"That's a good point," said George. "I can say that Mr. Washington's immunological picture is not grossly abnormal at present. He's scheduled for surgery next week, but we will be following his helper T-cell and cytotoxic T-cell populations for any sudden decline. Dr. Sorenson of the department of immunology does not think the AIDS is an absolute contraindication for surgery at this time."

A number of hands popped up in the audience, and George began to call on them. The animated discussion took the conference over its normal time, and even after it was officially over, groups of people stood in clumps to continue talking.

Thomas tried to leave immediately, but Ballantine had gotten up and blocked his way. "Good conference," he beamed.

Thomas nodded. All he wanted to do was get away. His head felt as if it were in a vise.

George Sherman came up behind Thomas and clapped him on the back. "You and I really entertained them this morning. We should have charged admission."

Thomas slowly turned to face George's smiling, self-satisfied face. "To tell you the honest truth, I think the conference was a goddamn farce."

There was an uncomfortable silence as the two men eyed one another in the midst of the crowd.

"Okay," said George at length. "I suppose you are entitled to your opinion."

"Tell me. Is this poor fellow, Jeoffry Washington, whom you paraded out here like some freak, occupying a cardiac surgical bed?"

"Of course," said George, his own ire rising. "Where do you think he'd be, in the cafeteria?"

"All right, you two," said Ballantine.

"I'll tell you where he should be," snapped Thomas while he jabbed George in the chest with his index finger. "He should be on the medical floor in case something can be done about his immunological problem. Having already had pneumocystic carini pneumonia there's a good chance he'll be dead before he ever gets into a life-threatening cardiac state."

George knocked Thomas's hand aside. "As I said, you're entitled to your opinion. I happen to think Mr. Jeoffry Washington is a good teaching case."

"Good teaching case," scoffed Thomas. "The man is medically ill. He should not be taking up a scarce cardiac surgical bed. The bed is needed for others. Can't you understand that? It's for this kind of nonsense that

I have to keep my patients waiting, patients with no medical problems, patients who will be making real contributions to society."

George again knocked Thomas's hand away. "Don't touch me like that," he snapped.

"Gentlemen," said Ballantine, stepping between them.

"I'm not sure Thomas knows what the word means," said George.

"Listen, you little shithead," snarled Thomas, reaching around Ballantine and grabbing a handful of George's shirt. "You're making a mockery of our program with the cases you're dredging up just to keep the so-called teaching schedule full."

"You'd better let go of my shirt," warned George, his face suffused with color.

"Enough," shouted Ballantine, pulling Thomas's hand away.

"Our job is to save lives," said George through gritted teeth, "not make judgments about who is more worthy. That's up to God to decide."

"That's just it," said Thomas. "You're so stupid you don't even realize that you *are* making judgments about who should live. The trouble is your judgment stinks. Every time you deny me OR space another potentially healthy patient is condemned to death."

Thomas spun on his heels and strode from the room.

George took a deep breath, then adjusted his disheveled shirt.

"God! Kingsley is such a prig."

"He is arrogant," agreed Ballantine. "But he is such a damn good surgeon. Are you all right?"

"I'm fine," said George. "I must admit I came close to slugging him. You know, I think he's going to be trouble. I hope he doesn't get suspicious."

"In that sense his arrogance will be a help."

"We've been lucky. By the way, have you ever noticed Thomas's tremor?"

"No," said Ballantine with surprise. "What tremor?"

"It's on and off," said George. "I've noticed it for about a month, mainly because he was always so steady. I even noticed it today when he was doing his presentation."

"Lots of people are nervous in front of groups."

"Yeah," said George, "but it was the same as when I was talking to him about the Wilkinson death."

"I'd rather not talk about Wilkinson," said Ballantine, glancing around at the slowly emptying amphitheater. He smiled at an acquaintance. "Thomas is probably just tense."

"Maybe," said George, not convinced. "I still think he's going to be trouble."

☐

Cassi dressed for her visit to Patricia as if it were the first time they were to meet. With great care she chose a dark blue wool skirt with a matching jacket to go over one of her high-necked white blouses. Just as she was about to leave, she noticed the atrocious state of her nails and thankfully postponed the visit while she removed her old polish and applied a new coat. When that was dry, she decided she didn't like her hair, so she took it down and put it back up again.

Finally having run out of reasons to delay, she crossed the courtyard between the house and the garage. It was freezing out. Ringing Patricia's bell, Cassi could see her breath in the crisp air. There was no answer. Standing on tiptoes, she looked through a small window in the door, but all she could see was a flight of stairs. She tried the bell again, and this time saw her mother-in-law slowly descend the stairs and peer out through the glass. "What is it, Cassandra?" she called.

Nonplussed that Patricia didn't open the door, Cassi was silent for a minute. Under the circumstances she didn't feel like shouting her reason for visiting. Finally she said: "I want to talk to you about Thomas."

Even with that explanation there was a long enough pause for Cassi to wonder if Patricia had heard her. Then several bolts snapped aside and the door opened. For a moment the two women eyed each other.

"Yes," said Patricia finally.

"I'm sorry to bother you," began Cassi. She let her sentence trail off.

"You're not bothering me," said Patricia.

"Could I come in?" asked Cassi.

"I suppose," said Patricia, starting up the stairs. "Be sure and close the door."

Cassi was glad to close the door on the cold, damp morning. Then she climbed after Patricia and found herself in a small apartment sumptuously furnished in Victorian red velvet and white lace.

"This room is beautiful," said Cassi.

"Thank you," said Patricia. "Thomas's favorite color is red."

"Oh?" said Cassi, who had always thought Thomas partial to blue.

"I spend a lot of time here," said Patricia. "I wanted it comfortable and warm."

"It is that," admitted Cassi, seeing for the first time a rocking horse, a kiddy car, and other toys.

Patricia, as if following Cassi's glance, explained: "Those are some of Thomas's old toys. I think they're rather decorative, don't you?"

"I do," said Cassi. She thought the toys did have a certain appeal but looked a little out of place in the lavish setting.

"How about some tea?" suggested Patricia.

Suddenly Cassi realized that Patricia was as uncomfortable as she was.

"Tea would be very nice," said Cassi, feeling more at ease herself.

Patricia's kitchen was utilitarian, with white metal cabinets, an old refrigerator, and a small gas stove. Patricia put on the kettle and got out her china. From the top of the refrigerator she produced a wooden tray.

"Milk or lemon?" asked Patricia.

"Milk," said Cassi.

Watching her mother-in-law search for a creamer, Cassi realized how few visitors the older woman saw. With a touch of guilt Cassi wondered why they hadn't become better friends. She tried to bring up Thomas's problem, but the rift that had always existed between them silenced her. It wasn't until they'd seated themselves in the living room with full teacups that Cassi finally got the courage to begin. "The reason I came over here this morning was to talk to you about Thomas."

"That's what you said," replied Patricia pleasantly. The old woman had warmed considerably and seemed to be enjoying the visit.

Cassi sighed and put her teacup down on the coffee table. "I'm concerned about Thomas. I think he is pushing himself too hard and . . ."

"He's been that way since he was a toddler," interrupted Patricia. "That boy was a hyperactive high achiever from the day he was born. And I tell you it was a twenty-four-hour-a-day job keeping him in line. Even before he could walk he was his own boss, and I had a devil of a time disciplining him. In fact from the day I brought him home from the hospital . . ."

Listening to Patricia's stories, Cassi realized exactly how central Thomas still was to the older woman's world. It finally made sense to her why Patricia insisted on living where she did, even though it was so isolated. Watching her mother-in-law pause to sip her tea, Cassi noted how strongly Thomas resembled Patricia. Her face was thinner and more delicate, but there was the same aristocratic angularity.

Cassi smiled. When Patricia put her cup back down, Cassi said, "Sounds like Thomas hasn't changed much."

"I don't think he's changed at all," said Patricia. Then with a laugh she added, "He's been the same boy all his life. He's needed a lot of attention."

"What I was hoping," said Cassi, "is that you might help Thomas now."

"Oh?" said Patricia.

Cassi could see the newly gained intimacy rapidly revert to the old suspiciousness. But she forged on. "Thomas listens to you and . . ."

"Of course he listens to me. I'm his mother. What exactly are you leading up to, Cassandra?"

"I have reason to suspect that Thomas may be taking drugs," said Cassi. It was a relief to finally get it out. "I've suspected it for a few months but hoped the problem would just go away."

Patricia's blue eyes became cold. "Thomas has never taken drugs," she said.

"Patricia, please understand me. I'm not just criticizing. I'm worried, and I think you might be able to help. He does what you tell him to do."

"If Thomas needs my help, then he should come and ask for it himself. After all, he chose you over me." Patricia stood up. As far as she was concerned, the little tête-à-tête was over.

So that was it. Patricia was still jealous that her little boy had grown up enough to take a wife.

"Thomas didn't choose me over you, Patricia," said Cassi evenly. "He was looking for a different relationship."

"If it is such a different relationship, where are the children?"

Cassi could feel her strength of will drain away. The whole issue of children was a sensitive and emotional one for her, since juvenile diabetics were cautioned against the risk of pregnancy. She looked down at her tea, realizing she never should have tried speaking to her mother-in-law.

"There won't be any children," said Patricia, answering her own question. "And I know why not. Because of your illness. You know it's a tragedy for Thomas to be childless. And he tells me you've been sleeping apart lately."

Cassi lifted her head, shocked that he would reveal such intimate matters. "I know Thomas and I have our problems," she said. "But that's not the issue. I'm afraid he is taking a drug called Dexedrine and that he has probably been taking it for some time. Even though he does it just to work harder, it can be dangerous both to him and his patients."

"Are you accusing my son of being an addict?" snapped Patricia.

"No," said Cassi, unable to explain further.

"Well, I should hope not," said Patricia. "Lots of people take a pill now and then. And for Thomas it is understandable. After all, he's been driven from his own bed. I think your relationship is the real problem."

Cassi didn't have the strength to fight back. She sat silently wondering if Patricia was right.

"Furthermore I think you should go," said Patricia, reaching across and taking Cassi's cup.

Without another word Cassi got up, descended the stairs, and let herself out.

Patricia collected the teacups and carried them into the kitchen. She had tried to tell Thomas that marrying that girl was a mistake. If only he had listened.

Back in the living room Patricia sat down at the telephone and called Thomas's exchange. She left a message for him to call his mother as soon as possible.

□

Thomas's patients were inconveniently sprinkled on all three surgical floors. After Grand Rounds he'd taken the elevator to the eighteenth to work his way down. Normally on Saturdays, he liked to make rounds before the conference and before visiting hours. But today he'd arrived at the hospital late and consequently lost a lot of time reassuring nervous families. They would follow him out of the room and stand asking questions in the hall until in desperation he cut them off to examine his next patient only to be further delayed by that person's relatives.

It was a relief to reach the ICU where visitors were rarely allowed. As he pushed through the door he allowed himself to think about the regrettable episode with George Sherman. As understandable as his reaction was, Thomas was surprised and disappointed in himself.

In the ICU, Thomas checked on the three patients he'd operated on the day before. All were fine. They'd been extubated and had taken something by mouth. EKGs, blood pressures, and all other vital signs were stable and normal. Mr. Campbell had had a few brief episodes of an irregular cardiac rhythm but that had been controlled when an astute resident found some unrelieved gastric dilation. Thomas got the fellow's name. He wanted to compliment him next time he had the opportunity.

Thomas walked over to Mr. Campbell's bed. The man smiled weakly. Then he started to speak.

Thomas bent over. "What did you say, Mr. Campbell?"

"I have to urinate," said Mr. Campbell softly.

"You have a catheter in your bladder," said Thomas.

"I still have to urinate," said Mr. Campbell.

Thomas gave up. He'd let the nursing staff argue with Mr. Campbell.

As he turned to leave, he glanced at the sorry case in the bed next to Mr. Campbell. It was one of Ballantine's disasters. The patient had embolized air to the brain during the operation and now was no more than a living vegetable totally dependent on a breathing machine, but with the quality of the nursing care at the Memorial, he could be expected to live indefinitely.

Thomas felt an arm on his shoulder. He turned and was surprised to find George Sherman.

"Thomas," began George. "I think it is healthy that we have disagreements if only because it might force us to examine our own positions. But it upsets me to think there has to be animosity."

"I was embarrassed at my own behavior," said Thomas. That was as close as he could come to an apology.

"I got a bit hot under the collar myself," admitted George. He let his eyes leave Thomas's face, noticing which bed Thomas had stopped at. "Poor Mr. Harwick. Talk about a shortage of beds. Here's another one we could use."

Thomas smiled in spite of himself.

"Trouble is," added George, "Mr. Harwick is going to be here for a long time unless . . ."

"Unless what?" asked Thomas.

"Unless we pull the plug, as they say," George smiled.

Thomas tried to leave, but George gently restrained him.

Thomas wondered why the man felt obligated to touch him all the time.

"Tell me," asked George. "Would you have the courage to pull the plug?"

"Not unless I talked with Rodney Stoddard first," said Thomas sarcastically. "What about you, George? You seem willing to do most anything to get more beds."

George laughed and withdrew his arm. "We all have our secrets, don't we? I never expected you to say that you'd talk to Rodney. That's a good one." George gave Thomas another of his little taps and walked away, waving good-bye to the ICU nurses.

Thomas watched him, then glanced back at the patient, thinking over George's comments. From time to time a brain-dead patient was taken off his life support system, but neither doctors nor nurses acknowledged the fact.

"Dr. Kingsley?"

Thomas turned to face one of the ICU clerks.

"Your service is on the line."

Giving Ballantine's patient one last glance, Thomas walked over to the central desk wondering how he could get Ballantine to refer his difficult cases. Thomas was confident these "unanticipated" and "unavoidable" tragedies would not happen if he did the surgery.

Thomas answered the phone with undisguised irritation. Invariably when the answering service looked for him it meant bad news. This time, however, the operator just said that he should call his mother as soon as he could.

Perplexed, Thomas made the call. His mother never called him during the day unless it was something important.

"Sorry to bother you, dear," said Patricia.

"What is it?" asked Thomas.

"It's about your wife."

There was a pause. Thomas could feel his patience evaporating.

"Mother, I happen to be rather busy."

"Your wife paid me a visit this morning."

For a fleeting moment Thomas thought that Cassi might have mentioned his impotence. Then he realized that was absurd. But his mother's next statement was even more alarming.

"She was suggesting you were some kind of addict. Dexedrine, I think she said."

Thomas was so angry he could barely speak.

"Wha-what else did she say?" he finally stammered.

"I think that's rather enough, don't you? She said you were abusing drugs. I warned you about this girl, but you wouldn't listen to me. Oh, no. You knew better . . ."

"I'll have to talk to you tonight," said Thomas, disconnecting the line with his index finger.

Still gripping the receiver, Thomas struggled to control his rage. Of course he took a pill now and then. Everybody did. How dared Cassi betray him by making a big deal of the fact to his mother? Abusing drugs! My God, an occasional pill didn't mean he was an addict.

Impulsively Thomas dialed Doris at home. She answered on the third ring out of breath.

"How about a little company?" asked Thomas.

"When?" asked Doris enthusiastically.

"In a few minutes. I'm at the hospital."

"I'd love it," said Doris. "I'm glad you caught me. I was just on my way upstairs."

Thomas hung up. He felt a twinge of fear. What if the same thing happened with Doris as happened last night with Cassi? Knowing it was better not to think about it, Thomas hurried through the rest of his rounds.

Doris lived only a couple of blocks from the hospital on Bay State Road. As Thomas walked to her apartment, he could not stop thinking about what Cassi had done. Why would she want to provoke him like that? It didn't make sense. Did she really think he wouldn't find out? Maybe she was trying to get back at him in some illogical way. Thomas sighed. Being married to Cassi had not been the dream he'd envisioned. He'd thought she was going to be such an asset. So many people had swooned over her that he'd been convinced she was something special. Even George had been crazy for her, wanting to marry her after a handful of dates.

Doris's voice mixed with static greeted him over the intercom when he pushed her bell. He started up the stairs and heard her door open.

"What a nice surprise," she called as he rounded the first landing. She was dressed in a skimpy jogging outfit of shorts and a T-shirt that barely covered her navel. Her hair was loose and seemed incredibly thick and shiny.

As she led him inside and closed the door, Thomas glanced around the apartment. He hadn't been there for months, but not much had changed. The living room was tiny, with a single couch facing a small fireplace. At the end of the room was a bay window that overlooked the street. On the coffee table were a decanter and two glasses. Doris walked up to Thomas and leaned against him. "Did you want to dictate a little?"

she teased, running her hands down his back. Thomas's fears about his potency quickly vanished.

"It's not too early for a little fun, is it?" asked Doris, pressing herself against Thomas and sensing his arousal.

"God, no," said Thomas, pulling her down onto the couch and yanking off her clothes in an ecstasy of excitement and relief at his own response. As he plunged into her he comforted himself that the problem that he'd experienced the night before was Cassi's, not his. It never occurred to him that he had yet to take a Percodan that day.

□

The nurses in the surgical intensive care unit knew that problems, particularly serious problems, had an uncanny way of propagating themselves. The night had begun badly with the eleven-thirty arrest of an eleven-year-old girl who'd been operated on that day for a ruptured spleen. Luckily things had worked out well, and the child's heart had begun beating again almost immediately. The nurses had been amazed at the number of doctors who had responded to the code. For a time there had been so many doctors that they'd been falling over each other.

"I wonder why there are so many attendings in the house?" asked Andrea Bryant, the night supervisor. "It's the first time I've seen Dr. Sherman here on a Saturday night since he was a resident."

"Must be a lot of emergency cases in the OR," said the other RN, Trudy Bodanowitz.

"That can't be it," said Andrea. "I spoke to the night supervisor there and she said that there were only two: an emergency cardiac case and a fractured hip."

"Beats me," said Trudy, looking at her watch. It was just after midnight. "Do you want to take first break tonight?"

The girls were sitting at the central desk finishing the paperwork engendered by the arrest. Neither was assigned to specific patients but rather manned the central station and performed the necessary administrative functions.

"I'm not sure either of us is going to get a break," said Andrea, looking around the large U-shaped desk. "This place is a mess. There's nothing like having an arrest right after shift change to spoil routine."

The nurses' station in the ICU rivaled the flight deck of a Boeing 747 for complicated electronic equipment. Facing the women were banks of TV screens giving constant readouts on all the patients in the unit. Most were set within certain limits so that alarms would go off if the values strayed too far from normal. While the women were speaking, one of the EKG tracings was changing. As crucial minutes passed, the previously regular tracing began to look more and more erratic. Finally, the alarm went off.

"Oh shit," said Trudy as she looked up at the beeping oscilloscope screen. She stood up and gave the unit a slap with her hand, hoping that an electrical malfunction was the cause of the alarm. She saw the abnormal EKG pattern and switched to another lead, still hoping the problem was mechanical.

"Who is it?" asked Andrea, checking for any evidence of frantic activities on the part of the nursing staff.

"Harwick," said Trudy.

Andrea's gaze quickly switched over to the bed of Dr. Ballantine's OR disaster. There was no nurse in attendance, which was not unusual. Mr. Harwick had been exceptionally stable over the last weeks.

"Call the surgical resident" said Trudy. Mr. Harwick's EKG was deteriorating even as Trudy watched. "Look at this, he's going to arrest."

She pointed to the screen where Mr. Harwick's EKG was showing typical changes before it either stopped or degenerated to ventricular fibrillation.

"Should I call a code?" asked Andrea.

The two women looked at each other.

"Dr. Ballantine specifically said 'no code,'" said Trudy.

"I know," said Andrea.

"It always gives me an awful feeling," said Trudy, looking back at the EKG. "I wish they wouldn't put us in this position. It's not fair."

While Trudy watched, the EKG line flattened out with just an occasional blip. Mr. Harwick had died.

"Call the resident," said Trudy angrily. She walked around the end of the ICU desk and approached Mr. Harwick's bed. The respirator was still inflating and deflating his lungs, giving him the appearance of life.

"Certainly doesn't make you excited about having surgery," said Andrea, hanging up the phone.

"I wonder what went wrong. He was so stable," said Trudy.

Trudy reached out and flipped off the respirator. The hissing sound stopped. Mr. Harwick's chest fell and was still.

Andrea reached over and turned off the IV. "It's probably just as well. Now the family can adjust and then go on with their lives."

CHAPTER

5

TWO WEEKS HAD PASSED since Thomas learned of Cassi's visit to his mother. While they had only fought briefly, the tension had been unbearable. Even Thomas had noted his increased dependency on Percodan, but he had to take something to allay his anxiety.

As he ran down the hall late for the monthly death conference, he felt his pulse race.

The meeting had already begun, and the chief surgical resident was presenting the first case, a trauma victim who had expired shortly after admission to the ER. The resident and intern had failed to notice warning signs that the sac covering the heart had been damaged and was filling with blood. Since no attending had been involved, the doctors happily raked the house staff over the coals.

If the case had belonged to one of the private staff men, the discussion would have progressed very differently. The same points would have been made, but the physician would have been reassured that the diagnosis of hemopericardium was difficult and he'd done the best he could.

Thomas had realized early in the game that the monthly death conference served more to relieve guilt than to punish, unless the offender was a resident. Lay people might have thought the death conference served as a kind of watchdog, but unfortunately such was not the case, as Thomas cynically observed. And the next case proved his point.

Dr. Ballantine was mounting the podium to present Herbert Harwick. When he finished, an obese pathology resident quickly ran down the results of the autopsy, including slides of the individual's brain, of which little remained.

Mr. Harwick's death was then discussed but with no mention that his trauma in the OR was the possible result of Dr. Ballantine's inept surgery. The general feeling among the attendings was, "There but for the grace of God go I," which was true to an extent. What made Thomas sick was that no one remembered that six months previously Ballantine had presented a similar case. Air embolism was a feared complication that at times occurred no matter what one did, but the fact that it occurred so often and at an increasing frequency to Ballantine was always ignored.

Equally amazing, as far as Thomas was concerned, was that nothing was said about Harwick's actual death in the ICU. As far as Thomas knew, the patient had been stable for an extended period of time before the sudden arrest. Thomas looked at the members of the audience and puzzled why they remained silent. It reconfirmed for him that bureaucracy and its committee method of dealing with problems was no way to run an organization.

"If there's no further discussion," said Ballantine, "I think we should move on to the next case. Unfortunately I'm still in the dock." He smiled thinly. "The patient's name is Bruce Wilkinson. He is a forty-two-year-old white male who had suffered a heart attack and who had shown focally compromised coronary circulation, suggesting he was a good candidate for a triple bypass procedure."

Thomas straightened up in his chair. He remembered Wilkinson very clearly, particularly the night he'd attempted to resuscitate him. He could still see the surrealistic scene in his mind's eye.

Ballantine droned on, presenting the case with much too much detail. The chin of the surgeon sitting next to Thomas slumped onto his chest and his deep, regular breathing could be heard as far away as the podium. Finally Ballantine got to the end and said, "Mr. Wilkinson did extremely well postoperatively until the night of the fourth postoperative day. At that time he died."

Ballantine looked up from his papers. His face, in contrast to its expression when they were discussing the previous case, had assumed a defiant expression as if to say, "Try to find a mistake here."

A slight, well-dressed pathology resident got up

from the first row and stepped behind the podium. He adjusted the small microphone nervously and bent over, thinking he had to speak directly into it. A high-pitched, irritating electronic sound resulted, and he backed away with apology.

Thomas recognized the man. It was Robert Seibert, Cassi's friend.

As soon as Robert began his presentation of the pathology, all evidence of his nervousness disappeared. He was a good speaker, especially when compared with Ballantine, and he had organized his material so that only the significant points were mentioned. He showed a series of slides and pointed out that, although the patient had been described as having been deeply and grossly cyanotic at the time of death, there was no airway obstruction. He next presented a photomicrograph that showed that there was no alveolar problem in the lungs. Another series of slides showed there were no pulmonary emboli. Another series of photomicrographs was presented that showed there was no evidence that there had been a rise in left or right atrial pressure prior to death. The final series of pictures indicated that the bypasses were skillfully sutured in place and that there was no sign of recent myocardial infarction or heart attack.

The lights came back on.

"All this shows, . . ." said Robert, pausing as if for effect, "that there was no cause of death in this case."

The audience responded with surprise. Such a statement was completely unexpected. There were even a few laughs as well as a comment from one of the orthopedic men who asked if this had been one of those cases that had awakened in the morgue. That inspired more laughter. Robert smiled.

"Must have been a stroke," said someone behind Thomas.

"That is a good suggestion," said Robert. "A stroke that shut down the breathing while the heart pumped the unoxygenated blood. That would cause deep cyanosis. But that would mean a brain-stem lesion. We went over the brain millimeter by millimeter and found nothing."

The audience was now silent.

Robert waited for more comments, but there were none. Then he leaned forward and spoke into the microphone: "With permission I'd like to present another slide."

Cleverly he'd caught the imagination of the gathering.

Thomas had an idea of what was coming.

Robert switched off the lights, then switched on the projector. The slide showed a compilation of seventeen cases, containing comparable data on age, sex, and points of medical history.

"I've been interested in cases such as Mr. Wilkinson for some time," said Robert. "This slide is to show that his is not an isolated case. I have found four similar cases myself over the last year and a half. When I went back in the files, I found thirteen others. If you'll notice, they have all had cardiac surgery. In each circumstance, no specific cause of death was found. I've labeled this syndrome sudden surgical death, or SSD."

The lights came back on.

Ballantine's face had turned bright red. "What do you think you are doing?" he spat at Robert.

Under different circumstances Thomas might have felt sorry for Robert. His unexpected presentation did not fit within the rather narrow protocol for a death conference.

Glancing around the room, Thomas saw many angry faces. It was an old story. Doctors did not like to have their expertise questioned. And they were reluctant to police their own.

"This is a death conference, not a Grand Rounds," Ballantine was saying. "We're not here for a lecture."

"In discussing the case of Mr. Wilkinson, I thought it would be enlightening . . ."

"You thought," repeated Dr. Ballantine sarcastically. "Well, for your information you're here as a consult. Did you have something specific to say when you presented this list of supposed sudden surgical deaths?"

"No," admitted Robert.

Although Thomas preferred to stay silent at such meetings, he had to ask a question: "Excuse me, Robert," he called. "Did all the seventeen cases have deep cyanosis?"

Robert could not have been more eager to field a question from the audience. "No," he said into the microphone. "Only five of the cases."

"That means that the physiologic cause of death was not the same in all these cases."

"That's true," said Robert. "Six had convulsions prior to death."

"That was probably air embolism," said another surgeon.

"I don't think so," said Robert. "First of all, the convulsions occurred three or more days after surgery. It would be hard to explain that kind of delay. Also when the brains were autopsied, no air was found."

"Could have been absorbed," said someone else.

"If there had been enough air to cause sudden convulsions and death," said Robert, "then there should have been enough to see."

"What about the surgeons?" called the man behind Thomas. "Were any more heavily represented than others?"

"Eight of the cases," said Robert, "belonged to Dr. George Sherman."

A buzz of conversation broke out in the back of the room. George rose furiously to his feet as Ballantine nudged Robert from the podium.

"If there are no further comments . . ." said Ballantine.

George spoke out: "I think Dr. Kingsley's comment was particularly cogent. By pointing out that there were different mechanisms of death in these cases, he indicated that there was no reason to try and relate the cases." George looked over at Thomas.

"Exactly," said Thomas. He would have preferred to let George sink or swim on his own, but he felt obligated to respond. "It occurred to me that Robert had correlated the cases because of some similarity he saw in their deaths, but that didn't seem to be the case."

"The basis of the correlation," said Robert, "was that the deaths, particularly over the last several years, occurred when the patients were apparently doing well, and there was no anatomic or physiologic cause."

"Correction," said George. "No cause was found by the department of pathology."

"It's the same thing," said Robert.

"Not quite," said George. "Maybe another pathology department would have found the causes. I think it's more of a reflection on you and your colleagues than anything else. And intimating that there is something irregular about a series of operative tragedies on such a basis is irresponsible."

"Hear, hear," shouted an orthopedic surgeon who began to clap. Robert quickly stepped down from the podium. There was an air of tension in the room.

"The next death conference will be one month from today, January seventh," said Ballantine, switching off the microphone and gathering his papers. He walked off the stage and over to Thomas.

"You seemed to know that kid," he said. "Who the hell is he?"

"His name is Robert Seibert," said Thomas. "He's a second-year pathology resident."

"I'm going to have the kid's balls in Formalin. Who does the little turd think he is, coming up here and putting himself up as our Socratic gadfly?"

Over Ballantine's shoulder, Thomas could see George making his way over to them. He was just as provoked as Ballantine.

"I got his name," said George menacingly, as if he were revealing a secret.

"We already know it," said Ballantine. "He's only in his second year."

"Wonderful," said George. "Not only do we have to put up with philosophers, but also smart-ass pathology residents."

"I heard there was a death this month in one of the cath rooms in radiology," said Thomas. "How come it wasn't presented?"

"Oh, you mean Sam Stevens," said George nervously, watching Robert leave the room. "Since the death occurred during the catheterization, the medical boys wanted to present it at their death conference."

While Thomas watched Dr. Ballantine and George fume, he wondered what they'd say if he told them that Cassi had been involved with the so-called SSD study. For everyone's sake he hoped they wouldn't find out. He also hoped that Cassi had had sense enough not to continue her association with Robert. All it could do was cause trouble.

□

In a totally dark examination room, Cassi was lying flat on her back and could not have been more uncomfortable. She wasn't in pain but close to it as she was forced to keep her eye still while Dr. Martin Obermeyer, chief of ophthalmology, shined an intensely bright light into her left eye. Worse than the discomfort was her fear of what the doctor would say. Cassi knew she'd been less than responsible about her eye problem. Desperately she hoped that Dr. Obermeyer would make some reassuring comment as he examined her. But he remained ominously quiet.

Without so much as a word, he shifted the light into

her good eye. The beam came from an apparatus that the doctor wore around his head, similar to a miner's light, but more intricate. Although the light seemed bright in her left eye, when it shifted to the good eye the intensity was so great it was difficult for Cassi to believe it did not cause damage in and of itself.

"Please, Cassi," said Dr. Obermeyer, lifting the light beam and peering at her beneath the eyepieces of the instruments. "Please hold your eye still." He pressed down with a small metal stylus.

Irritative tears welled up, and Cassi could feel them spill over and run down the side of her face. She wondered how much longer she could stand it. Involuntarily she gripped the sheet covering the examining table. Just at the moment she thought she could no longer remain still, the light disappeared, but even after Dr. Obermeyer turned on the overhead lights, she could not see well. The doctor was a blur to her as he sat down at his desk to write.

It concerned her that he was being so reticent. Obviously he was annoyed at her.

"Can I sit up?" asked Cassi hesitatingly.

"I don't know why you ask my opinion," said Dr. Obermeyer, "when you don't follow any of my other suggestions." The ophthalmologist didn't bother turning around as he spoke.

Cassi sat up and swung her legs over the side of the table. Her right eye was beginning to correct itself from the trauma of the bright light, but her vision remained blurry from the drops used to dilate her pupils. She watched Dr. Obermeyer's back for a moment, digesting his comment. She'd expected him to be annoyed that she'd canceled her last appointment, but she hadn't thought it would be this bad.

Only after he finished writing and closed his chart did he turn back to Cassi. He was sitting on a low stool with wheels, and he glided over to face her.

Cassi's line of vision from her perch on the exam table was a good foot higher than the doctor's. She could see the shiny area on the top of his head where his hair was thinning. He wasn't the world's best-looking man, with his full, heavy features and a deep line in the middle of his forehead. Yet the whole package was not unattractive. His face exuded intelligence and sincerity, two qualities that Cassi found appealing.

"I think I should be frank," he began. "There is no sign of the blood clearing from your left eye. In fact it appears as if there is new blood."

Cassi tried not to betray her anxiousness. She nodded as if she were listening to a discussion of another patient.

"I still cannot visualize the retina," said Dr. Obermeyer. "Consequently I do not know where the blood is coming from or if it is a treatable lesion."

"But the ultrasound test . . ." began Cassi.

"It proved that the retina is not detached, at least not yet, but it cannot show where the bleeding is coming from."

"Perhaps if we waited a little longer."

"If it hasn't cleared by now, it's extremely unlikely that it will. Meanwhile we could lose the only chance we have to treat. Cassi, I've got to see the back of your eye. We must do a vitrectomy."

Cassi glanced away. "It can't wait for a month or so?"

"No," said Dr. Obermeyer. "Cassi, you have already gotten me to postpone this longer than I wanted to. Then you canceled your last appointment. I'm not sure you understand the stakes here."

"I understand the stakes," said Cassi. "It's just not a good time."

"It's never a good time for surgery," said Dr. Obermeyer, "except for the surgeon. Let me schedule this thing and get on with it."

"I have to discuss it with Thomas," said Cassi.

"What?" questioned Dr. Obermeyer with surprise. "You haven't told him about this?"

"Oh yes," said Cassi quickly. "Just not the timing."

"When can you discuss the timing with Thomas?" asked Dr. Obermeyer with resignation.

"Soon. In fact tonight. I'll be back to you tomorrow, I promise." She slid off the table and steadied herself.

Cassi was relieved to escape from the ophthalmologist's office. Deep down she knew he was right; she should have the vitrectomy. But telling Thomas was going to be difficult. Cassi stopped at the end of the corridor on the fifth floor of the Professional Building, the same building where Thomas had his office. She stared out a window at the early December cityscape with its leafless tree-lined streets and densely packed brick buildings.

An ambulance was screaming down Commonwealth Avenue, its lights flashing. Cassi closed her right eye, and the scene vanished to mere light. In a panic she reopened her eye to let the world back in. She had to do something. She had to talk with Thomas despite the difficulties they'd had since her visit to Patricia.

Cassi wished that Saturday two weeks previously had never taken place. If only Patricia had not called Thomas. But of course that had been too much to ask. Expecting Thomas to come home angry, Cassi was shocked when he didn't come home at all. At ten-thirty, Cassi had finally called Thomas's exchange. Only then did she learn that Thomas had an emergency operation. She left word for him to call and waited up until two, finally falling asleep with book in hand and light on. Thomas finally came home on Sunday afternoon and, instead of screaming at her, refused to talk to her at all. With deliberate calm he moved his clothes into the guest room next to his study.

For Cassi the "silent treatment" was an unbearable strain. What little conversation they did have was just chatter. Dinner was the worst, and several times Cassi, pleading a headache, took a tray to her room.

After a week, Thomas had finally exploded in a rage. The triggering event had been insignificant; Cassi had dropped a Waterford glass on the tiled kitchen floor. As Thomas rushed over to her and started yelling, he accused Cassi of being deceitful and maneuvering behind his back. How dare Cassi go to his mother and accuse him of drug abuse?

"Of course I've taken an occasional pill," said Thomas, finally lowering his voice. "Either to help me sleep or keep me awake if I've been up all night. I dare you to name a single doctor who never took any of his own drugs!" He'd stabbed at her with his finger to make his point.

Having taken an occasional Valium herself, Cassi was not about to contradict Thomas. Besides, intuition told her to be quiet and let Thomas vent his anger.

In a more controlled tone Thomas asked her why in God's name had she gone to Patricia. Cassi, of all people, knew how much his mother nagged him without anyone giving her such a potentially frightening subject.

Sensing that Thomas had yelled himself out, Cassi tried to explain. She said that having found the Dexedrine, she'd been scared and had mistakenly thought that Patricia would be the best person to help if Thomas did have a problem. "And I never said you were an addict."

"My mother said you did," snapped Thomas. "Who am I to believe?" He threw up his arms in disgust.

Cassi didn't answer although she was tempted to say that if Thomas didn't know the answer after forty-two years of living with Patricia, he was never going to. Instead, Cassi apologized for jumping to conclusions after finding the Dexedrine and worse still for going to his mother. Tearfully she told him how much she loved him, silently acknowledging the fact she was more terrified of Thomas's leaving her than she was of his possible drug abuse. She wanted their relationship to return to normal. If the strain had started with her complaining about her diabetes, Cassi decided she would shield Thomas from any knowledge of her problems. But now her eye was forcing the issue. The arrival of another screaming ambulance brought Cassi to the present. As much as she did not want to upset Thomas, she knew she had no choice. She could not go into the hospital and have an operation without telling him even if she somehow found the courage to do so. With terrible foreboding Cassi pushed the elevator button. She'd see

Thomas now. Knowing herself, she was afraid that if she waited until they were at home that evening, she would not be able to broach the issue.

Trying not to think anymore lest she change her mind, Cassi made her way down to Thomas's office and pushed open the door. Fortunately there were no patients in the waiting room. Doris looked up from her typewriter and, as usual, turned back to her work without so much as acknowledging Cassi's presence.

"Is Thomas in?" asked Cassi.

"Yes," said Doris without interrupting her typing. "He's with his last patient."

Cassi sat on the rose-colored couch. She couldn't read because the blurring effect of the drops in her eye had not yet worn off. Since Doris didn't look at Cassi, Cassi did not feel uncomfortable watching her. She noticed that the nurse had changed her hairstyle. Cassi thought that Doris looked better without the severity of her usual bun.

Presently a patient emerged from the interior of the office. Brimming with good cheer, he smiled at Doris. "I feel terrific," he said. "The doctor told me that I'm completely better. I can do whatever I like."

Pulling on his coat, he said to Cassi, "Dr. Kingsley's the greatest. Don't worry about a thing, young lady." Turning to Doris he thanked her, blew her a kiss, and left.

Cassi sighed as she got up. She knew Thomas was a great doctor. She wished she could elicit the kind of compassion that she believed he gave to his patients.

Thomas was dictating when Cassi stepped into his office. "Thank you again, comma, Michael, comma, for this interesting case, comma, and if I can be of any further assistance in his management, comma, do not hesitate to call. Period. Sincerely yours, end dictation."

Clicking off the machine, Thomas swung around in his chair. He regarded Cassi with calculated indifference.

"And to what do I owe the pleasure of this visit?" he asked.

"I've just come from the ophthalmologist," said Cassi, trying to control her voice.

"That's nice," said Thomas.

"I have to talk to you."

"It had better be short," said Thomas, glancing at his watch. "I've got a patient in cardiogenic shock that I've got to see."

Cassi could feel her courage falter. She needed some sign that Thomas would not become irritated if she once again brought up her illness. But Thomas's posture just suggested an aggressive nonchalance. It was as if he were daring her to cross some arbitrary line.

"Well?" asked Thomas.

"He had to dilate my pupils," said Cassi, skirting the issue. "There's been some deterioration. I wondered if we could go home a little earlier."

"I'm afraid not," said Thomas, standing up. "I'm pretty sure the patient I'm seeing will need emergency surgery." He slipped off his white jacket and hung it on the hook on the door leading to the examining room. "In fact, I may have to spend the night here in the hospital."

He said nothing about her eye. Cassi knew she had to bring up her own surgery, but she couldn't. Instead she said, "You spent last night in the hospital. Thomas, you're pushing yourself too hard. You need more rest."

"Some of us have to work," said Thomas. "We can't all be in psychiatry." He pulled on his suit jacket, then stepped back to the desk to snap the tape out of the dictating machine.

"I don't know whether I can drive with this blurry eye," said Cassi. She knew better than to respond to Thomas's pejorative implication about psychiatry.

"You have two choices," said Thomas. "Hang around until the drops wear off or stay the night in the hospital. Whatever you think is best for you." Thomas started for the door.

"Wait," called Cassi, her mouth dry. "I have to talk to you. Do you think I should have a vitrectomy?"

There, it was out. Cassi looked down and saw she was wringing her hands. Self-consciously she pulled them apart, then didn't know what to do with them.

"I'm surprised you still care about my opinion," snapped Thomas. His slight smile had vanished. "Unfortunately, I'm not an eye surgeon. I don't have the slightest idea of whether you should have a vitrectomy. That's why I sent you to Obermeyer."

Cassi could feel his rising anger. It was just as she feared. Telling him about her eye condition was only going to make matters worse.

"Besides," said Thomas. "Isn't there a better time to talk about this kind of thing? I've got someone dying upstairs. You've had this problem with your eye for months. Now you show up when I'm in the middle of an emergency and want to discuss it. My God, Cassi. Think about other people once in a while, will you?"

Thomas stalked over to the door, wrenched it open, and was gone.

In a lot of ways Thomas was right, thought Cassi. Bringing up the problem of her eye in Thomas's office was inappropriate. She knew when he said he had a patient "dying upstairs," he meant it.

Her jaw clenched, Cassi walked out of the office. Doris made a show of typing, but Cassi guessed she'd been listening. Walking down to the elevators, Cassi decided to go back to Clarkson Two. It would keep her from thinking too much. Besides, she knew she couldn't drive, at least not for a while.

She got back to the ward while the afternoon team meeting was still in progress.

Cassi had arranged to take the rest of the day off and did not feel up to joining the group. She was afraid if she were among friends her delicate control would crumble and she'd burst into tears.

Thankful for the unexpected opportunity of reaching her office unobserved, she slipped inside and quickly closed the door behind her. Stepping around the metal and Formica desk, which practically spanned the width of the room, she settled herself into the aged swivel desk chair. Cassi had tried to liven the cubbyhole with several bright prints of Impressionist paintings she bought at the Harvard co-op. The effort hadn't helped much. With its harsh overhead fluorescent lighting, the room still looked like an interrogation cell.

Resting her head in her hands, she tried to think, but all she could concentrate on were her problems with

Thomas. She was almost relieved when there was a sharp knock on the door. Before she could answer it, William Bentworth stepped inside.

"Mind if I sit down, Dr. Cassidy?" asked Bentworth with uncharacteristic politeness.

"No," said Cassi, surprised to see the colonel entering her office on his own accord. He was carefully dressed in tan slacks and a freshly pressed plaid shirt. His shoes evidenced a spit-and-polish shine.

He smiled. "Mind if I smoke?"

"No," said Cassi. She did mind, but it was one of those sacrifices she felt she had to make. Some people needed all the help they could get in order to open up and talk. On occasion the process of lighting a cigarette was an important crutch. Bentworth leaned back and smiled. For the first time his brilliant blue eyes seemed cordial and warm. He was a handsome man, with broad shoulders, thick dark hair, and angular, aristocratic features.

"Are you all right, Doctor?" asked Bentworth, leaning forward again to examine Cassi's face.

"I'm perfectly fine. Why do you ask?"

"You look a bit distraught."

Cassi looked up at the Monet print of the little girl and her mother in the poppy field. She tried to collect her thoughts. It frightened her a little to realize that a patient could be so perceptive.

"Perhaps you feel guilty," offered Bentworth, considerately blowing smoke away from Cassi.

"And why should I feel guilty?"

"Because I think you have been deliberately avoiding me."

Cassi remembered Jacob's comment about borderline personalities being inconsistent, and she contrasted Bentworth's current behavior with his previous refusal to talk to her.

"And I know why you've been avoiding me," continued Bentworth. "I think I scare you. I'm sorry if that's the case. Having been in the army so long and being accustomed to giving orders, I suppose I can be overbearing at times."

For the first time in Cassi's short psychiatric career, something that she'd read in the literature was occurring spontaneously between herself and one of her patients. She knew, without any doubt, that Bentworth was trying to manipulate her.

"Mr. Bentworth . . ." began Cassi.

"Colonel Bentworth," corrected William with a smile. "If I call you Doctor, it's only reasonable you call me Colonel. It's a sign of mutual respect."

"Fair enough," said Cassi. "The fact of the matter is that you have been the one who has made it impossible for us to have a session together. I've tried, if you can remember, on numerous occasions to schedule a meeting, but you have always professed to have a prior commitment. Now I understand that you get more out of the group milieu than private conversation, so I haven't pushed the situation. If you'd like to meet, let's schedule it."

"I would love to talk with you," said Bentworth. "How about right now? I have the time. Do you?"

Cassi was not willing to fall prey to Bentworth's manipulation, thinking that it would ultimately have a negative effect on their relationship. She wasn't prepared now and Bentworth did frighten her despite his newly found charm.

"How about tomorrow morning?" said Cassi. "Right after team meeting."

Colonel Bentworth stood up and stubbed out his cigarette in the ashtray on Cassi's desk. "All right. I'll look forward to it. And I hope whatever is troubling you works out for the best."

After he was gone, Cassi breathed the smoky air while her mind envisioned Colonel Bentworth in a dress uniform. She could imagine he would be gallant and dashing, and his mental problems would seem fictitious. Knowing the depth of his disorder, she found the fact that it could be so easily camouflaged disturbing.

Before she could even dictate her notes, her door opened again, and Maureen Kavenaugh came in and sat down. Maureen had been admitted a month previously for recurrent major depression. She'd had a serious setback when her husband had come in and slapped her around. Seeing her out of her room was as much a surprise as having William Bentworth voluntarily pay a visit. Cassi wondered if some miracle drug were being secretly added to the patients' food.

"I saw the colonel go into your office," said Maureen. "I thought you said you weren't going to be here this afternoon." Her voice was flat and emotionless.

"I hadn't planned on it," said Cassi.

"Well, since you are here, can I talk to you for a moment?" asked Maureen timidly.

"Of course," said Cassi. She watched Maureen advance into the room, closing the door and sitting down.

"Yesterday when we talked . . ." Maureen hesitated and her eyes filled with tears.

Cassi pushed the box of tissues toward the woman.

"You . . . you asked me if I'd like to see my sister." Maureen's voice was so low that Cassi could barely hear. She nodded quickly, wondering what Maureen was thinking. The woman had not shown much interest in anything since her relapse even though Cassi had started her on Elavil. At team meeting several people had suggested electric shock, but Cassi had argued against it, thinking the Elavil and supportive sessions would be adequate. What amazed Cassi was Maureen's insight into the dynamics of her condition. But for Maureen an understanding of her illness did not automatically give her the power to influence it.

Maureen acknowledged her hostility to her mother, who had abandoned both Maureen and her younger sister when they were toddlers, and the repressed jealousy she felt toward that pretty younger sister who had run off and married, leaving Maureen to live by herself. Out of desperation she'd married an inappropriate man.

"Do you think my sister would want to see me?" asked Maureen finally, her face wet with tears.

"I think she might," said Cassi. "But we won't know unless you ask her."

Maureen blew her nose. Her hair was stringy and in need of a wash. Her face was drawn, and, despite her medication, she'd continued to lose weight.

"I'm afraid to ask her," admitted Maureen. "I don't think she'll come. Why should she? I'm not worth it. It's hopeless."

"Just thinking about talking to your sister is a hopeful sign," Cassi said gently.

Maureen let out a long sigh. "I can't make up my mind. If I call her and ask her and she says no, then everything will be worse. I want someone else to do it. Would you call her?"

Cassi flushed. She thought of her own indecisiveness in facing Thomas. Maureen's feelings of dependency and helplessness seemed all too familiar. She too wanted someone else to make her decisions. With exhausting effort, Cassi tried to concentrate on the woman sitting across from her.

"I'm not sure it's my place to contact your sister," said Cassi. "But it's something we can talk about. As far as seeing your sister, I think that is a good idea. Why don't we talk about it more tomorrow? I think you're scheduled for a session at two."

Maureen agreed and, after taking several more tissues, went out, leaving the door open.

Cassi sat for some time, staring blankly at the wall. She felt certain that identifying with one of her patients was a sign of her inexperience.

"Hey! How come you aren't in team meeting?" said Joan Widiker, doing a double take in the corridor after catching a glimpse of Cassi.

Cassi glanced up but didn't answer.

"What's going on?" asked Joan. "You look a little worse for wear." She stepped into Cassi's office and sniffed. "And I didn't know you smoked."

"I don't," said Cassi. "Colonel Bentworth does."

"He came to see you?" Joan raised her eyebrow.

"You're doing better than you think." She paused and then sat down.

"I thought I'd let you know that Jerry Donovan and I went out. Have you talked with him?"

Cassi shook her head.

"It didn't work out too well. All he wanted . . ." Joan stopped in midsentence. "Cassi, what's the matter with you?"

Tears overflowed Cassi's eyes and ran down her cheeks.

As she had feared, a friendly presence destroyed her self-control. She finally let go and, dropping her face into her hands, wept openly.

"Jerry Donovan wasn't that bad," said Joan, hoping a little humor might help. "Besides, I didn't give in. I'm still a virgin."

Cassi's body shook with sobs. Joan came around the end of the desk and put her arm around her friend's shoulder. For a few moments she said nothing. As a psychiatry resident, she didn't have the usual negative reaction to tears that lay people did. From the strength of Cassi's emotion Joan guessed that she needed the outlet.

"I'm sorry," said Cassi, reaching for the tissues just as Maureen had. "I didn't want to do this."

"Sounds like you needed it. Do you want to talk?"

Cassi took a deep breath. "I don't know. It all seems so hopeless." As soon as she said the word, Cassi remembered Maureen had said the same thing.

"What's so hopeless?" asked Joan.

"Everything," said Cassi.

"Give me an example," said Joan, challengingly.

Cassi pulled her hands away from her tear-streaked face.

"I went to the ophthalmologist today. He wants to operate, but I don't know if I should."

"What does your husband say?" asked Joan.

"That's part of the problem." As soon as Cassi spoke, she regretted it. She knew Joan, being both sensitive and clever, would piece together the whole picture, and, in the back of her mind, Cassi could hear Thomas telling her not to discuss her medical problems with anyone.

Joan took her hand from Cassi's shoulder. "I think you need someone to talk to. As the official department consult, I'm at your service. Besides, anyone can afford my fee."

Cassi managed a weak smile. Intuitively she knew she could trust Joan. She needed someone's insight, and God knows she wasn't doing too well on her own.

"I don't know if you have any idea of Thomas's schedule," began Cassi. "He works harder than anyone I know. You'd think he was an intern. Last night he stayed in the hospital. Tonight he'll stay in the hospital. He doesn't have a lot of extra time . . ."

"Cassi," said Joan politely. "I don't like to interrupt but why not save the excuses. Have you spoken to your husband about this operation?"

Cassi sighed. "I tried to bring it up a few hours ago, but it was the wrong time and place."

"Listen," said Joan. "I rarely make judgments. But when it comes to talking about eye surgery with your husband, there is no wrong time or place."

Cassi digested this comment. She wasn't sure if she agreed or not.

"What did he say?" asked Joan.

"He said he wasn't an eye surgeon."

"Ah, he wants to delegate his responsibility."

"No," said Cassi emphatically. "Thomas made sure I went to the best ophthalmologist."

"It still seems a rather callous reaction."

Cassi looked down at her hands, thinking Joan was too clever. She had the distinct impression that Joan could take this conversation further than Cassi would like.

"Cassi," asked Joan, "is everything all right between you and Thomas?"

Cassi could feel the tears filling her eyes again. She tried to stop them but was only partially successful.

"That's one way of answering," said Joan empathetically. "Do you want to talk about it?"

Cassi bit her trembling lower lip. "If something happened to my relationship with Thomas," she said, "I don't know if I could go on. I think my life would fall apart. I need him desperately."

"I can sense you feel that way. I also think that you don't really want to talk about the problem. Am I right?"

Cassi nodded. She felt torn between her fear of Thomas and her guilt at rejecting Joan's offer of friendship.

"Okay," said Joan, "but before I go, I think some advice is in order. Maybe it's presumptuous for me to say this, and it's certainly not professional, but I have a feeling that you should try to lessen your dependency on Thomas. Somehow I don't think you give yourself the credit you deserve. And that kind of dependence can really hurt a relationship in the long run. Well, enough unsolicited advice."

Joan opened Cassi's door, then stopped. "Did you say that Thomas was going to spend tonight in the hospital?"

"I think he has emergency surgery," said Cassi, preoccupied with the concept of dependency. "When he does, he usually sleeps over rather than suffer the forty-minute commute."

"Fine!" said Joan. "Why don't you come home with me tonight? I've got a sofa bed in the living room and a fully stocked refrigerator."

"And by midnight you'd know all my secrets," said Cassi, only half in jest.

"I'd be on my honor not to probe," said Joan.

"Anyway, I can't," said Cassi. "I appreciate the offer, but there's always the chance Thomas might not have surgery and, in that case, he could come home. Under the circumstances I want to be there. Maybe we'll talk."

Joan smiled sympathetically. "You do have it bad. Well, if you change your mind, give me a call. I'll be in the hospital for another hour or so." She opened the door again and this time really left.

Cassi stared at the Monet trying to decide if it was safe for her to drive. It was reassuring to note that her vision had significantly improved; the drops were finally wearing off.

□

Thomas felt his hands tremble as he opened his office door and switched on the light. The clock on Doris's desk indicated that it was almost six-thirty. It was already dark outside, making it hard to remember summer nights when it stayed light to nine-thirty. Closing the door, he held out his arm. It scared him to see his normally steady hand shake so violently. How could Cassi keep pressuring him when he was already so tense?

Approaching his desk, he opened the second drawer and pulled out one of his small plastic bottles. The combination of the child-proof top and his agitation made opening the package impossible. He had to restrain himself from dashing the thing on the floor and stomping on it with his heel. Finally he managed to extract one of the yellow tablets. He placed it on his tongue despite its bitter taste and walked into the small washroom, which still reeked of Doris's perfume.

Forsaking a cup, Thomas bent and drank directly from the faucet. He went back to his office and sat at his desk. His anxiety seemed to be increasing. Wrenching open the second drawer again, he fumbled for the same plastic bottle. This time he was unsuccessful with the top. Slamming the bottle down on the desk top only succeeded in denting the wood surface and bruising his thumb.

Closing his eyes, Thomas told himself that he had to stay in control. When he opened his eyes, he remembered that in order to open the bottle he had to line up the two arrows.

But he did not take another pill. Instead his mind

conjured up the image of Laura Campbell. There was no reason for him to be alone. "I wish there was something I could do for you," she had said. "Anything!" Thomas knew he had her phone number in her father's folder, ostensibly for emergency use. But wasn't this an emergency? Thomas smiled. Besides, there were many ways to camouflage his intentions if he'd misread her signals.

Thomas found Mr. Campbell's folder and quickly dialed Laura's number, hoping the woman was at home. She answered on the second ring.

"This is Dr. Kingsley. Sorry to bother you."

"Is something wrong?" asked Laura worriedly.

"No, no," assured Thomas. "Your father is doing fine. I'm terribly sorry about his jaundice. It is one of those unfortunate complications. I wish we could have anticipated it, but it should clear soon. Anyway the reason I'm calling is that your father will undoubtedly be discharged soon, and I thought, perhaps, you'd like to discuss the case."

"Absolutely," said Laura. "Just tell me when."

Thomas twisted the phone cord. "Well, that's why I'm calling. I'm sure you can guess what my schedule is like. But it so happens I'm waiting for a surgery and am presently alone in my office. I thought, perhaps, you might consider coming over."

"Can you give me thirty minutes?" asked Laura.

"I think so," said Thomas. He knew he had plenty of time.

"I'll be there," said Laura.

"One other thing," added Thomas. "To get into the Professional Building at this hour you must go through the hospital. The doors here are locked at six."

Thomas hung up. He felt much better. Excitement had replaced anxiety. Opening the desk drawer, he dropped in the container of pills. Then he called the cardiac catheterization lab to check on the patient in cardiogenic shock. As he had expected, the patient was still awaiting catheterization. No matter what the procedure showed, Thomas guessed he had several hours.

Thomas met Laura at the door to the inner office and motioned her inside. He was pleased to see that again she was wearing a thin, clinging silk dress. It was a light beige, almost the color of her skin. Thomas could see the faint line of her panties.

He didn't speak for a moment, plotting his opening so that if he'd misread her signals there wouldn't be any embarrassment. He began by reassuring her once again that her father would soon be discharged. Then he discussed Mr. Campbell's long-term care, and under the pretense of discussing his exercise limitations, Thomas brought up the issue of sex.

"Your father had asked me about this before the operation," he said, watching Laura's face. "I know that your mother passed away several years ago, and if this is an uncomfortable subject for you . . ."

"Not at all," said Laura with a smile. "I am an adult."

"Of course," said Thomas, letting his eyes run over her dress. "That is very obvious."

Laura smiled again and smoothed her long ponytail off her shoulder.

"A man like your father still has sexual needs," said Thomas.

"As a physician I'm sure you know that better than

most," said Laura. She'd uncrossed her legs and leaned forward. It was clear she wasn't wearing a bra under the sheer silk.

Thomas got up from his chair and came around in front of the desk. He was certain Laura hadn't come to talk about her father. "I understand these needs all too well myself because I have a wife with a chronic, debilitating disease."

Laura smiled. "As I said, I wish there was something I could do for you." She stood up and leaned against Thomas. "Can you think of anything?"

Thomas led her into the dimly lit examining room. Slowly he helped her out of her dress and then stepped out of his own clothes, folding them neatly on a chair. When he turned back to face her, he was pleased to find himself fully erect.

"What do you think?" he asked, with his palms spread out to the sides.

"I love it," said Laura huskily, reaching out for him.

☐

After having worried about driving, Cassi was glad that her trip home was pleasantly uneventful. The most hazardous part had been the walk from the garage to the house. She'd forgotten how early night came now that it was December.

The house itself was ominously black, particularly the windows, which shone like pieces of polished onyx. Inside Cassi found a note from Harriet explaining how to heat up dinner. Whenever Harriet got the word that Thomas was not coming home, she left early. As contrary as Harriet could be, Cassi would have preferred not to be alone.

She went through the house snapping on lights hoping to make the place a bit more cheerful. She found the rambling old house with its cavernous spaces particularly chilling, her footsteps echoing down the empty halls. The heat was supposed to be turned to sixty-five degrees, but Cassi could see her breath.

Upstairs the morning room was considerably warmer, almost comfortable. In the master bath she had a supplementary quartz heater, which she turned on. After testing her blood sugar, Cassi went ahead with her usual insulin dose, then took a shower.

She tried not to think too much. Her emotional outburst had left her drained and had settled nothing. She knew Joan was right about her dependency, and it reminded Cassi of the identification she'd felt with Maureen Kavenaugh. Just like her patient, Cassi felt hopeless, timid, and fearful. She wondered if she too lacked the ability to influence her life even when she understood her problem. Then in a flash of sudden horror, Cassi became aware of the power of her denial. One of the reasons she'd suspected that Thomas was abusing drugs was because of his pupils. So often of late they had been mere pinpoints, but Dexedrine caused dilated pupils! Other drugs caused small pupils. Other drugs that Cassi did not want to think about.

Cassi could feel perspiration appear on her palms. She did not know if it was from sudden terror or from her insulin. Praying that her fears were groundless, she forced herself down the hall to Thomas's study.

Flipping on the light, she stood there, her eyes recording all the details of the room. Against her will, she recalled the consequences of her previous visit, and she fought against the urge to flee.

The medicine cabinet in the bathroom was exactly as it had been two weeks earlier: a mess. It contained nothing that was suspicious. Getting down on her hands and knees, Cassi searched beneath the sink. Nothing. Then she went through the towel cabinets. Again nothing.

Feeling a modicum of relief, Cassi went back to the study itself. Besides the desk and burgundy reading chair, there was the sofa bed, bordered by two end tables with lamps, a hassock, an entire wall of bookshelves, a liquor cabinet, and an antique highboy with claw feet. The floor was covered with an enormous Tabriz carpet.

Cassi walked over to the desk. It was an imposing piece of furniture, which she knew had belonged to Thomas's grandfather. As she reached out and touched the cool surface, she had the same naughty sensation she'd felt as a child, snooping in her parents' bedroom. Shrugging her shoulders, she pulled out the center drawer. A plastic desk organizer was filled to overflowing with rubber bands, paper clips, and other odds and ends. She pulled the drawer out to its limit and carefully lifted the layers of papers toward the back. Nothing out of the ordinary. Satisfied, Cassi was about to push it closed when she thought she heard a door slam. Peering through the window, she could see the lights in Patricia's apartment over the garage. She hadn't heard a car, but that wasn't too surprising. With the storm windows down, sounds from the outside did not penetrate the house too easily. She could see the garage door was closed. Had she closed it? She couldn't remember. A moment later there were footsteps in the hall. Panic knotted her stomach. Obviously Thomas had come home. If he caught her in his study after the episode with Patricia, he'd be furious. She looked around frantically, wondering if she could slip out through the spare room. But before she could move, the door opened.

It was Patricia. She was as surprised to find Cassi as Cassi her. The two women stared at each other in disbelief.

"What are you doing in here?" Patricia said finally.

"I was about to ask you the same question," returned Cassi, standing behind the desk.

"I saw the light go on in here. Naturally, I thought Thomas had come home after all. As his mother I think I'm entitled to see him."

Cassi unconsciously nodded as if she agreed. Actually it had been a constant source of irritation for her that Patricia had a key to the house and felt no compunction about entering whenever she wanted.

"That's my excuse," said Patricia. "What's yours?"

Cassi knew she should have simply replied that it was her home and she could go into any room she pleased. But she didn't. Her sense of guilt made it impossible.

"I suppose I can guess," said Patricia disdainfully, "even though it upsets me. Snooping through his possessions like this when he's in the hospital saving lives! What kind of a wife are you?"

Patricia's question hung in the air like static electricity. Cassi didn't try to answer. She'd begun to wonder herself what kind of a wife she was.

"I think you should leave this room at once," rasped Patricia.

Cassi didn't object. She walked past her mother-in-law with her head bowed. Patricia followed her out and closed the door. Without looking back, Cassi descended the stairs and headed for the kitchen. She heard the front door close and presumed Patricia had left. The woman would tell Thomas that Cassi had been in his study. It was inevitable.

She looked at the meal Harriet had left on the stove with distaste, but she knew that after taking her normal insulin dose she required a certain amount of calories. Forcing down the warmed-over food, she made up her mind to return to the study and finish her search. Having already been caught, she no longer had anything to fear except what she'd find.

There was still the chance Thomas could appear, but Cassi was prepared to listen for the sounds of the Porsche. In order to keep from having to face Patricia again, Cassi pulled the heavy drapes over the windows, and she used a flashlight, like a real burglar. She went directly to the desk and tried the side drawers, starting at the top and working her way down. She didn't have far to go. In the back of the second drawer inside a stationery box, Cassi found a collection of plastic pill containers. Some were empty, but most were full. All of them had the same prescribing M.D., a Dr. Allan Baxter. The dates were all within the past three months.

In addition to the Dexedrine, there were two other types of pills, and Cassi carefully took one of each. She replaced the vials in the stationery box and closed the drawer. Switching off the flashlight, she reopened the curtains and walked quickly back to her room. When she got out her *Physician's Desk Reference* and compared the pills to the identification pictures, she realized that her suspicions were right. "Oh God!" she said out loud. "Dexedrine for exhaustion is one thing. Percodan and Talwin are something else entirely."

For the second time that day Cassi burst into tears. This time she did not even try to check her sobs. She flung herself down on the bed and wept uncontrollably.

☐

Despite his interlude with Laura, Thomas decided to keep his planned visit with Doris. He was disappointed enough that the man in cardiac cath had suffered a second heart attack and couldn't be scheduled for surgery. He certainly wasn't going to ruin the night further by the long drive home.

Doris buzzed him in the minute he touched the bell. When he reached the second floor, he found her peering coyly around the door. When she opened it, he realized why she'd stayed inside. She was dressed in a diaphanous, short black camisole that laced up the front and snapped between her legs. It covered about the same area as a one-piece bathing suit.

"Glenlivet with Perrier," said Doris, handing Thomas a tumbler and pressing herself up against him before he could get his coat off.

Thomas took the drink in one hand and put the other on Doris's backside. The only light in the room came from a Scandinavian-style oil lamp that painted the room with warm, golden tones. The coffee table was also laid for dinner with an uncorked bottle of wine standing nearby.

When Doris retreated to the kitchen, Thomas called the hospital page operator. He gave her Doris's number along with the admonition it was for the thoracic resident-on-call only. She was not to give it to anyone else, and if there were a question she should call herself.

CHAPTER

6

"I GOTTA BE MOVING," said Clark Reardon. "My woman told me not to be late." Clark had pulled a straight-back metal chair over to Jeoffry Washington's bed.

"Well, it was great to see you, man," said Jeoffry. "Thanks for coming in. I really appreciate it."

"No problem," said Clark, standing up. He raised his hand, and when Jeoffry put his out, he slapped it affectionately.

"So when you breaking outta here?" asked Clark.

"Pretty soon. Maybe in a couple days. I'm not sure. I still got this IV." Jeoffry raised his left arm, indicating the coiled plastic tubing. "I had some inflammation in my legs right after the operation. At least that's what Dr. Sherman told me, so they started giving me antibiotics. It was a little rough for a couple days, but it's better now.

The best thing that happened to me was when they took away the cardiac monitor. I tell you, the beep from that mother drove me crazy."

"How long you been in here so far?"

"Nine days."

"That ain't bad."

"Not from this end. But I tell you, I was pretty scared in the beginning. But I had no choice. They told me I was going to die if I didn't get operated on. So what can you do?"

"Nothing! I'll see you tomorrow night and I'll bring in those books you wanted. Anything else?"

"I'd love a little grass."

"Come on, man."

"I'm just joking."

Clark turned and waved at the door before disappearing down the hall.

Jeoffry surveyed his room. He was glad that he was leaving soon. The other bed in the semiprivate room was empty. His roommate had been discharged that day and no new patient had arrived. Jeoffry was sorry to be alone, especially now that Clark had left and he had nothing to look forward to. As far as Jeoffry was concerned, a hospital was not a place to be alone. There were too many frightening machines and procedures to face without support.

Jeoffry switched on the miniature TV set connected to the head of the bed. Toward the end of the second situation comedy, Miss DeVries, a spunky LPN, entered. Pretending she had some delectable treat for Jeoffry, she insisted he close his eyes and open his mouth. As he did so, he had a pretty good idea of what was coming, and he was right. It was a thermometer.

Ten minutes later she returned and exchanged the thermometer for a sleeping pill. Jeoffry took the pill with water he had on the side table while the LPN examined the thermometer.

"Do I have a temperature?" asked Jeoffry.

"Everybody has a temperature," said Miss DeVries.

"How could I forget," said Jeoffry. They'd been through this before. "Okay, do I have a fever?"

"That's classified information," said Miss DeVries.

Jeoffry never could understand why the nurses could not tell him if he had a temperature; correction, a fever. They always said that was up to the doctor, which was crazy. It was his body.

"What about this IV?" asked Jeoffry as Miss DeVries started for the door. "When's it coming out so I can take a real shower?"

"That's something I know nothing about." She waved before disappearing.

Jeoffry twisted his head and looked up at the IV bottle. For a moment he watched the regular fall of each drop in the small chamber. Turning back to the TV and the evening news, he sighed. It was going to be a relief when his tether was removed. He reminded himself to ask Dr. Sherman about it in the morning.

☐

When the phone first rang, Thomas sat up, confused as to where he was. On the second ring, Doris turned over to face him in the half-light of her apartment.

"Do you want to get it or should I?" Doris's voice was thick with sleep. She pushed herself up on one elbow.

Thomas looked at her in the semidarkness. She appeared grotesque with her thick hair radiating from her head as if a thousand volts of electricity had passed through her body. Instead of eyes she had black holes. It took him a moment to remember who she was.

"I'll get it," said Thomas, staggering to his feet. His head felt heavy.

"It's in the corner near the window," said Doris, flopping back onto the pillow.

Groping with his hands, Thomas went along the wall until he got to the open doorway of the bedroom. In the living room, the bay window let in more light.

"Dr. Kingsley, this is Peter Figman," said the thoracic resident when Thomas picked up the receiver. "I hope you don't mind my calling, but you asked me to let you know if any service cases were going to the OR. We have a stab wound of the chest that's due within the hour."

Thomas leaned on the small phone table. The chill in the room helped organize his mind. "What time is it?"

"A little after one A.M."

"Thank you," said Thomas. "I'll be right over."

As Thomas stepped out of Doris's vestibule to the street, the icy December wind sent a chill through his body. Pulling the lapels of his coat more tightly around his neck, he set off toward the Memorial. Every so often sudden gusts would swirl down the street, moving a line of papers and other debris against his feet, forcing Thomas to turn and walk backwards for a few steps. He was relieved when he rounded the corner and could see the complex of buildings that comprised Boston Memorial.

Approaching the main entrance, he passed the parking garage on his left. It was a cement structure, open to the elements. Although it was jammed during the day, now it was almost deserted. As he glanced in to admire his Porsche, he noticed another familiar car. It was a Mercedes 300 turbo diesel painted puke green. There was only one person in the whole hospital whose taste was that bad. The car belonged to George Sherman.

Thomas was practically at the hospital door, mulling over the absurdity of getting such a good car in such a terrible color, when he began to wonder why George was there. He turned to look again. It was his car all right. There was no chance of confusing it with another. Thomas glanced at his watch. It was 1:15 A.M.

Thomas went directly to the OR, changed, and while passing through the surgical lounge, saw one of the OR nurses knitting. He asked her if George Sherman had a case that night.

"Not that I know of," said the nurse. "Hasn't been a chest except for the stab wound you're covering."

Outside of OR room 18, Thomas met Peter Figman scrubbing. He was a baby-faced, slight fellow who appeared as if he didn't have to shave yet. Thomas had seen him on numerous occasions but never had the opportunity of working with him. He had a reputation of being smart, dedicated, and of having good hands.

As soon as he saw Thomas, Peter launched into a detailed presentation of the case. The patient had been stabbed during a hockey game at the Boston Garden but was in stable condition, although there had been some trouble with his blood pressure when he'd first been admitted to the emergency room. He'd been typed and crossed for eight units of blood, but none had been given yet. The first thought had been that the knife had punctured one of the great vessels.

While Thomas listened to the presentation, he took a

surgical mask from the box on the shelf above the scrub sink. He preferred the older-style masks that tied behind the neck and head as compared to the molded masks that were secured with a single elastic band behind the head. Tonight, however, he kept dropping one or the other of the straps. Then the mask slipped from his grasp and fell to the floor. Thomas cursed under his breath and took another. As he reached into the box, Peter noticed that the older man's hand had a slight tremor.

Peter stopped his presentation. "Are you all right, Dr. Kingsley?"

His hand in the box, Thomas slowly rotated his head to look directly at Peter. "What do you mean, am I all right?"

"I thought maybe you weren't feeling well," said Peter timidly.

Thomas snapped the mask out of the box, pulling an extra one with it which fell 'nto the scrub sink. "And why did you think I might not be feeling well?"

"I don't know, just a hunch," said Peter evasively. He was sorry now he'd said anything.

"For your information, I feel perfectly fine," said Thomas, making no attempt to conceal his anger. "But there's one thing I will not tolerate from the residents, and that is insolence. I hope you understand."

"I understand," said Peter, eager to drop the subject.

Leaving the resident to finish his scrub, Thomas pushed through the OR door. "For Christ's sake," thought Thomas, "doesn't the kid realize I was just awakened from a deep sleep; everybody has a little tremor until they have a chance to fully wake up."

The OR was a buzz of activity. The patient was already fully anesthetized and junior house staff were in the process of prepping the patient's chest. Thomas walked over to review the X rays. Then, while his back was to the room, he held up his hand. The tremor was slight. He'd had worse. "Just wait until that cocky kid rotates on cardiac surgery," Thomas mused with some satisfaction.

Thomas parked himself in the back of the OR and watched carefully as the case began. He was ready to intervene if needed, but to Peter's credit, he was a good technical surgeon. Thomas quizzed all the residents about possible hemopericardium. None of them, including Peter, had thought of the diagnosis despite the fact that it had been discussed at the last death conference. When Thomas was certain the case was routine and would go smoothly, he stood up and stretched. He wandered over to the door. "I'll be available if anything goes wrong. You fellows are doing a good job."

☐

When the OR door closed behind Thomas, Peter Figman glanced up and whispered: "I think Dr. Kingsley's had one too many tonight."

"I think you're right," said a junior resident.

☐

Thomas had felt a sudden sleepiness steal over him as he'd sat in the OR. Fear of nodding off had driven him out. On the way to the surgical lounge he took

several deep breaths. He couldn't remember how many
Scotches he'd had with Doris. He'd have to be more
careful in the future.

Unfortunately, the lounge was occupied by two
nurses on their coffee break. He'd planned to stretch
out on the couch but decided he'd use one of the cots in
the locker room instead. As he passed the window, he
glanced out and noticed a light in one of the offices
across the way in the Scherington Building. Counting
the windows from the end, Thomas realized that it was
Ballantine's. He looked up at the clock over the coffee
maker. It was close to 2:00 A.M.! Had the janitor just
forgotten to turn it off?

"Excuse me," called Thomas to the two nurses, "I'll
be in the locker room if they call me from surgery. In
case I fall asleep, would one of you mind coming in and
giving me a nudge?"

As Thomas went through the swinging doors to the
locker room, he wondered if the light in Ballantine's
office had anything to do with the fact that George
Sherman's car was in the parking lot. There was something disturbing about those two facts.

The windowless alcove with the two cots was not
completely dark. Light from the surgical lounge drifted
through the short hall to the locker room. As usual the
cots were empty. Thomas had the suspicion that he was
the only person ever to use them.

Reaching into the pocket of his scrub shirt, he found
the small yellow pill he'd placed there. Deftly he
snapped the tablet in half. One half went into his mouth
where he let it dissolve on his tongue. The other half

went back into his pocket in case he needed it later. Before he closed his eyes, he wondered how long he had before he would get called.

□

At 2:45 A.M., the stairwell seemed to belong in a gigantic mausoleum rather than a hospital. The long vertical drop acted like a chimney of sorts, and there was a low-pitched whine of wind coming from somewhere in the bowels of the building. As the figure in the stairwell opened the door on the eighteenth floor, air hissed out as from a vacuum jar.

In usual hospital dress, the man was not afraid of being seen but still preferred not to be. He checked carefully to make sure the corridor was deserted for its entire length before allowing the door to close behind him. As it swung shut there was the same rude sucking noise.

One hand thrust into the pocket of his white coat, the man moved silently down the hall to Jeoffry Washington's room. There he stopped and waited for a moment. There was no sound of activity coming from the nurses' station. All that could be heard were distant, muted sounds of the cardiac monitors and respiratory machines.

In a blink of the eye the man was inside the room, slowly closing the door to the hall. The only light came from the bathroom where the door was cracked an eighth of an inch. As soon as his eyes adjusted to the dimness, he pulled his hand out of his pocket, gripping a full syringe. He dropped the cap from the needle into the opposite pocket and moved rapidly to the bedside. Then he froze.

The bed was empty!

☐

His jaw straining to its limits, Jeoffry Washington yawned hard enough to bring tears to his eyes. He shook his head and tossed the three-week-old *Time* magazine onto the low table. He was sitting in the patient lounge across from the treatment room. Getting up, he pushed his IV pole ahead of him out of the lounge toward the semidarkened nurses' station. He'd hoped that a stroll down the corridor would have helped his insomnia, but it hadn't worked. He wasn't any sleepier than he'd been tossing in his bed.

Pamela Breckenridge watched his progress through the doorless opening of the chart room. She'd become accustomed to his appearances over the past two nights. To save money she'd been brown bagging it rather than using the cafeteria, and Jeoffry would appear just as she was ready to eat.

"Is it possible for me to have another sleeping pill?" he called.

Pamela swallowed, told him it was, and directed the LPN to get Jeoffry another Dalmane. Dr. Sherman had obliged by adding a "repeat × 1" after his initial order.

As if he were standing at a bar, Jeoffry accepted the pill and the miniature paper cup of water the LPN extended toward him over the counter of the station. Jeoffry popped the pill and tossed off the water. God, what he wouldn't have done for a few tokes of grass. Then he began the slow trip back up the corridor.

The hall darkened as he moved away from the nurses. Presently he saw his shadow appear in front of him on the vinyl floor, growing as he walked. The IV pole made it look as if he were some prophet clutching a staff. To open his door he thumped it with the wheeled footplate. Inside he hooked the door with his foot and shoved it closed. If there were any chance of dropping off to sleep, he had to shield himself from the noise and lights from the corridor.

Arranging the pole next to the bed, he turned and sat down, intending to lift his feet and stretch out. Instead he stifled a scream.

Like an apparition, a white-clad figure emerged from the bathroom.

"My God!" said Jeoffry, letting out his breath. "You really startled me."

"Lie down, please."

Jeoffry complied immediately. "I never expected you at this hour."

Jeoffry watched as the visitor pulled out a syringe and started to inject the contents into Jeoffry's IV bottle. He seemed to have some difficulty in the darkness as Jeoffry heard the bottle clank repeatedly against the pole.

"What kind of medication am I getting?" asked Jeoffry, unsure if he should say anything but sufficiently confused as to what was going on to overcome his hesitancy.

"Vitamins."

To Jeoffry it seemed like a strange time to be getting

vitamins, but the hospital was a strange place.

Jeoffry's visitor gave up trying to get the needle into the base of the IV bottle and switched to the injection site in the plastic tubing close to Jeoffry's wrist. This was far easier and the needle immediately slipped through the small rubber cap. Jeoffry watched as the plunger was rapidly depressed, causing the fluid to back up in the tubing, raising the level in the chamber above his head. He felt a twinge of pain but assumed it was just the rise in pressure in the IV.

But the pain did not disappear. Instead it got worse. Much worse.

"My God!" cried Jeoffry. "My arm! It's killing me!" Jeoffry could feel a white-hot sensation that began at the IV site rise up in his arm.

The visitor grabbed Jeoffry's hand to keep it still and opened the IV so it ran in a steady stream.

The pain that Jeoffry thought had been unbearable got worse and spread like molten lava into his chest. He swung his free hand over to grasp his visitor.

"Don't touch me, you friggin' faggot."

Despite the pain, Jeoffry let go. To his bewilderment was added fear . . . a terrible fear that something awful was happening. Desperately Jeoffry tried to free his arm with the IV from the intruder's grip.

"What are you doing?" gasped Jeoffry. He started to scream, but a hand was clamped roughly over his mouth.

At that moment Jeoffry's body experienced its first convulsion, arching up off the bed. His eyes rolled up and disappeared inside his head. Within seconds the spasms increased to become a grand mal seizure, rocking the bed back and forth. The intruder dropped Jeoffry's arm and pulled the bed away from the wall to reduce the banging. Then he checked the corridor and ran back to the stairwell.

Jeoffry convulsed in silence until his heart, which had begun to beat irregularly, fibrillated for a few seconds, then stopped. Within minutes Jeoffry's brain ceased functioning. He continued to convulse until his muscles exhausted their depleted store of oxygen . . .

□

Thomas felt as though he'd just closed his eyes when the nurse bent over and shook him awake. He rolled over in a daze and looked into the woman's smiling face.

"They need you in the OR, Dr. Kingsley."

"Be right there," he said thickly.

Thomas waited while the nurse beat a hasty retreat, then swung his feet to the floor. He paused a few minutes for the dizziness to clear. Sometimes, thought Thomas, sleeping for too short a time was worse than no sleep at all. He steadied himself at the entrance, then stumbled over to his locker. Getting out a Dexedrine, he washed it down with water from the drinking fountain. Then he changed into a fresh scrub suit, but not before he'd rescued the half pill he'd left in the soiled shirt's breast pocket.

By the time Thomas got down to OR 18, the Dexedrine had cleared his head. He considered scrubbing right away but then decided it was better to find out first what he was up against.

The residents were standing around the anesthetized patient, their gloved hands resting within the sterile field. The scene did not look auspicious.

"What's the . . ." began Thomas, his voice hoarse. He hadn't spoken since awakening except for the few words to the nurse. He cleared his throat. "What's the problem?"

"You were right about the hemopericardium," said Peter with respect. "The knife penetrated the pericardium and cut the surface of the heart. There's no bleeding, but we wondered if we should close the laceration."

Thomas had the circulation nurse locate a stool and put it behind Peter. From that vantage point, he could see into the incision. Peter pointed to the laceration and bent to the side.

Thomas was relieved. The laceration was inconsequential, having missed any significant coronary vessels.

"Just leave it as is," said Thomas. "The marginal benefits of suturing it aren't worth the possible problems the suture might cause."

"Good enough," said Peter.

"Leave the pericardium open, too," warned Thomas. "It will reduce the chances of running into a problem with tamponade in the postoperative course. It will serve as a drainage point if there is any bleeding."

☐

An hour later Thomas crossed from the hospital to the Professional Building. When he entered his office he felt unpleasantly wired from the Dexedrine. Over and over he kept worrying about Ballantine and Sherman's presence in the hospital that night. It was obvious they were having some kind of secret meeting, and, as he wondered what they were plotting, he felt his anxiety mount. Now he knew he would be unable to sleep unless he took something.

He rarely got such a surge from a single Dexedrine but decided it was probably due to his general exhaustion. Going over to his desk, he gobbled another Percodan. Then, fearful that he might have trouble waking up in the morning, Thomas called Doris. He had to let the phone ring a long time. Mentally he retraced the complicated route from her bed to the phone by the bay window. He wondered why she didn't get an extension.

"Listen," said Thomas when she answered. "You've got to come into the office at six-thirty."

"That's only a couple hours from now," protested Doris.

"Jesus Christ," shouted Thomas angrily. "You don't have to tell me what time it is. Don't you think I know? But I have three bypasses starting at seven-thirty. I want you over here to make sure I'm up."

Thomas slammed the phone down in its cradle, seething. "Goddamn selfish bitch," he said out loud as he punched his pillow into submission.

CHAPTER
7

CASSI'S EYES BLINKED OPEN. It was a little after five in the morning and was not yet light outside. The alarm wasn't scheduled to go off for another two hours.

For a while she lay still, listening. She thought perhaps some sound had awakened her but as the minutes passed, she realized that the disturbance had come from within her head. It was the classical symptom of depression.

At first Cassi tried turning over and drawing the covers up over her head, but she soon recognized it was useless. She couldn't go back to sleep. She got out of bed, knowing full well that she would be exhausted that day, especially since Thomas had made her accept an invitation to go to the Ballantines that evening.

The house was frigid, and she was shivering before

she got on her bathrobe. In the bathroom she turned on the quartz heater and started the shower.

Stepping under the water, Cassi reluctantly allowed herself to remember the reason for her depression— the discovery of the Percodan and the Talwin in Thomas's desk. And Patricia was undoubtedly going to inform her son that Cassi had again been snooping in his study. Thomas would guess that she'd been looking for drugs.

Getting out of the shower, Cassi tried to decide what to do. Should she admit she'd found the drugs and confront him? Was the presence of the drugs sufficiently incriminating? Could there be another explanation for their presence in Thomas's desk? Cassi doubted it, considering the additional fact of Thomas's frequently pinpointed pupils. As much as Cassi did not want to believe it, Thomas was most likely taking the Percodan and Talwin. How much, Cassi had no idea. Nor did she have any idea how much she was to blame.

The thought occurred to Cassi that maybe she should seek help. But who to turn to? She had no idea. Patricia obviously wasn't the answer, and if she went to any of the authorities, then Thomas's career could be ruined. Cassi felt almost too depressed to cry. It was a no-win situation. No matter what she did or didn't do, it was going to cause trouble. Lots of trouble. Cassi was aware that her relationship with Thomas could very well be at stake.

It took all her strength to finish getting ready for work and make the long drive to the hospital.

Cassi had no more than dumped her canvas bag on

her desk when Joan's head came through the door.

"Feeling any better?" asked Joan brightly.

"No," said Cassi in a tired, flat voice.

Joan could sense her friend's depression. From a professional point of view she knew Cassi was worse than she'd been the previous afternoon. Unbidden, Joan came into Cassi's office and closed the door. Cassi didn't have the energy to object.

"You know the old aphorism about the sick doctor," said Joan: "'He who insists on taking care of himself learns he has a fool for a patient.' Well, that applies in the emotional realm as well. You don't sound so good to me. I came in here to apologize for foisting my opinions on you yesterday, but looking at you now, I think it was the right thing to do. Cassi, what's happening to you?"

Cassi was immobilized.

There was a knock on the door.

Joan opened it and confronted a tearful Maureen Kavenaugh.

"Sorry, Dr. Cassidy is occupied," said Joan. She closed the door in Maureen's face before the woman could respond.

"Sit down, Cassi," said Joan firmly.

Cassi sat down. The idea of forceful direction was appealing.

"Okay," said Joan. "Let's hear what's going on. I know you have your hands full with your eye problem. But it's more than that."

Once again Cassi recognized the seductive pressure of the psychiatric interview on the patient to talk. Joan inspired confidence. There was no doubt about that.

And Cassi could be assured of confidentiality. And in the last analysis Cassi desperately wanted to share her burden with someone. She needed some insight if not merely support.

"I think Thomas is taking drugs," said Cassi in a voice so low Joan could barely hear. She watched Joan's face for the expected signs of shock, but there weren't any. Joan's expression didn't change.

"What kind of drugs?" asked Joan.

"Dexedrine, Percodan, and Talwin are the ones I know of."

"Talwin is very common among physicians," said Joan. "How much is he taking?"

"I don't know. As far as I am aware, his surgery hasn't suffered in the slightest. He's working as hard as ever."

"Uh huh," nodded Joan. "Does Thomas know you know?"

"He knows I suspect the Dexedrine. Not the others. At least not yet." Cassi wondered how soon Patricia would tell Thomas she'd been in his study.

"There's a euphemistic term for this," said Joan. "It's called the 'impaired physician.' Unfortunately it is not all that uncommon. Maybe you should read up on it; there's a lot of material in the medical literature although doctors themselves usually hate to confront the problem. I'll give you some reprints. But tell me, has Thomas exhibited any of the associated behavioral changes—like embarrassing social behavior or disruption of his appointment schedule?"

"No," said Cassi. "As I said before, Thomas is working harder than ever. But he did admit that he is getting less enjoyment from his work. And he seems to have less tolerance lately."

"Tolerance for what?"

"For anything. For people, for me. Even his mother, who essentially lives with us."

Joan rolled her eyes. She couldn't help it.

"It's not that bad," said Cassi.

"I'll bet," said Joan cynically.

The two women studied each other in silence for a few minutes.

Then Joan asked tentatively, "What about your married life?"

"What do you mean?" asked Cassi evasively.

Joan cleared her throat. "Often physicians abusing drugs will suffer episodes of impotence and actively seek extramarital affairs."

"Thomas has no time for extramarital affairs," said Cassi without hesitation.

Joan nodded, beginning to think that Thomas did not sound very "impaired."

"You know," said Joan, "your comment about Thomas's low frustration level and the fact that he's getting less enjoyment from his work these days is suggestive. Many surgeons are slightly narcissistic and share some of the side effects of the disorder."

Cassi didn't respond, but the concept made sense.

"Well, it's food for thought," said Joan. "It's an interesting idea that Thomas's success could be a problem. Narcissistic men need the kind of structure and constant feedback you get in a competitive surgical residency."

"Thomas did remark that there was no longer any-one for him to compete with," said Cassi, catching Joan's train of thought.

Just then Cassi's phone rang. As Joan watched her friend pick up the receiver, she was pleased. Cassi was already acting less depressed. In fact, she managed a smile when she realized it was Robert Seibert.

Cassi kept the conversation brief. After she hung up, she told Joan that Robert was in seventh heaven because he got another SSD case.

"That's wonderful," said Joan sarcastically. "If you're about to invite me to the autopsy, thanks but no thanks."

Cassi laughed. "No, in fact I declined myself. I've scheduled patients all morning, but I told Robert I'd come up at lunch to go over the results." Talking about time made Cassi glance at her watch. "Uh oh! I'm late for team meeting."

The meeting went well. There'd been no catastro-phes overnight nor any new admissions. In fact, the resident on call was pleased to report that he'd gotten nine hours of undisturbed sleep, which made everybody extremely jealous. Cassi got a chance to discuss Mau-reen's sister, and the consensus was that Cassi should encourage Maureen to contact her herself. There was general agreement that it was worth the risks to bring the sister into the treatment process if possible.

Cassi also described Colonel Bentworth's apparent improvement as well as his attempts to manipulate her. Jacob Levine found this particularly interesting but warned Cassi about jumping to premature conclusions.

"Remember, borderlines can be unpredictable," said Jacob, taking off his glasses and pointing them at Cassi for emphasis.

The meeting broke up early since there were no new admissions nor new problems. Cassi declined an offer of coffee, as she did not want to be late for Colonel Bentworth. When she got back to her office, he was waiting by the door.

"Good morning," said Cassi as brightly as she could, opening her office door and entering.

The colonel was silent as he followed Cassi in and sat down. She self-consciously took her place behind the desk. Cassi didn't know why, but the colonel exacerbated her professional insecurities, especially when he stared at her with those penetratingly blue eyes which she finally realized reminded her of Thomas's. They were both the same startling turquoise.

Bentworth again did not look like a patient. He was impeccably dressed and seemed to have totally regained his air of command. The only visible hint he was the same person Cassi had admitted several weeks earlier were the healing burns on his forearm.

"I don't know how to begin," said Bentworth.

"Maybe you could start by telling me why you've changed your mind about seeing me. Up until now you've refused private sessions."

"Do you want it straight?"

"That's always the best way," said Cassi.

"Well, to tell the truth, I want a weekend pass."

"But that kind of decision is usually made by the group."

Group was Bentworth's major therapeutic agent at the moment.

"That's true," said the colonel, "but the goddamn ignorant sons of bitches wouldn't let me go. You could overrule them. I know that."

"And why would I want to overrule the people who know you the best?"

"They don't know me," shouted Bentworth, slapping his hand on the desk.

The sudden movement frightened Cassi, but she said quietly, "That kind of behavior is not going to get you anywhere."

"Jesus Christ!" said Bentworth. He got up and paced the small room. When Cassi didn't react, he threw himself back into his chair. Cassi could see a small vein throbbing in his temple.

"Sometimes I think it would be easier just to give up," said Bentworth.

"Why didn't the members of your group think you should have a weekend pass?" asked Cassi. The only thing she was prepared for on Bentworth's part was manipulative behavior, and she wasn't going to fall for it.

"I don't know," said the colonel.

"You must have an idea."

"They don't like me. Is that good enough? They're all a bunch of jerks. Blue-collar workers, for Christ's sake."

"That sounds pretty hostile."

"Yeah, well, I hate them all."

"They happen to be people like you with problems."

Bentworth didn't respond immediately, and Cassi tried to remember what she'd read about treating borderline personalities. The actuality of psychiatry seemed a thousand times more difficult than the conceptualization. She knew that she was supposed to play a structuring role, but she wasn't sure exactly what that meant in the context of the current session.

"The crazy thing is that I hate them, yet I need them." Bentworth shook his head as if he were confounded by his own statement. "I know that sounds weird, but I don't like to be alone. The worst thing is for me to be alone. It makes me drink, and liquor makes me go nuts. I can't help it."

"What happens?" asked Cassi.

"I always get propositioned. It never fails. Some dude sees me and guesses I'm a stud, so he comes over and starts to talk to me. I end up beating the guy to a pulp. It's one thing the army taught me. How to fight with my hands."

Cassi remembered reading that both borderline personalities and narcissists wanted to protect themselves from homosexual impulses. Homosexuality could be a potentially fertile area for future sessions, but for the moment she didn't want to push into areas that were too sensitive.

"What about your work?" asked Cassi to change the subject.

"If you want to know the truth, I'm tired of being in the army. I liked the early competition. But now that I'm a colonel, that's over. I've arrived. And I'm not going to make general because too many people envy me. There is no more challenge. Every time I go into the office I get this empty feeling—like what's the use."

"An empty feeling?" echoed Cassi.

"Yeah, empty. I feel the same after I've been living with a woman for a couple of months. At first it's intense and exciting, but it always goes sour. It gets empty. I don't know how else to explain it."

Cassi bit her lip.

"The ideal relationship with a woman," said Bentworth, "would be one month long. Then, puff, she'd disappear and another one would take her place. That would be perfect."

"But you were married."

"Yeah, I was married. Only lasted a year. I just about killed the broad. All she did was complain."

"Are you living with someone now?"

"No. That's why I'm here. The day before they picked me up, she walked out. I'd only known her for a couple of weeks, but she met some other guy and took off. That's why I want to get out of here for the weekend. She's still got a key to my apartment. I'm afraid she might clean me out."

"Why not call a friend and have him change the lock?" said Cassi.

"There's nobody I can trust," said Bentworth, standing up. "Look, are you going to give me a weekend pass or is all this bull for nothing?"

"I'll bring it up at the next team meeting," said Cassi. "We'll discuss it."

Bentworth leaned over the desk. "The only thing I've learned in all my time in the hospital is that I hate psychiatrists. They think they're so goddamned smart, but they're not. They're a hell of a lot crazier than I am."

Cassi returned his stare, noticing how cold his eyes had become. The thought went through her mind that Colonel Bentworth should be committed. Then she remembered he was.

□

Cassi knocked on the doorjamb of Robert's tiny office. As he looked up from his binocular scope, his face broke into a broad and infectious smile. He jumped up so quickly to hug Cassi that his chair sped back on its wheels to the opposite wall.

"You look down," said Robert examining her. "What's wrong?"

Cassi looked away. She had had enough talk in the past few hours. "I'm just exhausted. I thought psychiatry was going to be so easy."

"Then maybe you should transfer back to pathology," said Robert as he pulled out a chair for Cassi. Leaning forward, he rested his hands on her knees. If any other man had done so, Cassi would have been annoyed, but she was comforted by Robert's gesture.

"What can I get for you? Coffee? Orange juice? Anything?"

Cassi shook her head. "I wish you could give me a good night's sleep. I'm beat, and I have to go to a party tonight at Doctor Ballantine's home in Manchester."

"Wonderful," cooed Robert. "What are you going to wear?"

Cassi rolled her eyes in disbelief, saying she hadn't given it a moment's thought, at which point Robert, who had some knowledge of Cassi's wardrobe, made several suggestions. Cassi interrupted to say that she'd come to hear about the autopsy, not for his fashion advice.

Robert made an exaggerated expression of being hurt and said, "The only thing that you come up here for is business. I can remember when we used to be friends."

Cassi reached out to give Robert a friendly shake, but he eluded her by pushing back on his chair, which glided smoothly out of the way. They both laughed. Cassi sighed and realized she felt better than she had all day. Robert was like a tonic.

"Did your husband tell you he saved me at the last surgical death conference?"

"No," said Cassi, surprised. She'd never mentioned Thomas's antipathy to Robert, but it was all too obvious the few times they'd met.

"I made a big mistake. I got this crazy notion that the cardiac surgeons would be overjoyed to hear about SSD, and I decided to make a preliminary presentation at yesterday's conference. It turned out to be the worst thing I could have done. I suppose I should have realized their egos are such that they'd consider the study a form of criticism. Anyway, when I finished talking, Ballantine started to chew me out until Thomas interrupted with an intelligent question. That sparked a few more questions, and what could have been a total disaster was averted. I did get a lot of heat this morning from the chief of pathology. It seems George Sherman had asked him to muzzle me in the future."

Cassi was impressed and grateful for her husband's intervention. She wondered why he hadn't mentioned it to her until she remembered that she hadn't given Thomas a chance. She'd brought up her eye surgery the second she'd seen him.

"Maybe I'll have to take back some of the nasty things I've said about your husband," added Robert.

There was an awkward silence. Cassi did not want to get into a discussion of her own feelings just then.

"Well," said Robert, rubbing his hands together enthusiastically. "To work! As I said on the phone, I think I found a new SSD case."

"Cyanotic like the last?" asked Cassi, eager to change the subject.

"Nope," said Robert. "Come on, I want to show you."

He leaped to his feet and dragged Cassi out of his office and into one of the autopsy rooms. A young, light-skinned black was laid out on the stainless steel table. The standard Y autopsy incision had been closed with heavy sutures and clumsy bites of tissue.

"I asked them to leave the body so you could see something," said Robert, his voice echoing in the tiled room.

He let go of Cassi and inserted his thumb into Jeoffry Washington's mouth, pulling down the lower jaw. "Look in here."

With her hands behind her back, Cassi bent over and looked into the patient's mouth. The tongue was a mangled piece of meat.

"Chewed hell out of it," said Robert. "Obviously had one hell of a grand mal seizure."

Cassi straightened up, a little sickened by what she'd seen. If this was an SSD case, he was the youngest yet.

"I think this one died of an arrhythmia," said Robert, "but I won't know for sure until the brain is fixed. You know, seeing this kind of case doesn't help my anxiety about my own surgery." Robert glanced over at Cassi.

"When are you going to have it?" she asked. Robert's statement sounded definitive.

Robert smiled. "I told you, but you wouldn't believe that I was going to get it over with. I'm being admitted tomorrow. What about yours?"

Cassi shook her head. "It's not definite yet."

"You chicken," accused Robert with an air of superiority. "Why don't you schedule yours for the day after tomorrow, too, so we can visit together in the recovery room."

Cassi didn't want to tell Robert about her difficulties talking the matter over with Thomas. Reluctantly her eyes went back to the corpse.

"How old?" asked Cassi, motioning toward Jeoffry Washington.

"Twenty-eight," said Robert.

"God, that's young," said Cassi. "And it's only been two weeks since the last case."

"That's a fact," said Robert.

"You know, the more I think about it, the more disturbing these cases are."

"Why do you think I've persisted?" said Robert.

"With the number you have now and the apparent increase in frequency, it's getting harder and harder to ascribe the deaths to chance."

"I agree," said Robert. "Ever since the last, I've had the nagging suspicion that these deaths are more closely related than we suspect. The only trouble with that idea is that it suggests a specific agent, and as your husband pointed out, the deaths are physiologically different. The facts don't fit the theory."

Cassi walked around the table to Jeoffry's right side. "Does this look swollen to you?" she said, reaching out and running her hand up the body's forearm.

Robert bent down to look. "I don't know. Where?"

Cassi pointed. "Was the patient on IV?"

"I think so," said Robert. "I think he was on antibiotics for phlebitis."

Cassi picked up Jeoffry's left arm and looked at the IV site. It was red and puffy. "Just for interest's sake, how about getting some sections of the vein where the IV was?"

"Anything if it will get you to come up and visit."

Cassi replaced Jeoffry's arm as carefully as if it were still sensate. "Do you happen to know if all the SSD cases were on IVs?" asked Cassi.

"I don't know, but I can find out," said Robert. "I have an idea what you're thinking, and I don't like it."

"The other suggestion I have," said Cassi, "is to collate the supposed physiological mechanisms of death and see if there is any pattern. You know what I mean."

"I know what you mean," said Robert. "I can probably do that today. And I'll get the sections of the vein, but you have to promise to come up and look at them. Agreed?"

"Agreed," said Cassi.

□

As Cassi pressed the elevator button in the corridor outside the pathology department, she was aware she was dreading her upcoming session with Maureen Kavenaugh. Without doubt, Maureen's depression exacerbated Cassi's own. The fact that Cassi had reason to be depressed, as Joan had pointed out, did not make the symptoms easier to live with.

Dreading the meeting with Maureen bothered Cassi because it forced her to admit that as a psychiatrist she was going to have to deal with her own value judgments. In other areas of medicine, if you were forced together with a patient you disliked, you concentrated on the pathology and cut the personal contact to a minimum. In psychiatry that was not possible.

Happily, when she entered her office, Maureen still was nowhere to be seen. Cassi knew she was going to have difficulty concentrating on what Maureen had to say because Robert's decision to have his surgery brought up the issue of her own. She knew Robert was right. After a moment's indecision, she dialed Thomas's office.

Unfortunately, he was still in surgery.

"I don't know when he will be out," said Doris. "But I know it will be late because he called me and told me to cancel his afternoon office hours."

Cassi thanked her and hung up. Blankly she stared at her Monet print. Joan's comment about the "impaired physician" disrupting his appointment schedule flashed into her mind. Then she dismissed the thought. Thomas had obviously canceled his office hours because he was stuck in surgery.

A knock interrupted her thoughts. Maureen's listless face appeared in the doorway.

"Come in," said Cassi as cheerfully as she could. She suspected that the next fifty minutes were going to be a good example of the blind leading the blind.

□

It was Doris, not Thomas, who called Cassi in the middle of the afternoon to say that Dr. Kingsley would meet her at the front entrance to the hospital at six o'clock sharp. She insisted Cassi be on time because of the party that night. Cassi was in the lobby promptly, but when the clock over the information booth showed twenty after six, she worried that she may have gotten the message wrong.

The entrance of the hospital was crowded with waves of people coming and going. The people leaving were primarily employees, and they chattered and laughed, glad to see the workday come to an end. Those arriving were mostly visitors who seemed subdued and intimidated as they lined up in front of the information booth to get directions from the volunteers in their green smocks.

Watching the crowds made time pass, and when Cassi looked back at the clock, it was almost six-thirty. Finally she decided to call Thomas's office, but as she moved toward the phone, she caught a glimpse of his head above the crowd. He looked as tired as Cassi felt. His face was shadowed, which turned out to be an irregular growth of beard as if he'd not shaved carefully that morning. As he came closer, Cassi could see that his eyes were red-rimmed.

Unsure of her reception, Cassi held her tongue. When she realized that Thomas had no intention of talking or even stopping, she hooked her arm in his and was carried toward the rapidly revolving door.

Outside Cassi was confronted by a mixture of rain and snow, which melted the instant the flakes touched the ground. Hefting her bag onto her shoulder, she shielded her face and stumbled behind Thomas toward the parking garage.

Once inside the garage, he stopped and, finally turning to Cassi, said, "Awful weather."

"We're paying for such a nice fall," said Cassi, encouraged that Thomas did not seem to be in a bad mood. Maybe Patricia would not tell him of the visit to his study.

The engine of the Porsche reverberated like thunder in the garage. As he watched the dials and gauges, Cassi carefully did up her seat belt. It took a conscious effort for her not to tell Thomas to do his, especially given the bad weather, but remembering his previous response, Cassi remained silent.

Whenever it snowed, traffic in Boston slowed to a frustrating stop-and-go mess. As Thomas and Cassi proceeded east on Storrow Drive, it was mostly stop. Although Cassi wanted to talk, she was afraid to break the silence.

"Did you hear from Robert Seibert today?" Thomas finally asked.

Cassi swung her head around. Thomas still had his

eyes on the road despite the fact that the car was immobilized in a sea of red taillights. He seemed hypnotized by the rhythmic click-clack of the windshield wipers.

"I did speak to Robert today," admitted Cassi, surprised at the question. "How did you know?"

"I'd heard that one of George Sherman's patients had died. Apparently it wasn't expected, and I wondered if your friend Robert was still interested in that series of his."

"Absolutely," said Cassi. "I went up after the autopsy. And when I did, Robert told me how you rescued him at death conference. I think that was very nice of you, Thomas."

"I wasn't trying to be nice," said Thomas. "I was interested in what he had to say. But he was a fool to do what he did, and I still think he should get his butt kicked."

"I think he did get his butt kicked," said Cassi.

With a faint smile Thomas took advantage of the thinning traffic and goosed his car up the grade to the expressway.

"Was this last death another suspicious one?" he asked as the car accelerated to seventy. He drove with both hands on the wheel, blinking his high beams furiously as he came up behind people traveling more slowly.

"Robert thinks so," said Cassi, her hands involuntarily gripping each other. Thomas's driving always scared her. "But he hasn't done the brain yet. He thinks the patient convulsed prior to death."

"So it wasn't like the last case?" asked Thomas.

"No," said Cassi. "But Robert thinks the situations

are related." Purposely she kept her own role in the discussion secret. "Most of the patients, particularly over the last several years, have died after their acute postoperative course was over. One point that occurred to Robert today was that all the patients may have been on IV when they died. He's checking on that now. It could be significant."

"Why? Does Robert think these deaths could be suspicious?" asked Thomas with shock.

"I guess it's occurred to him," said Cassi. "After all, there was a case in New Jersey where a series of patients were given something like curare."

"That's true, but they all died with the same symptoms."

"Well," said Cassi. "I guess Robert feels that he has to consider all possibilities. I know it sounds awful and it certainly accentuates any insecurities Robert has about his own imminent surgery." Cassi was hoping to shift the topic to her own operation.

"What kind of surgery is Robert going to have?"

"He's finally having his impacted wisdom teeth removed. Since he had rheumatic heart disease as a child, he has to be treated with prophylactic antibiotics."

"He'd be a fool not to," agreed Thomas. "Although he must have suicidal tendencies. That's the only way I can explain his behavior at that death conference. Cassi, I want you to be sure to stay away from this so-called SSD study, especially if there are going to be ludicrous accusations. With everything else going on, I certainly don't need that kind of grief."

Cassi watched the cars in front as the Porsche relentlessly passed them. The monotonous movement of the windshield wipers mesmerized her as she tried to find the courage to broach her own operation. She'd promised herself she'd start speaking as soon as they came abreast of that yellow car. But the yellow car soon dropped behind them. Then it was the bus. But they'd passed that, too, and still Cassi remained silent. She gave up in despair, hoping that Thomas would bring up the subject himself.

The tension exhausted her. The idea of Ballantine's party seemed less and less attractive. She had trouble understanding why Thomas, of all people, wanted to go. He hated hospital affairs. The idea occurred to Cassi that maybe he was going for her benefit. If that were the case, it was ridiculous. All Cassi could think about was clean sheets and their comfortable bed. She decided she'd say something when they got to the next overpass.

"Do you really want to go to this party tonight?" asked Cassi hesitantly as an overpass flashed above them.

"Why do you ask?" Thomas pulled the car sharply to the right, then gunned the engine to pass a car that had ignored his blinking high beam.

"If you're going for me," said Cassi, "I'm exhausted. I'd much rather stay home."

"Goddammit," shouted Thomas, banging the steering wheel. "Must you always think only of yourself! I told you weeks ago that the board of directors and the deans of the medical school are going to be there. Something strange is going on in the hospital that they are not telling me. But I don't suppose you think that's important?"

As Thomas reddened with anger, Cassi sank in her

seat. She had a feeling that no matter what she said, it would only make matters worse.

Thomas lapsed into a sullen silence. He drove even more recklessly, taking the car up to ninety as they crossed the salt marshes. Despite the seat belt, Cassi found herself being thrown from side to side as the car rounded the sharp bends. She was relieved when he began to down shift before turning into their driveway.

By the time they got to the front door, Cassi had become resigned about the party. She apologized for not understanding its implications and added gently, "You look tired yourself."

"Thanks! I appreciate your vote of confidence," said Thomas sarcastically. He started for the stairs.

"Thomas," called Cassi desperately. She could tell he'd interpreted her concern as an insult. "Does it have to be like this?"

"I think this is the way you want it."

Cassi tried to object.

"Let's not have a scene, please!" yelled Thomas. Then in a more controlled voice he said, "We'll leave in an hour. You're the one who looks terrible. Your hair is a mess. I hope you're planning on doing something with it."

"I will," said Cassi. "Thomas, I don't want us to fight. It terrifies me."

"I'm not getting into this kind of discussion," snapped Thomas. "Not now. Be ready in an hour."

Hurrying into his study he went directly to the bathroom, mumbling under his breath about Cassi's selfishness. He'd told her very specifically about the party and why it was important, but she'd conveniently forgotten because she was too tired! "Why do I have to put up with this," he said, running a hand over his beard.

Getting out his shaving paraphernalia, Thomas washed and lathered his face. Cassi was becoming more than a source of irritation. She was becoming a burden. First her eye problems, then her preoccupation with the fact he took an occasional drug, and now her association with Seibert's provocative paper.

Thomas began to shave with short, irritated strokes. It was beginning to feel as if everyone were against him, both at home and in the hospital. At work the key offender was George Sherman, who was constantly undermining him with all the supposed teaching bullshit. Just thinking about it filled Thomas with such frustration that he threw his razor into the shower with all the force he could muster. It richocheted off the tiled walls with a clatter before coming to rest near the drain.

Leaving the razor where it was, Thomas got into the shower. The running water always tended to soothe him, and after he'd stood under the spray for a few minutes, he felt better. While he was drying, he heard the door to his study open. Expecting it was Cassi, he didn't bother to look, but when he was done in the bathroom, he opened the door to find Patricia sitting in his armchair.

"Didn't you hear me come in?" she asked.

"No," said Thomas. It was easier to fib. He went to the cabinet below the bookshelves where he'd been keeping some of his clothes.

"I can remember when you used to take me to these hospital parties," said Patricia plaintively.

"You're welcome to come," said Thomas.

"No. If you'd really wanted me you would have invited me rather than making me ask."

Thomas thought it better not to respond. Whenever Patricia was in one of these "hurt" moods, it was safer to say nothing.

"Last night I saw the light come on in the study here, and I thought you'd come home. Instead I found Cassandra in here."

"In my study?" demanded Thomas.

"She was right over there behind your desk." Patricia pointed.

"What was she doing?"

"I don't know. I didn't ask her." Patricia stood up with a self-satisfied expression. "I told you she would be trouble. But, oh no! You knew better." She sauntered out of the room and closed the door gently behind her.

Thomas threw his clean clothes onto the sofa and went to his desk. Pulling out the drawer with his drugs, he was relieved to see the bottles of pills exactly as he'd left them behind the stationery.

Even so Cassi was driving him crazy. He'd warned her to stay away from his belongings. Thomas could feel himself begin to shake. Instinctively he reached into his cache of pills and extracted two: a Percodan for the headache he could feel behind his eyes and a Dexedrine to wake him up. If it was worth going to this party, he should at least be alert.

□

Cassi could sense a tremendous change for the worse in Thomas's mood as they drove toward Manchester.

She'd heard Patricia come into the house and guessed that she'd visited Thomas. It didn't take too much imagination to figure out what she'd told him. Since Thomas had already been in poor humor, she couldn't have chosen a worse time.

Cassi had made a real effort to look her best. After taking her evening insulin, which she'd upped because of sugar showing up in her urine, she'd bathed and washed her hair. Then she'd selected one of the dresses that Robert had suggested. It was a deep brown velvet with puffed sleeves and a tight bodice that gave her a charming medieval look.

Thomas said nothing about her appearance. In fact he said nothing at all. He drove the way he had coming from the hospital, recklessly and fast. She wished he had a close friend she could go to—someone who really cared for him, but in truth he didn't have many friends at all. For a moment she was reminded of her last meeting with Colonel Bentworth. Then she caught her breath. Identifying with Maureen Kavenaugh was one thing, but comparing her husband to a borderline personality was ridiculous. Cassi turned her attention to the window to keep from thinking and tried to see through the moisture. It was a dark, forbidding night.

The Ballantines' house fronted on the ocean, just like Thomas's. But that was where the similarities ended. The Ballantines' home was a large, stone mansion and had been in the family for a hundred years. In order to maintain the house, Dr. Ballantine had sold off some of the land to a developer, but since the original plot was so large, no other house could be seen from the main building. It gave the impression of being in the country.

As they got out of the car, Cassi noticed that Thomas had a slight tremor. His coordination seemed slightly off as they mounted the front steps. Oh God, what had he taken?

Thomas's demeanor changed as soon as he joined the party. Cassi watched with amazement, although she knew how easily he could abandon an angry mood and become charming and animated. If only he would still expend some of that charm on her. Deciding it was safe to leave him, Cassi began to look for the food. Having given herself her evening insulin, she shouldn't wait too long before eating. The dining room was to the right, and she made her way over to the arched entrance.

☐

Thomas was pleased. As he'd expected, most of the hospital trustees and the deans of the medical school were at the party. He'd seen them over the shoulders of the small group of people he'd joined when first arriving. He was particularly interested in finding the chairman of the board. Picking up a fresh drink, he began to make his way through the crowd toward the men when Ballantine came over to him.

"Ah, there you are Thomas." Ballantine had been drinking heavily, and the circles under his eyes were pronounced, giving him more the appearance of a Basset hound than usual. "Glad that you could make it."

"Wonderful party," said Thomas.

"You better believe it," said Ballantine with a forceful wink. "Things are really happening at the old Boston Memorial. God, it's exciting."

"What are you talking about?" asked Thomas, backing up a step. Dr. Ballantine had a habit of spitting when he pronounced "Ts" after he'd had a few drinks.

Ballantine stepped closer. "I'd like to tell you, but I can't," he whispered. "But maybe soon, and I think you should join us. Have you given any thought to my offer of full professorship?"

Thomas felt his patience evaporate. He didn't want to hear about joining the full-time staff. He had no idea what Ballantine was referring to when Ballantine said, "Things are really happening." But Thomas didn't like the sound of it. As far as he was concerned, any change in the status quo was worrisome. He suddenly recalled seeing Ballantine's office light blazing at 2:00 A.M.

"What were you doing in your office so late last night?"

Ballantine's happy face clouded. "Why do you ask?"

"Just curiosity," said Thomas.

"That's a strange question just coming outta the blue," said Dr. Ballantine.

"I was in surgery last night. I saw your office light from the lounge."

"Must have been cleaning people," said Ballantine. He raised his glass and stared at it. "Looks like I need a refill."

"I also saw George Sherman's car in the garage," said Thomas. "It seemed an odd coincidence."

"Ah," said Ballantine, with a wave of his hand.

"George's been having trouble with that car for a month. Something with the electrical system. Can I get you another drink? You're as low as I."

"Why not?" said Thomas. He was sure Ballantine was lying. The moment the chief edged toward the bar, Thomas recommenced his search for the chairman. It was more important than ever to find out what was going on at the Memorial.

□

Cassi stayed by the buffet table for a while eating and chatting with several other wives. When she was sure she had absorbed enough calories to balance her insulin, she decided she'd better find Thomas. She had no idea what drugs he'd taken, and she was nervous. She had just started for the living room when George Sherman stopped her.

"You look beautiful, as usual," he said with a warm smile.

"You look good yourself, George," said Cassi. "I like you far better in a tuxedo than that old corduroy jacket of yours."

George laughed self-consciously.

"I've been meaning to ask how you find psychiatry. I was surprised when I heard you'd made the switch. In a lot of ways, I envy you."

"Don't tell me you give psychiatry any credibility. I didn't think any surgeon did."

"My mother suffered a severe postpartum depression after my younger brother was born. I'm convinced her psychiatrist saved her life. I might have chosen it as a specialty if I thought I would have been successful. It takes a sensitivity I don't have."

"Nonsense," said Cassi. "You have the sensitivity. I think it would be the passivity that would give you trouble. It's the patient who has to do the work in psychiatry."

George was silent for a moment, and as Cassi watched his face she suddenly thought of fixing him up with Joan. They were both such nice people.

"Are you interested in meeting an attractive new woman these days?"

"I'm always interested in attractive women. Though few measure up to you."

"Her name is Joan Widiker. She's a third-year psychiatry resident."

"Wait a second," said George. "I'm not sure I can handle a psychiatrist. She'll probably ask me all sorts of tough questions when I drag out my whips and chains. I might be too self-conscious. Worse than when I was with you. Remember that first date?"

Cassi laughed. How could she forget? George had clumsily knocked her hand during dinner so that she'd spilled linguini Alfredo into her lap. Then, in his eagerness to help mop it up, he'd knocked her Chianti Classico into her lap as well.

"I don't mean to sound ungrateful," said George. "I do appreciate your thinking of me and I'll give Joan a call. But Cassi, I wanted to talk to you about something a little more serious."

Cassi unconsciously straightened, unsure of what was coming.

"As a colleague, I'm worried about Thomas."

"Oh?" said Cassi as casually as she could.

"He works too damn hard. It's one thing to be dedicated, quite another to be obsessed. I've seen it before. Often physicians can go along at nine hundred miles an hour for years and then suddenly burn themselves out. The reason I'm saying all this is to ask you to try to get Thomas to slow down, maybe take a vacation. He's been wound up like a coiled spring. There's gossip he's had a couple of bad arguments with the residents and nurses."

George's words awakened all Cassi's submerged tears. She bit her lip, but remained silent.

"If you could get him to take some vacation time, I'll be happy to cover his practice if need be." George was startled to see Cassi's eyes fill with tears. She turned away, hiding her face.

"I didn't mean to upset you," said George. Reaching out, he put his hand on her shoulder.

"It's all right," said Cassi, struggling to regain her composure. "I'm okay." She looked up and managed a smile.

"Dr. Ballantine and I have discussed Thomas," said George. "We'd like to help. We both think that when someone works as hard as Thomas, he has to recognize that there's an emotional price to pay."

Cassi nodded as if she understood. She gave George's hand a squeeze.

"If you feel uncomfortable talking to me, maybe see Dr. Ballantine. He thinks the world of your husband. Maybe you'd like the chief's private extension at the hospital?"

Cassi evaded George's warm gaze. Concentrating on her purse, she extracted a small notepad and pencil.

When George gave her the number, she wrote it down. When she looked up, her heart almost stopped. She found herself looking directly into Thomas's unblinking stare. With knowledge born of intimacy, she instantly knew he was violently angry. All at once, George's hand felt heavy on her shoulder.

She quickly excused herself, but by the time she moved toward the door, Thomas had disappeared.

☐

Thomas hadn't been so angry since he was a freshman in college and one of his roommates had dated Thomas's girl friend. No wonder George had been acting so strangely. He'd been renewing his affair with Cassi, and Cassi had no more sense than to display her interest in front of all Thomas's colleagues. The cold knot of fear in the pit of his stomach stirred. His hand shook so badly he almost spilled his drink. Quickly tossing it off, he stepped through the French doors onto the veranda, welcoming the sharp ocean breeze.

Frantically he searched his pockets for a pill. The evening had gone badly from the start. A trustee who'd already made several trips to the bar had stopped to offer congratulations on the hospital's new teaching program. When Thomas had stared blankly in response, the man had muttered a quick apology and backed out of the room. Thomas had been about to search out Ballantine and demand an explanation when he'd seen Cassi.

God, what a fool he'd been. Now that he thought about it, it was obvious George and Cassi were having an affair. No wonder she never complained when he stayed so often in the hospital. Mercilessly his mind teased him with the idea that they met in his house. The image of George in their bedroom made Thomas cry out in rage. Glancing over his shoulder, he saw a couple standing in the doorway, and Thomas was suddenly afraid they were aware of the affair. Obviously they were talking about him. He pulled out another pill, swallowed it, and went back inside for another drink.

□

Frantic to find Thomas, Cassi began to work her way around the living room, excusing herself as she squeezed among the guests.

She was on her way into the bar when she found herself face to face with Dr. Obermeyer.

"What a coincidence!" he said. "My most difficult patient!"

Cassi smiled nervously. She remembered she'd reneged on her promise to call him that day.

"Unless my memory fails, you were supposed to schedule your surgery today," said Dr. Obermeyer. "Did you talk to Thomas about it?"

"Why don't I come to your office tomorrow morning," said Cassi evasively.

"Maybe I should talk to your husband," said Dr. Obermeyer. "Is he here?"

"No," said Cassi. "I mean, yes he's here, but I don't think this is the time . . ."

A tremendous yell shook the room, halting all conversation and stopping Cassi in midsentence. Everyone looked confused; everyone but Cassi. She recognized the voice. It was Thomas! Running back toward the dining room, she heard another shout, followed by a crash of broken glass.

Pushing her way through the other guests, Cassi saw Thomas standing in front of the buffet, his face flushed with anger, a number of broken plates at his feet. Staring at him in horrified surprise was George Sherman, a drink in one hand and a carrot stick in the other.

As Cassi watched, George reached out and patted Thomas's shoulder with the carrot, saying, "Thomas, you're mistaken."

Thomas knocked George's arm away with a vicious snap of his wrist. "Don't touch me! And don't ever touch my wife. Understand?" He jabbed a threatening finger into George's face.

"Thomas?" said George helplessly.

Cassi ran between the two men. "What is the matter with you, Thomas?" she said, grabbing his jacket. "Control yourself!"

"Control myself," he repeated, turning toward her. "I think that applies more to you than me."

With a final sneer, he shook himself from Cassi's grasp and headed for the front door. Ballantine, who'd been in the kitchen, followed, calling his name.

Cassi apologized quickly to George and moved toward the door, her head bent to avoid the curious stares.

Thomas meanwhile had found his coat and was saying angrily to Ballantine, "I'm terribly sorry about all this, but learning that one of your colleagues is having an affair with your wife is hard to take."

"I, I can't believe that," said Ballantine. "Are you sure?"

"I'm sure," said Thomas. He turned to open the door as Cassi ran up and caught his arm.

"Thomas, what are you doing?" she said, fighting tears.

Thomas didn't answer. Buttoning his coat, he turned to leave.

"Thomas, talk to me. What happened?"

Thomas yanked his arm away from Cassi with such force she almost fell to the ground. She hesitated as he opened the door and stormed outside.

Cassi caught up to him at the bottom of the steps.

"Thomas, if you're going to leave, then I'm coming. Let me get my coat."

Thomas stopped short. "I don't want you with me. Why don't you just stay here and enjoy your affair!"

Confused, Cassi watched him walk away. "My affair? This is your affair. I didn't want to come tonight!"

Thomas didn't respond. Cassi gathered up the skirt of her long dress and ran after him. By the time she reached the Porsche she was shaking violently, but she didn't know whether it was from fear or the cold.

"Why are you acting this way?" she sobbed.

"I might be a lot of things, but I'm not stupid," snapped Thomas, slamming the car door against her. The engine started with a roar.

"Thomas, Thomas," called Cassi, beating against the window with one hand and trying to open the door with the other. Thomas ignored her and backed up quickly. If Cassi had not stepped back, letting go of the car, she would have been pulled down. Staring mutely, she watched the Porsche roar down the long driveway.

Mortified, she turned back to the house. Perhaps she could hide in one of the upstairs rooms until she could get a cab. When she reached the foyer, she was relieved to see the guests were again busy drinking and laughing. Only George and Dr. Ballantine were waiting at the door.

"I'm so sorry," Cassi said uneasily.

"Don't be sorry," said Dr. Ballantine. "I understand George has had a little talk with you. We are concerned about Thomas and think he's overworking. We have plans that will lighten his load, but he's been so upset lately that we haven't had the opportunity to discuss it with him."

Ballantine exchanged glances with George.

"That's right," agreed George. "I think this unfortunate episode tonight just underlines what we're saying."

Cassi was too upset and confused to respond.

"George also mentioned," said Ballantine, "that he gave you my private extension at the hospital. I'll be happy to see you any time you want, Cassi. In fact, why don't you stop by my office tomorrow?"

"Now, would you like to rejoin the party?" asked Ballantine, "or would you rather one of my boys drove you home?"

"I'd like to go home," said Cassi, wiping her eyes with the back of her hand.

"Fine," said Ballantine. "Just a moment." He turned and mounted the stairs to the second floor.

"I am sorry," said Cassi to George when they were alone. "I don't know what got into Thomas."

George shook his head. "Cassi, if he knew how I really felt about you, he'd have every reason to be jealous. Now smile. I was just paying you a compliment." He stood, gazing fondly at her until Ballantine's son brought the car around.

☐

Cassi didn't know what to expect when she turned the key in her front door. She was surprised to see a light in the living room. If Thomas was home and not in the hospital, she assumed he would be locked in his study. Nervously, she walked through the hall straightening her hair as best she could.

But it was her mother-in-law, not Thomas, who was waiting for her.

Patricia was seated in a wingback chair, her face lost in the shadowy light of a single floorlamp. Upstairs, Cassi heard a toilet flush.

For a long time neither woman spoke. Then Patricia stiffly stood up, her shoulders bowed as if under a heavy weight. Her face was drawn, accentuating the lines around her mouth. She walked directly up to Cassi and looked her in the eye.

Cassi held her ground.

"I'm shocked," she said at last. "How could you have done this? Maybe if he weren't my only child it wouldn't hurt so much."

"What on earth are you talking about?" demanded Cassi.

"And to pick one of Thomas's colleagues," Patricia

went on, ignoring the younger woman. "A man who has been steadily trying to erode his position. If you wanted an affair, why not a stranger?"

"I'm not having an affair," said Cassi desperately. "This is absurd. Oh God, Thomas is not himself."

She watched her mother-in-law for some sign of understanding, but Patricia stood rigidly looking at her daughter-in-law with a mixture of sadness and anger.

Cassi stretched her arms toward the woman. "Please," she pleaded. "Thomas is in trouble. Won't you help?"

Patricia remained unresponsive.

Letting her arms fall to her sides, Cassi watched as Patricia walked haltingly to the door. She seemed to have aged ten years since Cassi had last seen her. If only she'd listen. But Cassi realized at last that Patricia would rather break her heart over a lie than deal with the more frightening truth of Thomas's addiction. As much as Patricia criticized Thomas, Cassi knew that she could never conceive of the possibility of something significantly wrong with her son.

Cassi remained in the semidarkness of the living room for a long time after she heard the front door close. She'd cried more tears in the last forty-eight hours than she had for the previous twenty years. How could Thomas possibly believe she was having an affair? The idea was preposterous.

With heavy steps she finally ascended the stairs to find Thomas. There was no way she could just go to bed. She had to try to speak to him. For a moment she hesitated outside the study. Then she knocked softly.

There was no answer.

She knocked again, louder. When there was still no reply, she tried the door. It was locked. Determined to talk with him, she walked to the guest room and entered the study through the connecting bathroom.

He was sitting immobile in his easy chair, staring straight ahead, his eyes unfocused. If he heard Cassi, his expression did not change. A slight smile lifted the corners of his mouth. Even after Cassi knelt down and pressed his hand to her cheek, he did not move.

"Thomas," she called softly.

Thomas finally looked down at her.

"Thomas, I've never had an affair with George. I've never looked at anyone since we met. I love you. Please let me help."

"I don't believe you," Thomas said, badly slurring his words. Then his eyes rolled up and he passed out, leaving Cassi still holding his hand. She unfolded the sofa bed and tried to get him to move, but he refused. She sat with him for a while before going back to her own room to try to sleep.

CHAPTER

8

IN THE MORNING Cassi was up and dressed before she heard the alarm go off in the study. It kept ringing and ringing. Concerned, she ran down the hall and opened the door. Thomas was sprawled in his chair exactly as she had left him the night before.

"Thomas," she said, shaking him.

"Wha-what?" he whispered.

"It's quarter to six. Don't you have surgery this morning?"

"I thought we were going to Ballantine's party," he muttered.

"Thomas, that was last night. Oh God, maybe you should call in sick. You never take a day off. Let me call Doris and see if she can postpone your operations."

Thomas struggled to his feet. He swayed and steadied himself against the arm of the chair.

"No, I'm fine," his voice was still slightly slurred. "And with the cutback on my OR time, I won't be able to reschedule for weeks. Some of the patients this month have already waited too long."

"Then let someone else . . ." Thomas raised his hand so quickly Cassi thought he was going to hit her, but instead he lunged into the bathroom, slamming the door. A few moments later she heard him turn on the shower. When he came downstairs he seemed in better shape. Probably because he had taken a couple of Dexedrines, thought Cassi.

He quickly drank juice and a cup of coffee and then headed for the garage.

"Even if I can get home tonight, I'll be very late, so you better take your own car," he said over his shoulder.

Cassi remained sitting at the kitchen table for a long time before she, too, began the long trip to the hospital. "For the first time," she thought, "it's not just Thomas I'm worried about. It's his patients. I don't know if it's safe for him to operate anymore."

By the time she reached Boston Memorial, Cassi had made up her mind to do three things the minute she was finished with team meeting. She would make an appointment to have her eye surgery, arrange to take the necessary time off, and she would see Dr. Ballantine and confide her fears about Thomas. After all, the problem affected the hospital as well as her marriage.

Joan noted Cassi's preoccupation, but before she had a chance to ask any questions, at the end of the meeting Cassi said something about seeing her ophthalmologist and hurried off the floor.

Dr. Obermeyer interrupted his schedule the moment he heard Cassi had appeared. He came out of his inner office with his minerlike light still strapped to the top of his head.

"I trust you've come to the right decision?" he said.

Cassi nodded. "I'd like to be scheduled as soon as possible. In fact, the sooner the better before I have a chance to change my mind."

"I was hoping you'd say that," said Dr. Obermeyer. "In fact, I took the liberty of scheduling you as a semi-emergency for the day after tomorrow. Is that all right with you?"

Cassi's mouth went dry, but she nodded obediently.

"Perfect," said Dr. Obermeyer with a smile. "Don't you worry about a thing. We'll take care of all the arrangements. You'll be admitted to the hospital tomorrow." Dr. Obermeyer buzzed for a secretary.

"How long will I be unable to work?" said Cassi softly. "I will have to say something to the chief of psychiatry."

"That depends on what we find, but I'd guess a week to ten days."

"That long?" said Cassi. She wondered what would happen to her patients.

Walking slowly back from the Professional Building, Cassi decided to phone Dr. Ballantine before her courage failed her. He answered the phone himself and assured her he had no surgery and could see her in half an hour.

After arranging to take sick leave, Cassi decided to kill the rest of the time before her interview with Ballantine by visiting pathology. She could tell Robert about her surgery, and just seeing him always gave her confidence. But when she reached his office, it was empty. One of the technicians told her that Robert was not due in at all. He was being admitted early that afternoon for oral surgery, and he'd decided to go out to eat what would probably be his last real meal for a week.

Cassi was back out at the elevator when she remembered Jeoffry Washington. Turning back into the lab, she asked the technician for the slides. The woman located Jeoffry Washington's tray without difficulty but explained that only half the slides were finished. She said it took at least two days to do a case and suggested that Cassi come back the next day for the full set. Cassi said she understood, but was interested only in the H & E mounts of the vein, which were probably ready.

The slides Cassi wanted were available and, in fact, were the first slides she saw when she opened the tray. There were six in all, labeled LEFT BASILIC VEIN, H & E STAIN, followed by Jeoffry Washington's autopsy number.

Cassi sat down at Robert's microscope and, adjusting the eyepieces, focused on the first of the slides. There was a small collapsed ringed structure inside a smudge of pink tissue. Even under low power Cassi saw something strange. Looking closer, she identified multiple small white precipitates ringing the interior of the vein. Cassi then examined the walls of the vein. They looked completely normal. There was no infiltrate of inflammatory cells. Cassi wondered if the small white flakes had been introduced in the mounting process. There was no way to tell. She checked the rest of the slides and found the same precipitate in all but one.

Taking them back to the lab, Cassi showed them to

the technician, who was also perplexed. Cassi decided to tell Robert the moment she found out his room number. Glancing at her watch, she realized it was time to see Ballantine.

He was having a sandwich at his desk and asked Cassi if his secretary could bring her something from the cafeteria. She shook her head. Given what she had to say, she wasn't sure if she would ever want to eat again.

She began by apologizing for the scene Thomas had caused, but Dr. Ballantine cut her off and assured her that the party had been a great success and he doubted if anyone even remembered the incident. Cassi wished she could believe that; unfortunately she knew it was just the kind of scandalous scene that stayed in peoples' minds.

"I've talked with Thomas several times this morning," said Dr. Ballantine. "I happened to see him before surgery."

"How did he seem?" asked Cassi. In her mind's eye she could see Thomas unconscious in the leather armchair, then stumbling into the bathroom.

"Perfectly fine. Seemed to be in a good mood. I was pleased that everything was back to normal."

To her dismay Cassi's eyes filled with tears. She'd promised herself it wouldn't happen.

"Now, now," said Dr. Ballantine. "Everyone occasionally blows up under stress. Don't place too much importance on last night's incident. The way he's been working, it's entirely understandable. Maybe not excusable, but understandable. The house staff have even commented that he's spending an unusual number of nights in the hospital. Tell me, my dear, has Thomas been acting normally at home?"

"No," said Cassi, dropping her line of sight to her hands that lay immobile in her lap. Once she started talking, the words came out easily. She told Dr. Ballantine Thomas's reaction to her proposed operation and confessed that their relationship had been strained for some time, but she didn't think the cause was really her illness. Thomas had known she had diabetes before they were married, and, except for the eye problem, her condition had not changed. She didn't think her medical complications explained Thomas's anger.

She paused, beginning to perspire with anxiety.

"I think the real problem is that Thomas has been taking too many pills. I mean lots of people take an occasional Dexedrine or sleeping pill, but Thomas may be overdoing it." She paused again, looking up at Ballantine.

"I have heard one or two things," mused Ballantine. "One of the residents commented on a tremor. He didn't realize I was behind him in the hall. What exactly has Thomas been taking?"

"Dexedrine to keep awake and Percodan or Talwin to calm down."

Dr. Ballantine strode over to the window and stared into the surgical lounge directly opposite. Turning back to Cassi, he cleared his throat. His voice had not lost any of its warmth.

"The availability of drugs can be a severe temptation for a doctor, particularly if he is as severely overworked as Thomas." Ballantine moved back to his desk and eased into his chair.

"But availability is only part of the story. Many physicians also have a sense of entitlement. They take care of people all day and feel they deserve a little aid themselves if they need it. Drugs or alcohol. It's an all-too-common story. And since they have been trained to be self-sufficient, instead of talking to another doctor, they medicate themselves."

Cassi was enormously relieved that Dr. Ballantine absorbed the news about Thomas with such composure. For the first time in days she felt optimistic.

"I think the most important thing is that we keep this to ourselves," said Dr. Ballantine. "Gossip could be detrimental to both your husband and the hospital. What I will do is have a diplomatic talk with Thomas and see if we can't take care of the problem before it gets out of hand. Having seen this kind of thing before, I can assure you, Cassi, that Thomas's difficulties are minor. He has been carrying his usual surgical load."

"You're not worried about his patients?" asked Cassi. "I mean, have you seen him operate recently?"

"No," admitted Dr. Ballantine. "But I would be the first to hear if something were amiss."

Cassi wondered.

"I've known Thomas for seventeen years," Ballantine said reassuringly. "I'd know if there was something seriously wrong."

"How will you bring up the subject?" asked Cassi.

Dr. Ballantine shrugged. "I'll play it by ear."

"You won't mention that I spoke with you, will you?" asked Cassi.

"Absolutely not," said Dr. Ballantine.

□

Carrying a handful of irises that she'd purchased in the hospital flower shop, Cassi walked down the eighteenth floor corridor to room 1847. The door was open about halfway. She rapped and peeked in. A figure was lying in the single bed holding a sheet up to his eyes. He was shaking in apparent terror.

"Robert!" laughed Cassi. "What on earth . . ."

Robert bounced out of the bed dressed in his own pajamas and robe. "I happened to see you coming," he said. Eyeing the flowers, he asked, "Are those for me?"

Cassi surrendered the small bouquet. Robert took the time to arrange them carefully in his water pitcher before placing them on the nightstand.

Glancing around the room, Cassi could see she wasn't the first. There were a dozen bouquets blooming on every surface.

"Kinda looks like a funeral," said Robert.

"I don't want to hear that kind of humor," said Cassi, giving him a hug. "There is no such thing as too many flowers. It means you have a lot of friends." She settled down on the foot of the bed.

"I've never been a patient in a hospital," said Robert, pulling up a chair as if he were the visitor. "I don't like it. I feel so vulnerable."

"You get used to it," said Cassi. "Believe me, I'm a pro."

"The real problem is that I know too much," said Robert. "I can tell you, I'm terrified. I've convinced the anesthesiologist to double up on my sleep meds. Otherwise I know I'll be up all night."

"In a couple of days you'll wonder why you were nervous."

"It's easy for you to say, dressed in street clothes."

Robert held up his wrist with its plastic name tag. "I've become a statistic."

"Maybe it will make you feel better to know that your courage has prodded me into action. I'm being admitted tomorrow."

Robert's expression changed to one of compassion. "Now I feel foolish. Here I am worried sick over a couple of teeth while you face eye surgery."

"Anesthesia is anesthesia," said Cassi.

"I think you are doing the right thing," said Robert. "And I have a feeling that your operation is going to be a hundred percent successful."

"What about your own chances," teased Cassi.

"Um . . . fifty-fifty," said Robert, laughing. "Hey, I got something to show you."

Robert stood up and went over to the nightstand. Picking up a folder, he joined Cassi on the edge of the bed. "With the help of the computer, I collated the data we have on the SSD cases. I found some interesting things. First of all, as you suggested, all of the patients were on IVs. In addition, over the past two years, the cases increasingly involved patients who were in stable physical condition. In other words, the deaths have become more unexpected."

"Oh God," said Cassi. "What else?"

"I played around for a while with the data, punching in all the parameters for our study except surgery. The computer spat out some other cases, including a patient by the name of Sam Stevens. He died unexpectedly during cardiac catheterization. He was retarded but in excellent physical condition."

"Was he on IV?" asked Cassi.

"Yup," said Robert.

They stared at each other for several minutes.

"Finally," said Robert, "the computer indicated that there was a preponderance of males. Curiously enough, where the information was available, the computer pointed out an unusually high number of homosexuals!"

Cassi looked up from the papers to Robert's friendly gaze. Homosexuality had never been mentioned between them, and Cassi felt a reluctance to discuss it.

"I went to pathology to visit you this morning," she said, changing the subject. "I missed you, but I did find some of Jeoffry Washington's slides. When I looked at the sections taken from the IV site, I found white precipitate along the inside of the vein. At first I thought it was artifact, but they were present on all but one of the sections. Do you think they might be significant?"

Robert pursed his lips. "No," he said finally. "Doesn't ring any bells. The only thing I can think of is that when calcium is inadvertently added to a bicarbonate solution, it causes a precipitation, but that would be in the IV bottle, not the vein. I suppose the precipitation could run into the vein, but it would be so apparent in the bottle that everyone would see it. Maybe I'll have an idea when I look at the section. Meanwhile, enough of this morbid stuff. Tell me about the party last night. What did you wear?"

Cassi glossed over the evening. There was a chance Robert would hear what had happened on the hospital grapevine, but she didn't want to bring it up. In many ways Cassi was surprised Robert hadn't noticed her reddened eyes. He was usually so observant. She decided

he was understandably preoccupied with his admission
to the hospital. Promising to visit the next day, Cassi left
before she was tempted to burden him with her own
troubles.

☐

Larry Owen felt like a piano wire drawn out to its
limit, ready to snap at the slightest increase in tension.
Thomas Kingsley had arrived late that morning and was
furious that Larry had waited for him to physically appear before beginning to open the first patient's chest.
Even though Larry completed the procedure with record speed, Thomas's foul mood had not changed. Nothing pleased the surgeon. Not only had Larry done a
piss-poor job, but the scrub nurses weren't handing him
the instruments properly; the residents weren't giving
him adequate exposure, and the anesthesiologist was an
incompetent son of a bitch. As chance would have it,
Thomas was given a faulty needle holder, which he'd
thrown against the wall with such force it had snapped
in two.

Yet Larry had weathered this kind of abuse before.
What was making him crazy was Thomas's operative
performance. It had been obvious from the moment he
began work on his first patient that the surgeon was
exhausted. His usually flawless coordination was off and
his judgment faulty. And worst of all, Thomas had an
uncontrollable tremor. It almost gave Larry heart
failure to watch Thomas bend over the heart with a
razor-sharp needle and try to direct the instrument to
the dainty piece of saphenous vein he was attempting to
sew to the minute coronary vessel.

Vainly Larry had hoped the tremor would lessen as the morning progressed. Instead it got worse.

"Would you like me to sew this one on?" asked Larry on several occasions. "I think I can see a bit better from my position."

"If I want your help, I'll ask for it," was Thomas's only reply.

Somehow they got through the first two cases with the bypasses sewn reasonably in place and the patients off the heart-lung machine. But Larry was not looking forward to the third case, a thirty-eight-year-old married man with two little children. Larry had opened the patient's chest and was waiting for Kingsley to return from the lounge. The resident's pulse was racing, and he had begun sweating heavily. When Thomas finally burst through the OR door, Larry felt his stomach knot with fear.

At first, things went reasonably well, although Thomas's shaking was no better and his frustration level seemed even lower. But the open-heart team, wary after the first two cases, was careful not to cross him in any way. The hardest job fell to Larry, who tried to anticipate Kingsley's erratic movements and do as much of the actual work as Thomas would allow him. The real trouble didn't begin until they'd started sewing the bypasses in place. Larry couldn't watch and turned his head away as Thomas's needle holder approached the heart.

"Goddammit," shouted Thomas.

Larry felt his stomach churn as he saw Thomas yank his hand from the operative site, the needle buried in his own index finger. Inadvertently Thomas also pulled out one of the large catheters that took blood from the patient to the heart-lung machine. As if a faucet had been turned on, the wound filled with blood and in seconds began soaking the sterile drapes and dripping onto the floor.

Desperately Larry plunged his hand into the wound and groped blindly for the clamp holding the suture around the vena cava. Luckily his hand hit it immediately. Deftly he pulled up on the tape and the blood loss slowed.

"If I had decent exposure this kind of problem wouldn't happen," raged Thomas, pulling the needle out of his finger and dropping it on the floor. He stepped back from the table nursing his injured hand.

Larry managed to suck out the blood from the wound. As he reinserted the catheter from the heart-lung machine, he tried to think what he should do. Thomas wasn't fit to operate anymore that day, yet to say anything risked professional suicide. In the end Larry decided that he could no longer stand the tension. When he'd secured the operative site, he stepped away from the table and joined Thomas, who was being re-gloved by Miss Goldberg.

"Excuse me, Dr. Kingsley," said Larry with as much authority as he could muster. "This has been a trying day for you. I'm sorry we haven't been more on the ball. The fact of the matter is that you are exhausted. I'll take over from here. You needn't reglove."

For a moment Larry thought Thomas was going to slug him, but he forced himself to continue. "You've done thousands of these operations, Dr. Kingsley. No one is going to fault you for being too tired to finish one of them."

Thomas began to shake. Then, to Larry's astonishment and relief, he snapped off his gloves and left.

Larry sighed and exchanged glances with Miss Goldberg.

"I'll be right back," said Larry to the team. With his gloves and gown still on, Larry left the OR. He hoped that one of the other staff cardiac surgeons would be available and was relieved when he saw Dr. George Sherman coming out of OR No. 6. Larry took him aside and quietly related what had happened.

"Let's go," said George. "And I don't want to hear a word about this outside of the OR, understand? It could happen to any one of us, and if the public learned about the incident it would be disastrous, not just for Dr. Kingsley, but for the hospital."

"I know," said Larry.

☐

Thomas was angrier than he had ever been. How dared Larry suggest he was too tired to proceed? The scene had been a nightmare. It was the haunting fear of such disaster that had originally forced him to take an occasional pill to sleep. He'd been perfectly capable of finishing the operation, and if he hadn't been so upset over Cassi's infidelity, he certainly would not have left. Furiously he stomped into the surgical lounge and used the phone by the coffee machine. He called Doris to make sure there were no emergencies and asked her to reschedule his afternoon patients for another day. He was already late, and he didn't think he could stand to see patients. Doris was about to hang up when she remembered that Ballantine had called, asking if Thomas would stop by his office.

"What did he want?" asked Thomas.

"He didn't say," said Doris. "I asked him what it was in reference to, in case you'd need a patient folder. But he said he'd just like to see you."

Thomas told the nurse at the main desk that he'd be in Dr. Ballantine's office in case there was a call. To steady himself and relieve his headache, which had gotten steadily worse, he took another Percodan from his locker. Then he donned a white lab coat and left the lounge wondering what the meeting could be about. He did not think the chief would call him in to discuss the scene at the party with George Sherman, and it certainly couldn't have anything to do with the episode with Larry Owen. It must have something to do with the department in general. He remembered the trustee's odd comment the night before and decided Ballantine was finally going to let Thomas in on his plans. There was always the chance that Ballantine was thinking about retiring and wanted to discuss turning over the department to Thomas.

"Thanks for coming in to see me," said Dr. Ballantine, as soon as Thomas was seated in his office. He seemed somewhat ill at ease, and Thomas shifted in his chair.

"Thomas," Ballantine finally began. "I think we should speak frankly. I assure you that whatever we say will not leave this room."

Thomas rested an ankle on his knee, steadying it with his hands while his foot began to pump rhythmically.

"It's been brought to my attention that you might be abusing drugs."

Thomas's foot stopped its nervous movement. The low-grade headache became a pounding agony. Although anger flooded his consciousness, his expression stayed the same.

"I want you to know," said Dr. Ballantine, "that this is not an uncommon problem."

"What kind of drugs am I supposed to be taking?" asked Thomas, making a supreme effort to reign in his emotions.

"Dexedrine, Percodan, and Talwin," said Dr. Ballantine. "Not uncommon choices."

With narrowed eyes, Thomas studied Dr. Ballantine's face. He hated the older man's patronizing expression. The irony of being judged by this inept buffoon drove Thomas to the brink of frenzy. It was lucky that the Percodan he'd taken in the lounge was beginning to work.

"I'd like to know who brought this ridiculous lie to your attention," he managed to ask quietly.

"That is not important. What matters . . ."

"It's important to me," said Thomas. "When someone starts this kind of vicious rumor, they should be held accountable. Let me guess: George Sherman."

"Absolutely not," said Dr. Ballantine. "Which reminds me. I spoke to George about the regrettable incident last night. He was mystified by your accusation."

"I'll bet," snapped Thomas. "It's common knowledge that George tried unsuccessfully to marry Cassi before I met her. Then I gave them the opportunity by working so many nights . . ."

Dr. Ballantine interrupted. "That doesn't sound like much solid evidence, Thomas. Don't you think that you might be overreacting?"

"Absolutely not," said Thomas, uncrossing his legs and letting his foot down with a bang. "You saw them together yourself at your party."

"All I saw was a very beautiful girl who seemed only interested in her husband. You're a lucky man, Thomas. I hope you know that. Cassi is a special person."

Thomas was tempted to stand up and leave, but Ballantine was still talking.

"I believe that you have been driving yourself too hard, Thomas. You're trying to do too much. My God, man, what are you trying to prove? I can't even remember the last time you took a day off."

Thomas started to interrupt, but Dr. Ballantine cut him off.

"Everyone needs to get away. Besides, you have some responsibility to your wife. I happen to know Cassi needs eye surgery. Shouldn't she be getting some of your time?"

Thomas was now reasonably certain that Ballantine had talked with Cassi. As incredible as it sounded, she must have come to him with her wild stories about drug addiction. It wasn't enough, thought Thomas with anger, that she went to his mother. She also had to see his chief of service. Thomas suddenly realized that Cassi could destroy him. She could ruin the career that he'd spent his whole life constructing.

Luckily for Thomas, his sense of preservation was

stronger than his anger. He forced himself to think with cold, hard logic as Ballantine finished.

"I'd like to suggest that you take some well-earned vacation."

Thomas knew that the chief would love to have him out of the hospital while the teaching staff whittled away at his OR time, but he managed to smile.

"Look, this whole thing has gotten out of hand," Thomas said calmly. "Maybe I have been working too hard, but that's because there has been so much to do. As far as Cassandra's eye problem is concerned, of course I'm planning to spend time with her when she's laid up. But it really is up to Obermeyer to tell her how best to handle her retinal problems."

Ballantine started to speak, but Thomas interrupted him.

"I listened to you, now hear me," said Thomas. "About this idea that I'm abusing drugs. You know that I don't drink coffee. It's never agreed with me. So it's true that I occasionally take a Dexedrine. But it has no more effect than coffee. You just can't dilute it with milk or cream. I admit it has different social implications, especially if someone takes it to escape from life, but I only use it on occasion to work more efficiently. And as far as the Percodan and Talwin are concerned: yes, I've taken them at times. I've had a propensity for migraines since I was young. I don't get them often, but when I do, the only thing that helps is Percodan or Talwin. Sometimes the one, sometimes the other. And I'll tell you something. I'll be happy to have you or anyone else audit my prescribing habits. You'd see in an instant the amount of these drugs that I prescribe and for whom."

Thomas sat back and folded his arms. He was still trembling and did not want Ballantine to notice.

"Well," said Ballantine with obvious relief. "That certainly seems reasonable."

"You know as well as I," said Thomas, "that all of us take a pill now and then."

"True," said Dr. Ballantine. "The trouble comes when a physician loses control of the number he takes."

"But then they're abusing the drug," said Thomas. "I've never taken more than two in twenty-four hours, and that's only with a migraine."

"I must tell you that I feel relieved," said Dr. Ballantine. "Frankly, I was worried. You do work too hard. I still mean what I said about your taking some vacation."

I'm sure you do, thought Thomas.

"And I want you to know," continued Ballantine, "that the whole department only wants the best for you. Even if we see some changes down the line, you will always be the keystone of our service."

"That's reassuring," said Thomas. "I suppose it was Cassandra who came to you about the pills." Thomas's voice was matter of fact.

"It really doesn't matter who called it to my attention," said Dr. Ballantine, standing up. "Especially since you've laid my fears to rest."

Thomas was now positive it had been Cassi. She must have looked in his desk and found bottles. He was swept by another wave of anger.

He stood up, his fists lightly clenched. He knew he had to be alone for a while. Saying good-bye and forcing

himself to thank Ballantine for his concern, Thomas
hastily made his way out of the office.

Ballantine stared after him for a moment. He felt
better about Thomas, but not completely reassured.
The scene at the party nagged him, and there were
those persistent rumors that had cropped up recently
among the house staff. He didn't want trouble with
Thomas. Not now. That could ruin everything.

☐

When the door to the waiting room opened, Doris
quickly dropped the novel she was reading into a
drawer and closed it with one smooth, practiced motion.
Seeing Thomas, she picked up the telephone messages
and came around from behind the desk. After being
alone in the office all afternoon, she was happy to see
another human being.

Thomas behaved as if she were part of the furniture.
To her surprise, he went past her without the slightest
acknowledgment. She reached out to grasp his arm, but
she missed, and Thomas continued into his office as if
he were sleepwalking. Doris followed.

"Thomas, Dr. Obermeyer called and . . ."

"I don't want to hear about anything," he snapped,
starting to close his door.

In commendable saleswoman fashion, Doris got a
foot over the threshold. She was intent on giving
Thomas his messages.

"Get out of here," screamed Thomas. Doris stepped

back in fright as the door slammed in her face with jarring force.

The fury that he'd suppressed during the harrowing interview with Ballantine engulfed him. His eyes searched for some object on which he could vent his anger. He grabbed up a bud vase Cassi had given him when they were engaged and smashed it on the floor. Looking at the shattered pieces, he felt a little better. He went over to his desk, pulled out the second drawer, and grabbed a bottle of Percodan, spilling several of the tablets onto his desk. He took one, putting the rest back, then went into the washroom for a glass of water.

Returning to his desk, he put away the pill container and closed the drawer. He began to feel more in control, but he still could not get over Cassi's treachery. Didn't she understand that all he really cared about was his surgery? How could she be so cruel as to try to jeopardize his career? First going to his mother, the one person who really had the power to upset him, then George, and now the head of his department. He would not tolerate this. He had loved her so much when they were first married. She had been so sweet, so delicate, so devoted. Why was she trying to destroy him? He would not let her. He would . . .

Suddenly Thomas wondered if Ballantine was glad about all this. For some time he had the nagging feeling that something strange was going on with Ballantine and Sherman. Maybe it was all an elaborate play to undermine him.

Thomas again felt a thrill of fear. He had to do something . . . but what?

Slowly at first, and then more rapidly, ideas began to form. All at once he knew what he could do. He knew what he had to do.

☐

Still troubled by his meeting with Thomas, Ballantine decided to drop down to OR to see if he could find George. Sherman may have lacked Thomas's genius, but he was a consistently excellent surgeon and an evenhanded and unflappable administrator. The house staff admired him, and Ballantine was increasingly considering backing George as chief when he himself stepped down. For a long time, the trustees had pushed to get Thomas to switch to full-time so he would be eligible for the post, but now Ballantine had doubts even if Kingsley would agree.

Unfortunately George was still in surgery. Ballantine was surprised and hoped there was no trouble. He knew George had had only one seven-thirty case that morning. The fact that he was still in the OR in the middle of the afternoon was not auspicious.

Ballantine decided to use the time to visit Cassi on Clarkson Two. Even if he wasn't totally sanguine about her husband's future, Ballantine wanted to offer what reassurance he could. Despite the years Dr. Ballantine had been on the staff of the Boston Memorial, he'd never once set foot on Clarkson Two, and when he pushed through the heavy fire door, he felt as if he'd entered another world.

In a lot of ways it did not seem like a hospital at all. It

had more the feeling of a second-class hotel. As he passed the main lounge, he could hear someone plunking atonally on the piano, as well as some mindless television game show. There were none of the sounds that he traditionally associated with the hospital, like the hiss of a cycling respirator or the characteristic clink of IV bottles. Perhaps the thing that made him the most uncomfortable was that everyone was dressed in street clothes. Dr. Ballantine could not be sure who was a patient and who was on staff. He wanted to find Cassi but was afraid of approaching the wrong person.

The only place he could be sure of knowing who was who was the nurses' station. Dr. Ballantine walked to the counter.

"Can I help you?" asked a tall, elegant black woman whose name tag said simply, Roxane.

"I'm looking for Dr. Cassidy," said Dr. Ballantine self-consciously.

Before Roxane could respond, Cassi's head appeared around the door to the chart room.

"Dr. Ballantine. What a surprise!" Cassi stood up.

Ballantine joined her, again admiring her fragile beauty. Thomas must be crazy to spend so many nights in the hospital, he mused.

"Can I talk to you for a moment?" asked Ballantine.

"Of course. Would you like to go to my office?"

"Here's fine," said Ballantine, indicating the empty room.

Cassi pushed some of the charts away. "I've been writing summary notes on my patients for the other doctors to use while I'm in for my eye surgery."

Ballantine nodded. "The reason I stopped down was

to tell you in person that I've already spoken with Thomas. We had a very good talk. I feel he's been pushing it a bit, and he admitted a small reliance on Dexedrine to keep him awake, but he pretty well convinced me that he only took the pain-killers for his migraine headaches."

Cassi didn't reply. She was certain Thomas hadn't had a migraine since he was in his teens.

"Well," said Ballantine with forced joviality. "You get your eye taken care of and don't worry anymore about your husband. He's even offered to have his prescription roster audited." He stood up and patted Cassi on the shoulder.

Cassi wanted desperately to share Dr. Ballantine's optimism. But he had not seen Thomas's pupils or his staggering gait. And the chief was not the recipient of his unpredictable moods.

"I hope you're right," said Cassi with a sigh.

"Of course I'm right," said Dr. Ballantine, annoyed that his pep talk hadn't worked. He started to leave.

"And you didn't mention our conversation," Cassi added, seeing Ballantine was becoming impatient.

"Of course not. Anyway, Thomas's jealousy makes it obvious he adores you. And with good reason." Ballantine smiled.

"Thanks for coming down," said Cassi.

"Don't mention it," said Ballantine, waving. He headed down toward the fire door, glad to be leaving Clarkson Two. He had never understood why anybody would take up psychiatry.

Getting on the elevator, Ballantine shook his head. He hated getting mixed up with family problems. Here he had been trying to help both Kingsleys. He'd sought out Cassi in order to put her mind at ease. But she hadn't seemed willing to listen. For the first time he began to question Cassi's objectivity.

Getting off the elevator, Ballantine decided to see if George was out of the OR.

He found Sherman surrounded by house staff in the recovery room. When George caught the chief's eye, he excused himself and followed Ballantine out into the hall.

"I had a disturbing conversation with Kingsley's wife this morning," Ballantine said, getting straight to the point. "I thought she had wanted to see me to apologize about the incident last night. But that wasn't it. She was worried that Thomas might be abusing drugs."

George opened his mouth to reply, then hesitated. The residents had just been describing Kingsley's behavior in the OR that morning before George himself had taken over. If he told the chief that would mean real trouble for Kingsley. And it was always possible that Thomas had just drunk too much the night before, upset as he obviously was after the fight. George decided to keep his thoughts to himself for the time being.

"Did you believe Cassi?" he asked.

"I'm not sure. I spoke with Thomas, who had some very good answers, but even I have found his temper unusually erratic." Ballantine sighed. "You always said you didn't care about being chief of service, but even if Kingsley agrees to come full-time, he may not be right for the department when we are done reorganizing. He certainly opposes the new patients we're scheduling on the teaching service."

"Yes," said George. "And I can't see Thomas accepting the idea of free surgery for the mentally retarded in order to train new teams of vascular surgeons."

"His point of view isn't necessarily wrong. These new expensive procedures should be made available first to the patients with the best chances for long-term survival. But practically speaking, the residents rarely get such cases. And as far as the hospital favoring patients most valuable to society, who's to judge? As you said, George, we're just physicians, not God."

"Maybe he'll calm down," said George. "If our plans go through, we certainly will be needing him on the teaching staff."

"Let's hope," said Ballantine. "I've suggested he take a vacation with his wife. By the way, I assume his accusations were pure paranoia as far as you're concerned."

"Unfortunately yes. But I'll tell you, if she ever gave me a chance, I'd still fight for her. Aside from those amazing looks, she's one of the most caring women I've ever met."

"Just don't upset our genius any more than you have to," said Ballantine with a laugh. "In the meantime, do you think I should review Thomas's prescriptions?"

"How can it hurt? But there are other ways doctors can get hold of drugs," said George, thinking of Thomas's collapse in the OR.

"Let's just hope he takes his vacation soon and comes back his old self."

"Right," said George, though he personally had not been that fond of Thomas in happier days.

CHAPTER

9

CASSI WAS IN A STATE of shock. She couldn't believe the change that had come over Thomas. At around five o'clock he'd called her saying his surgery for that evening had been canceled and that he was free. He then offered to drive her home in the Porsche, saying she should leave her car at the hospital.

For the first time in months, dinner was a pleasant affair. Thomas had suddenly become his old charming self, the man Cassi had married. He tolerated Patricia's usual complaints with easy humor and was openly loving and affectionate toward Cassi.

Cassi was infinitely pleased although a little confused. It was hard to believe that Thomas had forgotten the wrenching events of the previous evening, but she watched in amazement as he hurried his mother back to her apartment and solicitously poured Cassi a Kahlua.

He fixed himself a cognac. They settled on the oval couch in front of the fire.

"I got a call from Dr. Obermeyer," he said, sipping his drink. "But by the time I called him back he'd left for the day. What's happening about your eye?"

"I saw him today. He said that since my vision hasn't cleared I must have the surgery."

"When?" Thomas's voice was mellow. He was swirling his cognac.

"As soon as possible," said Cassi hesitantly.

Thomas absorbed the news with apparent equanimity, and Cassi continued. "I guess Dr. Obermeyer was trying to reach you because he scheduled me for the day after tomorrow. Unless, of course, you object."

"Object?" asked Thomas. "Why would I object? Your eyesight is far too important to take chances with."

Cassi let out a sigh of relief. She had been so concerned about Thomas's response she hadn't realized she was holding her breath.

"Even though I know it's a minor operation, I'm still frightened to death."

Thomas leaned over and put his arm around her. "Of course you're scared. It's a natural reaction. But Martin Obermeyer is the best. You couldn't be in better hands."

"I know," said Cassi, with a weak smile.

"And I made a decision this afternoon," Thomas said holding her tighter. "As soon as Obermeyer gives you the green light, we'll take a vacation. Some place like the Caribbean. Ballantine convinced me that I need some time off, and what better time could there be than while you're recuperating. What do you say?"

"I say that sounds wonderful." She turned her face up to kiss him as the phone rang.

Thomas got up to answer it. She hoped he wasn't being called back to the hospital.

"Seibert," said Thomas into the phone. "Nice to hear your voice."

Cassi leaned forward and carefully set her glass on the coffee table. Robert had never called her at home. This was just the kind of interruption that could throw Thomas into a frenzy.

But he was saying calmly, "She's right here, Robert. No, it's not too late."

With a smile he handed the phone to Cassi.

"I hope it's all right that I called you at home," said Robert, "but I managed to sneak up to pathology and look at Jeoffry Washington's vein sections. After I got back to my room, I remembered where I'd seen such precipitates before. I had been doing the post on a man killed in an industrial accident. He had spilled concentrated sodium fluoride onto his lap. Even though he'd rinsed himself off, enough of the substance had been absorbed to prove fatal. He had the same kind of precipitation in his veins."

Cassi lowered her voice, turning her back to Thomas. She did not want him to know she was still following the SSD study. "But sodium fluoride isn't used as a medication."

"It is on teeth," said Robert.

"But it's not given internally," Cassi whispered. "And certainly not by IV."

"That's true," said Robert. "But let me tell you how this accident victim died. He had grand mal seizures, and finally acute cardiac arrhythmia. Sound familiar?"

Cassi knew that six patients in the SSD series had died with the same symptoms, but she didn't say anything. Sodium fluoride wasn't the only thing that could cause them, and there was no sense jumping to conclusions.

"As soon as I get back in the lab," said Robert, "I'll be able to analyze these precipitates. I'll find out if they are sodium fluoride. If they are, you know what that means, don't you?"

"I have an idea," said Cassi reluctantly.

"It means murder," said Robert.

"What was that all about?" asked Thomas when Cassi had rejoined him on the couch. "Does Robert have some new brainstorm about his SSD series?" To Cassi's surprise Thomas only seemed curious, not upset. She decided it was safe to tell him a little about Robert's progress.

"He's still working on it," she said. "He'd begun to collate the data just before he was admitted to the hospital. He got a computer printout that showed some rather interesting results."

"Like what?" asked Thomas.

"Oh, any number of possibilities," Cassi said evasively. "He can't rule out anything. I mean, all sorts of things can happen in hospitals. Remember those poor people in New Jersey who were given curare?" Cassi laughed nervously.

"Surely he doesn't suspect murder?" said Thomas.

"No, no," said Cassi, sorry she said so much. "He just noticed an odd precipitate at the last autopsy that he wanted to track through the data." Thomas nodded and appeared to be thinking. Hoping to restore his good humor, Cassi added, "Robert really appreciated your intervening on his behalf."

"I know," said Thomas, suddenly smiling. "I didn't do it for his benefit, but if he insists on seeing it that way, it's fine with me. Now I think we should go to bed."

As he tenderly guided her upstairs, Cassi wasn't sure just what she read in his extraordinary blue eyes. She shivered, not entirely sure if it was with pleasurable expectation.

CHAPTER

10

CASSI HAD NOT BEEN a hospital inpatient since college. Now with medical school and internship behind her, it was a very different experience, just as Robert had suggested. Knowledge of all that could happen made the process far more frightening. Since she'd ridden into the hospital with Thomas, she was there far too early to be admitted. In fact, she'd been told she would have to wait until ten before the proper clerks were available. When Cassi protested that people were admitted all night long through the emergency room, the secretary just repeated that Cassi had to come back at ten.

After spending three unproductive hours in the library, much too nervous to concentrate on anything more demanding than *Psychology Today*, Cassi went back to admitting. The personnel had changed, although their attitude hadn't. Instead of smoothing the way through the admitting procedure, they seemed intent on making it as harrowing as possible, as if it were a rite of passage. Now Cassi was informed that she had no hospital card, and without one she could not be admitted. A disinterested clerk finally told her to go to the ID office on the third floor.

Thirty minutes later, armed with a new ID which looked suspiciously like a credit card, Cassi returned to admitting. There she was confronted with another seemingly insurmountable problem. Since she used her maiden name, Cassidy, in the hospital because it was the name on her medical degree, and since Thomas had taken out her health insurance under Kingsley, the secretary claimed they needed her marriage certificate. Cassi said she didn't have it. It wasn't something she'd imagined she'd need to be admitted to the hospital, and surely they could just call Thomas's office and get it straightened out. The clerk insisted the computer had to have the certificate. She was only the machine's handmaiden, or so she said. This impasse was finally solved by the admitting supervisor who somehow got the computer to accept the information. Finally Cassi was assigned a room on the seventeenth floor, and a pleasant woman in a green smock, with a badge that said MEMO-RIAL VOLUNTEER, escorted Cassi upstairs.

But not to seventeen. First Cassi was taken to the second floor for a chest X ray. She said she had just had one six weeks ago during a routine physical and did not want another. X ray claimed anesthesia would not anesthetize anyone who was not X-rayed, and it took Cassi another hour to get the chief of anesthesia to call Obermeyer, who in turn called Jackson, the chief of radiology. After Jackson checked Cassi's old film, he called Obermeyer back, who called back the chief of anesthesia, who called back the radiology clerk to say that Cassi didn't need another chest film.

The rest of Cassi's admission went more smoothly, including the visit to the lab for standard blood and urine analysis. Finally Cassi was deposited in a nondescript light blue hospital room with two beds. Her roommate was sixty-one and had a bandage over her left eye.

"Mary Sullivan's the name," said the woman after Cassi had introduced herself. She looked older than her sixty-one years because she wasn't wearing her dentures.

Cassi wondered what kind of surgery the woman had had on her eye.

"Retina fell off," said Mary, as if noting Cassi's interest. "They had to take the eye out and glue it back on with a laser beam."

Cassi laughed in spite of herself. "I don't think they took your eye out," she said.

"Sure did. In fact, when they first took my bandage off I saw double and thought they'd put it back in crooked."

Cassi wasn't about to argue. She unpacked her things, carefully storing her insulin and syringes in the drawer of her nightstand. She would take her normal injection that evening, but after that she was not to medicate herself until she was cleared to do so by her internist, Dr. McInery.

Cassi changed into pajamas. It seemed a silly thing to do at that time of day, but she knew why it was a hospital

rule. Putting the patients into bedclothes psychologi-
cally encouraged them to submit to the hospital routine.
Cassi could feel the change herself. She was now a
patient.

After all her years at the hospital, she was amazed at
how uncomfortable she felt without the status of her
white coat. Just leaving her assigned room made her
feel uneasy, as if she were possibly doing something
wrong. And when she emerged on the eighteenth floor
to visit Robert, she felt as if she were an intruder.

There was no answer when she knocked on 1847.
Quietly she pushed open the door. Robert was flat on
his back, snoring gently. At the corner of his mouth was
a single drop of partially dried blood. Cassi went
alongside the bed and gazed at him for a few moments.
It was obvious he was still sleeping off his anesthesia.
Like a true professional, Cassi checked the IV. It was
dripping smoothly. Cassi kissed the end of her finger
and touched it to his forehead. On her way to the door,
she noticed a pile of computer printouts. She went over
and glanced at the first page. As she expected it was the
data from the SSD study. For a moment she considered
taking it with her, but the thought of Thomas's finding
it in her room made her hesitate. She'd read it with
Robert later.

Besides, it she were to take her friend's new theory
seriously, it was not the sort of evidence she cared to
have in her room the night before an operation.

□

Thomas opened the door to his waiting room and
crossed to the inner office. He nodded a greeting to the

patients and mentally cursed the architect for not providing a separate entrance. He'd prefer to be able to get to his office unseen. Doris smiled as he approached but didn't leave her seat. After the episode the day before, she felt a little gun-shy. She handed him his messages.

Inside his office, Thomas changed to the white coat he liked to wear when he saw his patients. He felt it encouraged not just respect but obedience. Sitting at his desk, he ran quickly through the multitude of phone calls until he got to Cassi's. He stopped and stared at the pink slip. Room 1740. Thomas frowned; it was a semi-private directly opposite the nurses' station.

Snatching the phone off the hook, Thomas put in a call to the director of admissions, Grace Peabody.

"Miss Peabody," said Thomas with irritation. "I've just learned that my wife has been admitted to a semi-private. I really wanted her to have her own room."

"I understand, but we are a little crowded right now, and she was classified as a semi-emergency."

"Well, I'm sure you can find her a private room since I feel it's important. If not, I'll be happy to call the hospital director."

"I'll do the best I can, Dr. Kingsley," said Miss Peabody with irritation.

"You do that," said Thomas and slammed the phone down.

"Damn!" He hated the pea-brained bureaucrats who were running the hospital these days. They seemed intent on creating maximum inconvenience. He had trouble imagining how anyone could be so shortsighted not to give the wife of Memorial's most famous surgeon a private room.

Glancing at the schedule that Doris had placed on his desk, Thomas massaged his temples. His head had begun to pound.

Hesitating only briefly, he yanked open the second drawer. After three bypasses and with twelve office patients on the agenda, he deserved a little help. He got out one of his peach-colored tablets and gulped it down. Then he pressed the intercom button and told Doris to send in the first appointment.

Office hours went better than Thomas had anticipated. Out of the twelve patients there were two postop visits that required no more than ten minutes each. Of the other ten, Thomas signed up five bypass cases and one valve replacement. The other four patients weren't operative and should not have been sent to Thomas in the first place. He got rid of them quickly.

After signing several letters, Thomas called Miss Peabody back.

"How does room 1752 sound?" asked Miss Peabody haughtily.

Room 1752 was a private corner room at the end of the corridor. Its windows faced west and north with a fine view of the Charles River. It was perfect, and Thomas said so. Miss Peabody hung up without saying good-bye.

Thomas changed back to his suit coat and, after telling Doris he'd see her later, left for the Scherington Building. He made a brief stop in X ray to see some films before going to visit Cassi.

When he reached seventeen, he was surprised to find his wife still in 1740. He pushed in without knocking.

"Why haven't you moved?" he demanded.

"Moved?" asked Cassi, confused. She'd been talking with Mary Sullivan about having children.

"I made arrangements for you to have a private room," said Thomas irritably.

"I don't need a private room, Thomas. I've been enjoying Mary's company."

Cassi tried to introduce Thomas, but he was already pressing the call button.

"My wife is going to be treated properly," said Thomas, glancing down the hall to see where the nursing staff was hiding out. "If any of these supposedly indispensable hospital administrators have a member of their family in this hospital, they always make sure they have a private room."

Thomas succeeded in causing an uproar and acutely embarrassing his wife. She had not wanted to bother the nurses when she was feeling well, but for almost a half hour, the entire staff was kept busy moving Cassi to her new room.

"There," said Thomas finally. "This is much better."

Cassi had to admit the room was more cheerful. From her position in bed she could see the wintry sun touching the horizon. While she hadn't liked all the fuss, she was touched by Thomas's apparent concern.

"Now I have some good news," he said, sitting on the edge of the bed. "I talked with Martin Obermeyer, and he said you should feel fine in a week for sure. So I went ahead and reserved a room in a small hotel on the beach in Martinique. How does that sound?"

"That sounds wonderful," said Cassi. The idea of a vacation with just the two of them was something to look forward to even if for some reason it didn't work out.

There was a knock at the partially opened door, and Joan Widiker peered around the edge.

"Come in," said Cassi, and introduced her to Thomas.

"I'm pleased to meet you," said Joan. "Cassi has spoken of you often."

"Joan is a third-year psychiatry resident," explained Cassi. "She's been a big help to me, especially in building up my confidence."

"It's nice to meet you," said Thomas, feeling an instant antipathy. He could tell she was one of those women who wore their feminity up front like a badge of privilege.

"I'm sorry to barge in like this," said Joan, sensing she was interrupting. "I really just stopped by to tell Cassi that all her patients are being well taken care of. They all wished you the best, Cassi. Even Colonel Bentworth. It's the strangest thing," laughed Joan. "Your having a medical problem seemed to have had a therapeutically beneficial effect on them all. Maybe all psychiatrists should have surgery once in a while."

Cassi laughed, watching her husband straighten his coat.

"I'll come back another time," he said. "I've got rounds." Turning back to Cassi he gave her a kiss. "I'll see you in the morning before surgery. Everything is going to be fine. Just get a good night's sleep."

"I can't stay either," admitted Joan after he left. "I have another consult on the medical floor. I hope I didn't chase your husband away."

"Thomas is just being wonderful," beamed Cassi, eager to share the good news. "He's been so considerate and supportive. We're even going on a vacation. I guess I was wrong about the extent of his drug taking."

Joan questioned Cassi's objectivity, remembering the degree of her dependency on Thomas. But she kept her thoughts to herself and just told Cassi how glad she was that things were working out well. Wishing her all the best, Joan departed.

For a while Cassi lay in her bed watching the sky change from pale orange to a silvery violet. She wasn't sure why Thomas was being so nice to her. But whatever the reason, Cassi was infinitely thankful.

As the sky finally became dark, Cassi began to wonder how Robert was doing. She didn't want to call in case he was still asleep. Instead she thought she'd run up there and see for herself.

The stairwell was conveniently opposite her room, and Cassi climbed quickly to the eighteenth floor. Robert's door was closed. She knocked quietly.

A sleepy voice told her to come in.

Robert was awake but still groggy.

In response to Cassi's question, he assured her that he had never felt better. His only complaint was that his mouth felt like a hockey game had been played in it.

"Have you eaten?" asked Cassi. She noticed the computer printout had been moved to his night table.

"Are you kidding?" asked Robert. He held up his arm with his IV. "Liquid penicillin diet for this guy."

"I'm having my surgery in the morning," said Cassi.

"You're going to love it," said Robert, his eyelids resisting his attempts to keep them open.

Cassi smiled, squeezed his free hand, and left.

□

The pain was so intense Thomas almost cried out. He'd stumbled against the antique trunk Doris kept at the foot of her bed. He was searching for his underwear in the dim light. Deciding he didn't care if he did wake her up, he switched on the lamp. No wonder he hadn't been able to find his shorts. She'd thrown them all the way across the room, where they had caught on one of the knobs on her bureau.

After finding all his clothes, Thomas switched off the light and tiptoed into the living room, dressing rapidly. Being as quiet as possible, he let himself out. When he reached the street, he checked his watch. It was just before 1:00 A.M.

He went directly to the surgical locker room, took off the clothes he'd just put on, and donned a scrub suit. Walking down the corridor, he paused outside the one OR that was in use. He tied on a mask and pushed through the door. The anesthesiologist told Thomas that the patient had suffered a dissecting aneurysm following a catheterization attempt that afternoon.

One of the staff abdominal surgeons was the attending on the case. Thomas went up behind him.

"Tough case?" asked Thomas, trying to see into the incision.

The doctor turned around and recognized Thomas. "Awful. We haven't determined yet how far up the aneurysm goes. May extend into the chest. If it does, you'd be a Godsend. Will you be available?"

"Sure," said Thomas. "I'll probably catch a little sleep in the locker room. Give me a call if you need me."

He left the OR and wandered back down the hall to the surgical lounge. Three nurses who'd just finished a

case were taking a break there. Thomas waved at them
and continued on to the locker room.

□

Cassi's evening had passed pleasantly enough. She'd
given herself her insulin, eaten a tasteless dinner, show-
ered, and watched a little television. She'd tried to read
her psychiatry journal but finally had given up, realizing
she could not concentrate. At ten o'clock she'd taken her
sleeping pill, but an hour later she was wide awake trying to analyze the consequences of Robert's findings. If
there really was sodium fluoride in Jeoffry Washington's vein, then someone in the hospital was a murderer.
Given the fact that she would be coming back from the
OR tomorrow groggy and helpless, it was not surprising
the thought kept her from sleeping.

She was restlessly turning from side to side in the
dark when she heard a sound. She wasn't positive but
she thought it had been the door.

Cassi lay on her side, holding her breath. There
were no more noises, but she felt a presence as if she
were no longer alone in the room. She wanted to roll
over and look, but she felt irrationally terrified. Then
she heard a very definite noise. It sounded like a glass
object touching her night table. Someone was standing
directly behind her.

Breaking the paralysis her terror engendered took
every ounce of mental strength Cassi possessed. But she
forced herself to turn toward the door.

She gave a muffled cry of fright as she found herself
staring at a shadowed figure in white. Her hand shot out
and flipped on her bedside reading lamp.

"My God! You startled me!" said George Sherman, pressing a hand to his chest in a theatrical demonstration of distress. "Cassi, you've just taken ten years off my life."

Cassi saw a huge bouquet of dark red roses in a vase on her night table. Attached to the side was a white envelope with "Cassi" written on it.

"I'm sorry. I guess we scared each other," said Cassi. "I had trouble falling asleep. I heard you come in."

"Well, I wish you'd said something. I expected you'd be asleep and didn't want to wake you."

"Are the beautiful roses for me?"

"Yes, I thought I'd be through much earlier, but I got tied up at a meeting until a few minutes ago. I'd ordered these flowers this afternoon and wanted to be sure you got them."

Cassi smiled. "That was so kind of you."

"I heard you were to be operated on in the morning. I hope everything goes well." He suddenly seemed to realize she was sitting up in her nightgown. He reddened, whispered a fast goodnight, and beat a hasty retreat.

Cassi smiled in spite of herself. The vision of him knocking her wine into her lap came back to her. She detached the envelope from the roses and slipped out the card. "All the best from a secret admirer." Cassi laughed. George could be so corny. At the same time she could understand his reluctance to sign his name after the scene Thomas had pulled at Ballantine's.

Two hours later Cassi was still wide awake. In desperation she threw back the covers and slid out of the bed. Her robe was draped over the chair, and she pulled it on, thinking maybe she'd see if Robert was awake.

Talking to him might finally calm her down enough to sleep.

If Cassi had felt out of place walking the hospital dressed as a patient that afternoon, now she felt positively delinquent. The corridors were deserted, and within the stairwell there wasn't a sound. Cassi hurried up to Robert's room hoping no one in authority would spot her and send her back to seventeen.

She ducked inside the darkened room. The only light came from the bathroom whose door was slightly open. Cassi could not see Robert but she could hear his regular breathing. Silently moving over next to the bed, she got a glimpse of his face; he was still fast asleep.

She was about to leave when she again noticed the computer printout on the night stand. As quietly as possible she picked it up. Then she moved her hand blindly over the surface of the table to search for the pencil she'd seen that afternoon. Her fingers found a water glass, then a wristwatch, and finally a pen.

Retreating to the bathroom, Cassi tore a blank sheet from the printout. Pressing against the edge of the sink she wrote: "Couldn't fall asleep. Borrowed the SSD material. Statistics always knock me out. Love, Cassi."

When she came out of the lighted bathroom, Cassi found it even harder to see as she made her way back to the night stand. Feeling her way, she propped her note on the water glass and was about to leave when the door slowly swung open.

Suppressing a cry of fright, Cassi nearly collided with a figure coming into the room. "My God, what are you doing here?" she whispered. Some of the computer papers slipped from her hands.

Thomas, still holding the door, motioned for Cassi

to be quiet. Light from the corridor fell on Robert's face, but he did not stir. Convinced he was not going to wake up, Thomas bent to help Cassi gather her papers.

As they stood up, Cassi whispered again, "What on earth are you doing here?"

In answer, Thomas silently guided her out into the hall, pulling the door shut behind them. "Why aren't you asleep?" he said crossly. "You've got surgery in the morning! I stopped by your room to make sure everything was in order only to find an empty bed. It wasn't hard to guess where you might be."

"I'm flattered you came to see me," whispered Cassi with a smile.

"This is not a joking matter," said Thomas sternly. "You're supposed to be asleep. What are you doing up here at two A.M.?"

Cassi held up the computer sheets. "I couldn't fall asleep so I thought I'd be industrious."

"This is ridiculous," said Thomas, taking Cassi's arm and leading her back to the stairs. "You should have been asleep hours ago!"

"The sleeping pill didn't work," explained Cassi as they went downstairs.

"Then you're supposed to ask for another. My word, Cassi. You should know that."

Outside her room, Cassi stopped and looked up at Thomas. "I'm sorry. You're right. I wasn't thinking."

"What's done is done," said Thomas. "You get into bed. I'll get you another pill."

For a moment Cassi watched Thomas resolutely walk down the corridor toward the nurses' station. Then she turned into her room. Putting the SSD data on her night table, she tossed her robe onto the chair and kicked off her slippers. With Thomas in charge she felt more secure.

When he returned with the pill, he stood by the bed watching as she swallowed it. Then, half-teasing, he opened her mouth and pretended to search inside to see if it was gone.

"That's a violation of privacy," said Cassi, pulling her face away.

"Children must be treated like children," he laughed.

He picked up the printout, carried it over to the bureau, and dumped it into a lower drawer. "No more of this stuff tonight. You're going to sleep."

Thomas pulled the chair over to the bed, switched off the reading light, and took Cassi's hand.

He told Cassi he wanted her to relax and think about their upcoming vacation. Quietly he described the untouched sands, the crystal water, and the warm tropical sunshine.

Cassi listened, enjoying the images. Soon she felt a peace settle over her. With Thomas there she could relax. Consciously she could feel the sleeping pill begin to work, and she realized that she was falling asleep.

□

Robert was caught in the netherworld between sleep and consciousness. He'd been having a terrifying dream: he was imprisoned between two walls that were relentlessly closing in on him. The space where he stood became smaller and smaller. He could no longer breathe.

Desperately he pulled himself awake. The entrapping walls were gone. The dream was over, but the awful sense of suffocation was still there. It was as if the room had been sucked dry of its air.

In panic he tried to sit up, but his body would not obey. Flailing his arms in terror, he thrashed around looking for the call button. Then his hand touched someone standing silently in the dark. He had help!

"Thank God," he gasped, recognizing his visitor. "Something's wrong. Help me. I need air! Help me, I'm suffocating!"

Robert's visitor pushed Robert back onto the bed so roughly the empty syringe in his hand almost dropped to the floor. Robert again reached out, grabbing the man's jacket. His legs kicked at the bed rails setting up a metallic clamor. He tried to scream, but his voice came out muffled and incoherent. Hoping to silence Robert before anyone came to investigate, the man leaned over to cover his mouth. Robert's knee flew up and thumped the man on the chin, snapping his teeth on the tip of his tongue.

Enraged by the pain, the man leaned his entire weight on the hand clamped over Robert's face, pushing his head deep into the pillow. For a few minutes more Robert's legs jerked and twitched. Then he lay still. The man straightened up, removing his hand slowly as if he expected the boy to struggle anew. But Robert was no longer breathing; his face was almost black in the dim light.

The man felt drained. Trying not to think, he went into the bathroom and rinsed the blood out of his mouth. Always before when he dispatched a patient, he had known he was doing the right thing. He gave life;

he took life. But death was only administered to further the larger good.

The man remembered the first time he had been responsible for a patient's death. He had never doubted it was the right thing to do. It had been many years ago, back when he was a junior resident on thoracic surgery. A crisis had arisen in the intensive care unit.

All the patients had developed complications. None could be discharged, and all elective cardiac surgery in the hospital had come to a halt. Every day at rounds the chief resident Barney Kaufman went from bed to bed to see if anyone was ready to be transferred, but no one was. And each day, they stopped last by a patient Barney had labeled Frank Gork. A shower of emboli from a calcified heart valve had been loosed during surgery and Frank Gork, formally Frank Segelman, had been left brain-dead. He'd been on the unit for over a month. The fact that he was still alive, in the sense that his heart was beating and his kidneys were making urine, was a tribute to the nursing staff.

One afternoon Kaufman looked down at Frank. "Mr. Gork, we all love you, but would you consider checking out of this hotel? I know it's not the food that's keeping you here."

Everyone snickered but the man who had continued to stare into Frank's empty face. Later that night, the man had gone into the busy intensive care unit and walked up to Frank Gork with a syringe full of potassium chloride. Within seconds Frank's regular cardiac rhythm degenerated with T waves peaking, and then flattening out. It had been the man himself who called the code, but the team only made a halfhearted attempt at resuscitation.

After the fact everyone was pleased, from the nursing staff to the attending surgeon. The man almost had to restrain himself from taking credit for the event. It had been so simple, clean, definite, and practical.

The man had to admit that killing Robert Seibert had not been like that. There wasn't the same sense of euphoria of doing what had to be done and knowing that he was one of the few with the courage to do it. Yet Robert Seibert had had to die. It was his own fault, dredging up all the so-called SSD series.

Returning from the bathroom, the man quickly searched the room for any papers relating to Robert's research. Finding none, he moved to the door and opened it a crack.

One of the night nurses was coming down the hall with a small metal tray. For a terrifying moment the man thought she might be coming to see Robert. But she turned into another room, leaving the corridor free.

His heart pounding, the man slipped into the hall. It would be a disaster to be seen on the floor. When he was a resident, he had reason to be in the corridors or patients' rooms or even the intensive care unit at all hours of the night. Now it was different. He had to be more careful.

When he reached the safety of the stairwell, panic overtook him. He plunged down three floors without pausing for breath and kept up this frantic descent until he'd passed the twelfth floor. Only then did he begin to slow down. At the landing on five, he stopped, flattening his back against the bare concrete wall, his chest heaving from his exertion. He knew he had to collect himself.

Taking a deep breath, the man eased open the stairwell door. Within a few moments he felt safe, but his mind wouldn't stop racing. He kept thinking about the SSD data, realizing that Robert probably had a source in his office, very likely a floppy disc. With a sigh the man decided he'd better visit pathology right away, before Robert's death was known. Then the only problem would be Cassi. He wondered exactly how much Robert had told her.

CHAPTER

11

CASSANDRA WOKE UP with a start, looking into the smiling face of a lab technician who was calling "Dr. Cassidy" for the third time.

"You do sleep soundly," she said, seeing Cassi's eyes finally open.

Cassi shook her head, wondering why she felt drugged. Then she remembered getting the second sleeping pill.

"I've got to draw some blood," apologized the technician. "You've got a fasting blood sugar ordered."

"Okay," said Cassi equably. She let the technologist have her left arm, remembering that for the next couple of days she would not be administering her own insulin.

A few minutes later a nurse came in and deftly started an IV in Cassi's left arm, hanging up a bottle of D5W with ten units of regular insulin. Then she gave Cassi her preop medication.

"That should hold you," said the nurse. "Try to relax now. They should be coming for you presently."

By the time Cassi was picked up and wheeled down to the elevator she felt a strange sense of detachment, as if the experience were happening to someone else. When she reached the OR holding area, she was only vaguely aware of the profusion of gurneys, nurses, and doctors. She didn't even recognize Thomas until he bent over and kissed her, and then she told him that he looked silly in his operating paraphernalia. At least she thought she told him so.

"Everything is going to be fine," said Thomas, squeezing her hand. "I'm glad you decided to go ahead with your surgery. It's the best thing."

Dr. Obermeyer materialized on Cassi's left. "I want you to take good care of my wife!" she heard Thomas say. Then she must have fallen asleep. The next thing she was aware of was being pushed down the OR corridor into the operating room itself. She didn't feel at all scared.

"I'm going to give you something to make you sleepy," said the anesthesiologist.

"I am sleepy," she murmured, watching the drops fall into the micropore chamber of the IV bottle hung over her head. In the next second, she was fast asleep.

The OR team moved swiftly. By 8:05 her eye muscles had been isolated and tapes had been passed around them. As soon as complete immobilization had been achieved, Dr. Obermeyer made stab wounds in the sclera and introduced his cutting and sucking instruments. Using a special microscope, he sighted through the cornea and pupil to the blood-stained vitreous. By 8:45 he began to see Cassi's retina. By 9:15 he found the source of the recurrent bleeding. It was a single aberrant loop of new vessel coming from Cassi's optic disc. With great care, Dr. Obermeyer coagulated and obliterated it. He felt very encouraged. Not only was the problem solved, there was no reason to expect it to recur. Cassi was a lucky woman.

□

Thomas had finished his only coronary bypass for the day. He'd canceled the next two. Happily the case had gone tolerably well although he again had trouble sewing the anastomoses. Unlike the previous day, though, he was able to finish, but the moment Larry Owen began to close, Thomas changed into his street clothes. Normally he waited until Larry brought the patient to the recovery room, but this morning he was too nervous to sit around with nothing to do. Instead he stopped down in the OR to see how things were going.

"Just fine," shouted Larry over his shoulder. "We're closing the skin now. The halothane's been stopped."

"Good. I've been called on an emergency."

"Everything under control here."

Thomas left the hospital, something he rarely did during a working day, and climbed into his Porsche. It thrilled him to hear the powerful engine as he turned on the ignition. After the frustration of the hospital, the car provided an enormous sense of freedom. Nothing on the road could touch him. Nothing!

Driving across Boston, Thomas left the car in a No Parking zone directly in front of a large pharmacy, confident his MD license plate would save him from a ticket.

Entering the store, he went directly to the prescription counter.

The pharmacist, in his traditional high-necked tunic, emerged from behind the high counter.

"Can I help you?"

"Yes," said Thomas. "I called earlier about some drugs."

"Of course. I've got it right here," said the pharmacist, holding up a small cardboard carton.

"Do you want me to write a script for it?" asked Thomas.

"Nah. Let me see your M.D. license. That'll be adequate."

Thomas flipped open his wallet and held it out for the pharmacist who just glanced at the license, then asked: "That'll be all?"

Thomas nodded, putting his wallet away.

"We don't have much call for that dosage," said the pharmacist.

"I'll bet," said Thomas, taking the parcel.

☐

Cassandra awoke from her anesthesia, unsure of what was dream and what was reality. She heard voices, but they seemed to be far away, and she couldn't make out what they were saying. Finally she realized they were calling her name. She heard them tell her to wake up.

Cassi tried to open her eyes but found that she couldn't. A sense of panic gripped her, and she attempted to sit up only to be immediately restrained.

"Easy now, everything is okay," said a voice by her side.

But everything wasn't okay. Cassi could not see. What had happened? Suddenly she remembered the anesthesia and the operation. "My God! I'm blind!" shouted Cassi, trying to touch her face. Someone grabbed her hands.

"Easy now. You have patches on your eyes."

"Why patches?" Cassi yelled.

"Just to keep your eyes quiet," said the voice calmly. "They'll only be on for a day or so. Your operation went smoothly. Your doctor said you are a lucky woman. He coagulated a troublesome vessel, but he doesn't want it to bleed again, so you must stay quiet."

Cassi felt a little less anxious, but the darkness was frightening. "Let me see, just for a moment," Cassi pleaded.

"I can't do that. Doctor's orders. We're not supposed to touch your bandages. But I can shine a light directly at you. I'm sure you'll see that. Okay?"

"Yes," said Cassi, eager for any reassurance. Why hadn't she been warned about this before the operation? She felt as if she had been cast adrift.

"I'm back," said the voice. Cassi heard a click and saw the light immediately. What's more, she perceived it equally with both eyes. "I can see it," she said excitedly.

"Of course you can," said the voice. "You're doing fine. Do you have any pain?"

"No," said Cassi. The light was switched off.

"Then just relax. We'll be right here if you want us. Just call."

As Cassi let herself relax, she listened to the various nurses as they moved about their patients. She realized she was in the recovery room and wondered if Thomas would come down to see her.

□

Thomas finished seeing his office patients early. By 2:10 he had just one appointment left at 2:30. While he waited he checked the OR to see which attending was on call that night for the thoracic service. Learning it was Dr. Burgess, Thomas gave him a call.

Thomas explained that he was planning to sleep in the hospital anyway to be near Cassi and suggested he take call as well. Dr. Burgess could pay back the favor when the Kingsleys were away.

Thomas hung up and, seeing he still had fifteen minutes to spare, decided to visit Cassi. She had just been brought up to her room, and Thomas could not tell if she were asleep or not. She was lying quietly, her face covered with bulky eye patches secured with heavy elasticized tape. An IV dripped slowly into her left arm.

Thomas went silently to the side of her bed.

"Cassi?" he whispered. "Are you awake?"

"I am," said Cassi. "Is that you, Thomas?"

Thomas grasped Cassi's arm. "How do you feel, honey?"

"Pretty well. Except for these patches. I wish Obermeyer had told me about them."

"I talked with him," said Thomas. "He called me right

after the surgery. He said everything went better than he could have anticipated. Apparently only one vessel was involved. He took care of it, but it was a large one and that made him opt for the patches. He didn't expect to use them either."

"It doesn't make this any easier," said Cassi.

"I can imagine," said Thomas sympathetically.

Thomas stayed for another ten minutes, then said he had to get back to the office. He gave her hand a squeeze and told her she should get as much sleep as possible.

To her surprise Cassi did doze and didn't wake up until late in the afternoon.

"Cassi?" someone was saying.

Cassi jumped, startled by the unexpected voice so close to her.

"It's me, Joan. I'm sorry if I woke you."

"It's all right, Joan. I just didn't hear you come in."

"I heard your operation went well," said Joan, pulling up a chair.

"So I understand," said Cassi. "And I'm going to feel a lot better when these patches come off."

"Cassi," said Joan. "I have some news. I've debated all afternoon whether I should tell you or not."

"What is it?" asked Cassi anxiously. Her first thought was that one of her patients had killed themselves. Suicide was a constant worry on Clarkson Two.

"It's bad news."

"I guessed that from the tone of your voice."

"Do you think you're up to it? Or should I wait?"

"You have to tell me now. If you don't I'll just keep worrying."

"Well, it's about Robert Seibert."

Joan paused. She could guess what effect the news was going to have on her friend.

"What about Robert?" demanded Cassi instantly. "Dammit, Joan, don't keep me in suspense." In the back of her mind she knew what Joan was going to say.

"Robert died last night," said Joan, reaching out and grasping Cassi's hand.

Cassi lay motionless. Minutes went by: five, ten. Joan wasn't sure. The only sign of life from Cassi was her shallow breathing and the force with which she gripped Joan's hand. It was as if Cassi were holding on for her own life. Joan didn't know what to say. "Cassi, are you all right?" she finally whispered.

For Cassi the news seemed like the final blow. Sure, everyone worried when they went into the hospital, but with no more seriousness than one expected to win the lottery if he bought a ticket. There was a chance, but it was so infinitesimally small that it wasn't worth thinking about.

"Cassi, are you all right?" Joan repeated.

Cassi sighed. "Tell me what happened."

"They don't know for sure," said Joan, relieved to hear Cassi speak. "And I don't know all the details. He apparently just died in his sleep. The nurses told me the autopsy showed that he had more severe heart disease than anyone suspected. I suppose he had a heart attack, but I don't know for sure."

"Oh God!" said Cassi, fighting tears.

"I'm sorry to bring you such sad news," said Joan. "I just felt if it were the other way around I'd want to know."

"He was such a wonderful man," said Cassi. "And such a good friend."

The news was so overwhelming that Cassi suddenly felt devoid of emotion.

"Can I get you anything?" asked Joan solicitously.

"No, thank you."

There was a silence that made Joan feel acutely uncomfortable. "Are you sure you're all right?" she asked.

"I'm fine, Joan."

"Do you want to talk about how you feel?" asked Joan.

"Not now," said Cassi. "I don't feel anything right now."

Joan could sense that Cassi had withdrawn. She questioned the advisability of having told Cassi, but what was done was done. She sat for a while holding Cassi's hand. Then she left, turning at the door to wish her a good night.

On her way out, she stopped at the nurses' station and spoke to the head nurse. She said she'd seen Cassi as a friend, not a consult, but she felt she should point out that Cassi was extremely depressed over the death of a friend. Maybe the nurses should keep an eye on her.

Cassi lay motionless for a long time. She'd not objected when Joan left, but now felt very much alone. Robert's death had triggered all her old fears of abandonment. She kept remembering the nightmare she had as a child that her mother would send her back to the hospital in exchange for a healthy child.

In a panic Cassi groped for the call button. She

hoped someone would come soon and help her.

"What is it, Dr. Cassidy?" asked a nurse coming into the room a few minutes later.

"I feel panicky," said Cassi. "I can't take the patches. I want them off."

"As a doctor, you know we can't do that. It's against orders. I'll tell you what I'll do," said the nurse. "I'll go call your doctor. How does that sound?"

"I don't care what you do," said Cassi. "I don't want eye patches."

The nurse left and Cassi was again plunged into darkness. Time dragged. When she allowed herself to listen, she could hear reassuring sounds of people moving up and down the corridor.

Finally the nurse came back. "I talked with Dr. Obermeyer," she said cheerfully. "He said to tell you he'd be stopping by shortly. He also told me that your operation went fantastically well but it is imperative that you rest. He ordered another sedative, so if you'll just roll over, I'll give it to you."

"I don't want another sedative! I want these patches off!"

"Come on now," urged the nurse. She pulled back Cassi's covers.

For a moment Cassi hovered between defiance and compliance. Then she reluctantly rolled over and got the shot.

"There," said the nurse. "That should make you feel a little calmer."

"What was it?" asked Cassi.

"That's a question you'll have to ask your doctor. Meanwhile, lie back and enjoy poor health. How about your television. Want it on?" Without waiting for an answer she turned on the set and went out.

Cassie found the voice of the newscaster reassuring. Soon the sedative began to have an effect and Cassi fell asleep. She woke briefly when Dr. Obermeyer stopped in to tell her in person how well her operation went. He said that he expected the vision in her left eye to be about normal when the patch came off, but that the next few days were critical and that she should try and be patient. He also told her that he'd left a standing order for sedatives and that she should ask for medication whenever she felt anxious.

Feeling better, Cassi drifted back to sleep. When she awoke some hours later, she could hear voices whispering in her room. Listening, she recognized one of them.

"Thomas?" she said.

"I'm here, dear." He picked up her hand.

"I'm afraid," she said, shocked to feel tears running out from under the bandages.

"Cassi, why are you crying?"

"I don't know," said Cassi, remembering that it was because Robert was dead. She started to tell Thomas but began to weep so hard she couldn't talk.

"You have to get control of yourself. It's important for your eye."

"I feel so alone."

"Nonsense. I'm here with you. You have a bevy of attentive nurses. You're in the best hospital. Now just try to relax."

"I can't," said Cassi.

"I think you need more sedative," said Thomas.

Cassi could hear Thomas talk to the other person in the room.

"I don't want another shot," she said.

"But I'm the doctor, and you're the patient," said Thomas.

Afterward Cassi was glad he'd insisted. She felt herself drift off into merciful sleep while Thomas was talking to her.

Thomas pressed the nurse's call button. When the nurse arrived, he stood up from his perch on the bedside. "I want you to give her two sleeping pills this evening. She was wandering the halls last night after one dose, and we certainly don't want her up tonight."

The nurse left, and Thomas waited a little longer to make sure Cassi remained asleep. Within minutes her mouth fell open and she began a throaty, uncharacteristic snoring. Thomas walked to the door, hesitated, then returned to the bureau and opened the bottom drawer. As he'd expected, the SSD data had not been touched. Under the circumstances he didn't want Cassi to be pulling it out as soon as her patches came off.

Quickly he picked up the computer printout and slipped it under his arm. With a final glance over at Cassi, Thomas left the room and walked down to the nurses' station. He asked for the head nurse, Miss Bright.

"I'm afraid that my wife is not standing up too well to the stress," said Thomas apologetically.

Miss Bright smiled at Dr. Kingsley. She knew him professionally very well. It was a surprise to hear him admit anyone might have a human weakness. For the first time she felt sorry for him. Obviously having his wife in the hospital was a strain on him, too.

"We'll take good care of Cassi," she said.

"I'm not her doctor and don't want to interfere, but as I told the other nurse, I think for psychological reasons she should be kept under pretty heavy sedation."

"I'll see to it," said Miss Bright. "And don't you worry."

☐

Cassi could not remember having had dinner, although the nurse who brought in sleeping pills assured her that she had.

"I don't remember it at all," said Cassi.

"That's not a very good recommendation for the hospital kitchen," said the nurse. "Nor for me. I fed it to you."

"What about my diabetes?" asked Cassi.

"You've been doing fine. We gave you a little extra insulin after your meal, but otherwise it's all in here." The nurse knocked the IV bottle with her knuckle so Cassi could hear. "And here's your sleep meds."

Cassi dutifully put out her right hand and felt two pills drop into her palm. She put them in her mouth. Then, reaching out again, she felt the glass of water.

"Do you think you need a sedative too?"

"I don't think so," said Cassi. "I feel like I've slept all day."

"It's good for you. Now your night table is right here."

The nurse took the glass from Cassi, then guided her hand over the bedside rail so she could feel the water glass, pitcher, telephone, and call button.

"Is there anything else?" asked the nurse. "Do you have any pain?"

"No, thank you," said Cassi. She was surprised she'd had so little discomfort from the operation.

"Do you want me to switch off the TV?"

"No," said Cassi. She liked the sound.

"Okay, but here's the switch." The nurse guided Cassi's hand to the button by the side of the bed. "Have a good night's sleep, and if you want anything, give us a call."

After the nurse left, Cassi did a little exploring of her own. Reaching out, she touched the side table. The nurse had pulled it away from the wall so it would be slightly more accessible. With some difficulty she pulled out the metal drawer and felt for her watch. Thomas had given it to her, and she wondered if she should have it put in the hospital safe. She didn't find it immediately. Her hand touched her own vials of insulin and a handful of syringes. The watch was under the syringes. It was probably safe enough.

She pulled her hand back under the covers. As the medicine took hold she realized why people were tempted to misuse it. It made reality recede. The problems were there, but at a distance. She could think of Robert without feeling the pain of his loss. She remembered how peacefully he had been sleeping last night. She hoped his death had been as calm.

Cassi suddenly pulled herself back from the abyss of sleep. With a jolt she realized that she must have been one of the last people to see Robert alive. She wondered at what time he'd died. If only she'd been there maybe she could have done something. Thomas certainly might have saved him.

Cassi stared into the darkness of her eyelids. The memory of Thomas coming into Robert's room replayed itself slowly in her mind. She remembered her shock at seeing him. Thomas had said that when he hadn't found Cassi in her room, he'd assumed she was visiting Robert. That had satisfied her at the time, but now Cassi wondered why Thomas would have been visiting her in the middle of the night.

Cassi tried to imagine what the autopsy on Robert showed, wondering specifically if a definitive mechanism of death was found. She didn't want to think about such things, but she found herself worrying if Robert had been cyanotic or if he'd convulsed at the time of his death. All at once Cassi began to fear that Robert might have been a candidate for his own study. He could have been case twenty. What if the last person to see Robert alive had been Thomas? What if Thomas had gone back to Robert's room after he'd left her? What if Thomas's sudden change of behavior was not as innocent as it appeared?

Cassi began to shake. She knew she was being paranoid, and knew how self-fulfilling delusions could be. She understood the stress she'd been under, and she'd had an enormous amount of drugs, including the sleep medication that she could already feel sapping her ability to think.

Yet her mind would not give up its horrifying thoughts. Involuntarily she found herself recognizing the fact that the first SSD case occurred at the same time as Thomas's residency. Cassi wondered if any of the deaths coincided with the nights Thomas had spent in the hospital.

All at once she became aware of her utter dependency and vulnerability. She was alone in a private room with an IV running, blindfolded and sedated. There was no way for her even to know when someone came into the room. There was no way for her to defend herself.

Cassi wanted to scream for help, but she was paralyzed with fear. She drew herself up into a ball. Seconds passed, then minutes. Eventually Cassi remembered the call button. Ever so slowly she inched her hand in its direction, half expecting her fingers to encounter some unknown enemy. When she touched the plastic cylinder, she pressed the button, holding it down with her thumb.

No one came. It seemed as if she had been waiting for an eternity. She let the button out and pushed it again several more times, praying for the nurse to hurry. At any second she expected something terrible to happen. She didn't know what, just something terrible.

"What is it?" asked the nurse curtly, pulling Cassi's hand away from the call button. "You only have to ring once, and we'll come as soon as we can. You have to remember there are a lot of patients on this floor and most are sicker than you are."

"I want to change rooms," said Cassi. "I want to go back to a semiprivate."

"Cassi," said the nurse with exasperation. "It's late at night."

"I don't want to be alone!" shouted Cassi.

"All right, Cassi. Calm down. As soon as we finish our medication records, I'll see what I can do."

"I want to talk to my doctor," said Cassi.

"Cassi, you do know what time it is, don't you?"

"I don't care. I want to talk with my doctor."

"All right. I'll put in a call if you promise to lie still."

Cassie allowed the nurse to straighten her legs.

"There, that must feel better. Now you relax and I'll call Dr. Obermeyer."

By the time the nurse left, Cassi's panic had lessened. She realized she was behaving irrationally. She was acting worse than her own patients. Thinking of Clarkson Two reminded her of Joan. She was the one person who would understand and wouldn't be angry at being awakened. Groping with her hand, Cassi found the phone and lifted it onto her stomach. With the receiver propped up between her shoulder and the pillow, she got the hospital operator. After Cassi explained who she was, the operator put the call through to Dr. Widiker.

The phone rang for a while, and Cassi began to worry that Joan had a late date. She was about to hang up when Joan answered.

"Oh, thank God," said Cassi. "I'm so glad you're home."

"Cassi, what's the matter?"

"I'm terrified, Joan."

"What are you terrified of?"

Cassi paused. With Joan on the line, she realized exactly how silly her fears were. Thomas was the most respected cardiac surgeon in the city.

"Has it something to do with Robert?" asked Joan.

"Partly," Cassi admitted.

"Cassi, listen to me," said Joan. "It's natural you're upset. Your best friend has just died and you've undergone surgery. Your eyes are bandaged. You mustn't let your imagination run riot. Ask the nurse for a sleeping pill."

"I've already had a lot of drugs," said Cassi.

"Either you had too little or the wrong kind. Don't try to be a hero. Do you want me to call Dr. Obermeyer?"

"No."

"Is there anything I can do?"

"Do you know if Robert Seibert was cyanotic when he was found or if there was evidence he convulsed?"

"Cassi, I don't know! And it's not the sort of thing you should be torturing yourself over. He's dead. That's more than enough for you to deal with right now."

"I guess you're right," said Cassi. "Just a minute, Joan. Someone's here."

"It's Miss Randall," said the nurse. "Dr. Obermeyer is trying to call you."

Cassi thanked Joan and hung up. The receiver was barely back in the cradle when it rang again.

"Cassi," said Dr. Obermeyer, "I got a call from the nursing office staff that you were upset. I don't know how to convince you that everything is fine. Your surgery went extremely well. I'd expected to find the usual diabetic pathology but I didn't. You should feel relieved."

"I think it's these patches over my eyes," said Cassi apologetically. "I feel terrified of being alone. I'd like to be transferred into a room with another patient. Now."

"I think that's asking a bit much from the nursing

staff, Cassi. Perhaps tomorrow we can think about transferring you. For now I'm more interested in getting you relaxed. I've advised the nurses to give you another sedative."

"The nurse is here right now," said Cassi.

"Good. Take the shot and go to sleep. I guess I should have expected this. Doctors and doctors' wives always make the worst patients. And you, Cassi, are both!"

Cassi allowed herself to be given yet another shot. She felt Miss Randall give her a final pat on the shoulder. Cassi was alone again, but it didn't matter. Drug-induced sleep descended like a silent avalanche.

☐

Cassi awoke from a violent dream filled with wild noise and clashing colors. Despite the heavy sedation, a faint throbbing pain in her left eye reminded her immediately that she was in the hospital.

For a moment she lay perfectly still, her ears straining to pick up the slightest sound. Behind the bandages wild colors continued to dance before her eyes, presumably caused by the pressure of the bandages. Cassi heard nothing save for the distant, muffled sounds of the sleeping hospital. Then she thought she felt something. She waited and felt it again. It was the plastic tube of her IV line. Her pulse quickened. Was it her imagination?

"Who's there?" called Cassi, suddenly finding the courage to speak.

There was no response.

Cassi lifted her right hand and swung it over the left side of the bed. No one was there. Reaching down, she felt the tape that secured the IV to her arm. Quickly she traced her finger up the plastic tube and pulled gently. The sensation was exactly the same twitch she'd felt. In the darkness someone had touched her IV line!

Trying to control her mounting fear, Cassi groped on the night table for the call button. It wasn't there. She touched the pitcher, the phone, the water glass, but nothing else. She felt over a larger area, moving her hand faster, feeling her sense of isolation and vulnerability mounting. There was no call button. It was gone.

Cassandra found herself frozen by the power of her own imagination. Someone was in her room. She could sense a presence. Then she smelled something familiar. Yves St. Laurent cologne.

"Thomas?" called Cassi. Pushing herself up with her right elbow, she called again. "Thomas!"

There was no answer.

Cassi felt herself break out in a profuse sweat. In seconds her entire body was drenched. Her heart, which had already been beating quickly, began to pound. Cassi knew instantly what was happening. It had happened before, but never with such devastating swiftness. She was having an insulin reaction!

Desperately she grabbed for the patches, trying to get her fingers under the plastered-down edges of the adhesive. Her left hand, previously immobilized because of the IV, also tore at the bandages.

Cassi tried to call out, but her voice had no strength. The bed began to spin. She threw herself to the side, against the raised rail. Thrashing wildly, she again tried to find the call button. Instead she inadvertently tipped over the bedside table sending the phone, the pitcher of ice water, and the glass crashing to the floor. But Cassi didn't hear. Her body was already locked into the grip of full-fledged grand mal seizure.

□

Carol Aronson, the night charge nurse on seventeen, was in the medication room drawing up an antibiotic when she heard the distant tinkle of breaking glass. She hesitated for a moment, then stuck her head into the chart area where she exchanged a questioning glance with Lenore, the LPN. Together the two women left the nurses' station to investigate. Both had the uncomfortable feeling that someone had toppled out of bed. They'd advanced only a short way down the hall when they heard the clatter of Cassi's side rails.

The women rushed into the room. Cassi was still convulsing wildly, her arms jammed through the rails, banging them back and forth.

Carol, who was aware Cassi was diabetic, knew immediately what was happening.

"Lenore! Call a code and bring me an ampule of fifty-percent glucose, a fifty cc syringe, and a fresh bottle of D5W."

The LPN ran out of the room.

Meanwhile Carol managed to pull Cassi's arms from between the rails. Next she tried to get a tongue depressor between Cassi's clenched teeth but that was impossible. Instead she stopped the rapidly running IV, and concentrated on keeping Cassi from hitting her head against the top of the bed.

Lenore returned and Carol took the D5W and immediately changed the IV bottle. She put the old bottle aside, knowing the doctor would want to check the insulin level. Then she opened the IV all the way and transferred the fifty-percent glucose from the ampule to the large syringe. When she finished, she debated using it. Technically she was supposed to wait for a doctor to arrive, but Carol had spent enough time in crisis medicine to know that under the circumstances the glucose should be the first thing tried and that it certainly couldn't hurt. She decided to give it. The amount of perspiration on Cassi's body suggested a severe insulin reaction.

Carol stuck the needle into the IV and depressed the plunger. Even before she'd injected the last few cc's, the result was dramatic. Cassi stopped convulsing and seemed to regain consciousness. Her lips opened and sounded as if she were trying to say something.

But the improvement didn't last. Cassi sank back again into unconsciousness, and, although she did not convulse again, the isolated muscles continued to contract.

When the code team arrived, Carol reported what she had done. The senior resident examined Cassi and began issuing orders.

"I want you to draw blood for electrolytes, including calcium, arterial blood gases, and a blood sugar," he said to the junior resident. "And I want you to run an EKG," he said to the medical student. "And Miss Aronson, how about another ampule of fifty-percent glucose?"

While the team fell to work, Lenore picked up the bedside table, replacing the phone. With her foot she pushed the shards of glass from the broken pitcher into the corner. The drawer had come out of the table and Lenore replaced it. It was then she found several used vials of insulin. Shocked, she handed them to Carol, who in turn handed them to the resident.

"My God," he said. "Was she supposed to give herself insulin blindfolded?"

"Of course not," said Carol. "She had insulin in her IV and was being supplemented according to the amount of sugar in her urine."

"So why did she give herself insulin?" asked the resident.

"I don't know," admitted Carol. "Maybe she was confused with all her sedatives and gave herself the medicine by rote. Hell, I don't know."

"Could she do that blindfolded?"

"Sure she could. Remember, she's been injecting herself twice a day for twenty years. She couldn't get the dose right, but she could certainly inject herself. Besides, there's another possibility."

"What's that?"

"Maybe she did it on purpose. The day nurse said she was depressed, and her husband said she'd been acting strangely. I guess you know who her husband is."

The resident nodded. He didn't like to think of the case being a suicide gesture because he hated psych cases, especially at three o'clock in the morning.

Carol, who had been filling another syringe with glucose while talking, handed it over. The resident injected it immediately. As before, Cassi improved for a few minutes, then again lost consciousness.

"Who's her doctor?" asked the resident, taking a third syringe of glucose from Carol.

"Dr. Obermeyer. Ophthalmology."

"Somebody give him a call," said the resident. "This isn't a case for a house officer to fool around on."

□

The phone rang and rang before Thomas groggily reached out and picked up the receiver. He had taken two Percodan before stretching out in his office, and he found it very hard to concentrate.

"You're a hard one to wake up," said the cheerful hospital operator. "You had a call from Dr. Obermeyer. He wanted to be put through immediately, but I told him you'd left specific orders. Do you want the number?"

"Yes!" said Thomas, fumbling on the desk for a pencil.

The operator gave Thomas the number. He started to dial and then stopped. Noticing the time, he was concerned. Obviously it was about Cassi. Going into the bathroom he splashed water on his face, trying to gather his wits.

He waited until some of the drug-induced fog receded before dialing.

"Thomas, we had a complication tonight," said Dr. Obermeyer.

"A complication?" asked Thomas anxiously.

"Yes," said Dr. Obermeyer. "Something we didn't expect. Cassi gave herself an overdose of insulin."

"Is she all right?" asked Thomas.

"Yes, she seems to be fine."

Thomas was stunned.

"I know this must be a shock for you," Dr. Obermeyer was saying. "But she is okay. Dr. McInery, her internist, is here and thanks to the quick thinking of the charge nurse, he says Cassi will be fine. We've moved her to the ICU for the time being just as a precaution."

"Thank God," said Thomas, his mind whirling. "I'll be right over."

As soon as he reached the hospital, Thomas rushed to Cassi's bedside. She seemed to be resting peacefully. He noticed that the patch on her right eye was gone.

"She's sleeping but she's arousable," said a voice at his side.

Thomas turned to face Dr. Obermeyer. "Do you want to talk with her?" he asked, reaching to shake Cassi's shoulder.

Thomas caught his arm. "No thanks. Let her sleep."

"I knew she was upset tonight," said Dr. Obermeyer contritely. "I ordered extra sedatives. I never expected anything like this."

"She was panicky when I saw her," said Thomas. "A friend of hers died last night, and she's been very upset. I hadn't planned to tell her, but I learned one of the psych residents had the poor judgment to do so."

"Do you think this was a suicide attempt?" asked Dr. Obermeyer.

"I don't know," said Thomas. "She could have just

been confused. She is accustomed to giving herself insulin twice a day."

"What do you think about a psychiatry consult?" asked Dr. Obermeyer.

"You're the doctor. I can't be very objective. But if I were you, I'd wait. Obviously she's safe in here."

"I took the patch off her right eye," said Dr. Obermeyer. "I'm afraid the bandages may have been a large factor in her anxiety reaction. I'm happy to say her left eye is still clear. Considering the fact she just had a grand mal seizure, which is probably the severest test imaginable for my coagulation of that vessel, I don't think we have to worry much about further bleeding."

"What's her blood sugar?" asked Thomas.

"Pretty normal right now, but they're going to follow it closely. They think she gave herself a whopping dose of insulin."

"Well, she's been careless at times in the past," said Thomas. "She's always tried to minimize her illness. But this seems like more than carelessness. Still, it's possible she just didn't realize what she was doing." Thomas thanked Obermeyer for his good work and walked slowly out of the ICU.

The nurses at the desk looked up as he went by. They had never seen Dr. Kingsley so depressed and anxious.

CHAPTER

12

CASSI BECAME CONSCIOUS of her surroundings around five o'clock in the morning. She could see the large wall clock over the nurses' station and thought she was in the recovery room. She had an awful headache, which she attributed to the eye surgery. Indeed, when she tried to look from side to side she got a sharp pain in her left eye. Gingerly she felt the bandage over the operative site.

"Well, Dr. Cassidy!" said a voice on her left. She slowly turned her head and looked into the smiling face of one of the nurses. "Welcome back to the land of the living. You gave us quite a scare."

Bewildered, Cassi returned the smile. She stared at the nurse's name tag. Miss Stevens, Medical ICU. That confused Cassi further.

"How do you feel?" asked Miss Stevens.

"Hungry," said Cassi.

"Could be your blood sugar is a bit low again. It's been bouncing up and down like a rubber ball."

Cassi moved slightly and felt an uncomfortable burning sensation between her legs. She realized she'd been catheterized.

"Was there a problem with my diabetes during surgery?"

"Not during surgery," said Miss Stevens with a smile. "The night after. As I understand it, you gave yourself a little extra insulin."

"I did?" said Cassi. "What day is it?"

"Five A.M., Friday morning."

Cassi felt very confused. Somehow she'd lost an entire day.

"Where am I?" she asked. "Isn't this the recovery room?"

"No, this is the ICU. You're here because of your insulin reaction. Don't you remember yesterday at all?"

"I don't think so," said Cassi vaguely. Somewhere in the back of her mind she began to remember a sensation of terror.

"You had your operation yesterday morning and were sent back to your room. Apparently you'd been doing fine. You don't remember any of that?"

"No," said Cassi without conviction. Images were beginning to emerge from the haze. She could recall the horrid sensation of being enclosed within her own world, feeling acutely vulnerable. Vulnerable and terrified. But terrified of what?

"Listen," said Miss Stevens. "I'll get you some milk. Then you try to go back to sleep."

The next time Cassi looked at the clock it was after seven. Thomas was standing by the side of her bed, his blue eyes puffy and red.

"She woke up about two hours ago," said Miss Stevens, standing on the other side. "Her blood sugar is slightly low but seems stable."

"I'm so glad you're better," said Thomas, noticing Cassi had awakened. "I'd visited you in the middle of the night, but you were not completely lucid. How do you feel?"

"Pretty good," said Cassi. Thomas's cologne was having a peculiar effect on her. It was as if the smell of Yves St. Laurent had been part of her devastating nightmare. Cassi knew that whenever she'd been unlucky enough to have an insulin reaction, she'd always had wild dreams. But this time she had the sensation that the nightmare wasn't over.

Cassi's heart beat faster, accentuating her pounding headache. She could not tell the difference between dream or reality. She was relieved a few minutes later when Thomas left, saying, "I've got surgery. I'll be back as soon as I'm done."

By noon, Cassi had been visited by Dr. Obermeyer and her internist, and released from the unit. She was taken back to her private room at the end of the corridor, but she raised such a fuss about being alone that they finally moved her to a multibed unit across from the nurses' station. She had three roommates. Two had had multiple broken bones and were in traction; the other, a mountain of a woman, had had gallbladder surgery and was not doing too well.

Cassi had had one other insistent request. She

wanted her IV out. Dr. McInery tried to reason with her, arguing that she'd just had a severe insulin reaction. He told her that had she not had the IV originally and gotten the sugar when she had, she might have slipped into irreversible coma. Cassi had listened politely but remained adamant. The IV was removed.

In the middle of the afternoon Cassi felt significantly better. Her headache had settled down to a tolerable level. She was listening to her roommates describe their ordeals when Joan Widiker walked in. "I just heard what happened," she said with concern. "How are you?"

"I'm fine," said Cassi, happy to see Joan.

"Thank God! Cassi, I heard that you'd given yourself an insulin overdose."

"If I did, I can't remember it," said Cassi.

"You're sure?" asked Joan. "I know you were very upset about Robert . . ." Her voice trailed off.

"What about Robert?" asked Cassi anxiously. Before Joan could respond, something clicked in Cassi's mind. It was as if some missing block fell into place. Cassi remembered that Robert had died the night after his surgery.

"You don't remember?" asked Joan.

Cassi let her body go limp, sliding down into her bed. "I remember now. Robert died." Cassi looked up into Joan's face, pleading that it wasn't true, that it was part of the insulin-induced nightmare.

"Robert died," agreed Joan solemnly. "Cassi, have you been dealing with your sorrow by trying to deny the fact?"

"I don't think so," said Cassi, "but I don't know." It seemed doubly cruel to have to learn such news twice.

Could she have suppressed it or did the insulin reaction just remove it from her disturbed memory?

"Tell me," said Joan, pulling over a chair so she could talk privately. The other three women pretended not to be listening. "If you didn't give yourself the extra insulin, how did it get in your bloodstream?"

Cassi shook her head. "I'm not suicidal, if that's what you're implying."

"It's important you tell me the truth," said Joan.

"I am," snapped Cassi. "I don't think I gave myself the extra insulin even in my sleep. I think it was given to me."

"By accident? An accidental overdose?"

"No. I think it was deliberate."

Joan regarded her friend with clinical detachment. Thinking that someone in the hospital was trying to do you harm was a delusion that Joan had heard before. But she had not expected it from Cassi. "Are you sure?" Joan asked finally.

Cassi shook her head. "After what I've been through it's hard to be sure about anything."

"Who do you think could have done it?" asked Joan.

Cupping her hand over her mouth, Cassi whispered. "I think it might have been Thomas."

Joan was shocked. She was not a fan of Thomas's, but this statement smacked of pure paranoia. She wasn't sure how to react. It was becoming obvious that Cassi needed professional help, not just advice from a friend. "What makes you think it was Thomas?" Joan finally asked.

"I awoke in the middle of the night and smelled his cologne."

If Joan had had the slightest concern that Cassi was

schizophrenic, she would not have challenged her. But she knew Cassi was an essentially normal person who'd been placed under extreme stress. Joan felt it was advisable not to let Cassi build on her delusional thought patterns. "I think, Cassi, that smelling Thomas's cologne in the middle of the night is awfully weak evidence."

Cassi tried to interrupt, but Joan told her to let her finish.

"I think that under the circumstances, you are confusing a dream state with reality."

"Joan, I've already considered that."

"Furthermore," said Joan, ignoring Cassi, "insulin reactions include nightmares. I'm sure you know that better than I. I think you experienced an acute delusional psychosis. After all, you've been under enormous stress, what with your own surgery and Robert's unfortunate death. I think in that state it's entirely possible you gave yourself the injection and then afterward suffered all sorts of nightmares you now think may be real."

Cassi listened hopefully. She'd had trouble sorting out the real from insulin-induced dreams in the past.

"But it is still very difficult for me to believe that I could have given myself an overdose of insulin," she said.

"It might not have been an overdose. You could have just given yourself your usual dose. You may have thought it was time for your evening shot."

It was an attractive explanation. Certainly an easier one to accept than that Thomas wanted her to die.

"My real concern," Joan went on, "is whether you are depressed now."

"I guess a little, mostly about Robert. I suppose I

should be happy about the results of the surgery, but under the circumstances, it's difficult. But I can assure you, I don't feel self-destructive. Anyway, they've taken away all my insulin."

"It's just as well," said Joan, standing up. She was convinced Cassi was not suicidal. "Unfortunately I've got two legitimate consultations to do. I've got to get a move on. You take care and call if you need me, promise?"

"I promise," said Cassi. She smiled at Joan. She was a good friend and a good doctor. She trusted her opinion.

"Was that lady a psychiatrist?" asked one of Cassi's roommates after Joan left.

"Yes," said Cassi. "She's a resident like I am, but further along in her training. She'll be finishing this spring."

"Does she think you're crazy?" the woman asked.

Cassi thought about the question. It wasn't as stupid as it sounded. In a way Joan did think she was temporarily crazy. "She thought I was very upset," said Cassi. Euphemisms seemed easier. "She thought that I might have tried to hurt myself in my sleep. If I start doing anything weird, you'll call the nurses, won't you?"

"Don't worry. I'll scream my bloody head off."

Cassi's other roommates, who had been listening, enthusiastically concurred.

Cassi hoped she hadn't scared the three women, but in a way it made her feel more comfortable that they would be watching her. If it were true that she had given herself an overdose without knowing it, she could use a little nervous concern.

She closed her eyes and wondered when Robert's

funeral was. She hoped she'd be released in time to go. Then she thought of the SSD project and wondered what would happen to it. Remembering the printouts she'd taken from his room, she decided to see if someone could locate them for her.

She rang for the nurse, who promised to check Cassi's former room. A half-hour later, the nurse returned and said that the two LPNs who had helped move Cassi had not seen the computer printout. The nurse added that she'd checked all the drawers herself without success.

Maybe the SSD data had been a hallucination, too, thought Cassi. She seemed to recall going into Robert's room, picking up the material, and then bumping into Thomas. But perhaps it was all a dream. Cassi wondered how she could check. The easiest way would be to ask Thomas, but she wasn't sure she wanted to do that.

Glancing around the room, Cassi was glad to see her three roommates getting ready for dinner. Just having them there made her feel safe.

☐

Thomas stopped short of the bridge over the marsh inlet. He switched off the engine and checked for any traffic before opening the door. Getting out of the car, he walked out onto the arched wooden bridge, his shoes making a hollow noise on the old planks. The tide was on its way out and the current rushed beneath the small bridge, swirling in frenetic eddies about the support pilings.

Thomas needed a breath of air. The two Talwin he'd

taken before leaving the office had had disappointingly little effect on his mood. He'd never felt such anxiety before. The Friday afternoon conference had been a disaster. And on top of that were the mushrooming problems with Cassi.

Thomas stood on the deserted bridge for almost half an hour, letting the damp breeze chill him to the bone. The discomfort was therapeutic, making it possible for him to think. He had to do something. Ballantine and his cohorts were intent on destroying everything Thomas had carefully built. In his hand he gripped a drug vial, intending to throw it into the water. But he didn't. Instead he returned it to his coat.

Slowly Thomas felt better. He had an idea, and as the idea took form, he began to smile. Then he laughed, wondering why he hadn't thought of it before. With a new surge of energy he returned to his car and warmed his fingers by holding them over the defroster vent.

After pulling into the garage, he crossed the courtyard to the house at a run. He moved the drug container to his suit pocket when he took off his coat and, feeling better than he had all day, went in to greet his mother.

"I'm so glad you're on time," she said. "Harriet is just putting dinner on the table." She took his arm and led him into the dining room. He knew she was in a good mood because she had him to herself, but she managed to inquire politely about Cassi before serving herself from the platter of Yankee pot roast.

When Harriet had gone back into the kitchen, she began asking about Thomas's day.

"Are things going better at the hospital?"

"Hardly," said Thomas, not eager to discuss the worsening hospital situation.

"Have you spoken with George Sherman?" asked Patricia with disgust.

"Mother, I don't want to talk about hospital politics."

They ate in silence for a few minutes, but Patricia could not contain herself and again spoke up. "You'll know what to do with the man when you become chief."

Thomas put down his fork.

"Mother, can't we talk about something else?"

"It's hard to avoid the issue when I can see how much it is bothering you."

Thomas tried to calm himself with a series of deep breaths. Patricia could see him tremble.

"Look at you, Thomas, you're like a spring wound too tightly." Patricia reached over to stroke her son's arm, but Thomas evaded her touch by pushing back his chair and standing up.

"The situation is driving me crazy," admitted Thomas.

"When do you think you'll be chief?" asked Patricia, watching her son begin to pace back and forth like a caged lion.

"God, I wish I knew," said Thomas through clenched teeth. "But it better be soon. If not, the department will be in shambles. Everyone seems to be going out of their way to destroy the cardiac vascular program I set up. Boston Memorial is famous because my operating team made it so. Yet instead of letting me expand, they are constantly cutting down my time in the OR. Today I learned that my surgical time is being reduced again. And you know why? Because Ballantine made arrangements for the Memorial Teaching Service to have free access to a large state mental institution out in the western part of the state. Sherman went out there and said the place was a cardiac surgical gold mine. What he didn't say was that the average mental age of the patients was less than two years. Some of them are actually deformed monsters. It makes me furious!"

"Well, won't you be backing the house staff on those cases?" asked Patricia, trying to think of the positive side of the issue.

"Mother, they are mentally defective pediatric cases, and Ballantine plans to recruit a full-time pediatric cardiac surgeon."

"Well, then, that won't affect you."

"But it will," shouted Thomas. "It will put more pressure on me to cut back my OR time." Thomas felt his temper rising. "My patients will either have dangerous delays before surgery or will have to go elsewhere."

"But surely your patients will be scheduled first, dear."

"Mother, you don't understand," said Thomas, making an effort to speak slowly. "The hospital doesn't care that I only take on patients who not only have a good chance of survival but are worth saving. To build the reputation of the teaching school, Ballantine would rather sacrifice valuable OR time for a bunch of imbeciles and defectives. Unless I become chief I won't be able to stop them."

"Well, Thomas," said Patricia, "if they don't give you the position, you'll just have to go to another hospital. Why don't you sit down and finish your dinner?"

"I can't just go to another hospital," shouted Thomas.

"Thomas, calm down."

"Cardiac surgery requires a team. Don't you understand that?" Thomas threw his napkin into his half-eaten food.

"You've upset me!" he shouted irrationally. "I come home for once expecting a little peace and you upset me!" He stormed out of the room, leaving his mother wondering what on earth she had done.

Walking down the upstairs corridor, Thomas could hear the surf breaking on the distant beach. The waves must be four to six feet high. He loved the sound. It reminded him of his childhood.

Snapping on the light in the morning room, he looked around. The white furniture had a harsh, cold appearance. He hated the way Cassi had insisted on redecorating the room. There was something brazen about it despite the lace curtains and flowered cushions.

He stayed for only a short time before going back to his study. With trembling hands he found his Percodan. For a while he entertained the idea of returning to town to see Doris. But soon the Percodan began to make him feel calmer. Instead of going out into the frigid night, he poured himself a Scotch.

CHAPTER
13

CASSI HAD HOPED that she'd become accustomed to the ophthalmologist's light, but each time Obermeyer examined her was as uncomfortable as the last. It had been five days since her surgery, and except for the insulin reaction, the postoperative course had been smooth and uneventful. Dr. Obermeyer had come by each day to peer into her eye for a moment, always saying that things were looking good. Now on the day of her scheduled discharge, Cassi had been escorted over to Dr. Obermeyer's office for one last "good" look, as he called it.

To her relief, he finally moved the light away.

"Well, Cassi, that troublesome vessel is in good shape, and there's no rebleeding. But I don't have to tell you that. Your vision has improved dramatically in that eye. I want to follow you with fluorescein studies and at some point in the future you may need laser treatments, but you're definitely out of the woods."

Cassi was not certain what laser treatments involved, but it didn't dampen her enthusiasm for getting out of the hospital. Convinced that her fear of Thomas had been imaginary and that a good deal of their problems were at least partially her own fault, she was anxious to get home and try to put her marriage back on course.

Although Cassi was entirely capable of walking, the green-smocked volunteer who came to escort her back to her room in the Scherington Building insisted that she ride in a wheelchair. Cassi felt silly. The volunteer was almost seventy and had a disturbing wheeze, but she wouldn't give in, and Cassi had to allow the woman to push her back to the room.

After she was packed, Cassi sat by her bed and waited for her formal discharge. Thomas had canceled his office hours and was going to drive her home around one-thirty or two. Since she had been admitted, his loving attention had not faltered. Somehow he'd managed to find time to visit four or five times a day, often eating dinner in the room along with Cassi's roommates, whom Thomas had charmed. He'd also completed plans for their vacation, and now with Dr. Obermeyer's blessings they were to leave in a week and a half.

The thought of the vacation alone was enough to make Cassi feel enormously happy. Except for their honeymoon in Europe, during which Thomas had taken time out to operate and lecture in Germany, they'd never been away together for more than a couple of days. Cassi was anticipating the trip like a five-year-old waiting for Christmas.

Even Dr. Ballantine had visited Cassi during her hospital stay. Her insulin overdose seemed to have particularly unnerved him, and Cassi wondered if he felt responsible because of their talks. When she tried to bring up the subject, he refused to discuss it.

But what really made the rest of the hospitalization so pleasant was Thomas. He had been so relaxed the last five days, Cassi had even been able to talk to him about Robert. She had asked Thomas if she really had met him in Robert's room the night Robert died or if she'd dreamt it. Thomas laughed and said that he indeed did find her there the night before her surgery. She had been heavily sedated and hadn't seemed to know what she was doing.

Cassi had been relieved to know she had not hallucinated all the events that night, and although she still questioned certain vague memories, she was willing to ascribe them to her imagination. Especially after Joan made Cassi comprehend the power of her own subconscious.

"Okay," said Miss Stevens, bustling into the room to see if Cassi was ready. "Here are your medicines. These drops are for daytime use. And this ointment is for bedtime. I also tossed in a handful of eye patches. Any questions?"

"No," said Cassi, standing up.

Since it was a little after eleven, Cassi carried her suitcase down to the foyer and left it with the people at the information booth. Knowing that Thomas would be busy for at least another two hours, Cassi took the elevator back up to pathology. One of the vague memories she'd not wished to discuss with Thomas concerned the

SSD data. She could remember something about the data, but it wasn't clear, and the last thing she wanted to do was suggest to Thomas she was still interested in the study.

Reaching the ninth floor, Cassi went directly to Robert's office. Only it was no longer Robert's. There was a new name plate in the stainless steel holder on the door. It said Dr. Percey Frazer. Cassi knocked. She heard someone yell to come in.

The room was in sharp contrast to the way Robert had kept it. There were piles of books, medical journals, and microscopic slides everywhere she looked. The floor was littered with crumpled sheets of paper. Dr. Frazer matched the room. He had unkempt frizzed hair that merged into a beard without any line of demarcation.

"Can I help you?" he asked, noting Cassi's surprised reaction to the mess. His voice was neither friendly nor unfriendly.

"I was a friend of Robert Seibert," said Cassi.

"Ah, yes," said Dr. Frazer, rocking back in the chair and putting his hands behind his head. "What a tragedy."

"Do you happen to know anything about his papers?" asked Cassi. "We'd been working on a project together. I was hoping to get hold of the material."

"I haven't the slightest idea. When I was offered this office, it had been completely cleaned out. I'd advise you to talk to the chief of the department, Dr. . . . ."

"I know the chief," interrupted Cassi. "I used to be a resident here myself."

"Sorry I can't help you," said Dr. Frazer, tipping

forward again in his chair and going back to his work.

Cassi turned to go, but then thought of something else. "Do you know what the autopsy on Robert showed?"

"I heard that the fellow had severe valvular heart disease."

"What about the cause of death?"

"That I don't know. They're waiting on the brain. Maybe they haven't finished."

"Do you know if he was cyanotic?"

"I think so. But I'm not the one to be asking. I'm new around here. Why don't you talk to the chief?"

"You're right. Thanks for your time."

Dr. Frazer waved as Cassi left the office, closing the door silently behind her. She went to look for the chief but he was out of town at a meeting. Sadly Cassi decided to sit in Thomas's waiting room until he was ready to go. Seeing Robert's old office already occupied had brought his death back to her with unpleasant finality. Having been forced to miss the funeral, Cassi sometimes had trouble remembering her friend was gone. Now she wouldn't have that problem anymore.

When Cassi reached Thomas's office she found the door locked. Checking her watch, she realized why. It was just after twelve and Doris was on her lunch break. Cassi got security to open the door to the waiting room and settled herself on the rose sofa.

She tried flipping through the collection of outdated *New Yorker* magazines, but she couldn't concentrate. Looking around, she noticed that the door to Thomas's office was ajar. The one thing Cassi had been effectively denying for the past week was Thomas's drug taking.

With the change in his behavior, she wanted to believe that he'd stopped. But when she was sitting in his office, curiosity got the better of her. She got up, walked past Doris's desk, and entered the inner office.

It was one of the few times she'd been there. She glanced at the photos of Thomas and other nationally known cardiac surgeons that were arranged on bookshelves. She couldn't help noticing that there were no pictures of herself. There was one of Patricia, but that was with Thomas Sr. and Thomas himself when he was in college.

Nervously, Cassi seated herself behind the desk. Almost automatically her hand went to the second drawer on the right, the same one where she'd found the drugs at home. As she pulled it out, she felt like a traitor. Thomas had been behaving so wonderfully the last week. Yet there they were: a miniature pharmacy of Percodan, Demerol, Valium, morphine, Talwin, and Dexedrine. Just beyond the plastic vials was a stack of mail-order forms for an out-of-state drug firm. Cassi bent over to look more closely. The firm's name was Generic Drugs. The prescribing doctor was an Allan Baxter, M.D., the same name that had been on the vials she'd found at home.

Suddenly she heard the waiting room door shut. Resisting a temptation to slam the drawer, she quickly eased it shut. Then, taking a deep breath, she walked out of Thomas's office.

"My God!" exclaimed Doris with a start. "I had no idea you were here."

"They let me out early," said Cassi with a smile. "Good behavior."

After recovering from her initial shock, Doris felt compelled to inform Cassi that she'd spent the entire previous afternoon canceling today's office patients so that Thomas could take her home. Meanwhile, she glanced at the inner office, then closed the door.

"Who is Dr. Allan Baxter?" asked Cassi, ignoring Doris's attempt to make her feel like a burden.

"Dr. Baxter was a cardiologist who occupied the adjoining professional suite that we took over when we added the extra examination rooms."

"When did he move?" asked Cassi.

"He didn't move. He died," said Doris, sitting down behind her typewriter and directing her attention at the material on her desk. Without looking up at Cassi, she added, "If you'd like to sit down, I'm sure that Thomas should be along soon." She threaded a sheet of paper into her machine and began to type.

"I think I'd prefer to wait in Thomas's office."

As Cassi passed behind her desk, Doris's head shot up. "Thomas doesn't like anyone in his office when he's not there," she protested with authority.

"That's understandable," returned Cassi. "But I'm not anyone. I'm his wife."

Cassi went back through the door and closed it, half expecting Doris to follow. But the door didn't open, and presently she could hear the sound of the typewriter.

Going back to Thomas's desk, she quickly retrieved one of the mail order forms, noting that it was not only printed with Dr. Baxter's name, but also his DEA narcotics number. Using a direct outside line, Cassi placed a call to the Drug Enforcement Administration. A secretary answered. Cassi introduced herself and said she had a question about a certain physician.

"I think you'd better talk with one of the inspectors," said the secretary.

Cassi was placed on hold. Her hand was trembling. Presently one of the inspectors came on the line. Cassi gave her credentials, mentioning that she was an M.D. on the staff at the Boston Memorial. The inspector was extremely cordial and asked how he could be of assistance.

"I'd just like some information," said Cassi. "I was wondering if you keep track of the prescribing habits of individual physicians."

"Yes, we do," said the inspector. "We keep records on computer using the Narcotics and Drugs Information System. But if you are looking for specific information on a particular physician, I'm afraid you can't get it. It is restricted."

"Only you people can see it, is that right?"

"That's correct, Doctor. Obviously we don't look at individual prescribing habits unless we are given information by the board of medical examiners or the medical society's ethics committee that suggests there is an irregularity. Except, of course, if a physician's prescribing habits change markedly over a short period of time. Then the computer automatically kicks out the name."

"I see," said Cassi. "There's no way for me to check a particular doctor."

"I'm afraid not. If you have a question about someone, I'd suggest you raise it with the medical society. I'm sure you understand why the information is classified."

"I suppose so," said Cassi. "Thanks for your time."

Cassi was about to hang up when the inspector said, "I can tell you if a specific doctor is duly registered and actively prescribing, but not the amount. Would that help?"

"It sure would," said Cassi. She gave Dr. Allan Baxter's name and DEA number.

"Hang on," said the inspector. "I'll enter this into the computer."

As Cassi waited, she heard the outer door close. Then she heard Thomas's voice. With a surge of anxiety she stuffed the drug order form into her pocket. As Thomas came through the door the inspector came back on the line. Cassi smiled self-consciously.

"Dr. Baxter is active and up-to-date with a valid number."

Cassi didn't say anything. She just hung up.

☐

Thomas was both talkative and solicitous as he drove Cassi home. If he'd been angry at her presence in his office, he'd hidden the fact beneath a welter of questions about how she was feeling. Although Cassi insisted she felt fine, Thomas had made her wait by the hospital entrance so that he could run and bring the car around.

Cassi was thankful for Thomas's attentiveness, but she was so upset by what she had just learned from the Drug Enforcement Administration that she remained silent most of the way home. She now understood how Thomas managed to procure his drugs without detection. He'd supply Allan Baxter's narcotics registration.

All he had to do was fill out a form every year and send in five dollars. With the number and some idea of the level at which Dr. Baxter had been prescribing before he died, Thomas could obtain plenty of drugs. Probably more than he could consume.

And the fact that he had resorted to such deception made it clear that his problem was more extensive than Cassi had allowed herself to believe. His behavior had been so normal this last week she let herself hope that he had already begun to control his abuse. Perhaps they could talk further when they were away.

"I have some bad news," said Thomas, breaking into her thoughts.

Cassi turned. She saw his eyes flick over at her for the briefest instant as if to make certain he had her attention.

"Before I left the OR today I got a call from a hospital in Rhode Island. They're bringing in a patient for emergency surgery tonight. I tried to get someone else to take the case because I wanted to be with you, but there was no one available. In fact, after I make sure you're comfortable, I'll have to be on my way."

Cassi didn't respond. She was almost glad Thomas would stay over at the hospital. It would give her a chance to decide what to do. Maybe she could document the amount of drugs Thomas was taking. There was still the chance he'd stopped.

"You do understand?" asked Thomas. "I didn't have any choice about it."

"I understand," said Cassi.

Thomas drove up to the house, insisting on getting out and opening the car door for Cassi. It was something he hadn't bothered to do since their first dates.

As soon as they were inside, Thomas insisted that she go directly up to the morning room.

"Where is Harriet?" asked Cassi when Thomas followed her with a pitcher of ice water.

"She took the afternoon off to visit her aunt," said Thomas. "But don't worry. I'm sure she made something for you to eat."

Cassi wasn't worried. She could certainly make herself dinner, but it seemed odd not to have Mrs. Summer bustling about.

"What about Patricia?" asked Cassi.

"I'll take care of everything," said Thomas. "I want you to relax."

Cassi lay back on the chaise and allowed Thomas to settle a comforter over her lap. With her backlog of psychiatric reading at her fingertips, she had plenty to do.

"Can I get you anything else?" asked Thomas.

Cassi shook her head.

Thomas bent and kissed her forehead. Before he left he dropped a travel folder in her lap.

Cassi opened it and found two American Airlines tickets.

"Something for you to look forward to while I'm gone. Meanwile, get a good night's sleep."

Cassi reached up and put her arms around Thomas's neck. She hugged him with as much force as she could muster.

Thomas disappeared into the connecting bathroom, being careful to close the door quietly. Cassi heard the toilet flush. When he reappeared, he kissed her again and told her he'd call after surgery if it wasn't too late.

After a quick stop in the study as well as the living room and kitchen, Thomas was ready to go.

With Cassi back home from her stay in the hospital, Thomas felt better than he had for many days. He even looked forward to surgery, hoping it would be a challenging case. But before he could be on his way, he had one more job: to see his mother.

Thomas rang her bell and waited while Patricia came down the stairs. She was pleased to see him until he told her he was returning directly to the hospital.

"I brought Cassi home today," he said.

"Well, you know Harriet's off. I hope you're not expecting me to look after her."

"She's fine, Mother. I just want you to leave her alone. I don't want you going over there tonight and upsetting her."

"Don't worry. I certainly won't go where I'm not wanted," said Patricia, contrary to the last.

Thomas walked away without saying anything more. A few minutes later, he climbed into his car and, after wiping his hands on the rag he kept under the front seat, started the engine. He looked forward to the drive back to Boston, knowing there would be very little traffic. Carefully he eased the powerful car out into the crisp afternoon air.

Arriving at the hospital, Thomas was pleased there was a spot next to the attendant's booth. He called a loud hello as he climbed from the car. He went into the hospital and took the elevator directly up to surgery.

☐

As evening approached, Cassi let the pale, wintry light fade without turning on the lamp. She watched the windswept sea change from pale blue to gunmetal gray. The airplane tickets still in her lap, she hoped that once they were away she and Thomas could honestly discuss his addictive problem. She knew that recognition and acknowledgment were more than half the problem. Trying to take a positive attitude, Cassi closed her eyes and conjured up visions of long talks on the beach and the beginning of a whole new relationship. Still tired from her ordeal in the hospital, she fell asleep.

It was completely dark when she awoke. She could hear the wind rattling the storm windows and the steady beat of the rain on the roof. True to form, the New England weather had made another about-face. She reached up and snapped on the floor lamp. For a moment the light seemed glaringly bright, and Cassi shielded her eye to look at her watch. She was surprised to see that it was almost eight o'clock. Irritated at herself, she tossed off the comforter and got to her feet. She did not like to be so late with her insulin.

In the bathroom, Cassi noted that she was showing two-plus sugar. Returning to the morning room, she went to the refrigerator and took out her medicine. Carrying the paraphernalia over to her desk, she meticulously drew up the correct amounts, fifty units of the regular and ten units of the Lente. Deftly she injected herself in her left thigh.

She carefully broke off the needle and dropped the syringe into the wastebasket, then put the insulin containers back into the refrigerator. Cassi kept the regular and Lente insulins on different shelves just to make sure she did not confuse them. Then she unpacked her eye medication, removed her eye patch, and managed to put the drops in her left eye. She was on her way down to the kitchen when she felt the first wave of dizziness.

She stopped, thinking it would pass quickly. But it didn't. Cassi felt perspiration break out on her palms. Confused as to why eyedrops would cause such a rapid systemic effect, she returned to the morning room and checked the label. It was an antibiotic as she'd suspected. Putting the eye medication down, Cassi wiped her hands; they were drenched. Then her whole body began to sweat, accompanied by a rush of unbelievable hunger.

Cassi knew then that it wasn't the eyedrops. She was having another insulin reaction. Her first thought was that she'd misread the calibration on the syringe, but retrieving it from the wastebasket proved that to be false. She checked the insulin bottles, but they were just as they'd always been, U100. Cassi shook her head, wondering how her diabetic balance could hve been thrown off so much.

In any case the cause of the reaction was less important than treating it. Cassi knew she'd better eat without delay. Halfway down the hall to the kitchen, she felt streams of perspiration began to run down her body and her heart began to beat wildly in her chest. She tried to feel her pulse, but her hand was shaking too much. This was no mild reaction! This was another overwhelming episode like the one in the hospital.

In a panic Cassi dashed back to the morning room and threw open the closet. The black leather doctor's bag she'd gotten in medical school was somewhere there. She had to find it. Desperately she pushed the clothes to the side, searching the shelves in the back. There it was!

Cassi pulled the bag down and ran over to her desk. Undoing the catch, she dumped out the contents, which included a container of glucose in water. With shaking hands, she drew some up and injected herself. There was little or no effect. The shaking was getting worse. Even her vision was changing.

Frantically Cassi snatched up several small IV bottles of fifty-percent glucose which had also been in the doctor's bag. With great difficulty she got a tourniquet around her left arm. Then with a spastic hand managed to jam a butterfly needle into one of the veins on the back of her left hand. Blood squirted out of the open end of the needle, but she ignored it. Loosening the tourniquet, she connected the tubing from the IV bottle. When she held the bottle above her head, the clear fluid pushed the blood slowly back into her hand, then started to run freely.

Cassi waited for a moment. With the glucose running she felt a little better and her vision immediately returned to normal. Balancing the bottle between her head and shoulder, Cassi put a few pieces of adhesive tape over the site where the butterfly needle entered her skin. The adhesive did not stick too well because of the blood. Then, taking the IV bottle in her right hand, she ran into the bedroom, lifted the telephone receiver, and dialed 911.

She was terrified she would pass out before anyone answered. The phone was ringing on the other end. Someone answered, saying "911 emergency."

"I need an ambulance . . ." began Cassi, but the person on the other end interrupted her, saying, "Hello, hello!"

"Can you hear me?" asked Cassi.

"Hello, hello!"

"Can you hear me?" screamed Cassi, her panic returning.

Cassi could hear the person on the other end of the line say something to a colleague. Then the line went dead.

Cassi tried again with the same result. Then she dialed the operator. It was the same maddening problem. She could hear them, but they couldn't hear her.

Grabbing the second IV bottle in her left hand and carrying the running bottle above her head, Cassi ran on wobbly legs down the corridor to Thomas's study.

To her horror his phone also wasn't working. She could hear the other party vainly saying hello, but it was obvious they couldn't hear her. Bursting into tears, she slammed the phone down and picked up the second IV bottle.

Cassi's panic mounted as she struggled to descend the stairs without falling. She tried the phones in the living room and kitchen without success.

Fighting against a powerful drowsiness, she ran back through the hall to the foyer. Her keys were on the side table, and she clutched them along with the unused IV bottle. Her first thought was to try to drive to the local hospital, which wasn't far—ten minutes at most. With the IV running, the insulin reaction seemed to be controlled.

Getting the front door open was an effort that ultimately required Cassi to put down her IV bottle for a moment. Blood backed up into the IV but cleared again when she raised the bottle over her head.

The cold, rainy night seemed to revive her as she ran for the garage. Juggling the IV, she managed to open the car door and slide behind the wheel. Tilting the rearview mirror, Cassi slipped the ring of the IV bottle over it. She pushed the key into the ignition.

The engine turned over and over, but it would not start. She took out the key and closed her eyes. She was shivering violently. Why wouldn't the car start! She tried again with the same result. Looking at the IV she realized the bottle was almost empty. Shaking, she removed the cover from the second bottle. Even during the few minutes it took to make the exchange she could feel the effect. There was no doubt in her mind that when the glucose ran out, she'd most likely lose consciousness.

She decided her only chance now was Patricia's phone. Emerging from the garage into the rain, Cassi rounded the building and ran to Patricia's door. Still holding the IV bottle above her head, she rang the buzzer.

As on her previous visit, Cassi was able to see Patricia descend the stairs. She came slowly, warily peering out into the night. When she recognized Cassi and saw her holding aloft an IV bottle, she quickly fumbled with the door and threw it open.

"My God!" said Patricia, noticing Cassi's pale, perspiring face. "What happened?"

"Insulin reaction," managed Cassi. "I have to call an ambulance."

Patricia's face registered concern, but seemingly paralyzed with shock, she did not get out of the way. "Why didn't you call from the main house?"

"I can't. The phones are out of order. Please."

Cassi blundered forward, pushing clumsily past Patricia. The movement caught Patricia by surprise and she stumbled back. Cassi didn't have time to argue. She wanted a phone.

Patricia was incensed. Even if Cassi wasn't well, she didn't have to be rude. But Cassi had turned a deaf ear to her mother-in-law's complaints and was already dialing 911 when Patricia caught up to her in the living room. To Cassi's relief, this time she could be heard by the emergency operator. As calmly as she could, she gave her name and the address and said she needed an ambulance. The dispatcher assured her that one would be there immediately.

Cassi lowered the receiver with a trembling hand. She looked at Patricia, whose face reflected confusion more than anything else. Exhausted, Cassi sank to the couch. Patricia did the same, and the two women sat quietly until they heard the sirens coming down the drive. The years of unspoken antagonism made communication difficult, but Patricia helped Cassi, who was now nearly unconscious, down the stairs.

As Patricia watched the shrieking ambulance race back across the salt marsh, she had a moment's real sympathy for her daughter-in-law. Slowly she went back upstairs and called Boston Memorial. She felt her son should try to meet his wife at the local hospital. But Thomas was in surgery. Patricia left word that he should call as soon as possible.

☐

Thomas glanced down at the clock on the instrument panel. It was 12:34 A.M. The charge nurse had given him Patricia's message the moment he came out of the OR at 11:15. When he'd spoken to his mother she'd been very upset, telling him what had happened. She chided him about having left Cassi alone and urged him to go to the local hospital as fast as he could.

Thomas had called Essex General, but the nurse hadn't been able to say yet how Cassi was doing. She just told Thomas that she'd been admitted. Thomas didn't need any urging to hurry. He was desperate to find out Cassi's condition.

At the red light the block before the hospital, Thomas slowed but did not stop. When he reached the hospital grounds, he turned so sharply the wheels of his car squealed in protest.

The front desk of the hospital was deserted. A small sign said INQUIRIES GO TO EMERGENCY. Thomas sprinted down the hall.

There was a tiny waiting area and a glassed-in nurses' station. A nurse was having coffee and watching a miniature TV set. Thomas pounded on the glass.

"Can I help you?" she asked with a strong Boston accent.

"I'm looking for my wife," said Thomas nervously. "She was brought in here by ambulance."

"Would you mind sitting down for a moment."

"Is she here?" asked Thomas.

"If you'll sit down, I'll get the doctor. I think you'd better talk to him."

Oh God, thought Thomas as he turned and obediently sat down. He had no idea what was coming. Luckily he didn't have to wait long. An Oriental man in a crumpled scrub suit appeared, blinking in the bright fluorescent light.

"I'm sorry," he said, introducing himself as Dr. Chang. "Your wife is no longer with us."

For a moment Thomas thought the man was telling him Cassi was dead, but then the doctor went on to say Cassi had signed herself out.

"What?" shouted Thomas.

"She was a doctor herself," apologized Dr. Chang.

"What are you trying to say?" Thomas tried to stifle his fury.

"She arrived suffering from an insulin overdose. We gave her sugar and she stabilized. Then she wanted to leave."

"And you allowed her to."

"I didn't want her to leave," said Dr. Chang. "I advised against it. But she insisted. She checked out against medical advice. I have her signature. I can show you."

Thomas grabbed the man's arms. "How could you let her leave! She was in shock. She probably wasn't thinking clearly."

"She was lucid and signed a release form. There wasn't much I could do. She said she wanted to go to the Boston Memorial. I knew she'd get better care there. I'm not a specialist in diabetes."

"How did she go?" asked Thomas.

"She called a taxi," said Dr. Chang.

Thomas ran back down the corridor and out through the front door. He had to find her!

Thomas drove recklessly. Luckily there was almost

no traffic. After a brief stop at home, he headed back into Boston. When he pulled into the parking garage at the Memorial it was just before 2:00 A.M. He parked and ran into emergency.

In contrast to Essex General, the ER at the Memorial was flooded with patients. Thomas ran straight to the admitting office.

"Your wife hasn't come into the ER," one of the clerks told him.

The other clerk punched Cassi's name into the computer. "She hasn't been admitted either. It shows she was discharged this morning."

Thomas felt a sinking feeling in the pit of his abdomen. Where could she be? He had only one other thought. Maybe she'd gone up to Clarkson Two.

Although he'd never stopped to wonder why, Thomas did not like to be on the psychiatry floor. It made him feel uncomfortable. He didn't even like the sound the heavy fire door made when it closed behind him with its airtight seal.

As he walked down the dark corridor, his heels echoed loudly. He passed the common room where the TV was still on although no one was watching. At the desk a nurse who'd been reading a medical journal looked up at him as if he were one of the patients.

"I'm Dr. Kingsley," said Thomas.

The nurse nodded.

"I'm looking for my wife, Dr. Cassidy. Have you seen her?"

"No, Dr. Kingsley. I thought she was on medical leave."

"She is, but I thought she might have come in here."

"Nope. But if I see her I'll tell her you're looking for her."

Thomas thanked the woman and decided to go to his office while he tried to figure out what to do.

As soon as he opened the door he went to his desk to get several Talwin. He took them with a splash of Scotch, then sat down. He wondered if he were getting an ulcer. He had a boring pain just below his sternum that he also felt in his back. But the pain he could live with. What was worse than the pain was the pervasive anxiety. He felt as if he were about to shatter into a million pieces. He had to find Cassi. His life depended on it.

Thomas pulled over the phone. Despite the hour, he called Dr. Ballantine. Cassi had spoken to him before, and there was a chance she'd approach him again.

Dr. Ballantine, groggy with sleep, answered on the second ring. Thomas apologized and asked if he'd heard from Cassi.

"I haven't," said Dr. Ballantine, clearing his throat. "Is there some reason I should?"

"I don't know," admitted Thomas. "She was discharged today, but after I took her home I had to come back to the hospital for an emergency. When I got out of surgery there was a message to call my mother. She told me Cassi had apparently given herself another overdose of insulin. An ambulance took her to the local hospital but by the time I got there she'd signed herself out. I have no idea where she is or what state she's in. I'm worried sick."

"Thomas, I'm so sorry. If she calls, I'll get in touch with you immediately. Where will you be?"

"Just call the hospital. They'll have my number."

As Dr. Ballantine replaced the receiver, his wife rolled over and asked what the trouble was. As chief of service, Ballantine got few emergency calls at night.

"It was Thomas Kingsley," said Ballantine, staring into the darkness. "His wife is apparently very unstable. He's afraid she may have tried to kill herself."

"The poor man," said Mrs. Ballantine as she felt her husband throw off the covers and get up. "Where are you going, dear?"

"No place. You go back to sleep."

Dr. Ballantine put on his robe and walked out of the bedroom. He had an awful feeling that things were not happening the way he'd planned.

CHAPTER

14

CASSI AWOKE with the same violent headache she'd had in the intensive care unit. The difference now was that her mind was clear. She remembered everything that had happened the previous night. After checking out of Essex General she headed into Boston thinking she should call Dr. McInery, but when she reached the hospital she no longer felt she needed emergency care. But before she could face her fears about what had happened, she knew she needed sleep. She'd gone to the empty on-call room on Clarkson Two and stretched out on the cot.

As she fell asleep she knew she'd have to find someone to talk to about Thomas. Had he been involved in her second insulin overdose? She didn't see how since she had taken her regular medicine herself. But the fact that all the phones except Patricia's were out seemed too much of a coincidence to be an accident, and her car had never in the past failed to start. What if her fears about Thomas's connection to the SSD cases were true? What if she hadn't been hallucinating and he was responsible for Robert's death?

If it were true, he had to be ill, mentally ill. He needed help. Dr. Ballantine had said he would do anything he could if Thomas needed counseling. Cassi decided to see him in the morning. For the moment she was safe.

Checking her urine a final time, she decided she might as well fall asleep. Hopefully Patricia couldn't alarm Thomas until morning.

When she awoke well before dawn, the psychiatry ward was still deserted. Cassi washed up as best she could and ran down to the lab where she persuaded a sleepy technician to draw some blood for a sugar level, only to have the night lab supervisor refuse to run it because Cassi didn't have her hospital card with her. Not up to arguing, Cassi left the sample and told the man to do whatever his conscience dictated. She said she'd stop back later. Then she went up to Ballantine's office and parked herself in the hall opposite his door.

An hour and a half passed before he appeared. He saw Cassi as he came down the hall.

"If you have a moment, I'd like to talk to you," she said.

"Of course," said Dr. Ballantine, turning to unlock his door. "Come in." He acted as if he'd expected her.

Cassi walked into the office, looking out the window to avoid meeting Dr. Ballantine's gaze. She could see over the Charles River to the MIT building directly opposite. Although she wasn't sure why, Cassi thought that Dr. Ballantine seemed somewhat annoyed to see her.

"Well, what can I do for you?" he asked.

"I need help," said Cassi. Dr. Ballantine was standing before his desk. He was not making her feel comfortable, but she didn't know who else to turn to.

"And what kind of help do you need?" asked Dr. Ballantine. He made no gesture for Cassi to sit down.

"I'm not entirely sure," said Cassi slowly. "But before dealing with anything else I must get Thomas into therapy. I know he's abusing drugs."

"Cassi," said Dr. Ballantine with patience. "Since we last talked, I've checked Thomas's prescribing habits. If he errs, he errs on the side of caution as far as narcotics are concerned."

"He doesn't get pills under his own name," said Cassi. "But drugs are only part of the story. I think Thomas is ill. Mentally ill. I know that I haven't been on psychiatry long, but Thomas is definitely sick. I'm afraid he considers me a threat."

Ballantine didn't respond immediately. He looked at Cassi with surprise and, for the first time since he'd seen her, concern. His expression softened and he put an arm around her shoulders. "I know you've been under a lot of stress. And I think the problem has gone beyond my capabilities. What I'd like you to do is sit down and rest for a few minutes. There is someone else I think you should talk to."

"Who?" asked Cassi.

"Please sit down," said Dr. Ballantine softly. He moved his wing chair from the corner and placed it in front of the desk, facing the window. "Please." He took

Cassi's hand and gently encouraged her to sit down. "I want you to be comfortable."

This was the Dr. Ballantine Cassi had remembered. He would take care of her. He would take care of Thomas. Gratefully she sank into the soft leather cushions.

"Let me get you something. Coffee? Something to eat?"

"I could use something to eat," said Cassi. She felt hungry and guessed her blood sugar was still low.

"All right, you wait here. I'm sure everything is going to work out fine."

Dr. Ballantine left the room, closing the door quietly.

Cassi wondered whom Dr. Ballantine was calling. It had to be someone in a position of authority who would have some influence over Thomas. Otherwise he wouldn't listen. Cassi began to rehearse her story in her mind. She heard the door open behind her and glanced around expecting to see Dr. Ballantine. But it was Thomas.

Cassi was stunned. Thomas pushed the door shut with his hip. In his hands he had a plate of scrambled eggs and a carton of milk. He came over and handed her the food. He was unshaven and his face looked haggard and sad. "Dr. Ballantine said you needed something to eat," he said softly. Cassi took the plate automatically. She was hungry but too shocked to eat. "Where is Dr. Ballantine?" she asked hesitantly.

"Cassi, do you love me?" asked Thomas in a pleading voice.

— GODPLAYER —

Cassi was nonplussed. It wasn't what she'd expected to hear. "Of course I love you, Thomas, but . . ."

Thomas reached out and touched her lips, interrupting her.

"If you do, then you should understand that I'm in trouble; I need help, but with your love I know I can get better."

Cassi's heart turned over. What had she been thinking? Of course Thomas had nothing to do with the terrible events of the previous night. His sickness was making her equally crazy.

"I know you can," said Cassi with encouragement. She'd not thought Thomas was capable of having such insight into his own problems.

"I have been taking drugs," said Thomas, "just as you suspected. I've been better this last week, but it's still a problem, a major problem. I've been fooling myself, trying to deny it."

"Do you really want to do something about it?" asked Cassi.

Thomas's head shot up. Tears streaked his cheeks. "Desperately, but I can't do it alone. Cassi, I need you with me, not against me."

All at once Thomas appeared like a helpless child. Cassi put the plate down and took his hands in hers.

"I've never asked for help before," said Thomas. "I've always been too proud. But I know I've done some awful things. One thing has led to another. Cassi, you must help me."

"You need psychiatric attention," said Cassi, watching Thomas's response.

"I know," said Thomas. "I just never wanted to admit it. I've been so afraid. And instead of admitting it, I just took more drugs."

Cassi stared at her husband. It was as if she'd never known him. She struggled with the desire to ask if he'd been responsible for her insulin overdose, or if he had anything to do with Robert's death, or with any of the cases in the SSD series. But she couldn't. Not then. Thomas was too broken.

"Please," he begged. "Stand beside me. It's been so difficult to admit all this."

"You'll have to be hospitalized," said Cassi.

"I understand that," said Thomas. "It just cannot be here at the Memorial."

Cassi stood up and put her hands on his shoulders.

"I agree, the Memorial would not be a good idea. Confidentiality is important. Thomas, as long as you agree to professional care, I'll stand beside you for as long as it takes. I'm your wife."

Thomas clasped Cassi in his arms, pressing his wet face against her neck.

Cassi hugged him reassuringly. "There's a small, private hospital in Weston called the Vickers Psychiatric Institute. I think we should go there."

Thomas nodded in silent agreement.

"In fact I think we should go immediately. This morning." Cassi pushed Thomas away so she could see his face.

Thomas looked directly at her. His turquoise eyes seemed clouded with pain. "I'll do anything you think I should, anything to relieve the anxiety I feel. I can't bear it any longer."

The doctor in Cassi conquered all other reservations. "Thomas, you've driven yourself so hard. You wanted to succeed so much that the process of winning became more important than the goal. I think it's a common problem with doctors, particularly surgeons. You mustn't think you are alone."

Thomas tried to smile. "I'm not sure I understand, but as long as you do and you won't leave me, it doesn't matter."

"I wish I'd understood sooner."

Cassi pulled Thomas back into her arms. Despite everything, she felt she had her husband back. Of course she'd stand by him. She of all people knew what it was like to be ill.

"Everything is going to be all right," she said. "We'll get the best doctors, the best psychiatrists. I've done some reading about impaired physicians. The rate of rehabilitation is almost one hundred percent. All it takes it commitment and desire."

"I'm ready," said Thomas.

"Let's go," said Cassi, taking his hand.

□

Like lovers, Thomas and Cassi ignored the morning crowds pouring into the Boston Memorial. Walking arm in arm to the garage in the early morning light, Cassandra kept up a steady stream of enthusiastic conversation about the Vickers Psychiatric Institute. She even told Thomas she had a specific psychiatrist in mind who'd had lots of experience treating other doctors.

After they'd climbed into the Porsche, Cassi asked

Thomas if he felt well enough to drive. Thomas assured her that he was fine. Cassi reached up and pulled down her seat belt. As usual she had the urge to tell Thomas to do the same, but she thought better of it. She had the feeling that his emotions were so volatile, he would explode at the slightest frustration.

Thomas started the car and carefully backed out of the parking lot. After they'd passed through the automatic gate, Cassi asked how Dr. Ballantine had found Thomas so quickly.

"I called him during the night when I couldn't find you," said Thomas, stopping for a red light. "I had a feeling you might go to see him. I asked him to call me in my office if he heard from you."

"Didn't he think it was a little odd? What exactly did you say?"

The light changed and Thomas accelerated toward Storrow Drive. "I just told him you had another insulin reaction."

Cassi considered her own behavior. She recognized that her actions would appear irrational, especially signing out of a hospital against medical advice when she had barely been stabilized. Then hiding from everyone.

As usual Thomas drove recklessly, and when they reached Storrow Drive Cassi braced herself against the door for the sharp left turn that would take them toward Weston. Instead Thomas swung the wheel to the right, and Cassi had to grab the dash to keep from falling against him. He must have turned out of habit, thought Cassi.

"Thomas," she said. "We're heading home rather than to Vickers."

Thomas didn't answer.

Cassi turned to look at him. He seemed to be holding the wheel in a death grip as the speedometer gradually inched upward. Cassi reached over and put her hand on his neck, massaging the tight muscles. She wanted to get him to calm down. She could sense that he was becoming enraged.

"Thomas, what is the matter?" asked Cassi, trying to keep her fear in check.

Thomas did not respond, driving the car as if he were an automaton. They rose up the ramp, banked, and merged into the multiple lanes of Interstate 93. At that time of the morning there was no outbound traffic, and Thomas let the car go.

Cassi turned toward him as much as her seat belt would allow. She let her hand trail down Thomas's side, at a loss as to what to do. Her fingers hit something sharp in Thomas's jacket pocket. Before he could react, Cassi reached in and pulled out an opened package of U500 insulin.

Thomas snatched the package away, returning it to his pocket.

Cassi turned and watched the road rush toward her in a bewildering blur. Her mind was racing as she began to understand the cause of her last insulin reaction. There could only be one reason for Thomas to have U500 insulin. It was a rarely used drug. He must have replaced her U100 insulin with the more concentrated drug, forcing her to give herself five times her normal dosage. It would have been easy enough to do, forcing a syringe through the sealed cap in the same way that she drew out her regular dosage. If it had not been for her glucose solution, she'd have been in a coma now, or maybe worse. And the hospital episode? She hadn't been dreaming when she smelled the Yves St. Laurent cologne. But why? Because she, like Robert, was analyzing the sudden death data. Suddenly it was clear that Thomas's performance before they left the hospital had been a trick. With horror she realized that Ballantine must have thought she was the mentally troubled person, not Thomas.

Cassi felt the emergence of a new emotion: anger. For a moment it was directed almost as much at herself as at Thomas. How could she have been so blind?

Turning, she studied Thomas's sharp profile, seeing it in a different light. His lips looked cruel and his unblinking eyes appeared deranged. It was as if she were with a stranger . . . a man whom she intuitively despised.

"You tried to kill me," hissed Cassi, tightening her hands into fists.

Thomas laughed with such harshness that Cassi jumped.

"Such clairvoyance! I'm impressed. Did you really think the broken phones and your car not starting were coincidences?"

Cassi looked out at the blur of scenery. Desperately she tried to control her anger. She had to do something. The city was falling behind them.

"Of course I tried to kill you," snapped Thomas. "Just like I got rid of Robert Seibert. Jesus Christ! What did you think I was going to do, sit and let you two destroy my life?"

Cassi's head shot around.

"Look," shouted Thomas, "all I want to do is surgery on people who deserve to live, not a bunch of mental defectives or people who are going to die of other illnesses. Medicine has to understand that our resources are limited. We can't let worthy candidates wait while people with multiple sclerosis or gays with autoimmunal deficiencies take valuable beds and OR time."

"Thomas," said Cassi, trying to control her fury, "I want you to turn this car around immediately. Do you understand?"

Thomas stared at Cassi with unconcealed hatred. He smiled cruelly, "Did you really think I would go to some quack hospital?"

"It's your only hope," said Cassi, while she tried to tell herself that he was sick crazy. But all she felt was an overwhelming loathing.

"Shut up!" screamed Thomas, his eyes bulging, his skin flushed with anger. "Psychiatrists are full of shit, and no one is going to sit in judgment of me. I'm the best goddamn cardiac surgeon in the country."

Cassi could feel the irrational power of Thomas's narcissistic rage. She had little doubt as to what was in store for her, especially since everyone thought she'd already given herself two overdoses of insulin.

Ahead, Cassi could see the Somerville exit rapidly approaching. She knew she had to do something. Despite the speed at which they were traveling, she reached across and grabbed the steering wheel, pulling the car sharply to the right, hoping to force them off the interstate.

Thomas struck out and slapped the side of Cassi's head, throwing her forward with the force of his blow. She released her hold on the steering wheel to protect herself. Thomas, thinking she still had hold of the wheel, jerked it back with all his strength, and the car, which was already out of control, careened wildly to the left. Thomas desperately swung the wheel to the right and the Porsche skidded sideways, then rammed into the concrete abutment in a crescendo of broken glass, twisted metal, and blood.

CHAPTER
15

CASSANDRA COULD HEAR someone calling her name from a great distance. She tried to answer but couldn't. With great effort, she opened her eyes. Joan Widiker's concerned face emerged as if from a dense fog.

Cassi blinked. Slowly glancing upward, she could see a tangle of IV bottles. To her left she heard the incessant beep of a cardiac monitor. She took a deep breath and felt a stab of pain.

"Don't try to talk," said Joan. "It may not feel like it, but you're doing fine."

"What happened?" whispered Cassi with great difficulty.

"You were in a car accident," said Joan, smoothing back the hair from Cassi's forehead. "Don't try to talk."

As if recalling a dream, Cassi remembered the nightmare ride with Thomas. She could remember her anger and grabbing the wheel. She had a vague memory of being slapped and then bracing herself against the dash. But after that, it was as if a curtain had been dropped over the scene. It was blank.

"Where is Thomas?" said Cassi, struggling up in fear.

"He was hurt too," said Joan, urging her to lie quietly.

Cassi suddenly knew that Thomas was dead.

"Thomas didn't have his seat belt on," said Joan.

Cassi hesitated, then said the word aloud. "Dead?"

Joan nodded.

Cassi let her head fall to the side. But as the tears poured down her cheeks, the memory of her last conversation with Thomas returned. She thought of Robert and all the others. Gripping Joan's hand, she said, "I thought I loved him, but thank God . . ."

EPILOGUE

(six months later)

Dr. Ballantine pushed through the swinging door into the surgical lounge. He'd finished his only case for the day and it hadn't gone smoothly. Perhaps it really was time to slow down. Yet he loved to operate. He loved the triumphant feeling that came at the end of a successful case.

Pouring himself a cup of steaming black coffee, he felt a hand on his shoulder. Turning, he found himself looking into the smiling face of George Sherman.

"You'll never guess who I had dinner with last night," said George.

Dr. Ballantine examined George's worn face. Since Thomas's death, the inpatient load was taking its toll on all the staff, but George was perhaps the most over-worked. Under the pressure he had matured. Although he still had a ready smile and ready joke for his colleagues, he seemed increasingly thoughtful. But now he looked at Ballantine with the old roguish grin.

"So who did you have dinner with?" the chief asked.

"Cassandra Kingsley."

Dr. Ballantine's eyebrows lifted in a gesture of admiration. "Very good. How is that one-sided romance coming?"

"I think the opposition is weakening," smiled George. "I have her convinced to go down to the Caribbean come January. That would be wonderful. She really is a fabulous person."

How's that eye of hers doing?" said Dr. Ballantine.

"Just fine. And every one of those bones healed flawlessly. She's really got courage, especially getting back to work so fast. And she seems to making quite a name for herself on Clarkson Two. One of the attendings told me she has all the makings of a chief resident."

"Does she ever talk about Thomas?" asked Dr. Ballantine on a more serious note.

"On occasion. I have a feeling there is part of that story that no one but Cassi knows. She's still confused as to what she should do, but personally I think she's going to let it go."

Dr. Ballantine sighed with relief. "God, I hope so. At our last meeting I thought I'd convinced her that making Thomas's story public would do more harm than good. But I wasn't sure."

"She doesn't want to hurt the hospital," said George. "Her main point is that she thinks peer review doesn't work. People like Thomas are allowed to go on destroying themselves and their patients because their colleagues won't take action."

"I know. At least I contacted the Drug Enforcement Administration and suggested they force the medical licensing board to contact them whenever a physician dies. That way no one can abuse a dead physician's license."

"That's a good idea," said George. "Did they do it?"

Dr. Ballantine shrugged. "I don't know. To tell you the truth, I never followed up on it."

"You know," said George, "the thing about Thomas that bothers me the most is that he seemed so normal. But he must have been taking a lot of pills. I wonder how it got out of hand. I take a Valium now and then myself."

"So do I," said Ballantine. "But not every day like Thomas apparently did."

"No, not every day," admitted George, shaking his head. "You know I never could understand why he wouldn't face the fact the whole department was going full-time. Maybe the pills did blunt his sense of reality. After that late-night meeting with the trustees, he could have written his own ticket. The money men were wild to keep him happy. Even if they did want him to give up an independent practice."

"As good a surgeon as Thomas was," said Dr. Ballantine, "he had trouble seeing beyond his own nose. He was like the subject of all those jokes. You know, the doctor who plays God."

George was silent for a minute, thinking they all made decisions affecting their patients' lives. "What about that triple valve replacement you mentioned last week," George said, following his train of thought. "What have you decided to do?"

Ballantine took a careful sip of his coffee: "I'm not even going to present the case. The woman's got questionable kidneys; she's over sixty; and she's been on welfare for years. Some of Thomas's objections to our teaching cases were valid, and I don't even want the committee to know about her. If that goddamn philosopher hears about this woman, he'll probably insist we operate."

George nodded, ostensibly agreeing. But in his mind he recognized they all played God to a degree, and he knew that was Cassi's real concern. He'd promised her that when he became chief, which he'd already been guaranteed, he'd let such decision-making rest with the committee, including the philosopher.

George broke off from Ballantine and passed through the crowded lounge into the locker room. Passing by the phone he realized he felt more and more uncomfortable concerning Ballantine's decision about the triple valve case. Abruptly he picked up the phone, called the operator, and put in a page for Rodney Stoddard.